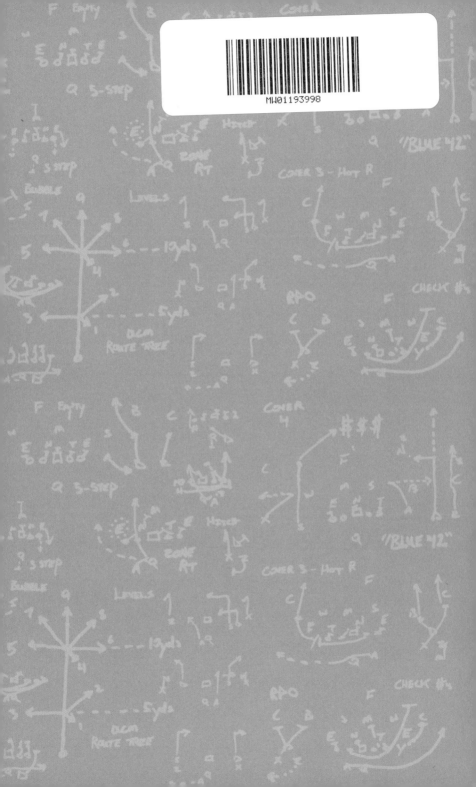

MISSISSIPPI
BLUE 42

Also by Eli Cranor

Don't Know Tough
Ozark Dogs
Broiler

MISSISSIPPI BLUE 42

ELI CRANOR

Published by Soho Press, Inc.
227 W 17th Street
New York, NY 10011
www.sohopress.com

Library of Congress Cataloging-in-Publication Data

Names: Cranor, Eli, 1988- author.
Title: Mississippi blue 42 / Eli Cranor.
Other titles: Mississippi blue forty-two
Description: New York, NY : Soho Crime, 2025.
Identifiers: LCCN 2025005717

ISBN 978-1-64129-697-7
eISBN 978-1-64129-698-4

Subjects: LCGFT: Sports fiction. | Detective and mystery fiction. | Novels.
Classification: LCC PS3603.R38565 M57 2025 | DDC 813/.6—dc23/
eng/20250221
LC record available at https://lccn.loc.gov/2025005717

Title page art by Jeff Wong
Interior design by Janine Agro, Soho Press, Inc.

Printed in the United States of America

10 9 8 7 6 5 4 3 2 1

EU Responsible Person (for authorities only)
eucomply OÜ
Pärnu mnt 139b-14
11317 Tallinn, Estonia
hello@eucompliancepartner.com
www.eucompliancepartner.com

for Johnny Wink, the one and only

This novel takes place during the 2013–14 season, around the same time I was wrapping up my collegiate quarterbacking career. A lot has changed since then.

Or has it?

William Faulkner once wrote, "The past is never dead. It's not even past." Close your eyes and let your mind rewind to the "glory days" of college football, prior to the College Football Playoff, the transfer portal, or the NIL. Before "student athletes" could legally receive payments of any sort. Now picture a coach feeding his team that same Faulkner line after a frustrating loss.

Can you hear him?

A multimillionaire coach, trying to motivate his unpaid players. Do you see the connection between America and its most beloved sport, a contest held on surrogate battlefields where flagship universities clash every Saturday in the fall?

If not, that's okay. This game's just getting started.

E.C.

FIRST QUARTER

Work hard, never quit, and good things'll happen.
—Chuck Johnson,

Arkansas footbwall coach

1

Rae Johnson said, "The one with his hands up, number four? He's what's called the quar-ter-back," taking it slow as she explained the rules of American football to Madeline Mayo instead of mentioning her first week as a federal agent, her rookie case. "Hear him? He's calling out the snap count. UCM just got a first down—"

"I know quarterbacks, but first downs?" Mad said, frown framed in a light blue window on the left side of Rae's laptop screen. "How many points are those worth again?"

Rae rolled her eyes a couple inches to the right, studying the college football game she had going there, ignoring her own face displayed in a smaller window on the Skype app. The screen made Rae's hair look redder than it really was. Almost orange, like it'd been back when she was a girl. No makeup. Not even any eyeliner. She hadn't showered once over the last six days. Her armpits reeked, a funky, locker-room tang, but Rae wasn't even in the game. She was trapped inside an unfurnished studio apartment with pizza boxes everywhere, bankers boxes and accordion files too.

"*Touch*downs get you six points," Rae said. "Field goals three. Two-point conversions, two, obviously, and a PAT is just worth one."

Mad said the letters "P-A-T?" like a question.

"It stands for point-after-touchdown. Sorry."

"This is crazy. You know that, right?"

"What? No. This is football, and it's—"

"—not the first time you've tried to explain it to me," Mad said, a scrim of smoke drifting up from the bottom of her display. "*Me.* Your best friend who also happens to make a living decoding complex computer systems."

The former roommates were ten minutes into their Skype call and still not getting anywhere. Rae'd first tried to explain basic football rules to Mad sometime around the end of the FBI Academy's eighth week, a hellacious five-day span chock-full of pass-or-fail firearm, academic, and athletic tests. There'd been a college game on that Friday, two mid-majors duking it out in Idaho, or maybe Iowa. Rae couldn't remember. The teams didn't matter. Neither did the score or the fact that Madeline Mayo was too high to get it.

The drug test the next morning was the only test Mad ever failed, but it was enough. She was back home in Missouri that same night. The infraction almost took Rae down as well. She'd pissed clean, of course. Too clean. "Diluted." That's the word they'd used. The instructors in charge of drug testing didn't want to hear why some New Agent Trainee was overly hydrated; they wanted tickets to the Smithfield Commonwealth Clash, the Virginia versus Virginia Tech rivalry game, a donation that Chuck Johnson, Rae's father and longtime college football coach, was able to make after placing a single call.

"Cut the crap and just tell me about your case." Mad coughed as she snuck another off-camera hit. "Where are you? What are you doing?"

Mad's hair was longer now than it had been at Quantico, or at least the top was. Somewhere between a Mohawk and a mullet. Rae grinned at the digital image of the cyberpunk hacker from just outside of Springfield, Missouri, thinking if

Mad ever decided to write a memoir, *Between a Mohawk and a Mullet* might work for the title.

"That's classified information," Rae said.

"Your partner, then. Is he hot?"

"Who said my partner's a he?"

"I might not have made it through the Academy, but I learned enough at Quantico to know the Bureau's not putting two women on the same investigation." Mad ran her hands along the shaved sides of her head. "The only thing more patriarchal than football is the federal fucking government."

It was getting late, almost ten. The purple and orange Trapper Keeper on Rae's lap was closed, the Velcro strap fastened. She'd finally finished her homework. Otherwise, she would've never called Mad. She wouldn't have been watching that football game either, the one that was taking place less than a mile away at Sutpen Stadium.

The University of Central Mississippi Chiefs—the 2012 defending national champions—were somehow losing to the Southern Miss Golden Eagles in what should've been a non-conference, cupcake game. Brett Favre, Southern Miss's most notable alum, was propped up in the south end zone like a cutout cowboy silhouette. The announcers couldn't get enough of the retired gunslinger. According to the duo of broadcast analysts, Favre—his presence in general—was the reason behind the Golden Eagles' shocking success. Rae knew better. The Chiefs' senior quarterback, Matt Talley, had committed more turnovers than completions. The coach's daughter had never seen a sorrier performance from such a highly accomplished QB.

"Earth to Rae." Mad flicked her joint at the screen. "I see

those boxes behind you. You wanna tell me about all those classified files or your partner?"

Rae wanted to tell Madeline Mayo about the files. The six straight days she'd spent working through them, recording everything she'd found in her retro Trapper Keeper because Trapper Keepers couldn't be hacked. Her first case was a lot like football; it was complicated. There were so many moving parts, so many different players. Rae decided to start at the beginning, right after she'd gotten off Delta Air Lines Flight DL674.

"My partner, he, uh . . ." Rae took a strand of hair out from behind her ear. "He thought I was a guy."

"A dude? I was right! Wait, *you*? I mean, I know you've got the whole sporty vibe going, but come on . . . You're five, what, nine? Ten, probably, in heels? You're a babe. A total knockout . . ."

Rae didn't think of herself as a "babe" or a "total knockout." Maybe once, back in her track star days. No, not even then. Not really. Rae only noticed her beauty from certain angles: her jawline in profile, her calves, and sometimes her thighs, flexed. Mostly, Rae tried not to look at herself at all. Instead, the rookie agent focused on her fitness. Just that morning, she'd completed a vigorous jump rope cycle and four sets of static lunges. Rae'd gotten her workouts off whiteboards in her father's weight rooms. Glute-ham raises, side straddle hops, Romanian dead-lifts, and fifty-yard prowler pushes when she wasn't locked inside a six-hundred-square-foot apartment.

"It was my name," Rae said.

"Rae?"

"He'd written it on the back of a Papa Johns flyer, an ad from the newspaper or something. Three black letters in all caps, except he got the last one wrong."

"No way."

"Yeah. R-A-Y," Rae said. "You should've seen him, standing at the baggage claim wearing this baby-blue blazer over a Hawaiian shirt, gold-rimmed aviators pushed back in what was left of his hair. An old guy, late fifties, at least, with this thick Yankee accent, wadding the pizza coupons up as he said, 'Ray? *Jesus.* You, uh . . . You're Ray Johnson?'"

"Did you tell him the story? Your full name and all that?"

Rae's first name was Raider, and she did tell her new partner that. Even hinted at what her father did for a living—why he would've named his only child, his baby girl, "Raider"—by connecting it back to the case she was there to help close. All the guy did was ask about the spelling. "Why not R-A-I?" Lips moving as he sounded it out then shook his head and said, "Or what about your middle name?"

Rae's middle name was Indigo, which had been her mother's contribution, but Rae didn't mention Lola Johnson. Didn't even say much about the history of her first name either. How her daddy had coached all over the country but spent the late 1970s as a graduate assistant at a string of Division II colleges in California. The Oakland Raiders left such an impression on the young coach from Arkansas, Chuck knew exactly what he'd name his own little QB, or heck, maybe even a linebacker. What he never considered, though, was what he'd do if he had a baby girl.

Rae said, "We didn't talk much," being honest about the drive out from the Jackson–Medgar Wiley Evers International Airport, the Boeing 747s and the Airbus A320s framed in the rearview of her partner's cherry-red Subaru Outback. The ride was like the rest of Rae's rookie investigation had been up to that point, all twelve minutes of it. *Weird.* Nothing at all like what she'd pictured in her mind.

A month ago, the FBI Director had been handing Quantico's Leadership Award to Rae, top of her class again, but where had that gotten her? Stuck with a past-his-prime field agent investigating a possible NCAA fraud case in Compson, Mississippi. The White-Collar Crime division of the FBI wasn't exactly the trajectory Rae had imagined for her career. A Joint Terrorism Task Force would've been more her speed. More contact. More action. A badass in a black jacket with JTTF stamped across the back, chasing down leads, collecting counterintelligence, and nullifying national security threats. Then again, how many agents' daddies were college football coaches? Rae knew why she was in Compson; she was there because of her father.

But what about her partner? Did he know her story? He could've. He *should've.* There were no secrets in the FBI, at least not for rookies. When Rae finally asked him about the case— why were they looking into UCM, exactly?—he'd said, "We follow the money, kid, and the highest-paid state employee in Mississippi also happens to be the Chiefs' head football coach." He'd added that it was the same in almost every state, but UCM's recent success had caught the Bureau's attention. The Chiefs had gotten too good too fast. "Haven't seen a turnaround like that since SMU won the big dance back in the eighties," he'd said, "and *every*body knows what happened to the Mustangs after that."

Rae knew about the Pony Express but kept quiet for the rest

of the drive, watching as gas stations hawking tall boys and fried chicken blurred together through the passenger-side window. Toss in a couple firework stands, a string of tiny white churches with signs out front that read JESUS SAVES, or Rae's personal favorite, MOSQUITOS KNOW THERE'S POWER IN THE BLOOD, and that was it. Mississippi in a nutshell.

"Anyway, all Frank said was—"

Mad jabbed a finger at her laptop screen. "*Frank?*"

"Ranchino. Frank Ranchino. That's the guy's name. My partner. He's old, getting close to mandatory retirement age."

"He's lazy? That's what you're saying?"

"He's something. Listen to this. Frank pulls into the parking lot," Rae said, reminding herself not to say too much, not even to Madeline Mayo, "and starts explaining how there aren't any federal buildings within a two-hour drive in any direction. Tells me that's why I'll be working from my new apartment, but doesn't get out of the car. Just says he left me a 'housewarming' gift."

"Bottle of bourbon?" Mad said. "No, you drink vodka, right? But the guy, Frank, he didn't know that. What was it?"

"This." Rae held both arms up, the way a referee signals a touchdown. "All of this."

"The files?"

"A whole year's worth. That's what Frank had been doing, collecting intel but going about his work 'incognito.' Said he didn't want to tip our hand. He says stuff like that. 'Tip our hand.' Talks in poker lingo, and quotes movies a lot too, but I got it. He couldn't subpoena anybody because he didn't want them to know the feds were in town. That's why he spent a year gathering up bank statements, emails, phone records. It's all here."

Rae watched Mad's eyes, glassy but widening, as the rookie agent rotated the webcam, giving her friend a panoramic view of the mess Frank had left in her apartment.

"You spend twenty straight weeks going through hell at Quantico, you make it through all that," Mad said, "just to graduate and be some greaseball agent's secretary?"

"I'm sitting on a bankers box," Rae said. "I used a stack of file folders for a pillow last night. But I did it. I went through everything."

The laptop was turned so that Rae couldn't see the screen. She could just hear Mad's voice, saying, "Well, what did you find? *Wait* . . . What were you even looking for?"

Rae was looking for evidence of fraud, any indication that the University of Central Mississippi, their football program in particular, was misusing federal funds. Namely, paying players more than their already allotted scholarships. Rae knew about such shenanigans, of course. She'd seen the documentaries, read the breaking news. Her dad had even told her a little bit about the dirty side of the sport, but Chuck Johnson was one of the good guys. Chuck played the game straight.

Work hard, never quit, and good things'll happen.

Rae's father was a walking, talking, motivational jukebox, and that one line was his mantra. Rae's too. It had propelled her through her own decorated athletic career, a pole vaulter at the University of Arkansas. Those same eight words got Rae through law school. She'd chanted them as she defended the public up in DC. But the courtroom didn't thrill her like the gridiron had. Nothing did. That's why, when the time was finally right, Rae submitted her application to the FBI. She didn't tell Chuck about it, though. She wanted to make it on her own, and for eight straight weeks, she did. All the way up until Madeline Mayo got caught smoking weed and Chuck had to swoop in with those damn tickets to save the day.

"Come on," Mad whined as Rae spun her laptop around. "You gotta tell me something. What's all this—"

Rae felt her phone vibrate at the same time she saw the game still going on the computer screen. She brought the device up to one ear, muted her laptop, and said, "Hey, Coach. What's up?"

The boxes, the files, the entire apartment evaporated when Rae heard her father's voice, a gruff baritone similar to Sam Elliott playing Wade Garrett in *Road House*. Unlike Wade, Chuck Johnson kept his hair short, a close-cropped crew cut going gray at the temples. A little thin on top too but he was so tall it made the bald spot hard to detect. Rae couldn't read his voice. She hadn't talked to him all week, not once since she'd arrived in Compson. He knew she was on her first case, but Rae hadn't told him what it was. Which was funny because Chuck was calling to ask if Rae was watching the game, the one that was taking place just down the road.

Rae said, "Does a shark fart bubbles?" and smiled when her father laughed. She'd worked hard at honing her humor. She'd had to. It wasn't easy being the only woman on a football field, but a handful of dirty jokes helped.

"Well, yeah. I guess they do," Chuck said. "But, hey, the Chiefs just got the ball back, a minute twenty-seven left on the clock, down five, and . . ."

Madeline Mayo flailed around on the left half of the computer screen. Rae looked past her and refocused on the game, trying to see what she'd missed, the reason her dad had called.

"...and they've got sixty yards to go," Rae said, finishing the thought for him. "No field goals."

"Nope. Touchdown or bust."

"How many timeouts?"

Chuck said, "That's my girl," and Rae glanced again at her former roommate. Mad had her thumb in her mouth, cheeks puffed, middle finger inching up from her fist. Before Mad's finger reached full mast, Rae ended the Skype call and expanded the game stream to fill the screen.

"Just one timeout," Chuck said, "but that's—"

"—enough."

"Damn straight. UCM loses, they're out of it. No shot at a second title. What's the call?"

"Something short. Out route to the home sideline."

"Formation?"

"Trips, maybe? Ten personnel."

"Gotta keep that UCM running back in the game."

Rae said, "Cergile Blanc," and watched one of the players she'd been investigating, a name she'd read countless times over the last week, take his position in the backfield beside Matt Talley.

There was a break in the rhythm of their back and forth, just long enough for Rae to check the phone screen. Her dad was there. They were still connected, and the Chiefs were lining up in a trips formation, three receivers split out to the field.

Chuck said, "Hey, look. You called it."

Rae's cheeks flushed the color of her hair as the quarterback caught the snap and the first play of the Chiefs' final drive was officially underway. Her eyes went to the offensive line. The big boys were shuffling back into a three-step protection, setting up a quick pass just like Rae had said, when two knocks rattled her apartment door.

The rookie federal agent turned as the ball sailed high out of bounds. Her dad was explaining how the UCM quarterback had let his elbow get ahead of his wrist, that's why the pass had gotten away from him. Rae cut him off, saying, "Hey, Coach. Gotta go," then ended the call without worrying what Chuck might think. He knew enough to know that his daughter was working her first case, and in the Johnson household, work always came first.

Three more knocks and Rae opened the door. Frank Ranchino had his light blue blazer off, folded over the crook of one arm, revealing the straps of a shoulder holster bisecting the palm trees and coconuts on his Hawaiian shirt.

"Made it through the files yet? Hope so. I got—" Frank nodded over Rae's head to the laptop, the live stream still flickering across the screen. "You're watching the game?"

Rae could see her reflection in the shades hanging from the neck of Frank's shirt, and *holy shit*, she wasn't wearing any pants. Just panties and an oversized Razorback Track sweatshirt. Rae tried to think of a joke, something she could say that might defuse the situation. Frank beat her to it.

"Twelve months I been stuck in this cotton patch, one whole year," he said without looking at her legs. "No partner. No nothing. Just old Frank in the butthole of America, watching Speer Taylor make millions coaching a kiddie game. You learned anything about Speer yet?"

"He's the coach. UCM's head coach."

"That's right, but the players are the ones out there getting their bells rung. You imagine an announcer saying that these days? 'That kid just got his *bell rung*.' Guy'd get canned faster than Howie Cosell."

Rae said, "I'm sorry?"

"Don't be. Just go get some clothes on, shorts at least—Jesus, this heat in November, you believe it?—and meet me at the Waffle House here in, oh, how about five minutes?"

Rae stared up at her new partner, trying to make sense of Frank Ranchino, the leather straps on his shoulder holster tightening him up somehow, holding him together. She thought of her father and realized she hadn't asked him about his game. Arkansas at Auburn, the noon slot on ESPN. Rae hadn't even checked the score. She wondered what Madeline Mayo was thinking. How much damage control would it take to get her best friend to answer another call?

"But the game," Rae said, tugging at her sweatshirt, pulling it down. "This is the last drive. Can't we wait until it's over? I'd like to see how it ends."

"You meet me at the Waffle House in," Frank said, and flicked his left wrist, getting his watch face turned where he could see it, "*four* minutes now, and I'll show you how the game ends. How it always ends. Capeesh?"

2

There were five seconds left in the game when the University of Central Mississippi's senior quarterback Matt Talley scrambled free of the pocket. If he'd just thrown the ball away, right then, there would've still been time for another play. But Matt had already noticed the man standing in the south end zone, the gray beard, the broad shoulders, bottom lip bulging from an oversized pinch of snuff. All of that converged in Matt's mind and the years fell away until he was a boy again, lying in his double bed tossing a football at the Super Bowl XXXI poster hanging on the wall, playing catch with his hero.

Stunned by the realization that Brett Favre was now less than twenty yards away, Matt forgot what he was supposed to be doing out on that field. He'd already fumbled, thrown two interceptions, and missed every open receiver in the second half. He'd singlehandedly given the undermanned Golden Eagles the game. Right in front of Brett Favre. Pathetic.

UCM trailed Southern Miss by five, and time was still ticking. There were only two seconds left when Matt stopped running altogether. It was so sudden, so unpredictable—like Matt was in his backyard playing two-hand touch, not trying to keep the Chiefs' undefeated season alive—that it caused the Eagles' blitzing middle backer to misjudge his angle and whiff, arms flailing as he stumbled past Matt in a blur.

The clock hit zero, the scoreboard buzzed, and Matt finally snapped out of his Favre-induced daze. This was it. The senior quarterback had however long it took to make his next move—or get tackled for a loss—and then, either way, the game would be over. Matt was still ten yards from the goal line. Ten yards beyond that stood Favre, calling to the senior quarterback in a way that went beyond words, gunslinger to gunslinger.

In the far-left corner of the end zone, Cergile Blanc spun off a defender and reversed field, cutting horizontally across the blue-and-red letters that spelled CHIEFS. Matt saw Cerge but couldn't make sense of him. Matt was no longer thinking, just reacting, everything on autopilot now, movements repeated thousands of times down through the practice fields and dreams of his youth.

Matt's feet started up again. He sprinted for the end zone, scrambling instead of passing the ball to his wide-open running back. It was too late anyway. Matt had already crossed the line of scrimmage and could no longer make a legal pass downfield.

There were only seven yards to go, but at six-foot-six, Matt Talley was a pure pocket passer. Probably the slowest guy on the field, excluding the offensive linemen, of course. It didn't matter. Everyone, including the strong safety barreling straight at him, paled in comparison to Favre. Matt was so close, he thought he could see his hero smiling. Or maybe it was just the snuff.

The Chiefs' senior quarterback pumped his throwing arm like he was going to lob a pass to Cerge—a move he'd seen Brett Favre work to perfection ten, sometimes fifteen yards downfield—and the safety jumped. Matt couldn't believe it.

His lips peeled back, revealing a bright blue mouthpiece as he loped like a racing camel toward the touchdown that would change his life forever.

3

Driving south on College Street, Rae Johnson had both hands on the wheel of the Chevy Impala she'd rented on the government's dime. She was wearing a pair of beige Jordans with jeans, not shorts like Frank Ranchino had suggested. The top two buttons on her dress shirt were undone, the sleeves rolled up. Rae was ready, ecstatic, *thrilled* to finally be out of that apartment, but she was still in desperate need of a shower.

As the Impala approached the corner of College and Main, Rae spotted Frank's cherry-red Subaru Outback parked in the Waffle House parking lot. She eased the Impala to a stop at the intersection, trying not to think of how much the classic diner reminded her of home.

Arkansas sat ninety miles northwest across the Hernando de Soto Bridge, just past Memphis. Chuck Johnson had finally put down his roots in the Natural State after dragging Rae all across the country for the first half of her youth. She barely remembered the early days, one-year stopovers at schools with weird names nobody knew. The Delaware Fightin' Blue Hens. Kent State Golden Flashes. Stephen F. Austin Lumberjacks. Florida Atlantic Owls. There was a slew of Tiger teams Rae got mixed up and a few seasons in Division II that were so tough Rae'd felt sorry for her father, riding beside him in those stinking sleeper buses, traveling hundreds of miles every weekend to play games nobody watched. The Southern Arkansas *Mule*riders weren't exactly prime time, but Chuck was, even back in the dark days. Rae's daddy never lost his shine.

Chuck worked his way out of Division II and eventually landed a string of smaller D-I jobs before finally becoming the head coach at his alma mater. News broke the night before Rae turned thirteen. The shitty birthday was a small price to pay for four straight years at the same high school. Rae trained with the Fayetteville Bulldogs track team while Chuck whipped the University of Arkansas Razorbacks into shape. His first championship came during Rae's freshman year at the U of A, the same year the track team won its twenty-ninth and nobody cared. Chuck stayed on after Rae graduated. He just kept building those Hogs up, adding more blue-chip recruits to his roster.

Despite Rae's itinerant childhood, she loved her daddy like only a daughter could. Chuck was all she had, after all. Lola Johnson had left for the Keys shortly after Rae started kindergarten. Rae always wondered if she was the reason her mother had hauled ass for Marathon, or if Lola simply couldn't stomach the thought of another season, another cross-country move, with a little girl in tow.

Chuck did what he could, but there was no way to shield Rae from the spotlight, no way to protect her from the public eye. She'd grown up under a microscope. Always "the coach's daughter," instead of an honor-roll student or a record-setting track star. The money helped, though. Before his long-running stint at Arkansas, Chuck Johnson had been the head coach at Texas Tech for two abysmal seasons. His record was so atrocious, the board of trustees in Lubbock was willing to fork over a truckload of cash just to get him out of there. For the next five years, the Red Raiders were contractually obligated to pay Chuck $5,500 a day to *not coach*. When Rae'd first realized what she'd be making as a federal agent, she'd considered sending

Texas Tech a letter, explaining how, for only $1,000 a day, she'd also agree to *not coach*. In addition, she was willing to accept payments to not do the following: ride in elevators, watch soccer games, or listen to "country" music released after the year 2000. Rae knew better, though. Texas Tech would never hire her, or fire her, for any football-related operations. Rae was a woman.

That fact had been cemented Rae's senior year at the University of Arkansas. She'd not only excelled in the classroom and on the track, Rae had also spent every second of what little free time she had helping Chuck prepare for his games. She knew her way around the sideline, the coaches' office, and the film room, especially. That's where her daddy had taught her how to scout an opponent.

Chuck had risen through the ranks in a time before cell phones and the internet. There were no instant replays on colossal video boards, no online databases of game film. He'd had to gather his information as it happened, vibrant bursts of action, offensive and defensive schemes revealed one play, one second, at a time. Chuck recorded everything in a specifically designed three-ring binder. Inside were reams of paper devoted to the opposing team's players, tells, tendencies, and more.

So much more.

Her father's binder had cast a spell on young Rae. His notes, on the other hand, were incomprehensible. They might as well have been written in another language, hieroglyphics on a cave wall. The strangeness, the mystery of it all, only upped his daughter's curiosity. So much so, Rae made her own binders, the same way some children keep diaries. Rae's binders had MTV, *Goosebumps*, and Game Boy stickers on the covers, but the pages weren't filled with the worries of a nine-year-old girl. They were brimming with blitzes and play diagrams. Rae took notes, whole boxes full, even though she didn't have a clue what was happening on the field.

As the seasons wore on, the clutter eventually gave way to a kind of organized chaos. Rae soon learned a football field was called a gridiron for a reason. The yard lines and hash marks provided boundaries for the game. They defined what the players could do, the same way the squares on a chess board restrict the pawns, the kings, and, most importantly, the queens.

By college, Rae didn't just understand the game, she'd mastered it.

Which was why Chuck let her sit in on his coaches' meetings. Why he allowed her to take film to her dorm. When Rae returned with notes, Chuck read them. He listened to her. He was thankful for his daughter's help, all the extra, unpaid hours she was giving him and his team. The experience was so impactful, Rae decided she wanted to be a coach, the first female coach in the history of college football. Rae wasn't asking for any special favors. She'd start off at the bottom as a graduate assistant, just like everybody else. But Chuck wouldn't hear it. He wouldn't hire her either.

Chuck claimed Rae was better than football, too smart to devote her life to a game. Rae didn't understand. She'd already devoted her life to the sport. Football was what she knew best, and then, just as soon as she'd graduated, it was gone. Maybe that's why she'd wanted something else for her first case. Something far away from the fields she'd grown up on.

Compson, at least, was different.

Rae could tell that much already. The sleepy Mississippi

town sat smack dab in the heart of the Delta, steeped in the blues. Son House. Muddy Waters. Robert Johnson. There were no mountains like there'd been back in Fayetteville, barely any hills except for a few Native American burial mounds. There was nothing outside of Compson except dusty fields and dilapidated silos. The Chiefs and their multimillion-dollar football program were the heartbeat of the dying Delta town.

The Waffle House, located less than a mile from campus, was one of the few buildings that remained unaffected by the Chiefs and all their football money. It looked just like the one in Fayetteville. Just like every other Waffle House Rae had ever seen, yellow and black, a throwback with its red barstools cemented into the greasy tile floors.

Rae pulled into the parking space next to Frank's Subaru. He had his window cracked and the radio on, loud enough Rae could hear the announcers recapping the game.

"Come on. Get in," Frank said. "You're late."

"We're not eating? I had my heart set on some pecan waffles."

"We got about fifteen minutes before a mob of college kids comes storming out that stadium, itching for a taste of the All-Star Special."

Blue JanSport backpack in tow, Rae hustled around the Subaru and slid into the passenger seat, knocking a mound of Diet Mountain Lightnings and wadded-up McDonald's bags to the floor. Frank turned the radio down, put the car in reverse, and they were off, cutting back across College Street and into a Dollar General parking lot, its black-and-yellow sign similar to the Waffle House's in a way Rae'd never noticed before. Frank left the Subaru running and settled in.

Six days after first meeting Frank Ranchino and all the patience Rae'd brought with her to Compson was gone. She said, "I was joking about the waffles, but this, whatever kind of rookie crap you're trying to pull? It's not funny."

"Easy," Frank said. "The Chiefs won."

"Who cares, right? That's what you said. The game doesn't matter. It's about—"

"Oh, it's about winning and losing, kid. The Chiefs pulled it out thanks to some last-second acrobatics by their flat-footed quarterback." Frank unbuckled his seatbelt. "And that's good. It'll make this run smoother. The stuff I gotta show you tonight."

"Show me what, Frank? I made it through all those files, that whole damn apartment full of paperwork you left me."

"And? What'd you find?"

"Some suspicious calls to the Compson Police Department. A few unidentified numbers here and there, but outside of that, nothing. Not a single shred of evidence that indicated fraud."

"No shit."

"No shit? I'm serious. I didn't find anything."

"Yeah, me neither."

As the daughter of a football coach, Rae'd witnessed her fair share of crackback blocks, busted noses, and sideline brawls. She had a mean right hook and almost used it when Frank Ranchino told her he'd already gone through the files, the very same documents she'd spent the last six days poring over, tackling each page, every line, the same way her father had taught her to study game film.

"I thought you hadn't . . ." Rae took a breath. "I mean, shit, I thought you were—"

"Oh, trust me, kid, I am. Whatever you thought and more, but yeah, I went through the files. Just wanted you to double check, make sure I didn't miss something before I sent my report back to Barb."

Rae's fist loosened but flexed again when she realized Frank was talking about Barbara Lawrence, their Special Agent in Charge. Rae'd never called her SAC by her first name, much less "Barb." Even worse, if Frank really was about to send in the report, then that meant the investigation was already over, Rae's rookie case closed.

"So the Chiefs are clean?" she said through clenched teeth. "That's what you're saying?"

Frank lifted one finger from the steering wheel. "Not exactly."

Rae followed his aim, watching as a blacked-out SUV—a vehicle like FBI agents drive in movies—turned off College Street and into the Waffle House parking lot. A cute little blond emerged wearing a pair of high heels and a miniskirt, leading a stampede of college girls toward the diner's glass doors.

Frank grinned and said, "Exhibit A."

"College girls?"

"*Gridiron* Girls, or at least that's what they call them at UCM. It's like this little club, an offshoot of the athletic department, for—"

"—cleat chasers," Rae said, remembering the type of women who hung around her father's players, helping out on and off the field.

"Your term, not mine. But, yeah, you get the picture. The Gridiron Girls get a free T-shirt, a chance to hang with next year's stars, and all they gotta do is go to a party, hit a couple bars downtown. A girl like that pays some kid from Nebraska a little attention on a visit, and *boingo*—UCM's got a new four-star tight end."

"You're saying Coach Taylor is using college girls as a recruitment tool? Frank, that's—"

"—not what I'm saying. That shit goes down at every college program in America. Just let me play this thing out for you, okay?"

It came to Rae then, what this was all about. Frank wasn't lazy; he was lonely. He'd spent the last year down here, a thousand miles away from home, gathering intel and following up on leads with nothing to show for it except the story he was trying to tell Rae now. She already had an idea about how it worked, of course, but she unzipped her backpack anyway, interested enough to hear her partner out.

Frank said, "The hell's that?" nodding at the three-ring binder Rae'd just removed from her backpack. It wasn't just any binder, though. This was her Trapper Keeper, the one with the Velcro flap and an orange synthwave sunrise set against a smattering of purple palms. Rae'd first purchased it in 1993, back when she was still learning how to scout teams with her dad.

"It's a binder, Frank. I like to take notes."

"Notes? Shit, kid. You ever heard of a steno pad?"

Steno pads were too small. The inside of the Trapper Keeper was organized much like her father's scouting binder had been. Except, instead of formation charts and rosters, Rae's tabs had headings like LOCATIONS and LEADS. She'd owned other binders over the years but had always liked this one best. The beach theme reminded her of her mother.

"It helps me keep my thoughts in order." Rae ripped the Velcro flap open and glared sideways at her partner. "Okay?"

"Sure, yeah, take some notes. I don't care." Frank swiped at his hair. "Anyway, the girls, that's where I started. A bunch of white girls driving Beamers and wearing three-hundred-dollar dresses running around Compson with these six-foot-six home-boys off the streets. Black kids. Like Cergile Blanc. Straight out the 305 . . ."

Rae tapped her pen against the binder's middle ring.

"What I'm saying is, the Chiefs are clean. You checked out all the local PD reports, just like I did, and no UCM player has ever been convicted of a crime in Compson. Not so much as a traffic violation. Only problem the Chiefs got now is with the Choctaws."

"The mascot, right?"

"It's not so much the name that's got the Choctaws worked up, it's the fans and all that warpaint they wear every Saturday. The powwow drums, the plastic tomahawks and shit."

Rae nodded, watching the girls through the oily windows, remembering the calls her daddy used to get at all hours of the night, his boys out howling at the moon, getting snatched up and thrown in the drunk tank until Chuck came to bail them out. But the Chiefs hadn't had a single assault charge? No DUIs? *Nothing?* Rae flipped to her INQUIRIES tab and made a note.

"I still haven't figured that part out," Frank said. "I mean, it's one thing to pay some high school boys off, get 'em to come play ball. It's another thing entirely to get local law enforcement in your back pocket. Sure, by this point the Chiefs are already in the national spotlight, getting some airtime on ESPN. There's a lot of pride involved in college football, especially down here. Like these yahoos are making up for something."

A blue Ford F-150 with red accents turned off College Street toward the Waffle House and parked in the back corner of the lot. It didn't look like a college kid's vehicle. No rims, not even a lift kit, just an expensive truck, a "Limited" or "Deluxe" edition decked out in the home team's colors. Rae waited for the door to open, expecting to see some big-money booster slide out.

"It's more than just pride, though," Frank said. "This whole operation is their lifeblood. You notice all the hotels around the stadium?"

Rae had noticed the hotels. A string of DoubleTrees, Hilton Gardens, and Fairfield Inns. Nothing fancy, no five-star resorts, but they were new and there were lots of them. Every single one with freshly planted trees out front. A few still had tags attached to the branches and plastic support straps around the trunks.

"Made a couple calls. You'll never believe how much a room in the Fairfield Inn goes for on game day." Frank waited, shrugged, then shrugged again. "Go on. Guess."

"I don't know. A couple hundred bucks?"

"Try five hundred, a grand, even, depending on who the Chiefs are playing, or if, say, it's a conference game."

"A thousand bucks for a room in the Fairfield Inn?" Rae wrote the words down as she said them.

"*An oasis of culture and thought.* That's the Compson city slogan, and it's new too. Just like the hotels."

The slogan wasn't just new, it was stupid. *An oasis?* Rae thought. The Delta was the birthplace of the blues. You could find more culture in a single Mississippi juke joint than almost anywhere else in the world. She held her tongue and said, "Okay, so Compson's capitalizing off the home team," thinking of her father, that buyout from Texas Tech, and his latest contract extension with Arkansas. "Can you blame them?"

"No, you're right," Frank said, digging around in the breast pocket of his Hawaiian shirt. "I needed more than that. So I kept waiting, hoping to see some report about a Gridiron Girl getting a backside blitz run on her ass, or hell, a speeding ticket—that would've done it. But no charges come through. Zero cases. The Chiefs are clean, and I don't believe it for one friggin' minute."

Frank's hand was out of the pocket now, holding what Rae took to be a single cigarette, like the guy was trying to quit but kept one stashed away just in case.

Frank said, "E-cig," and placed the plastic cylinder between his lips. "Got it at the Walgreens when I heard you were coming down." He exhaled and a small cloud materialized above his head. The Subaru's cab smelled faintly of cherries.

"But you kept looking, right? You're still trying to figure out who's covering up the crimes? Paying the players is one thing, Frank, but this stuff with the police"—Rae slapped her Trapper Keeper—"that's the heart of the case."

Frank took another long drag off his e-cig. The tip glowed electric red. He didn't exhale this time, holding it in as he said, "Bet your ass I'm still looking, Agent Johnson," raising his eyebrows and wheezing a little with the cherry-flavored vapor in his lungs. "Matter of fact, you notice that blue Ford just pulled into the Waffle House a second ago?"

Rae leaned forward, narrowing her eyes.

"Here in about, oh," the veteran special agent said, talking in a high-pitched tone of voice, still holding that last hit down, "four, maybe five min—" Frank coughed and a puff of vapor shot out of his nose, his mouth. "Whatever. Listen. You got your pen ready?"

Rae lifted her blue Pilot V7, the same brand her father favored.

"Good, 'cause you're about to meet the star of this show," Frank said, "the whole damn reason UCM's files are squeaky clean."

4

Brett Favre was kind of short. That was the first thing Matt Talley remembered about meeting his hero. Favre had found him out around the fifty-yard line after the game. There'd been so many people—the whole student section plus some other drunk fans—that Matt never saw him coming. Favre was just *there*, reaching his right hand out, a sign of respect, a peace offering coming from the other side. When their hands finally met, Matt felt the calluses running along the ridge of the old gunslinger's palm, the two of them connecting again like they'd done for that final, magical moment of the game.

Favre said, "A downfield pump fake on the goal line? Hot damn, son. Reminds me of my favorite play: *Mississippi Blue 42*," and then he was gone, dissolving back into the crowd as reporters shoved cameras and cell phones into Matt Talley's face, the bright stadium lights burning the moment into his mind forever.

And now Matt was driving down College Street in his tan Jeep Wrangler with the top off, still getting a few cheers when a diehard fan recognized his vehicle. Matt whispered, "*Brett Favre*," and turned into the Waffle House parking lot. "Brett fucking *Favre* . . ."

Matt parked his Jeep in the far back corner, right next to the blue Ford sitting alone in the dark. He took a deep breath and started for the truck, hoping none of the Gridiron Girls in the Waffle House could see him.

Before he opened the Ford's passenger-side door, Matt

paused, trying to ignore the shadowy figure behind the wheel, letting his mind drift back to the special moment he'd shared with his hero. What was it Favre had said?

The door opened. Matt half expected the retired QB to be sitting behind the wheel, offering him the keys to his castle, but instead it was just a heavyset redneck holding a bulging red gym bag. Matt pulled himself into the cab and said, "Hey, Eddie. You ever heard of Mississippi Blue 42?"

5

"Introducing Eddie Pride Junior," Frank Ranchino said as the starting quarterback for the top-ranked college football team in the country disappeared inside the blue Ford. "Mr. Pride's what's known as a bagman. Heard of it?"

"I just graduated from the Academy, Frank. I've heard of bagmen."

"Different kind of bagman, kid. Here in Compson, the bagmen pay the players, usually in bags full of cold, hard cash."

Rae ran two fingers over her Trapper Keeper's back flap, feeling the words she'd written there over twenty years before. *Work hard, never quit, and good things'll happen.* The blue ink had faded, and Rae's handwriting was messier now than it was then, but her father's core message remained. Rae looked up from the binder and said, "What's with the bags?"

"I'm getting there. But first we got to go back to the beginning. Back in high school, when a player's just starting to get recruited."

"A kid comes to Compson," Rae said, "goes on a visit, gets a Gridiron Girl, and a bag full of cash? No wonder the Chiefs are undefeated."

"This isn't just any kid we're talking about. This special sort of treatment is only for the best. The four- and five-star recruits. You familiar with the ranking system?"

Rae recalled Rivals.com and 247sports, online databases that assigned each potential recruit a certain number of stars, like they were in kindergarten, getting good marks on spelling tests.

"Yeah," Rae said. "Think I dated a three-star once."

"Bet you did. Anyway, a kid like Matt Talley gets four stars coming out of Jackson Prep, and that's good enough to draw the attention of a man like Mr. Pride."

The truck across the street, the one that belonged to the bagman, was cloaked in darkness. Shadows moved behind the glass. Rae tried to imagine what was going on in there: the handoff, the drop, whatever the hell it was called when a college QB got paid.

"They start by making house calls, stopping in, oh, about once a week, and leaving a bag behind every time. Some prefer gym bags, or duffels," Frank said. "I heard about this one Black guy used to work around here—think he plays guitar, the blues—this guy made his drops using *shopping* bags. Like from department stores? Dillard's and JCPenney. The payments are always in cash and it's never too much. Just enough to make a kid feel special."

Frank held his e-cig loose between his index finger and thumb, painting a picture for Rae in the space between his words.

"Usually—not always—but *usually*, the recruit winds up going to the highest bidder. You gotta remember, most these kids, especially the Black ones, they're coming from nothing. Got dollar signs in their eyes, dreams of making it to the NFL and buying their moms Cadillacs and shit."

"I get it, Frank, but what happens after they get to campus?"

Frank nodded across the street to Eddie's Ford. "You're looking at it. No more free meals. Once they get a kid on the roster, he's paid based on production. Throw a couple touchdown passes, make a few sacks, and the same guy that was there back in high school sets up a meeting at some skeevy place like a Waffle House parking lot where he says thank you with a bag full of Benjamins."

"Then why haven't you made a bust already? I mean, what's keeping us from going over there, flashing our badges, and catching Eddie giving Matt the business?"

"Jesus, kid, this ain't prison. Nobody's getting the business. It's just a bag full of cash. And what's keeping me from walking over there and flashing my badge is the fact that it's not illegal. Eddie Pride Junior doesn't have ties with UCM. He's not a coach. Not even a booster. A booster leaves a paper trail. Eddie's just a bagman."

Rae read back over the notes she'd taken: *Gridiron Girls. Fairfield Inn. Bagmen. Five star. Four star. Boosters?* Rae knew boosters. She could spot one from a mile away. They always had the newest gear, the best seats in the stadium. They were the men, and sometimes women, who coaches thanked at Touch-down Clubs. Boosters gave money to the universities, or more specifically, the football programs. In any other business they would've been called donors, rich people whose names went up on the sides of buildings.

"If a bagman's not a booster," Rae said, "then what is he?"

"A ghost." Frank stuck the e-cig behind his ear. "And that's the friggin' problem. That's why we don't got nothing on UCM. All these bagmen, they're private citizens who spend their free time bribing the country's best players into signing with the Chiefs. Bagmen don't even talk to the recruits on their personal phones. They use burners, or the way Eddie likes to say it, his 'Bat Phone.' You believe that shit?"

"And I'm guessing he's got a thing for the Waffle House?"

"They all do," Frank said. "Every bagman I ever tailed does most his business in or around a Waffle House. The place is open twenty-four hours a day, every day. And the coffee's not half bad, neither."

Rae snapped her fingers and watched Frank's forehead wrinkle. "If the bagmen aren't affiliated with the schools, then why do they do it? There must be some sort of incentive, a connection we're missing."

"Now there's the million-dollar question." Frank stared up at the Subaru's sunroof, on past it, maybe. "Remember how I said there's a lot of pride on the line with football, especially down here?"

Rae flipped back to her GENERAL NOTES tab and said, "Sure."

"For a guy like Eddie, it's more than that. It's a sickness. That's what it is, and you can see it spreading across the country you look close enough." Frank the philosopher now, still leaned back, head in the stars. "I blame it on the Civil War."

Rae didn't bite, guessing this was the final act in the Frank Ranchino Show.

"Namely, the fact that the South lost. See, college football's their second chance. Every Saturday in the fall, these people get to wage a new war, sometimes even against teams from the North, although football up there's nothing like it is down here, and that's why we didn't find jack shit in all those files. Things are so backwards in the South, the teams don't have to cheat, their fans do it for them."

Rae leaned forward in her seat, trying to make sense of everything Frank had said. He wasn't wrong. She knew how much football meant to her, her father, all their friends and family.

Frank poked the side of his head, trying to make a point.

The e-cig fell out from behind his ear and into the crack between the console and the driver's seat. Frank went after it, elbow deep with his eyes on Rae, saying, "Okay. I think that covers it. Any questions?"

"You've been down here a year," Rae said, "and that's all you've got? Some lame theory about the Civil War?"

"Huh?" Frank grunted, still scrounging for the e-cig. "Speak up. Don't hear so good in my left ear."

"Let's say all these *bagmen*," Rae said, louder now, "really do have middle-aged hard-ons for college football players, and they're somehow pulling the behind-the-scenes strings for the country's top programs . . . If all that's true, then there's got to be more to it than just pride."

Frank said, "Shit. Almost forgot," and made a sound like a laugh without looking up. "Eddie played left guard for the Chiefs. A four-year letterman during the '88 to '92 seasons. Wanna take a stab at the Chiefs' overall record during that run?"

The Gridiron Girls were exiting the Waffle House now, toting black and yellow to-go bags.

"Eddie won six games," Frank said. "That means he lost the other forty-something. You imagine what that does to a man? I can't, but if you're asking my personal opinion, I think the guy just got tired of losing, decided to do something about it."

The girls' faces glowed red in the Ford truck's taillights. Rae guessed they liked to get their bellies full of hashbrowns before they got their drink on, some sort of pregame ritual, a protective measure. She said, "But the Chiefs didn't start really winning until Coach Taylor showed up."

"So?"

"And Eddie's been delivering bags for how long?"

"Years. Decades. Who knows?"

"How, then, does Eddie all the sudden start bringing in the country's top recruits? And you said the Chiefs haven't had a single crime reported in the last two seasons?" Rae didn't wait for him to answer. "It has to have something to do with Speer Taylor. He's the connection."

Frank sat up and slapped the wheel. "Lazy Dayz. Shit. I forgot to tell you about Lazy Dayz."

Rae's eyes were still on the girls squeezing into that black SUV when she noticed movement in the back of the lot. The passenger-side door on the blue Ford, opening. She pointed, trying to get Frank's attention, but his mouth was moving again, saying, "Eddie runs a beach chair business out of Gulfport called Lazy Dayz. A few years back, right around the time Speer Taylor was hired, Brett Favre's on vacation with his family . . ."

"You see that? The side door on Eddie's Ford just opened."

"And I'll tell you what happens next," Frank said. "Matt Talley's about to step out sporting a gym bag full of cash. Eddie likes gym bags for some reason. Me, personally, I'd go with a duffel." Frank pushed up from the steering wheel, stretching a little. "Like I's saying, Favre's on vacation down in Gulfport, and somehow, he winds up in a Lazy Dayz beach chair. Probably passed out in the damn thing. The guy flips for it. Posts the shit all over his social media, saying it's the most comfortable chair he's ever sat in. What happens next is—"

"The money, Frank. *Look.*"

"What?" Frank tapped his bad ear and laughed. "Just kidding. I heard you, and you're right. It's money, kid. *That's* the point. Eddie's into some serious dough now. He's expanded Lazy Dayz all the way from the Emerald Coast down to South Beach, charging fat-ass tourists seventy-five bucks a day for a foldout chair with an umbrella and a built-in cup holder." Frank stuck his hand back in his breast pocket but the e-cig was already in his lips, just hanging there. "And that's when the Chiefs' record got a facelift. That's when Cerge and Matt Talley showed up. That's when UCM started winning ball games. Speer Taylor? The guy's a total Zelig."

Rae frowned, too distracted to take notes now.

"You seen that movie? Think Woody Allen did it. Anyway, that's what Speer is: part coach, part youth pastor, with a little politician thrown in. Drinks his own Kool-Aid by the gallon. Yeah," Frank said, "Coach Taylor's the luckiest bastard on the planet, and Matt Talley's right behind him."

Rae reached across the center console and took hold of Frank's chin. The veteran agent flinched like he thought the redhead was about to choke him.

"Matt Talley just got out of that truck," Rae said, rotating her partner's head back toward the Waffle House, "and he doesn't have a bag in his hands."

6

"**Look at** him, baby," Cergile Blanc said, talking to UCM's backup quarterback, Moses McCloud, as Matt Talley walked through the front doors of the Buffalo Nickel, a college bar nestled between Backyard Books and Snack Rack Bakery in the heart of Compson's downtown square. "That should be you with all them Gridiron Girls."

Moses was taller than Cerge by a few inches, a solid six-foot-three, but leaner, built more like a wide receiver than a quarterback. Standing on the Buffalo Nickel's second-story loft looking down at Matt Talley tossing back tequila shots at the bar, Moses appreciated Cerge's vote of confidence, but he knew he wasn't ready. Moses was just a freshman, using his redshirt year to learn the playbook and settle in. Besides, there was only one game left in the regular season, and if the Chiefs won it, they'd play in the SEC Championship game. If they won that, they'd be headed to the Cotton Bowl for a shot at their second straight national championship. All that pressure, Moses thought, taking a sip of his carbonated water, Matt could have it.

"Know what you thinking." Cerge ran a hand through the dreads he'd told Moses he started growing back in sixth grade, a rite of passage for a kid from South Florida. "You thinking about how Matt just won the big game, diving into the end zone like his life depended on it, sacrificing his body for the good of the team. What could be better?"

Moses wasn't thinking that. He was watching the Gridiron Girls now, one in particular, a curvy blond junior by the name of Ella May Pride. She was half the reason Moses had signed with the Chiefs in the first place, all the things she'd said and done the night of his official visit in room 217 of the Fairfield Inn, her breath hot in Moses's ear as she whispered, "Daddy ever gets wind of this, he'll skin you alive."

Moses took another sip of his sparkling water, trying to wash the memory away. A mistake, a risk, that's what Ella May had been. What she still was. The Gridiron Girls, just like everything else in Mississippi, were segregated. Back at Clarksdale, there were still two homecoming queens, a Black one and a white one, the Mexican girls lost in the shuffle. It wasn't that clear-cut in Compson. Stuff just went that way most of the time. Like how Moses's bagman, or at least the brother who looked out for him, was Black and Matt's guy was white. Not just any white man either. Matt's bagman was Ella May's daddy. Eddie Pride Junior. One of those swolled-up short guys looked like maybe he'd been buff once.

Nobody said anything straight out about the Gridiron Girls when Moses had first arrived for his visit. Each player was assigned a host, a special friend, or something. Moses couldn't remember the exact term. What he could remember was how Ella May Pride had come to him on the Buffalo Nickel's dance floor, nudging Moses's preassigned female companion of color out of the way with her perky can and staring the young quarterback straight in his eyes. A week later, Moses signed his National Letter of Intent, declaring his allegiance to UCM, and he never heard from Ella May Pride again.

"People all the time asking me if we gonna win," Cerge was saying, slurping down his fourth Tipsy Tomahawk, the Buffalo Nickel's signature drink, "like I got The Eye the way my Gran

Blanc had it. I mean, shit, I *know* we gonna win. But if it's you and me in the backfield, two brothers that can really run? Then there ain't no need for a last-second play. Know what I'm saying?"

"Yeah."

"I'm trying to get drafted. Trying to make it to *the* League. Get me a contract, a signing bonus. Make me some that real money, man."

Moses raised his cup, peering over the rim at Ella May, Cerge's voice lost in the churn of a postgame Saturday night. He still had the cup to his lips when he realized his drink was empty, and—*shit*—Ella May was staring up at him, swaying her hips to the bass as she cut her way through the crowd, Matt Talley's drunk ass stumbling along behind her.

Cerge said, "All them girls out there, and you get stuck on the quarterback's girlfriend."

"What?"

Cerge nodded toward the couple coming up the stairs. "You ain't got a damn clue the kinda trouble you gonna get in you start sniffing around Ella May Pride again."

She was at the top of the steps now, standing close enough Moses noticed the red gym bag in her hand, the kind her boyfriend was always toting around when he wasn't driving his brand-new Jeep Wrangler. Matt was a few feet behind her, trying to find the last two steps. Moses watched Ella May pass Matt the bag, using the handle like a leash to tug him along. He never understood what she saw in him. The tall white boy looked like an ostrich the way he walked, or maybe a flamingo, whatever kind of bird it was where the knees bent backward. Maybe it was the fact that Matt was the starting quarterback for the Chiefs. Maybe that's why Ella May liked him. Moses had never thought of that before. He was thinking it now.

"There he is," Cerge said, putting it on thick as he bypassed Matt's outstretched hand and went in for a hug. "Celebrating big, ain't you, baby? Should be, shit, after that game you played?"

Mouth pressed against the top of Cerge's dreads, Matt said, "We need to talk, man. I gotta—"

"*Talk?* I'm right here, baby. Big Cerge's all ears."

"Matt just needs some fresh air," Ella May said, stepping between them.

Cerge was wearing acid-washed jeans that had holes down the front and a baggy white T-shirt, the words HE IS RIZZEN stamped across his chest along with a picture of Black Jesus in a pair of Gucci shades. "Go on, then," Cerge said. "Take Matt's drunk-ass up to my office. Get him some air."

Moses had visited Cerge's "office" the night of his official visit, right before his rendezvous with Ella May at the Fairfield Inn, the All-American running back of Haitian descent standing on the bar's roof telling Moses if he came to UCM, he could change things. "*A Black quarterback in Compson, Mississippi. You know what that would mean? And the spot's all yours, baby. That Talley guy ain't shit.*"

But now, there Cerge was leading Matt across the loft toward the stairwell, even holding the door open for the gangly QB. Ella May hadn't moved, hanging back with this look in her eyes like her daddy got sometimes. Moses never knew what to expect when it came to Eddie Pride Junior. It was the same way with Ella May.

Before Moses could think of what to say, his dream girl turned and started for the door Cerge was still holding open.

Moses was following along behind them, his mind back in the Fairfield Inn, room 217, when Ella May stepped into the stairwell and Cerge slammed the door shut behind her.

"Nope," Cerge said, blocking Moses's path with one hand, a stiff arm. "Do *not* go up there, man. This some white people shit. We need to get gone, like now."

Blood boomed in Moses's ears the same way it did anytime Ella May walked past him on campus. Cerge lifted his chin. His lips were moving, forming words Moses couldn't hear, and then Cerge walked away, shaking his head as he hustled back down to the bar's first floor.

Moses watched Cerge disappear into the crowd and felt his phone vibrate against his thigh. He checked it, frowning as he scanned the article his grandmother'd just sent him, the headline big and bold across the top of the screen: USC QB SCRAMBLES AMID DUI CHARGES. Momma G was all the time texting him stuff like that, but Moses took it as a sign. A reason to do like Cerge had said and get the hell out of there.

7

Ella May Pride was thinking about her daddy and the men who would come for him—how they might already be there, at her house, right now—all because Matt Talley saw Brett Favre in the back corner of the end zone. Like he'd seen Jesus or something.

That's basically what he'd told her on the drive over to the bar, Matt sitting in the Denali's backseat, knees scrunched, saying, "I don't care what you think, Ella May. It was worth it. You know what Mr. Brett said to me?"

Mississippi Blue 42.

The hell was that supposed to mean? Maybe it was something Favre liked to say back in his glory days, before he sent those dick pics to that model and came back from retirement one time too many, or maybe the guy was just drunk. The way Matt kept whispering the phrase under his breath after every tequila shot—"*Mississippi Blue 42*"—Ella May knew her boyfriend was wasted, and something was bad wrong.

Her daddy knew it too.

That's why Eddie had flashed his Ford's high beams right before Ella May followed Matt into the Buffalo Nickel. Eddie didn't say anything when she walked up to his driver-side window. He just took her Waffle House to-go bag and handed her a red one, a look on his face Ella May had never seen before. She pushed one arm through the gym bag's straps, carrying it the same way she would a purse. Ella May wasn't sure what the money was for, but she guessed it was something like a parting gift, a going-away present. Her father's last will and testament.

Ella May took some pride in accepting the bag from her father. She'd watched him offer payments to so many players down through the years. Recently, Eddie'd been promoted to recruiting upper-class white boys. Quarterbacks, mostly. It was an honor and a chore, so far from the offensive linemen he'd dealt with forever. Eddie'd been poor most his life, right up until Lazy Dayz hit it big. He didn't understand the rich boys. Boys like Matt didn't give a damn about money, not even a red gym bag stuffed full of fifty thousand bucks.

Matt had been so loaded he could barely make it up the steps to the second floor. Ella May handed him the bag as a counterweight, something to keep him balanced. Last thing she needed was for Matt to fall flat on his face and cause a scene. The place was packed, the whole student section still buzzing after the big win. Cergile Blanc was waiting for them at the top of the steps with Moses McCloud, drinking what Ella May guessed was water and looking at her the same way he always looked at her. Ella May wondered how much they knew, or if they knew anything at all. Cerge knew enough not to come upstairs, but what about Moses?

Standing on the college bar's roof now, Ella May kept her distance, remembering the sad look on her daddy's face, knowing his quarterback had gone rogue and run Blue 48 Mississippi, or whatever the hell it was Favre had said. The bagman's daughter closed her eyes and whispered, "Dammit, Matt. You realize what you've done?" streaks of purple and green lighting up the darkness, the shape of her boyfriend's body still silhouetted in her mind.

Matt said, "What?" slurring the word so it sounded like *Waa?*

Ella May opened her eyes to find the same scene as before. The same game. That's all this was to Matt, but it was her daddy's life he was playing with. Ella May took a breath and said, "I asked if you knew what you'd done."

Matt made another sound that was supposed to be a word then said, "*Whooops,*" real loud and slow, the same way he'd been saying that line he'd heard from Favre for the last couple hours. Like a dumbass. That's how Ella May felt when she noticed how her boyfriend was leaning way out over the ledge, looking down.

A breeze picked up from the west and blew back his frat-boy hairdo. Matt wobbled as he turned. All those tequila shots, he was white-girl wasted. Ella May was staring at his freakishly white forehead, guessing it had something to do with his bangs, or maybe his helmet, when the thought of rushing her boyfriend entered the Gridiron Girl's mind. Matt's pocket awareness was shit. He'd never see it coming.

Ella May took a step forward then stopped, thinking she'd have to hit him low, down around the knees, and lift with her hips. Matt was really tall. Another step and a memory slipped through: Moses McCloud, the way he'd been staring at her in the loft. The way he was *always* staring at her.

The thought was enough for Ella May to pause and consider her game plan. Maybe she was taking the wrong approach. Maybe, instead of blitzing Matt, she should send for backup— Matt's backup—and go on the offensive.

It was a tough call.

8

Rae was starting to think she liked Frank the loudmouth Yank better than the current version of her partner: quiet and reserved, almost pouty. He'd made this sad, rattling sound in the back of his throat when Matt Talley stepped out of Eddie's blue Ford empty-handed, and that was it. Frank didn't say another word. Didn't even follow the black SUV with the Gridiron Girl behind the wheel and the quarterback in the backseat. Frank just kept sitting there, watching the one empty space in the far corner of the Waffle House parking lot, the place where the deal had gone wrong.

After five minutes of sitting quiet and still, Rae tried snapping her partner out of it, saying, "Okay, so Matt didn't take the money. It doesn't mean—"

"Thought I had it all figured," Frank said, shoulders slumped against the leather holster straps. "Had you double-check the files. I was *this* close to filing the report . . ."

"It was just one drop. We weren't even going to make a bust."

"I know." Frank shifted the Subaru into gear, nosing the front end back onto College Street. "It would've just been nice to get this one in the books before I called it quits. Felt like, maybe, if I gave you all the pieces, let you write everything down in that big ass binder . . ." Frank sighed, staring down the road. "Something like that."

They were headed south on College Street: the opposite direction the Gridiron Girls had gone. A few miles later, they were out of town. A cotton field materialized through the passenger-side window. The rows between the bolls blurred together like a stick man running, sprinting faster and faster until the field was gone, replaced by the dim lights of Compson once again. The two-lane highway turned back into College Street as soon as the Subaru passed the CITY LIMITS sign.

And that's where they were now, coming into the downtown square, Frank still doing his crybaby routine, saying, "They give you this little plaque, the word 'Retired' etched into it. You can keep the badge if you want, but I got this nephew lives in Brooklyn says he's about to get in. Maybe it'll mean something to him."

Rae rolled her window down, wanting to get a better look at the Compson Square: the line of mom-and-pop shops, first a bookstore, then a bakery, followed by a row of crowded college bars. The busiest one had BUFFALO NICKEL written in jagged black letters across a wooden sign above the door.

The Subaru came to a stop at a red light almost even with the bar. Frank said, "You gotta turn your gun in, but they got this special kind of concealed carry permit for retirees. Long as you pass a test at the end of the year, you can still pack heat. The problem? You're on your own. Buddy of mine mentioned this retired agents' insurance policy the other day . . ."

Frank was still talking, maybe feeling better after his drive through the cotton fields, when a hundred-dollar bill fell from the sky and stuck to the Subaru's windshield.

Rae reached through the rolled-down window and had the C-note in her hand before Frank said, "Hey, look, it's your lucky day."

The bill felt cool between her fingers, the cotton-infused paper worn and smooth like old money.

Frank shrugged. "Anyway, that retired agents' insurance, it's for when I'm sitting at home a few years from now, minding my own business, and some crackhead comes crawling through the window . . ."

The Buffalo Nickel was the tallest building on the square. Rae squinted, noticing movement in the shadows on the roof.

"Let's say I shoot the guy. Put one in his kneecap. Maybe his upper thigh?" Frank had his fingers cocked like guns, waiting for the light to change. "Then the bastard tries to sue me. I gotta go to court and—"

Rae sat her Trapper Keeper in the backseat and popped open the Subaru's passenger-side door. She started to get out, but Frank said, "*Hey!*" and reached over the center console, taking hold of her shirttail. "The hell you think you're going?"

Rae looked up again, answering Frank with her eyes. The movement on the roof was different now: a faint red light pulsing behind a whirlybird vent. Rae shrugged and was starting to slide one of her Jordans back into the Subaru when a bag hit the asphalt and exploded.

The partners watched a flurry of hundred-dollar bills twirl against the backdrop of the Delta night sky, covering the square in a sea of dirty green.

Rae gripped the door handle. This was it, what her daddy would've called a "game-changing moment." Rae was ready to blow the case wide open until she felt Frank's hand on her shoulder, giving his rookie partner a gentle squeeze as he said, "A muddy puddle clears best when left alone."

"You get that off a fortune cookie?"

"I'm serious. Don't go rushing into this thing."

"I'm counting to three," Rae said, still holding the door

handle, "then I'm getting out of this vehicle. This is our chance, Frank."

"Fine, but you do the count in Mississippis."

Frank stared back at Rae, serious now. She blew a strand of red hair out of her face and started counting: "One Mississippi. Two Mississippi . . ." She paused, rolled her eyes, then said, "*Three* Mississippi."

A body hit the pavement twenty feet away. A puff of pink stuff shot out of the guy's mouth, covering the crinkled bills with his final breath.

"Ruptured lung," Frank said, and squeezed his partner's shoulder again.

A knot formed in Rae's throat. Her ears started to ring.

"I was in the city on nine-eleven," Frank said. "All those people jumping out the Towers, bodies friggin' vaporizing when they hit Greenwich. That kid there, he's still in one piece, but I don't think he's breathing."

Frank's fingers felt cold through the thin fabric of Rae's white dress shirt. She jerked away and pulled the passenger door shut.

"Hey, take it easy. Everything's coming together now. See?" Frank shifted the Subaru into reverse. "Matt Talley got his money bag, just like I said he would."

9

Headlights poked holes through the oak grove surrounding Eddie Pride's recently refurbished mansion. The whole compound had once been nothing more than a double-wide with a homemade front porch. The remodel happened after Favre passed out in that Lazy Dayz chair. Eddie had only one goal in mind for the renovation—he'd wanted his whole new estate to scream old money.

Things were different now.

Staring out at the fleet of squad cars in the driveway, Eddie pined for the double-wide he'd grown up in. All that remained from the original structure was the porch. It cost an arm and a leg, but Eddie had the contractor reattach it to the front of his new house and give it a few minor updates. Exposed overhead beams. A couple new fans.

There were four vehicles in total. Three Compson PD cruisers out ahead of a rusty Ford Ranger. Looked just like the tiny truck PawPaw Pride had driven forever. Eight men exited the patrol cars before the Ford came to a stop. Eddie peeked through the venetian blinds and whispered, "*Shit*," then took off for the door.

Standing barefoot on his front porch, Eddie placed both hands on his hips and stared into the darkness. He saw the men but didn't notice the rope in the smallest cop's hands or the way one end had been fashioned into a noose. It made no difference. Eddie knew what would happen. He'd known it as soon as Matt Talley went diving for the end zone instead of fumbling, or even just getting his lanky ass out of bounds. All the Chiefs had to do was lose. It didn't matter how.

Eddie shifted his weight from one foot to another. The wraparound porch groaned beneath him, the same planks that had held his family up for decades. Ella May had taken her first steps on that porch. PawPaw Pride used to sit and shell purple-hull peas for hours in the faded white rocking chair positioned neatly in one corner. A brand-new palm blade fan hung motionless from the porch's sky-colored ceiling. "Haint Blue." That's what Eddie's mother had called it, a homemade paint meant to keep the Devil away.

Eddie finally saw the rope in the lead boy's hands. That's what the one up front was, a boy, a young officer of the law, ready and willing to hurt somebody if that's what it took to get in good with the boss. "Bruiser" Brandt Conrad, former UCM-linebacker-turned-Compson-chief-of-police, was back there too. Bruiser was still in good shape outside of his beer gut, but he wasn't the boss.

Eddie'd never met the boss. None of the bagmen had. That was part of the deal. Everything was done in code, secret messages delivered by the very same men who were now standing on Eddie's front steps. Cops did most of the dirty work in Compson. Eddie didn't know if it was like that in Baton Rouge or Athens, but it sure as hell made things easier. Eddie'd go out to check his mail and find a fancy envelope in the box, the paper thick as cardboard with one of those red wax seals melted onto the flap. The notes inside were simple, usually just names of players, recruits to target, grandmothers and uncles to track down. Biological parents sometimes too. That sort of thing.

And money.

Up until just recently, before Favre made that Lazy Dayz post, the money'd been the most important part. Eddie already knew where to find the best players. He'd been following the recruiting message boards, sites with names like "Fearless Friday" and "Prep Gridiron" for decades. Hell, he even knew the names of the brightest, most innovative coordinators in every state. Eddie'd done his homework, and he didn't mind sharing his hard-earned answers. Even though Eddie had mostly just recruited offensive linemen, he'd discovered some of the Chiefs' best talent. Made him proud to see those players sign on over the years. Made him hungry for more.

So hungry, Eddie lost his wife, Darlene, when she found one of his burner phones. Darlene thought Eddie was having an affair even after she called and a teenage boy answered. She was gone a week later. Eddie didn't stop. He couldn't. Football would never leave him. There was always another season, another fresh crop of high school seniors, itching to play college ball. Eddie's devotion eventually paid off. Three winters ago, right around the same time the remodel wrapped up, Eddie got a card with Matt Talley's name on it. His first quarterback.

The bagman laughed, staring past the men to the racehorse tied to the live oak behind the cars.

"You think this is funny, fatty?" the lead boy said, working the noose around Eddie's neck. The kid had a shaved head and a tattoo under his left eye. A teardrop, or maybe a dog turd. Good bad cops must be getting harder to come by, Eddie thought, then flexed his neck as the noose pulled tight.

"Think it'll hold him?" The skinhead tossed the end of the rope up over one of the porch's new beams. The other cops didn't answer. Not one word from the Compson chief of police.

Eddie used to play church-league softball with "Bruiser" Brandt Conrad. Bruiser had this wicked knuckleball that gave the Methodists fits. Some claimed it was cheating. Eddie and Brandt played for the Baptist Blitz, league champs three years straight. Would've been four but Brandt tore his hamstring trying to stretch a double into a triple during the last game of the regular season.

"Hey, Bruiser," Eddie hollered. "How's the hammy?"

The police chief glanced sideways at the yellow Ford. An early '90s model. Ugliest little trucks ever made. It didn't add up to the image in Eddie's head.

Bruiser scratched his neck and said, "Still pretty tight."

"The price you pay. Lord knows my time's coming."

"You still play?"

"Brother John calls me up sometimes, when they're down a guy. Nothing serious. But I could still knock that knuckleball of yours out the park."

"That pitch only works on Methodists, Eddie."

The two men laughed like they were back in the dugout over at Hickey Park, spitting sunflower seeds through the chain-link fence. If only it were that simple. Truth was, Bruiser was the one who'd convinced Eddie to bribe Matt Talley and get him to throw the game. Said it was what was best for the Chiefs, even if it didn't look that way. What Bruiser didn't say, what he didn't have to say, was anything about Eddie Pride's gambling problem. The fifty grand Eddie had agreed to pay Matt Talley after UCM lost to Southern Miss had come straight from his own wallet, a nice chunk of dough, but it was nothing compared to what the bagman owed his bookie. Once it was all over, Bruiser had promised to drive over to the Horseshoe Casino in Tunica and make Eddie's debt disappear. No strings attached.

"*Methodists*," Eddie said and slapped his thigh. "Hot damn. That's a—"

The Ford's driver-side window creaked as it started down, silencing the former teammates. Eddie watched the red-hot tip of a cigarillo materialize in the gap. A quick flick, a scattering of ash, and the skinny cigar was gone. Eddie kept staring through the crack in the window, wanting to see the big boss more than he'd ever wanted anything in his life. The window started up again. Eddie shouted, "Hey!" and the window stopped.

"After everything I've done?" Eddie hollered, ignoring the way the rope scratched his throat. "Least you could do is show yourself."

"Shut your pie hole," the skinhead said, crouching beneath the truck's dented grill. He was doing something with his hands Eddie couldn't make out beneath the headlights' glare. Eddie scanned the shadows for Bruiser. The former linebacker with the mean knuckleball was out of the game now, sitting back in his cruiser with the door still open.

"I trusted you," Eddie said, talking straight to the big boss. "Did just what you said. I told Matt to throw the game. Told him about his pocket presence, his footwork, how he'd never make it in the NFL. This was his only shot at a big payday, but Matt didn't care about the money."

"No duh, he didn't care about the money," the skinhead said.

Eddie tried giving the kid a real hard look but his jowls got hung in the rope. "You're right about that." Eddie craned his neck, nodding past the truck to the thoroughbred.

The skinhead said, "You bought him a horse?"

"That ain't just any horse, pard. That one there's from Ireland. Guess how much that thing cost me."

"Hundred grand?"

"*Shiiit.*" Eddie liked the way the word slithered through his teeth. He tried shaking his head. The rope wouldn't allow it. "Bought Matt that horse, even tacked on an extra fifty grand, cold cash, but then, well . . . You know the rest." Eddie raised up on his tiptoes, talking over the boy. "How was I supposed to know the kid had a thing for Favre?"

A couple seconds of complete silence, not even any leaves rustling—there was no breeze—and then the window started down again.

Eddie was finally going to meet the man who'd orchestrated the Chiefs' meteoric rise to the top of the college football universe. The window stopped after only a few cranks. A hand emerged. Despite the dark, Eddie could still see the liver spots and wrinkles marring every inch of pale flesh. Each weathered finger began to curl until only a thumb remained, sticking out sideways, perfectly parallel to the ground. The other men were watching the truck now too, watching as the old man's forearm twisted and the thumb turned down.

The skinhead howled.

Eddie could see what the boy'd done with the rope now, how he'd fed the loose end into the winch on the front of the truck. The skinhead took the handle in both hands and started cranking.

The rope slithered over the beam like a cottonmouth. The noose constricted, yanking Eddie up, a portly puppet on a string. The bagman punched at the rope, his toes prodded for the planks, but it was pointless. As Eddie's eyeballs bulged, his life rewound forty years until he was back on that very same porch, watching his mother paint the ceiling. A nine-year-old Eddie held the ladder steady beneath her, whispering, "Haint Blue keeps the Devil away, Momma."

Eddie was still looking up, realizing for the first time how much Ella May favored Wanda Pride, when his cell phone called him back from the past.

The UCM fight song, a melody similar to "She'll Be Coming 'Round the Mountain," underscored the footsteps on the porch. Eddie blinked but his eyes weren't working. He felt fingers slide his phone up from his pocket, followed by a voice, saying, "Is that right? Well, I surely do appreciate the tip, hon." A pause. A click. Then: "Somebody fetch me that mission-style rocker."

A moment later, PawPaw Pride's rickety rocking chair was beneath Eddie's feet and he was finally able to breathe again. Still couldn't see shit, though. Eddie thought he'd gone blind until he felt his lashes brush against something slick. A bag of some sort. A feed sack. Purina Strategy Professional Formula GX Horse Feed. Cost thirty bucks a pop and smelled sort of like licorice.

"A rocker like this," said the voice from before, "might bring a pretty penny, Mr. Pride. You ever considered going on the *Antiques Roadshow?*"

"The wha—" Eddie's Adam's apple got hung up under the rope.

"The Antiques Roadshow. Tickets are free to the public."

The voice was soaked in Mississippi mud, so thick, Eddie finally realized who stood before him.

"Holy shit, mister. Is it really you?"

"Afraid so."

Eddie kept sucking the feed sack into his mouth. Despite the smell, it didn't taste one bit like licorice. "You—you blindfolded me," Eddie managed. "You don't want me to see your face, and that means—"

"It means you're a lucky man."

Eddie felt a new pressure on his thigh, one of those gnarled fingers he'd seen pinching the cigarillo. The man's digit was sharp and cold. Eddie felt the chill even through his Wranglers.

"Lucky or desperate, I haven't quite decided." The man coughed, and it sounded like something from one of those "Tips From Former Smokers" commercials. "Never imagined you'd get your family involved in this. Must say, I'm impressed."

Eddie's hand moved from the rope to his heart. The UCM fight song replayed in his mind. Ella May was the only person in his contacts with that ringtone. Eddie remembered handing her the red gym bag, thinking he'd never see his daughter again.

"What'd she do?" Eddie croaked. "What'd my baby girl tell you?"

Duty boots clacked across the porch planks. The skinhead hissed. A moment later, car doors were slamming, but Eddie could still feel the old man's finger on his leg.

"It appears our quarterback finally took his fall, Mr. Pride. Better late than never."

"Matt?"

"Yes, young Matthew has shuffled off this mortal coil, but your daughter says she's found a replacement. And if that's true, then we still have a deal."

Eddie knew what was being wagered. He knew what he'd have to do, but he wanted to hear the man say it. "A deal?" He said, "What kinda deal?" and waited.

There were no footsteps. Not even a single plank creaked. The patrol cars came to life, revving their engines then roaring away. Eddie cocked an ear, expecting to hear that little Ford fire up next.

"Mister?"

The feed sack pulsed over Eddie's lips. He shifted his weight, working hard to stay balanced on PawPaw Pride's antique rocking chair. The rope around his neck was looser now, but it was still there. The racehorse whinnied from the grove.

"How the hell am I supposed to get down from here?"

SECOND QUARTER

Mama wanted me to be a preacher. I told her coachin' and preachin' were a lot alike.

—Paul "Bear" Bryant,
Alabama football coach

10

The special agents ended up back at the Waffle House around the same time the tow truck came to take Matt Talley's Jeep away. It was real late, or extra early. A little past three in the morning. Rae was tired but trying not to show it; Frank about the same as always, bitching about how the one kid who might've eventually snitched was dead.

"Matt Talley wins the biggest game of his life," Frank said, holding the diner's front door open for Rae, "goes out, just trying to have a good time, and falls off a friggin' roof."

"Who said he fell?"

A cowbell rattled as the rookie agent walked under it. A snaggletoothed waitress looked up from wiping down a table just long enough to say, "Welcome to Waffle House," then went right back to it.

Frank said, "The service is . . . *meh* . . ." shrugging off his partner's question as he led Rae toward a back-corner booth. *Typical agent move*, she thought. Stay aware of the exits. Know your surroundings. Count the civilians. Rae took a quick step past her partner and slid into the bench against the wall. Frank just stood there, staring down at Rae as she propped up her Jordans. She was still a little jittery but feeling better than when she'd first arrived in Compson. Things were moving now.

"You're one of those broads," Frank said, still standing beside the booth, "always has to be in charge, huh? Should've known it when I saw those sneakers. And now you're sitting on my side of the booth, same spot I've been sitting for the last year." He paused, giving Rae time to move. When she didn't, he said, "Whatever," and plopped down in the bench across from her. "You think this deal at the Buffalo Nickel changes things? That's it?"

"Matt Talley's dead, Agent Ranchino." Rae gave Frank the same look her father used to give his players after they'd dropped a pass, missed a tackle, or messed up in general. "A human being died on our watch, twenty feet in front of us. If that doesn't change things, what does?"

"We're white-collar crime, kid." Frank put his elbows on the table. "We don't do murder investigations or whatever it is you're thinking. We deal in money. That's it."

"You mean the green stuff in the bag that hit the pavement right before the quarterback?"

Frank leaned back, glanced over both shoulders, then said, "Listen, we start digging around, find out Matt Talley's got some skeletons, shit, maybe some bullwhips in his closet, then what?"

Bullwhips? Rae thought and pulled her hair up into a bun. She slipped a rubber band off her wrist as her eyes went to work casing the diner. One cook: white male, forty-something, overweight. Two waitresses: ol' snaggletooth and a Black woman with blond hair. There was only one other patron in the Waffle House, which Rae thought was weird until she remembered UCM's star quarterback had just died on College Street. The Black guy in the far corner looked like an athlete, or at least what was left of one. Traces of muscle in all the right places, wide shoulders, defined chest and toned biceps stretching the sleeves of a canary-yellow polo shirt. He was hunched forward over his coffee. An attractive man, alone in a Waffle House at a little past three in the morning.

"You gave me thirty minutes' worth of Eddie Pride Junior's personal history," Rae said and flipped open her Trapper Keeper, "but somehow forgot to mention the guy had a daughter? Ella May Pride's a Gridiron Girl for shit's sake, Frank. She was driving that big black Denali. The one that picked up Matt."

"What're you busting my balls for?" Frank reached into his sports coat and produced a folder of his own. "I got this, didn't I?"

An hour before, Rae had finally gotten to witness her partner in action. Frank had walked straight into the Compson Police Department wearing that ridiculous outfit and fiddled with the coffee machine until there weren't any cops in the lobby. He'd been careful with the secretary too, pushing just hard enough to get early copies of the statements. They'd soon be public record anyway, but Frank had been nice about it. Didn't flash his badge or throw his weight around.

"Ella May Pride," Frank said, index finger moving along the paper as he read the girl's full name. "Says here she was Matt Talley's girlfriend."

"Seriously?" Rae said, eyes down, scribbling furiously, adding a new note, a whole new tab titled SUSPECTS, to her binder. "The Chiefs' starting quarterback was banging the bagman's daughter? How could you not know this?"

"I try to stay out of the players' personal lives, Agent Johnson. They're just kids."

"Was she up there?"

"On the roof?"

"Yes, Frank. Was Ella May on the roof when Matt Talley went down?"

"I hear what you're saying, but I don't know." Frank produced a pair of tortoiseshell reading glasses from another pocket in his coat. "Says here Ella May refused to talk."

"Was anybody else up there with her? A third party who could back up her story?"

Frank was flipping through the folder again when the snaggle-toothed waitress reappeared. "What can I get y'all to drink?"

Frank said, "*Drink?* We been waiting ten minutes already. Jesus."

"You ain't even looked at them menus. Usually, people come in, they look at the menus before they place a order."

The nametag over the woman's left breast read TWYLA. Rae tried guessing her age. She looked sixty but Rae figured she was younger; life in the Waffle House could wear a woman down.

"I know what I wanna eat," Frank said. "Shit. I been coming in here, sitting at this same goddamn booth for . . ."

Twyla turned to Rae and said, "I just hate the way he talks. All that cursing. How do you stand it? Pretty little thing like you."

Rae realized the woman thought she was with Frank, like *with him* with him. *Gross.*

"How does *she* stand it?" Frank said. "I'm the guy stuck down here with all you inbred knuckle-draggers. Sounds like every-body's talking with mouths full of peanut butter."

Twyla tongued her tooth hole and took a pen out from behind one ear. "Let me guess, a guy like you comes to the *Waffle* House and orders *grits*."

Twyla chewed that last word, staring back at Frank until they both started laughing. "Twyla, I'd like you to meet a friend of mine, goes by the name of Rae."

Twyla said, "How do you do?"

"You wanna know what's happening in Compson," Frank said, nodding up at the waitress, "this is the woman you come see. Twyla's got a front row seat to the whole show. And Rae here, she's from the other side of the Big Muddy. Little place called Arkansas."

"My cousin Clementine stays somewhere up north of Russellville," Twyla said. "But listen, Big Steve's on the grill tonight. If I don't get your order in quick, you won't never get your food."

"Just give me the usual, black coffee and grits." Frank removed the glasses and rubbed his eyes. "Same for my friend here, but don't worry. We're not in any rush."

Twyla's eyes jumped to the man in the corner booth. Something about the nervous glance made Rae think the waitress wasn't just being friendly with Frank.

Rae said, "I'll take a coffee. No grits," and squared her shoulders on her partner. The waitress tapped the pen against her chin then turned and walked away. Rae waited until she was out of earshot to say, "She knows something, Frank."

"No shit. You think I brought you in here to read the Compson police reports?" Frank slapped the file folder closed then tried to slide it across the syrup-stained table. The surface was so sticky, it only made it halfway. "Ella May Pride and Moses McCloud. Those are the only statements you need to see."

"Moses McCloud?" Rae flipped to the new SUSPECTS section in her Trapper Keeper, wondering if she should add his name. "The backup?"

"That's right, or at least he was till just a couple hours ago. Here. Look at this."

Frank extended his cell phone. A game was going on the screen. Rae guessed it was high school, judging by the speed of the players, all the players except one. It wasn't just Moses's agility that caught Rae's attention, it was his savvy. She could tell, just from those few plays on his high school highlight reel, that Moses McCloud was the real deal.

"Everybody's got him billed as a runner, a 'dual threat,' but I dunno," Frank whispered. "I think the kid can sling it around a little too."

"Hey, Frank?" Rae waited until her partner looked up from his phone. "Why are you whispering?"

"See that Black guy sitting back there? Last booth on the left."

"You mean the only other guy in here?"

"Okay, smartass. What about the bag he's got beneath his bench? You notice that?"

Rae took a quick peek and saw it, a white plastic bag with a big red square in the middle. She was surprised, and a little disappointed, to realize she'd noticed the guy's physique, the way his shirtsleeves clung to his arms, but had somehow missed the bag.

"Looks like a JCPenney bag." Rae started to shrug, got halfway into it, then said, "*Wait.* That's the guy. The department-store guy. The—"

"—bagman. Yeah. What I hear, he's real tight with Moses. His name's Darren Floyd." Frank frowned and flipped the case folder open again. "But, hey, there's another question on the table here. A big one."

Rae's eyes darted between her Trapper Keeper and the police report, scanning the officer's barbwire scrawl, all the words he'd used to describe the scene that was etched into Rae's mind: her first body, Matt's body, sprawled on the pavement, surrounded by—

"*Money*. Shit, Frank. It's not in the report. Which means, the Compson PD . . ." Her tone was steady despite her mind, her heart. "They hid the money, just like they've been covering for the Chiefs."

"Sure looks that way," Frank said, "but looks can be deceiving. What we need is proof. Hard evidence. Somebody on the inside to slip up in the next few days. Somebody like Mr. Floyd over there."

Twyla was back with the coffee and a plate of slimy grits. Rae ignored her, turning back to the corner booth. The coffee mug was still sitting square in the middle of the table, but the guy was gone.

"Bet you're the sorta girl," Twyla said, spilling Rae's coffee a little as she set it down, "drinks your jitter juice black."

Rae forced a smile, expecting the woman to take the hint and leave. When she didn't, Rae cupped both hands around her mouth and whispered, "The guy, Frank. Darren Floyd. Where'd he go?"

Frank tore open three packs of Sweet'N Low then dumped them into his coffee. "You're asking the wrong question, kid. It ain't where Mr. Floyd went you need to be worried about. Where will he be tomorrow morning, after you've had some time to think this thing through?"

"You want me to go talk to Darren Floyd?"

"We don't *talk* to nobody. We keep an eye out. We sit back and gather intel. That's it."

Rae watched Twyla slide Frank's grits onto the table, wondering if sitting back was really the best plan of action. Things were getting serious, and thus far, Frank Ranchino had seemed anything but. In fact, the way he was talking about the investigation, right there, in front of a Waffle House waitress, was more than a little unnerving. Frank was still her partner, though. Her *senior* partner.

"Okay, but if I'm tailing Darren," Rae said, "where does that put you?"

"I'm heading over to the field house first thing tomorrow. See, I know Speer Taylor likes to get to work real early, even on Sundays. How about you?" Frank made a face that reminded Rae so much of Robert De Niro it was kind of creepy. "You know where Mr. Floyd likes to spend his Sunday mornings?"

"You know I don't."

Frank took a sip of his coffee, still doing De Niro as he said, "Twyla's standing right there, kid. Why don't you ask her?"

11

Speer Taylor's phone vibrated. The clock beside the bed read 3:04 A.M. Speer blinked the world into focus and reached for his device, wondering why the Lord had woken him at such a strange hour. Thirty-seven text messages and sixteen missed calls glowed up from the screen. Apparently, the Lord wasn't the only one who needed the forty-three-year-old football coach.

The news was bad—wretched, actually—but it was all part of God's plan. Speer would keep the faith, just like he'd been doing since the first week he arrived in Compson, Mississippi. That was as long as it had taken him to realize that this level of football was too much for him, the stage too big, but then the Chiefs won their first game, and the next, and the one after that. The Chiefs couldn't lose, not even when they got into the meat of the schedule. Not even when they played for UCM's first-ever national championship, and won it too.

Speer was just as surprised as everyone else. What came next amazed him even more. In the months that followed, the tiny Southern town became the epicenter of college football and Speer was Compson's shining star. Local business boomed, along with the university. Enrollment was up. Two new frat houses were under construction, the student union was being renovated, but still, Speer worried. After just one season, he'd accidentally set the bar as high as it would go.

Through it all, Speer stuck to his routine, even today, *especially* today. Coach Taylor worked seven days a week. He felt guilty about that on Sundays. Then again, Jesus Christ, Speer's Lord and Savior, had healed a dropsy-stricken man just outside of Capernaum on the Sabbath.

Still lying beside his wife, all five of their children sound asleep on the second floor, Speer began his routine by breathing in through his nose. The air tickled the hair in his nostrils. He exhaled out through his mouth, lips pursed as if he were blowing into a steaming bowl of soup.

"Chicken soup," Speer whispered, "for the *soul.*"

The football coach continued this practice for fifteen minutes. He called it "Waiting for My Happy Place," which he imagined as a small summer cabin in the Rockies, somewhere outside of Colorado Springs. There was a tire hanging from a low branch. Speer pictured himself in that place, throwing footballs through the hole until he got to where he couldn't miss.

At half past three, Speer was still in bed instead of his happy place. Lately, it'd been getting harder and harder to find. Speer put both feet on the ground and started the next stage of his routine: one hundred push-ups, sit-ups, and pull-ups, followed by an ice-cold shower. The water stung Speer's chest and face. He liked it. Three organic turkey links and one decaffeinated cup of coffee later, Speer Taylor was walking out the door just as the clock struck four.

At four fifteen, Speer's Mercedes-Benz E-Class pulled into the State Farm Field House parking lot. Speer listened for sirens but found the night quiet. Too quiet. There wasn't a light on in the field house, a looming structure that looked like a mix between a cathedral and a McDonald's PlayPlace. The front of the building was all glass. A lime-green tube slide wound its way down from the second floor to the first. Speer had asked the UCM boosters for the slide when he'd first arrived, saying, "Football's a game, and I want to be sure our players are having fun."

He swiped his badge at the door. A red light blinked and Speer Taylor entered the "Great Teepee," a name he liked to call the field house inside his head but was smart enough to never say aloud. The soles of his tennis shoes squawked across the tile floors. Speer tried to forget what he'd seen on his phone as he climbed the ladder to the slide, but he couldn't.

Yes, things were worse, Speer decided, perched atop the slide, holding onto the handles attached to the tube. Much worse. Now that Speer was without his star quarterback, he didn't know what he'd do. He'd never dealt with anything like this before, at least not in Compson. The UCM players were surprisingly well behaved. At previous jobs, Speer was always handling off-the-field incidents: local police, lawyers, college girls. Sometimes all three at once. There'd been none of that in Mississippi. Not until today, the coach thought, and then he let go.

As he zipped down the slide, Speer's golden hair—which the Chiefs' fan base had complained about until he won enough games to change their minds—billowed out behind his ears. Both Speer's hands were clasped over his chest, knees locked, toes pointed forward, whipping around the turns like an Olympic luger and then it happened.

Speer found his Happy Place.

Sometimes it came to him in the freezing shower, or on the seventy-eighth pull-up. Lately, the slide had been the ticket. Speer guessed it had something to do with childhood, innocence lost. He felt like a kid again, nine or ten years old, young enough for his mom to still make him her world-famous PB&J "sammies." That's what Speer'd called his mother's sandwiches back when he didn't have a worry in the world, back when things were still pure and football was just a game like he'd told the UCM boosters his first week on the job. Swept up in his fantasy, Speer could smell the ponderosa pines as he threw perfect spiral after perfect spiral through the tire hanging from that tree outside the cabin in Colorado Springs.

Back in the real world, four seconds passed, and then Speer Taylor's wild ride was over. Still, he felt recharged, ready to face the day and everything that would come as a result of Matt Talley's death. Everything, that is, except the old man waiting for him at the base of the slide.

The man was smoking a skinny cigar and wearing a pair of loose-fitting cargo pants. There was a small tear in the rib-knit trim sleeve of his navy-blue windbreaker. His shoes were so worn-in Speer couldn't make out the brand. The hat atop his head, a houndstooth fedora like the one worn by legendary Alabama coach Paul "Bear" Bryant, was the only thing on him that was halfway clean. Speer knew who the man was, and the fact that he was standing in the field house a little after four in the morning scared Speer more than the dire news he'd seen on his phone.

"We've got a problem, Coach."

Speer stood. He was taller than the old man by a solid six inches. The height advantage bolstered his confidence enough to say, "I don't believe in problems. Every single thing that happens in this world—right or wrong, good or bad—it's all just a tiny part of God's big plan."

"Okay, then . . ." The man took a long drag off his little cigar then dropped it. Nodding to the line of gray smoke rising from the still-smoldering tip, the man said, "What was the point of that?"

Speer stared down at the cigarillo.

"Have you talked to anyone else?" the old man said. "Any assistants or publicists?"

Speer shook his head.

"Not even your family?"

"No."

"Meet me at your house in ten minutes, Coach."

"*My house?* My wife's still asleep. My kids—"

"I know," the man said, snuffing out the skinny cigar with the toe of his discolored orthopedic shoe. "And don't you forget it."

The old man tipped his hat and turned, taking slow, shuffling steps toward the field house's glass doors. Speer breathed in through his nose, out through his mouth, but he was a long-ass way from that cabin in Colorado.

12

Five girls smiled up at Congressman Harry Christmas from a picture on the coach's desk. The dimples in their cheeks reminded the old man of home.

Harry lit another cigarillo. Same brand as always. Black & Mild. Same way he wore the same getup most days. Sometimes he traded the khakis out for jeans but never strayed far from the windbreaker. Not even in the heat of an Indian summer. Harry couldn't stand being cold. He was getting old. Seventy-eight or nine. There was some speculation regarding his birth certificate. Harry'd never met his biological father, or mother for that matter. He'd heard all sorts of stories, though, and not a one of them was any wilder than what his childhood turned out to be.

Harry had been adopted by a woman named Maxine Christmas soon after his ninth birthday, still a cute age for boys, the last full year of baby fat. Harry'd never forget watching that tall, beautiful woman in her knee-length fur coat come waltzing through the Apple Blossom Orphaned Boys' Home, moving from bunk to bunk as if she were at an animal shelter, raising her nose at the walleyed boys, shaking her head at the sickly, and stepping past the husky ones altogether.

Maxine Christmas stopped for young Harry. She didn't like his ears but said the right hat would fix that. Was it strange for a single lady dressed in a fur coat to adopt a child? A boy, especially? Yes, of course, but Maxine never worried much with strange. She had money. Gobs of it in a silk purse she produced from a secret fold in her coat. The bills smelled sweet and somewhat salty, a doughy scent Harry didn't recognize at the time but would learn well as the years wore on and the men came and went from his mother's house.

Maxine's place, a rundown plantation she'd purchased and renamed "Sudan," was the premier brothel north of Jackson for the better part of the 1930s, '40s, and '50s. A classy establishment with heavy burgundy curtains and a stained-glass window in the dormer above the entryway. At night, the window glowed red, calling out to the men of Chickalah County, a silent siren's song. Harry Christmas learned everything he ever needed to know from his mother, but each lesson came at a price. He was, and would forever be, the son of a whore—or a pimp—depending on one's perspective. Which, as fate would have it, gave Harry a leg up in the wild world of politics.

"Is this about the Choctaws?" Speer Taylor said, pacing the confines of his surprisingly well-decorated home office. "If it is, I've been thinking. Nobody gets up in arms about 'The Fighting Irish,' and well, I just don't see much difference between the *Irish* and the *Chiefs*."

Harry nodded, knowing the young coach was well aware of Matt Talley's fall. Of course he was. There were so few secrets left in the world. Harry nodded again, admiring the built-in bookshelves, what appeared to be a Persian Bakhtiari rug, and an attractive antique banker's lamp, the dim light through the green shade setting the tone for the early morning meeting.

"Started looking into the Notre Dame program," Speer continued, "trying to get ahead of the Choctaws, and you'll never guess what I found."

Harry lifted a hand.

"The Fighting Irish, they actually *play* in Ireland," Speer said, missing the congressman's signal. "Just once every five years or so. What if we called up the Choctaws over in Tunica, see what they thought about hosting a game at the casino? Non-conference, of course, but you get the—"

"Sit down."

Congressman Christmas appreciated the way the football coach went scrambling for his high-back leather chair. He'd never taken such a tone with Speer Taylor before. He'd never had to.

"Do you remember," Harry said, "what I told you the day you were hired?"

The young man—"young," at least by Harry's standards—nodded, two times, quick. The gesture told the congressman the coach hadn't forgotten how Harry'd cornered him in the field house after his first press conference, all the cameras and the microphones already packed away.

"I told you if things went right, you'd never see me again."

"But we've done good. We're undefeated. One more win and we're headed back to the SEC Championship, then the Cotton Bowl after that."

"Too good."

Harry sucked his teeth, recalling the greatest lesson he'd ever learned from his mother. For much of his childhood, he'd believed Maxine to be invincible, a force of nature capable of bending the world to her every whim. As Harry grew older, though, his mother's weaknesses became more apparent, none more so than her belief that she was destined for something greater than what she already was. By the time Harry turned sixteen, Maxine Christmas damn near ran Compson, ruling over the tiny Delta town from her castle made of dirt. Powerful men had darkened Harry's mother's door, their faces cast red in the light coming down from that stained-glass window. The light played tricks on Maxine. It boosted her confidence, bolstered the myth of her destiny. So much so, Maxine decided to come out from behind Sudan's dark curtains and make a legitimate run for mayor. Even at that age, Harry foresaw the dangers of the democratic process. He knew those men wouldn't give a damn about whatever blackmail Maxine thought she had. All they had to do was call her a liar, a *whore*, and that's just what they did. Red-faced men, the very same men who'd so enjoyed themselves in his mother's house, tore Maxine Christmas's reputation apart, one lie, one truth, at a time.

"Too good?" Speer Taylor rocked back in his chair, relaxing a little. "You're kidding, right?"

Harry Christmas was many things—an avid antiques collector, an aficionado of cheap bourbon and even cheaper cigarillos, a longtime state-level legislator for the Forty-Eighth Congressional District of Mississippi—but a *kidder* wasn't one of them.

After the election of 1956, Harry knew what his mother was too, what she'd always been, even if she never did. The lesson remained lodged deep in her son's heart, guiding Harry's every move. He took his mother's weakness and turned it into his greatest strength. Harry Christmas became the king of the long game. He was cautious, extraordinarily careful. He understood his place, his lot in life, which was why he'd never tried moving up the political ranks. There was power in such knowledge, and once he discovered college football, Harry flourished.

The hierarchy of the sport fortified the congressman's core belief. Yes, quarterbacks and coaches received the lion's share of public praise. Some even became legends, statues outside the stadium gates. But the ultimate power belonged to men like Harry Christmas. Men who ruled from the shadows were untouchable. There was no expiration date, no contracts to renegotiate, no fan base to please. There was, of course, a limit to all things, a balance, and the University of Central Mississippi's football program had finally reached its tipping point.

Through the window behind the coach's desk, a faint red glow appeared in the east. Harry could see the outline of his little truck now in the Taylors' front drive, a marble fountain bubbling behind it.

"People hear the name 'Harry Christmas' and they think it's a joke. Think I'm some sort of Santa Claus."

"I'm sorry?"

"Don't be. My mother gave me that name, and it's been my single greatest advantage. This cheap cigar? That truck out there?" Harry nodded and watched Speer turn, getting a good look at the man's shock of golden hair. "These clothes I wear? It all helps."

"Helps what?"

There was no way to convey how much Harry had done for the University of Central Mississippi. His shrewd political prowess and eye for detail had singlehandedly saved Compson, the town where his mother was born and buried out back of the house that had serviced all those men, the very same structure Harry Christmas now called home.

More than anything, Harry had wanted to protect Sudan. The plantation house was his mother's legacy, after all. That's why he'd called up all the old-money farmers in Compson. Great-great-grandsons and nephews of lawful slave owners. The very same men who'd once plowed through Maxine's stable. Harry called them into his study, one by one, and told them what they already knew. The days of bountiful harvests were over, at least in the Delta. The summers had grown too hot, the storms damn near biblical. Harry kept from mentioning "climate change." He knew his clientele. Instead, he focused on the Blacks and how they were taking over Mississippi, county by county, town by town. People of color (Harry knew better than to use that term too) were everywhere in the Delta, and they were at the very heart of the congressman's masterplan. Harry told the farmers it was time to put all those Black boys back to work, and he had just the ticket.

College football.

Now, Harry'd never earned any sort of degree, but college football programs across the South were already pumping millions into good, God-fearing communities like Compson, Mississippi. And UCM was right there, ripe for the picking. The football team had been up and down—mostly down—over the years. But Harry saw potential in the remote college town. Which was why he borrowed the governor's private jet and stopped off at every Southern football powerhouse from College Station to Gainesville. There were men like Harry lurking in the shadows of each stadium, men who held the keys to success, the secrets to winning that never got talked about on ESPN. In Dallas, Harry received a crash course in player payments from some old-school bagmen who used to run the Pony Express. In Athens, he learned how to coerce local law enforcement. In Clemson, a town of less than twenty thousand, Harry learned what would prove to be his most invaluable lesson—how to build an entire town around a college football team, one game, one win, one player at a time.

When Harry landed back in Compson, he took some flak for jet-setting across the country on the taxpayers' dime, but the congressman doubled down, telling any reporter who'd listen that he'd used the governor's jet to visit churches across the South. Which wasn't far from the truth. With that mess behind him, Congressman Christmas was finally able to relay what he'd learned to his prospective investors. The rich old farmers were hesitant at first, wary of handing family money over to a politician, but what choice did they have? They'd felt the heat. They'd seen the dark tide rising. Seemed like there were more muscly-armed Black boys roaming the streets of Compson now than ever before. Why let the strong ones, the fast ones, get plucked up by Bama, or even worse, Ole Miss?

The thought was enough to get Compson's upper crust to make significant donations to Congressman Christmas's interminable campaign. Harry went straight to work, covertly bankrolling every diehard fan who had the inside scoop on a hot new recruit. He broke bread with the Compson chief of police too, a former UCM linebacker by the name of "Bruiser" Brandt Conrad. The dirty cop became Harry's righthand man. Bruiser was the only person in town who knew the depth of Harry's involvement with the Chiefs, and the congressman worked hard to keep it that way.

It took fifteen seasons and three head coaches before UCM was finally established enough to get a real shot at the four- and five-star players. Turns out, the country's top athletes were like

Maxine's girls in one very important way—both could be purchased.

After word got around about the money, the Chiefs finally started winning. Nothing crazy. Not at first. Just enough success to get the boosters' attention, enough to fill the seats in Sutpen Stadium once again. Harry soon realized it was much easier to run a crooked operation in a tiny farming town than, say, a city like Dallas, chock-full of reporters, camera crews, and worst of all, liberals. Once the Chiefs had a few winning seasons under their belts, Harry called all those farmers back and relayed the next step in his scheme, a truly Southern take on gentrification.

It didn't take them long to renovate all the abandoned buildings downtown into upscale restaurants and bars, just like Harry had told them to do. They built hotels by the dozens. After the national championship win, fans flocked to Compson by the tens of thousands. Nowadays, one home-game weekend could bring in twenty million dollars' worth of citywide revenue. UCM's new investors were in high cotton, along with everyone who had ties to the team. Everyone, that is, except the players.

"Uh, Mr. Christmas?"

Harry said, "*Congressman*," reflexively, and blinked. Speer was still sitting on the other side of his desk, a single finger raised, pointing at the ceiling.

"I think the girls are up."

"The *girls*?"

"My daughters. Yeah. Sounds like they're awake."

A quarter-inch worth of ash hung from the tip of the congressman's cigarillo. Harry flicked it onto the floor. "I'll make this quick. What we're dealing with here, it's bigger than just poor Matthew's accident. Are you aware of the death penalty?"

"Listen, Mr. Christmas. I—"

"*Congressman.*" Harry brought the cigarillo to his lips but the heat was gone, the tip cold and gray. "I'm speaking of the NCAA's 'death penalty,' Coach Taylor. The National Collegiate Athletic Association's power to ban a school from competing in a sport."

Harry waited, studying the coach's eyes for signs of recognition, wondering if maybe Speer wasn't up for what the congressman had in mind. The other coaches, the ones Harry had watched come and go, had shown him what he needed. What UCM needed. Harry hadn't hired any of these men, of course. He didn't sit in on the interviews. There was a wall between Harry and the university's administration, the boosters and the bagmen too, an added layer of protection for all parties involved. Everyone understood the rules of the game. And that's what Harry wanted in a coach. No more hotheads. No more narcissists. Harry needed someone he could control.

He'd first seen Coach Taylor on YouTube a little over two years ago. Eddie Pride had sent the link to Bruiser, a video of a handsome young coach shaking his ass in a locker room after a game. Speer was surrounded by his players, boys with rippling chests and rock-hard thighs. It wasn't the coach's moves that caught Congressman Christmas's attention; it was the color of his players' skin. Harry'd never seen anything like it. A white man juking and jiving with a bunch of Black boys? After Coach Taylor finished his little jig, he addressed the team, speaking to the group in a voice that sounded like a mix between a Memphis bluesman and a Southern Baptist preacher. The video ended mid-speech, but Harry found another one, a professionally edited interview with Action News 5. The coach looked different in the bright lights, more civilized, almost clean-cut with his hair slicked straight back behind his ears. Speer sounded different too. The Southern drawl was gone, replaced by a neutral Midwestern delivery. Speer sounded so much like the broadcaster, Harry had trouble telling the two apart.

Speer Taylor was decent when it came to game planning. Somewhat subpar on the player-management front. But he was a world-class chameleon. So good, in fact, Speer didn't even seem aware of his God-given talent, but the congressman was.

"The death penalty," Harry said, "would be the end of UCM, of Compson, as we know it. The NCAA has only ever passed down such a sentence *once* in its hundred-plus-year history."

"SMU, right?"

"Why, yes," Harry said. "Fast forward forty years and the Southern Methodist Mustangs have bounced around conferences, gone through a stable of coaches, and recorded just *one* winning season since the NCAA dropped the proverbial hammer."

"But they were paying the players. We're not—"

"We were a Cinderella story. Last year's championship run? That was a dream we've used to sell more season tickets, more merchandise than ever, but it's time to wake up."

Harry leaned forward, inspecting the framed photograph of Coach Taylor's family: his beautiful wife, their five smiling daughters, all of them huddled together on a sandy dune. The congressman cocked an ear, listening to the footsteps still thudding overhead.

"As you well know, Coach, America loves an underdog, but we're not underdogs anymore. The Chiefs are at the very tip-top of the college football food chain now. Which is bad business. You see, a real winner knows when to lose."

Harry waited for Speer to say something, anything. When he didn't, the congressman realized such a scheme was outside the young coach's comprehension. If Matt Talley had simply stuck to the plan, Coach Taylor could've gone on thinking of football as "America's Game," instead of the highly lucrative business it had become. Speer would never understand how losing a game could've saved UCM in the long run. A loss to Southern Miss would've restored the balance. It would've kept the NCAA, or worse, the federal government, from investigating the University of Central Mississippi. If either of those organizations started sniffing around, there was no telling what might happen to a man in Congressman Christmas's position. Harry's dream had never been to create a football powerhouse. He didn't give a damn about championships. Harry cared about Compson, about Sudan, and he'd do whatever he could to protect his home. There was a limit to all things. Harry had learned his mother's fatal lesson well.

"The young quarterback's death," Harry said, "how you manage it moving forward, that's of utmost importance. That's why UCM needs to lose. You understand that now, don't you?"

"So we don't get investigated," Speer said, "or slapped with the death penalty?"

"That's right, but let me be clear. There's no *we* involved here. I'm not affiliated with the University of Central Mississippi in any official capacity. This is all on *you*. How *you* handle this very delicate situation will greatly impact what comes next."

Speer frowned. "What comes next?"

"The end of your coaching career, I'm afraid."

"But—"

"*But* the beginning of what could be a successful venture into politics."

The footsteps were in the hallway now, a stampede of chubby toes and tiny feet. Speer Taylor was still frowning, but his eyes were moving, darting beneath his furrowed brow, seeing a way out, maybe? Harry wasn't sure, not until the coach said, "Politics? Geez, Congressman Christmas. I'm just an ol' ball coach. You really think I could cut it as a baby kisser?"

"Keep talking like that," Harry said, then stood, watching as a line of little girls paraded into the office, "and you'll do fine, Coach. Just fine."

13

A sagging border of yellow police tape was all that remained outside the Buffalo Nickel. The dirty money had been swept away, Matt's body bagged and tagged, any evidence of the previous night's tragedy—gone.

Rae surveyed the recently scrubbed crime scene as she turned her Impala west onto College Street. Four hours earlier, Twyla had scribbled the address on the back of an order slip: *6009 Durant Avenue.* The location of a restaurant named "Floyd's Fresh Fish." The waitress hadn't told Rae the name of the eatery, or the fact that Darren Floyd was the sole proprietor. She'd just said, "You wanna talk to D, you get to this address early tomorrow morning and hope he ain't having a meeting."

What kind of meeting? Rae thought, still not sure what she'd do when she got there. Frank had told her to sit back, scope the place out and gather intel, but was that really what was best? Rae had passed what was left of the previous night flipping through her Trapper Keeper. All the notes she'd taken, the names: Matt Talley, Speer Taylor, Moses McCloud, Darren Floyd, Eddie and Ella May Pride. A lesser agent would've had trouble knowing where to begin. Not Rae. She'd been training for this since she was a child, sitting beside her father in the bleachers, watching as twenty-two athletes crashed together on a hundred-yard field. Rae knew to start small. It worked the same way in law school. Focus on one problem, one question, and solve it.

What happened to Matt Talley?

Despite everything Frank had said—his claims that they were White-Collar Crime and the quarterback's death was out of their jurisdiction—Rae knew Matt was the key to cracking her rookie case.

Matt's body had been sent to the forensics laboratory in Pearl, Mississippi, for an autopsy. The cause of his death was obvious, but what about the money? The towers of files in Rae's apartment stood as stark reminders that UCM was clean, which didn't make them innocent. Frank's bagman theory was still in play, even if Rae had trouble believing a top-ranked college football program would hand over that much control to a handful of rabid fans.

What was a girl to do? Or better yet, what would Chuck Johnson have done? What would he have told his daughter, his team, his quarterback?

In case of doubt, attack.

The line had come to Rae an hour before sunrise. It was so simple, so direct, she knew exactly what she had to do. She needed to call Madeline Mayo.

It took three calls for Mad to answer. The hacker hadn't been asleep; Mad was nearly nocturnal. She'd ignored the first two calls because she was still pissed about Rae hanging up on her. It was confession time, and although Rae didn't tell her old roommate everything about her investigation, the juicy details of Matt Talley's death were enough to win Mad over. Rae played up the moment of impact, the blood splatter on the soon-to-be-missing money, and then, when Mad was good and primed, Rae had asked her to help set up a new plan of attack.

Rae eased her Impala into the Floyd's Fresh Fish parking lot. The restaurant's façade had been built to resemble some sort of boat. Staring up at the stern, Rae took a moment to think back over her plan and get into character. She'd even dressed for the part. Skinny jeans tucked into her Jordans and a deep-cut Dave Matthews Band tour tee she'd gotten in college, a woman stitched across the front, on fire and dancing.

As soon as she started across the gravel lot, Rae smelled cigarette smoke and heard voices coming from an outdoor dining area. Back pressed against the fake ship's bow, she peeked around the corner.

There were six of them sitting in a circle of foldout chairs smoking cigarettes. Darren Floyd was wearing green tapered joggers, white Chuck Taylors, and a simple beige shirt that contrasted nicely with his skin. But what were they doing at his catfish restaurant so early on a Sunday morning?

"Back during my dark days," a long-necked dude with a buzzcut was saying, "I kept waking up in Momma's bed. Momma'd been dead since I's twelve. Didn't stop ol' Lucky Tucker. I'd snuggle up close to Daddy and feel his foot in the small of my back. Never would let me sleep in Momma's spot." The man paused and pushed two fingers under his wire-frame glasses. "Always worried I's gonna piss the bed."

The others nodded like they could relate.

The restaurant owner stood, lit another cigarette, and said, "My name's Darren Floyd, and I'm an alcoholic."

The group said, "Hi, Darren," all together at the same time, and then Darren started in talking about his dark days, a hard-headed kid trying to survive the mean streets of Detroit.

• • •

By the time Darren Floyd finished telling his story, the ground beneath the circle of alcoholics looked like a miniaturized cemetery, all those cigarette butts sticking straight up in the grass.

Rae liked watching Darren smoke, how he really took his time with it, raising the cigarette to his lips then taking a considerable drag. He'd leave the smoke in and strum the guitar Lucky Tucker had brought over at some point. A six-string made of steel. What were those called? Rae wasn't sure, but she liked listening to Darren talk too, offering up memories of his childhood in Detroit: "Never knew food could save a man's life, not till I got me a taste of Grandy's." Smoke drifting out his nose in wisps, Darren picked a blues riff as he said, "Blank-Face Nate, my big brother, had him a Monte Carlo, always blasting WJLB. Johnny Smooth spinning Anita Baker's 'I Just Wanna Be Your Girl' damn near on repeat. Anita coming out cool through the speakers, like a quiet storm."

That last line mixed with the way Darren exhaled—just breathing out, letting the smoke fall easy from his mouth—made Rae's neck get hot. Damn, she wanted a cigarette, but what about Darren Floyd? Did she want him too?

Rae blinked and realized he was headed her way, limping a little, his left leg a second behind his right. "You're late," the bluesman said, and extended what Rae thought was a hand until she looked down and saw the pack of Marlboro Red 100's.

She said, "That's funny," and thought of her partner, everything Frank had told her, but she'd already called Madeline Mayo. It was all set up now. "Thought I was early."

Rae placed the cigarette between her lips, watching as Darren produced a book of matches with "Floyd's Fresh Fish" stamped across the front. Hands cupped, he offered Rae a light. She inhaled and tried not to cough, hoping the fire dancer on her Dave Matthews shirt wouldn't give her heart away.

Darren folded the matchbook and said, "Early for what?"

"I'm supposed to meet some people here," Rae said, "for breakfast."

"Thought maybe you came here for the meeting."

Darren had great lips. Rae had dated a guy with lips like that once, a receiver with soft hands too. Poor guy was soft all over, or at least that's what Chuck said after he got word that one of his players was dating his daughter. The relationship, if you could call it that, lasted three weeks, and the receiver never stepped foot on the field again.

"Yeah, I saw you," Darren said, "making faces when Lucky Tucker got to telling how he used to crawl up in his dead momma's bed."

"His name's really Lucky?"

"Luck's just another alcoholic."

Rae took a quick puff and gazed past Darren to the parking lot. She'd had to leave her Trapper Keeper in the Impala. She felt naked without it.

"All right, then," he said and turned. "You want another smoke, you can find me in the captain's quarters."

Rae let him take a few steps, then said, "The captain's quarters? That's cute."

"White people eat this boat shit up."

"Bet they eat a lot of catfish too."

"You should see them get after my Blacktip Special."

"You serve shark? At a catfish restaurant? I didn't know it was edible."

"Got to know how to cook a shark. Besides, without the Blacktip Special, what'd be the point in having a building looks like a boat?" Darren laughed. "Be like a Waffle House that didn't sell waffles."

A feeling washed over Rae, a bad one, like she'd been caught doing something silly. But what was it? Wearing her skinny jeans and DMB concert tee to go follow up on a lead? Close but not quite. It wasn't even the fact that she'd directly disobeyed her senior partner. It was the way Darren made her feel, all warm and jittery on the inside like the cigarette smoke.

"That song you were playing on the guitar, that was the blues, right?"

Darren said, "What else is there?" and peeked around the boat's bow.

Rae took a step forward. Five minutes she'd been talking to the bagman—flirting with him really—and now it was finally time to put her plan into action.

"I'm a journalist."

Darren, still with his back to her, said, "Nice shoes."

"I'm working on a story."

"A redhead wearing Jordans in Compson, Mississippi. Never thought I'd see the day."

"I'm serious. Google me. Rae Jo—" She caught herself at the vowel, remembering the moniker and numerous fake articles Madeline Mayo had uploaded to an online portfolio shortly after their early morning call. "*Joyce*. Rae Joyce."

"If you say you're a journalist," Darren said, "you're a journalist. What I need to look you up for?"

Okay. That part was over. Rae was journalist. Darren still had his back to her, watching as a crowd gathered outside his restaurant's front doors.

"This story I'm working on," Rae said, "it's a tell-all piece about college football."

Darren said, "Yeah?" and turned.

"Yeah," Rae said, going against everything she'd learned in Intermediate Undercover Techniques and Survival, the thirty-six-hour course she'd aced at the Academy. All those perfect scores didn't amount to much in the field. Chuck Johnson always used to say, "Everybody's got a plan till they get punched in the mouth," a line he'd stolen from former heavyweight champion Mike Tyson. It reminded Rae of this Helmuth von Moltke quote she'd encountered at Quantico: *No plan survives first contact with the enemy.* In the real world, everything came down to feel. Rae got the feeling Darren was a nice guy, a little flirty, maybe, but she didn't think he was the enemy.

"The Chiefs are going for back-to-back national championships after decades of subpar seasons." Rae waited, just long enough to run a hand through her hair. "I want to know how they did it. How they got so good so fast, and don't forget Matt Talley. What happened to him."

"He tripped."

"And landed on a bag full of money?"

Darren bit his puffy bottom lip, holding back a grin. "And here I was thinking you were really into sharks."

"I was—I mean, I am, but we're just getting to know each other. I'd love to hear about your other hobbies."

"My *other* hobbies? You move fast, huh?"

"You have no idea."

Darren scratched at his chin. "All right, then. Meet me tonight at the Love Handle, this little juke joint ten miles outside town, and I'll tell you all about the blues."

"The blues? No, I was talking about—"

"I know what you was talking about, but it's all the same. There ain't nothing but the blues in Mississippi." Darren's eyes went to her shoes, the Jordans Rae'd worn since college. "You know MJ didn't like the original colors? Not at first. Said the red reminded him too much of the Devil."

"The red was for the Bulls. Jordan's team. The Chicago Bulls."

"That ain't what I'm saying." Darren brought the matchbook back up from his pocket again. "What I'm saying is, do you know what you're doing, sniffing around down here, trying to talk to me about my business?"

Rae's feet were hot, sweating inside her premium leather kicks. She swiped the matchbook from Darren's hands and scribbled her number on the flap.

"MJ wanted blue, baby blue, Tar Heel blue, to match his college team," Rae said and tossed him the matchbook. "You get a wild hair, call me, or better yet, text. I'd love to learn more about the blues."

14

Moses McCloud turned his silver 1999 model Nissan Altima, a vehicle that had once belonged to his mother, out of the Starlight Apartments parking lot. He'd driven the Altima since high school, but it felt weird now that he was the starting quarterback for the top-ranked college football team in the country.

It wasn't how he'd seen the end of his first college semester going. If the Chiefs won their next game, they'd play in the SEC Championship on December 4 at 4 P.M. Eastern Time, smack dab in the middle of finals. If they won that, they'd play in the Cotton Bowl on January 6. That was two weeks before his first spring class. When was Moses supposed to get ready for General Microbiology, a course he'd need to ace if he ever wanted to make it into vet school?

As far back as Moses could remember, he'd wanted to be a veterinarian, maybe even more than he'd wanted to be a quarterback. Football was his ticket out of Clarksdale. His chance to get the education he needed to make his real dream come true. Moses couldn't really explain why, exactly, he wanted to be a vet. He just liked dogs. Pit bulls, especially. Big square-headed ones everybody thought were mean. Moses wanted to help dogs like that, get them out of their cages and give them a shot at a better life. Maybe it was because he hadn't had a dog growing up. Kids always want what they can't have, and Moses had never had any sort of pet at all. His grandmother always claimed she had enough mouths to feed; she didn't have time to worry with little furry ones too.

The UCM field house came and went through the passenger window. All Moses saw was a cage. An expensive one, sure, way better than anything his boys back in Clarksdale had, the former high school teammates whose careers had ended the night the Wildcats won the Mississippi state championship. Sometimes—not always, just sometimes—Moses envied their freedom. After one semester on a college football team, going through all the early-morning workouts, followed by class, then practice, then study hall after that, Moses would've given his left big toe for just one normal Saturday night. Go get a couple tamales from Abe's like back in his Wildcat days. Put some *Boondocks* on the TV and just veg out.

Moses pulled onto College Street. Two more blocks and he'd be at Ella May Pride's place, a three-bedroom apartment within walking distance of Sutpen Stadium. She lived there with two other Gridiron Girls. Trina Masters and Ashley Something. Trina was Cerge's main girl. Looked sorta like a white chick, or maybe a Latina. Long dark hair parted straight down the middle. Cerge liked to call Trina his "Little Warrior Princess." When Trina got real pissed, she'd say she was "getting her Irish up." Whatever that meant. Trina wasn't Irish, but that wasn't what had Moses worried. It wasn't even the fact that Matt Talley's memorial service had been scheduled for the day after the quarterback died. It was the idea of walking into an apartment where three girls used the toilet and left stringy thongs hanging from doorknobs, towel racks, and Lord knows where else.

Just thinking about Ella May made Moses's tongue get heavy, and there sat her Denali parked outside an apartment door with three golden numbers—*1-0-7*—drilled into the metal frame. Less than twelve hours ago, while the blue lights were still spinning but before they'd zipped Matt up in that black body bag, Ella May had called Moses and said, "Lucky number seven, Moses, just like that number on the back of your jersey? One-oh-*seven*. Meet me there, tomorrow morning. Deal?" Moses remembered thinking the number was on the front of his jersey too, but he hadn't told Ella May that. He'd just let her say what she had to say and then he hung up.

Ella May was like vet school—she was a part of Moses's big plan. Cerge liked to give Moses shit, always saying it was because Ella May was white. Race didn't have a thing to do with it. It was that one time at the Fairfield Inn, the freshman quarterback's only night with a girl, ever, and how much it had scared him.

What if Ella May'd gotten pregnant? Or worse, what if she'd told her daddy? That would've been the end of everything, the freshman quarterback's big dream down the drain before his first college semester even started.

Moses slid out of his Nissan and felt his stomach clench. Why had he come there? Was he making another mistake? He stopped at Ella May's door, that golden seven glowing in the morning sun. It had to mean something, but what? He shook his head and noticed his knuckles were ashy. It was enough to get him to stop thinking about Ella May Pride until the door swung open and there she was, looking better than ever, curly blond hair, bright blue eyes, all hundred and twenty pounds of her athletic little body stuffed into a tiny pair of cheer shorts and a neon-green sports bra.

The bra had a highlighter effect on Moses, blinding him to the point where he didn't notice the man in the neck brace sitting on the sofa. Moses was already in the living room, watching his dream girl lock the door behind him, when Eddie Pride Junior rocked forward and said, "Grab a seat, pard. This won't take long. Ella May's done told me all about you."

15

Ella May snuck a peek at Moses's hands as she turned the dead-bolt, wondering if it was wrong for her to notice the quarterback's cuticles after everything that had happened. She blinked and saw Matt face-up on the pavement, her daddy's money fanned out like a thin green blanket beneath him. Too thin. The opposite of Moses's thick nails. His fingers were long but not skinny surgeon's fingers like Matt's had been. Moses's digits were well-proportioned, thick enough to balance out the eleven inches between his pinky and his thumb, a quarterback measurement her daddy had mentioned once. Something to do with grip strength.

Moses's hands hung at his sides now. Eddie was on the couch, patting the cushion to his left. The neck brace had surprised Ella May. Scared her. It was one thing to know that men were coming for her father. To realize they'd been there—to see the tire tracks in the gravel drive, the rope still hanging from the porch—that was different. That was enough to get her to agree to this, whatever was about to happen to Moses at the meeting she'd scheduled the night before.

"Moses Mc*Cloud*," Eddie said, still petting the sofa cushion. "Clarksdale's finest. You know I'm the one found your highlight?"

Moses said, "Nah, Darren—"

Eddie lifted his hand from the couch. "Yeah, yeah. Darren's your main man, your *home*boy and all that, but I found you. You weren't on Rivals. Didn't even have a Twitter, or a single highlight on Hudl. First time I talked to your high school coach he told me you were different. The way he said it, it was like he was warning me or something. *Diff*-rent. Yeah. Then he said you were the best damn quarterback he'd ever coached. Best he'd ever *seen*."

"I was in middle school," Moses said, "when Darren first started coming by my grandmamma's house."

"That's what I'm saying. We were late. Scared as hell Ole Miss already had their hooks in you." Eddie patted the cushion again, but his heart wasn't in it. "Anyway, listen. I really appreciate you answering my daughter's call last night."

Moses turned his head just far enough Ella May could see his profile, his recently trimmed hairline a shade darker than his skin. She thought of Matt again, her memory of him compared to what Eddie had mentioned of Moses's home life. How his grandmother had raised him. How they lived in a house smaller than her apartment. The way Eddie explained it, they were helping Moses. He was still young, eighteen, nineteen in the spring. A true freshman. Had three full seasons ahead of him. One game wouldn't change anything.

"When Ella May called me," Moses said, head still turned, speaking into the space between the Prides, "I was already gone. Me and Cerge were headed over to the Burger King. You can ask him. I wasn't at the bar when—"

"Nobody's saying you were," Eddie said. "That ain't what this is about."

Moses's lips parted but no words came out. Ella May felt bad for him. She watched her daddy rise from the sofa, holding his neck brace with one hand. The foam pad pushed his cheeks up. Purple bruises blossomed out from behind his ears. Eddie hadn't said anything about what those men had done to him. Not one word. Ella May didn't need to hear it. She'd seen enough.

Eddie said, "I'd like to help you out," and reached behind the sofa. "That's all."

Ella May remembered Matt, wobbling around on the roof, holding the same thing her father was reaching for now. The bag bothered her. Then and now. She didn't know why the money wasn't locked up at the police department. She didn't know how her father had gotten it. She didn't care. Ella May just wanted this next part over with, the sooner the better.

"Now, this don't change whatever you got going with Darren. This here's for one game and one game only." Eddie stood and held the red gym bag up in both hands. "Fifty thousand big ones, and they're all yours, Moses, so long as the Chiefs lose."

The bag looked dirty. It was dirty, the once-white handles cream-colored in the apartment lights. The whole thing felt just like that.

"Not bad for a couple hours' work." Eddie cupped the bag's bloated bottom, extending it out for the Chiefs' new starting quarterback. "Well, pard. What do you say?"

16

Three hours later, Rae was back in Frank Ranchino's Subaru watching men in black suits and women in knee-length dresses wipe their eyes and blow their noses. She didn't know what her partner hoped to glean from the daytime stakeout. Did he really expect a backdoor deal to go down here? The only thing Rae was sure of was that Frank didn't know anything about her date with Darren Floyd. Which was why she'd spent the last ten minutes pointing out the stranger aspects of Matt Talley's memorial service.

"Is that the mascot?" Rae nodded to a shirtless young man wearing a headdress, both cheeks streaked red with war paint.

"No way," Frank said. "The Chiefs' mascot is this real deal Cherokee dude named Moytoy. I met him at the Waffle House one night after a game. Seemed like a nice guy."

Rae couldn't tell if Frank was serious. The grim carnival taking place in the center of UCM's campus felt the same way. Hundred-year-old magnolia trees lined the grassy opening, ten acres of prime tailgating real estate affectionately referred to as the "Glades." The lawn was littered with college students holding posterboards of varying shapes and sizes. The only thing all the homemade signs had in common was the hashtag "#TalleyLives." Apparently, the recently deceased QB was trending. The bevy of local news vans rimming the lawn probably had something to do with that. Rae counted five, along with a few food trucks on either side of the stage.

"Look at that one. 'Nothing Butt Pork'?" Frank said,

squinting through a pair of binoculars as he read the name off a truck. "I don't get it."

"Y'all don't have BBQ up north?"

"Pork *butt*. Ah, it's a barbeque truck." Frank lowered the binoculars. "Anyway, I tell you Coach Taylor never showed? I spent the whole morning over at the field house. There's this slide, a big green number with a—"

"Coach Taylor didn't go to the field house?"

"Nope, but a bunch of players did. It was like watching a parade. White boys rolling up in big trucks, blaring country music. Willie and Waylon and Christ knows what else. Texas plates, mostly. Then here come these chopped-up Chevys, windows rattling from the bass. Think I lost a filling just sitting there. Most of the bass thumpers had Florida tags. The white boys, the Black boys, their rigs had one thing in common," Frank said. "They all cost a boatload of cash."

Rae tried to recall the parking lot outside her father's field house. She remembered the music. The players' stereos were loud in Arkansas too, but what about the vehicles? Were they as flashy as the ones Frank had just described?

"Can't say I blame Coach Taylor for staying home. The guy's got a lot on his plate." Frank pressed the binoculars back to his eyes. "I mean, there weren't this many people at the Ernest Borgnine funeral."

"Who?"

"Ernest Borgnine. Major General Worden from *The Dirty Dozen*. Think he was on that kiddie show. The one with the talking sponge? Mermaid Man. Yeah, that's it."

"SpongeBob."

"What?"

"SquarePants. The show, Frank. The one you were just—"

"His *character* was called Mermaid Man. Ran around with this other old coot. Barnacle Boy. Something like that," Frank said, nodding. "Always had a thing for Ernie. He was born in Connecticut, but there's no denying his Italian roots. Think his mother was from . . ."

In the time between leaving Darren and finding Frank, Rae had worried over how much to tell her new partner, or if she should tell him anything at all. One week into her first investigation, Rae was breaking all the rules. She'd already had Mad set her up that fake alias online. She'd gone undercover and made direct contact with Darren Floyd. If she got caught, her entire career would be in jeopardy. If she cracked the case, however, she'd be the Bureau's brightest rising star.

It was a gamble, similar to starting the season with an onside kick. It felt right. A call her dad would've made back in the early days of his career. Chuck Johnson hadn't climbed the ranks by playing it safe, and neither would Rae. Her knowledge of the game gave her an advantage. If she was careful, she could stay three plays ahead of the defense, but what about Frank? What would he do if he got wind of his partner's game plan?

Listening to him still rambling on about that Nickelodeon cartoon, Rae wished she hadn't wasted the mental energy. Frank Ranchino was a lost cause, dead weight, a lot like Mermaid Man. Madeline Mayo, on the other hand, was quick.

Rae felt her phone vibrate and read MAD above an incoming text. Having a hacker for a best friend was like having an assistant coach in the press box, a pair of eyes in the sky. Mad hadn't just made that fake portfolio, she was also keeping watch over the Mississippi Forensics Laboratory system. As soon as that pathologist in Pearl logged into the MSFL to file Matt's autopsy report, Mad would see it, possibly even before it went online.

Rae unlocked her phone and read Mad's text:

forgot to tell you, i'm doing some freelance work 4 this digital media outlet. they've got a crew down there, covering that quarterback's service.

"So how'd your morning go?" Frank said, holding the binoculars out for Rae.

The eye cups were still warm. Rae could smell Frank on the plastic, an aftershave she couldn't place but reminded her somewhat of her father. Brut, maybe? Was that even still a thing? Rae rolled the focus wheel. The memorial service was magnified through the convex lenses, revealing details she'd overlooked. There were six food trucks in total and seven news vans. Through the binoculars, Rae read PRISM NEWS stamped in rainbow letters on the van parked closest to the stage. It had to be Mad's crew, that digital media outlet she'd mentioned.

Rae turned the binoculars on the UCM football team sitting in numerical order behind the podium. She scanned the front row. There were two number ones: a Black kid and a jug-headed white boy, a receiver and a linebacker if Rae had to guess, both good enough to get promised the same number, and since they were never on the field together, they could have it. Nifty little recruiting tactic, Rae thought, then moved the binoculars farther down the line until they stopped on the eighth seat, the place where a player wearing jersey number seven should've been sitting.

Rae said, "Where is he?" and felt her phone buzz as the binoculars fell to her chest.

"Coach Taylor's standing stage left, back behind the curtain." Frank pointed. "And would you look at what that clown's wearing . . ."

17

The television in Harry Christmas's dingy study was tuned to Action News 5. A male reporter stood in the middle of the screen, stone-faced as he gave a recap of Matt Talley's twenty-three years on earth.

Harry wasn't listening. He knew everything there was to know about the recently deceased quarterback, all the way down to the fact that Matt had cheated on his SATs. The kid had conned his way through Jackson Prep, but he wouldn't throw a football game?

In five days, the Chiefs played Mississippi State, a heated rivalry. A loss to the Bulldogs would bump the Chiefs out of the national championship conversation. The fans would be upset, sure, but what those ignorant Mississippians and nearly every other college football fan in the country didn't know was that the game they worshipped was in danger.

Way out west, the acronym "NIL" was spreading like wildfire. The term had originated because of a video game. *EA Sports NCAA Football.* All the kids loved it, even the players, and that was the problem. The game was using their likenesses to make money, boatloads of cash. And now, those players out west were starting to think maybe their universities had been taking advantage of them too, selling their jerseys, using their highlights on recruitment videos. Those Cali boys wanted to get paid, compensated for their "name, image, and likeness."

Harry Christmas had lived through the Jim Crow era, the Civil Rights Movement, and all the assassinations that followed.

He knew it wouldn't be long before the UCM players started asking for their slice of the pie, and that just wouldn't fly. Not with all those good ol' boy farmers Harry had sold his plan to twenty years ago. They could stomach offering scholarships to Black boys, even dishing out a couple hundred dollars to the players on the side. But the thought of actually paying them real money, with real contracts—that would be the end.

Turning Speer Taylor into a United States senator was Harry's only hope, a Hail Mary pass as time expires. With Speer in the Senate, the former coach could fight the NIL case, keep it from ever making it to the federal courts. Speer could look all those smooth-palmed policymakers dead in the eye and tell them his tales of the gridiron.

Couldn't he?

The young coach was good in the locker room, even better at press conferences, but politics was a different beast. Could Speer Taylor handle the heat?

Before he'd left the coach's mansion, Harry had warned Speer that if he didn't play along, the congressman would make sure he never coached again. All it would take was one call, to the right person, and Coach Taylor would be finished. Harry kept receipts from every dirty deal he'd ever done. The way the young man had stared back at him, Harry wasn't sure what to make of it. Which was why he'd called the Compson police chief that morning and invited him to come out to Sudan. He wanted Bruiser there to help gauge how Speer was taking the news.

The sounds of the memorial service emanated from the portable Panasonic television set on the corner of the congressman's pedestal desk, an antique rumored to have once belonged to Robert E. Lee. Beside the TV there was a framed photograph of a woman in her thirties perched way up high on a camel's hump. Harry smiled down at his mother as a car door slammed.

The congressman turned in time to spot Brandt Conrad stomping up the front walkway. On the television, the service was in full swing. Speer Taylor hadn't taken center stage yet, but he was scheduled to deliver the eulogy, just as soon as the preacher finished giving the Lord's Prayer.

"Morning, Congressman," the police chief said, lumbering his way into Harry's study. "Or hell, guess it's the afternoon already."

"And we have miles yet to go."

Bruiser Brandt pulled out a chair. Dust coated the leather. He stared down at his soiled fingers, then out the window to the overgrown lawn, the crumbling stairs. "All the money you got, ain't there somebody you could hire to come clean?"

"All the money I have goes to the Chiefs, and the price of winning is higher than ever."

There was more to it than that. The house was just like the congressman's truck, his windbreaker, his cigarillo—it fortified his façade. Truth was, Congressman Christmas was one of the richest men in Mississippi—if not, the richest.

"A family of Mexicans," Harry said, "used to live here. Did good work for the most part. Kept things clean enough. I just couldn't bring myself to trust them. They didn't speak a lick of English."

"They never do."

"I'd come into the drawing room and they'd be huddled up in the corner making strange noises. I could understand bits and pieces, words everybody knows: *Si. Por que? Bien.* They were all the time saying, 'Bien,' and nodding their heads. 'Bien. Bien. *Bien.*'" Harry produced a letter opener, the handle shaped like a fleur-de-lis, up from his desk. Using the blade to pick at his teeth, he said, "Nothing is that good, Chief Conrad. Especially not around here. This is Sudan."

Brandt nodded as if he knew the story behind the name. Harry couldn't remember if he'd told him about Maxine's ill-fated trip to Egypt. Now was not the time. Harry nodded at the television set. "Have you been watching the service?"

"Been listening to it on the radio." Brandt stared down at the dusty chair, his dark blue uniform stretched tight over his chest and thighs. The man lived up to his name. Harry had once seen "Bruiser" Brandt Conrad pull the right ear clean off a homeless man, yet there he stood, still trying to decide whether to get dust on his duty pants.

"Took some doing to convince Mr. Talley that the service needed to happen today," Bruiser said.

"I imagine it did. Max Talley is a lawyer, if I'm not mistaken?"

"An ambulance chaser, yeah, but he played for the Chiefs back around the same time I did. A walk-on, I think. Those guys always wind up being the biggest fans. I told him this was what was best for UCM. The boys needed to move past it, get it out of their system and get focused on the game."

"And what'd he say to that?"

"We're having the service today, ain't we?"

"Why, yes, Brandt," Harry said. "Yes, we are."

"You got a rag, a paper towel or something?"

"You've never been one to worry about getting your hands dirty before."

"It's my pants I'm worried about. See, my wife's got to be extra careful when she washes these slacks or else the stripe on the side—"

"Good *Lord.*" Harry Christmas jabbed his letter opener at the television screen.

"That hat," Bruiser said, still standing. "It's the same as yours."

Speer Taylor's fedora did resemble the one Congressman Christmas was touching now, running two fingers along the band, but it wasn't the same. Harry's houndstooth hat didn't just look like the one made famous by Paul "Bear" Bryant—it had once belonged to the Hall of Fame coach. Harry'd purchased it at auction for an ungodly sum after it had been discovered in the glove box of a 1972 Cadillac. Harry had spent his whole life searching for the right hat, one with a brim that helped hide his ears. The fedora had become his trademark, which was why seeing a similar style on Speer Taylor's head made the aged congressman feel as if the young coach was mocking him, and Harry did *not* take well to teasing.

"Well, Brandt," Harry said, listening as Speer addressed the crowd in a syrupy Southern accent, so thick, so familiar, the congressman switched off the television set. "It appears Coach Taylor is sending us a message."

18

Sometimes, real late at night, Speer Taylor would sit up and listen for the voice that had led him to Compson, the same voice Hagar, the slave girl, had heard before she gave birth to Ishmael. The voice wasn't saying anything now, at least not to Speer.

Which was a shame, because all Speer really wanted to do was to save as many souls as possible. So much so, he'd once asked his preacher about going around and evangelizing with a pistol. Just walk up, put a gun to some stranger's head, and say, "Do you believe in Jesus Christ as your Lord and Savior?"

If only it were that easy.

Lately, Speer had been questioning himself like he did back before he was named starting quarterback for the Texas Long-horns and God blessed him with a national championship his senior year. That one game, a magnificent performance by the handsome QB—19–24, 345 yards, 4 TDs—had led Speer to this very moment, standing before thousands of teary-eyed Chiefs fans at Matt Talley's memorial service.

"The only thing we have to fear," Speer said, summoning the different political speeches he'd studied shortly after Congressman Christmas left his house, "is fear itself."

Speer adjusted the houndstooth hat he'd found packed away with his grandfather's Easter suit. The hat had helped him unlock his new character the same way he'd transitioned from an option-style quarterback to a pocket passer his senior year. Back then, it was a haircut that did the trick.

For the better part of his time at Texas, Speer Taylor had rocked a shoulder-length mullet he sometimes called his "beaver paddle" among friends, and even once during an interview (which, by some stroke of luck, had never been uploaded to the internet). Speer let his bangs grow long the summer before his final season then got it all trimmed up in late August. His new do made him feel more professional, like a real quarterback. The hat worked the same way. It made Speer feel like the man Congressman Christmas had told him to be, a transformation the young coach was ready to make.

Ever since Speer had arrived in Compson, there'd been too much pressure and not enough preaching. Politics, on the other hand, offered Speer what he'd always wanted—a way to save souls without a Beretta M9. Speer had, of course, prayed about the transition during his quiet time after his wife hauled their daughters off to school. He didn't hear anything, but he knew what he had to do. Which was why he was taking full advantage of the podium, summoning every drop of his God-given oratory skills and pouring the whole pitcher into Matt Talley's eulogy.

"Ask not what this team can do for you—ask what you can do for this team." Speer smiled and performed his first "thist," or "thumb-fist," the classic politician's gesture. Speer liked former President Bill Clinton's style best, a two-handed approach where the thumbs were pressed atop curled fingers as if tugging down on a pair of perky nipples. "The Chiefs need each and every one of y'all," Speer said, "now more than ever."

His hair wasn't the only thing Speer changed before his senior year. He also became a card-carrying Christian a month before the Longhorns played the Aggies. The transformation happened at Kanakuk, a megachurch camp just outside of

Colorado Springs. Speer spent one week there as the camp's recreational director, which meant he got to do all the fun stuff and the campers loved him for it. Speer loved the kids too. Most of all, he loved the way they loved him. He was a rockstar, a college quarterback who could strum an acoustic guitar, sing well enough, work a sock puppet, run faster, jump higher, and bench press more free weights than just about all the other counselors.

On the last night of camp, a Christian magician sawed a woman in half with a hacksaw then put her back together in the name of Jesus Christ. The magician had long hair like Speer's except it was jet-black and shiny. Speer approached the magic man after the show and asked him how he'd performed the trick. The magician said, "Trick? What trick? That, my boy, was a miracle." That very same night that very same magician baptized Speer Taylor in the Manitou Mineral Springs.

Armed with his new do and a piping hot faith, Speer Taylor ventured into his senior season at the University of Texas and quickly became the talk of college football. After every game Speer won, he thanked Jesus and pointed to the sky. During halftime of the national championship, one of the broadcasters attributed Speer's magnificent on-the-field play to the young quarterback's new haircut and his recent "spiritual transformation." It truly was a miracle, just like that magician at Kanakuk had said, the first of many to come.

It made sense for a quarterback, especially a successful one, to try his hand at coaching, so that's what Speer did. His first job was working with the receivers at Tyler High, his alma mater. He listened to the way the players talked. He mimicked their slang. He bought a new cowboy hat before the first practice, a big suede Stetson. Two years later, he was named head coach of the Tyler High Lions and everybody in his hometown went wild.

The exact opposite of what the crowd was doing now. Cringing, mostly. Everyone except Speer's wife and daughters, all five of them. Speer let his gaze drift down the line of Taylor girls: Sarah, Susan, Samantha, Sally, and Savannah (there were only so many women in the Bible whose names started with *S*). Speer drew strength from his daughters' innocent smiles and followed "nattering nabobs of negativism" with a classic Teddy Roosevelt line: "... which is why we must speak softly and carry a big stick."

Five years after his first season at Tyler High, Speer piggybacked his star QB and landed a college job at a Division II school in Georgia. It took some doing, but by the time Speer left the Bisons, he could rap every verse of "Jesus Muzik," a chart-topping hit by Christian hip hop artist Lecrae. For more than a decade, Coach Taylor pulled the same trick, riding his best players to another job where he morphed his style to fit the local aesthetic.

Most of Speer's success was luck, but he didn't think of it that way. Speer considered himself *blessed*. His greatest blessing, or so he thought, came when he got a call from the University of Central Mississippi, his first shot at a power-conference team. It was a huge jump and a whole lot more pressure. Speer prayed about the offer for two straight nights, drifting in and out of sleep until finally his wife rolled over and said, "Jesus, Speer. Just do it."

So, he did. Speer jumped in with both Nikes, and his journey had led him here, staring out at the throng of dumbstruck faces gathered before him. The crowd numbered in the thousands but was nothing compared to how many people there'd be in Sutpen Stadium on Saturday. Matt's parents sat side by side in the front row, their expressions a mixture of grief, fear, and embarrassment. The toxicology report hadn't come back yet, but everybody knew Matt enjoyed a couple cold beers after big wins. Tequila, sometimes too. Speer felt himself frowning, mimicking Matt's father's expression until he remembered that whatever had happened to Matt hadn't been an accident. It was just another page out of God's great playbook.

"In football and in life," Coach Taylor concluded, riffing off a line he'd pulled from an anonymous online quote, "ignorance is not a virtue. It's not cool to not know what you're talking about, but now you do. Matt Talley was a good young man. The very best we had to offer."

A woman in the front row clapped both hands over her mouth.

"Thank you," Speer said, "and may God continue to bless the University of Central Mississippi."

19

"**The hell** was that?" Frank said.

Rae felt her phone vibrate for the fourth time. She hadn't checked it. She'd been so mesmerized by Speer Taylor's speech she'd forgotten all about Madeline Mayo. Rae squeezed the phone between her palms as the grumbling crowd dispersed.

"The hat," Frank said. "That accent . . ."

Rae stared past the masses to the only empty seat on the stage, the place where Moses McCloud should've been sitting.

"Silent treatment, huh? Or maybe you're at a loss for words. That was some weird shit." Frank brought his aviators down from his hair to his nose. "But, hey, you never told me how things went this morning." Brown eyes peering out over his shades, Frank added, "At the catfish place, with Darren. You get any leads?"

Rae's phone vibrated again. The text was from Darren, not Mad, and it was more than just a lead; it was an invitation. She said, "I've got to go, Frank. I'm sorry."

"Yeah?"

"I'm not feeling too great."

Frank stared at her sideways, grunting as he jerked the Subaru into gear. "Okay, then. Let's call it a day."

Darren picked Rae up in his gold 1981 Monte Carlo exactly six minutes after Frank dropped her off at her apartment, just enough time for the rookie agent to hustle inside and grab her electric toothbrush. Rae ran the vibrating bristles over her teeth as she flipped through her Trapper Keeper, prepping her mouth and her mind for the ride with Darren Floyd. The sound of a car horn honking cut the refresh session short. Rae sat the toothbrush beside the sink, grabbed her JanSport backpack, and sprinted down the stairs.

Even after all that running, the rookie's legs were still restless, her right knee bouncing against the Monte Carlo's dash. *Giddy.* That's the word her daddy would've used. Rae couldn't help it. She'd done good. She was in a possible informant's car, headed down Highway 49 toward Clarksdale, Mississippi.

A Fairfield Inn & Suites came and went through the passenger window. Rae's eyes moved to the side mirror, reading the words engraved on the glass: OBJECTS IN MIRROR MAY BE CLOSER THAN THEY APPEAR. She waited until the hotel was gone, the entire town of Compson in the Monte Carlo's rearview, and then she said, "I take it we're not going to the Love Handle? What made you change your mind?"

Darren lit a cigarette and cracked his window. "Saw your news van on the TV. *Prism News.* Never heard of it."

Rae said, "You looked me up, huh?" playing the part Madeline Mayo had created for her.

"Saw all them articles on your website too."

"Read any?"

"Read enough to know what I needed to know."

The portfolio Mad had put together included pieces with titles like "Outcome of Trayvon Martin Trial Will Shape America's Future" and "Migrants Still Packed into Detention Camps along US–Mexico Border." Bless that mullet-rocking hacker's heart.

"Was it as bad as it looked?" Darren said. "At the memorial service?"

"Speer's speech was weird, yeah, but what was weirder was the fact that Moses never showed."

Darren exhaled out the crack in the window. The smoke scattered toward a water wheel inching its way over a soybean field. Rae watched the irrigation system, trying to gauge its progress, comparing it against her own. After a minute she said, "Come on. I thought we were—"

"*We?*" Darren said. "You don't know the first thing about me, Ms. Joyce."

Hearing him say her alias aloud made Rae pause, made her nervous like she hadn't been since she'd left her apartment. Instinctively, she unzipped the backpack between her knees. Staring down into the main compartment, Rae saw an unopened protein bar, a half-finished water bottle, and a paperback edition of *The 7 Habits of Highly Effective People*. The book was good, or at least the start of it was (Rae'd only made it through Habit 1: Be Proactive), but where the hell was her Trapper Keeper?

By the sink in her apartment, right where she'd left it.

Had she made a mistake? The first miscue of her rookie investigation? Rae was posing as a journalist, after all. She could've brought her binder along. Something to take notes with, at least. If her father had been watching her performance on film, he might've given her a missed assignment, the same way he gave quarterbacks demerits for bad reads. Then again, the Trapper Keeper might've been hard to explain. All those tabs. The dates, locations, the names. Darren Floyd's name, especially. This wasn't a football game. It wasn't even practice. This was a federal investigation and Rae was on her own now, making the plays up as she went along.

After a solid sixty seconds of silence, Darren shook his head and said, "I played ball for the Chiefs. Came all the way down from Detroit back in 1996 . . ."

Rae ran the numbers. Darren was older than he looked. Older than her by almost ten years, closer to forty than thirty.

". . . just to play some college ball. Things were different back then, but not much. Thought I was hot shit, let me tell you."

"What position did you play?"

"Guess."

Rae studied him. His lips, his hands, both soft, smooth. Smooth like the way he was leaned back in the seat, long legs stretched straight out. "Receiver," she said. "With your height, I'm guessing you were on the outside, a possession guy, or did you run deep routes? Were you fast?"

A forest of Little Trees "Black Ice" air fresheners swayed beneath the rearview mirror. Other than that, all was still inside the Monte Carlo's cab. Darren Floyd included. Rae feared she'd said too much, leaned too heavy on her football knowledge and exposed herself.

"Yeah, I was fast." Darren switched his hands on the wheel, holding it with the one closest to Rae, turning away from her a little. "But now I can barely walk, much less run."

Rae remembered the limp, how Darren had hobbled around the AA meeting.

"Got two busted knees, a bum shoulder, and a catfish joint. That's it, all I got out of my four years at the University of Central Mississippi."

"Why don't you go back to Detroit?"

"I visit, sometimes, but it ain't the same. In Compson, people still remember that catch I made against Ole Miss in overtime my senior year. That's why they come eat at my restaurant. They wanna talk about it."

"And that's bad?"

"What's bad was all the money I blew after that game."

Rae's right leg started to twitch again.

"See, I was getting paid, we all were, but nobody knew what to do with it. You got to remember, we were poor. Five hundred bucks was crazy money. You should've seen my shoes. Had every pair of Jordans ever made, kept them clean too, but kicks don't count for shit after college."

Rae brought her heels up against the passenger seat, trying to hide her feet.

"That's what nobody understood, not back then, not now," Darren said. "That's why I decided to do something with what little influence I had left. Something besides just selling catfish."

"That's why you became a bagman?"

The Monte Carlo swerved then straightened out again. Darren's fingers tightened around the wheel. "You put all this in your story, you know you can't use my name, right? Nobody's name."

"No names. Got it. But what made you want to talk to me?"

"Somebody needs to hear it. Somebody needs to know how messed up it is. And that word you just used—*bagman*—that ain't me. Never was."

"Then what were you doing at the Waffle House last night?"

Darren raised his chin. "Eating waffles."

"It was damn near three in the morning," Rae said, "and I saw that JCPenney bag."

Darren brought the cigarette to his lips. "Okay, so maybe I was waiting to meet somebody, but not like what you're thinking. There wasn't any money in that bag."

"A pair of slacks?"

"A shirt, actually. A decent button-down shirt, something Moses could wear to church, but he never showed."

Rae could see the name *Moses McCloud*, the exact place she'd written it in her Trapper Keeper, beneath the new SUSPECTS tab next to Ella May Pride.

"These boys," Darren said, "they're the most recognizable students on campus. They deserve to look good, wear something other than the same hoodies, the same kicks they had back in high school. So I hook them up with fresh clothes now and then. Maybe take them out to eat, someplace other than the caf."

"And that makes you different from a bagman, how?"

"I don't deal in cash, and I never ask for nothing in return. Like to think of myself as a agent. Yeah. A brother that's been there before, who's using what he knows, the mistakes he made, to help these kids out. That's why, when Moses called and said he was skipping the memorial service today, told me to meet him at his grandmamma's place—I called you."

"You want me to put Moses in my story? That's why you brought me out here?"

"I want you to listen," Darren said, steering with his knees, the highway a straight flat line ahead of them, each mile marker another minute closer to the truth. "Something's got Moses scared. Could hear it in his voice."

Rae waited. It took everything in her, but she waited.

"Shit rolls downhill in Compson," Darren said and flicked his cigarette out the window. "The players, boys like Moses and Cerge, they're at the bottom. They're the ones down on the field, taking the hits."

"Who's at the top?"

"Now that's a good question."

A structure appeared in the distance. A water tower, maybe? Rae glanced at it and said, "You're telling me you don't know?"

"Told you to listen. When we get out to Geraldine's place, you let me do the talking, okay?"

"Geraldine? That's Moses's grandma? That's where we're going?"

The Monte Carlo eased to a stop at the intersection of Highways 49 and 61. What Rae had mistaken for a water tower was actually two giant hollow-body electric guitars rising out of the ground.

"Geraldine stays just on past the Crossroads," Darren said. "You know why they call it that?"

"Yeah," Rae said, staring up at the guitars, thinking of her father. "This is where Robert Johnson made his deal with the Devil."

"That's right." Darren lit another cigarette. "Now let's go make sure Moses ain't about to do the same thing."

20

When King Tutankhamun's tomb was discovered in 1922, Maxine Christmas left Mississippi and headed for the Gift of the Nile, ready to turn her dreams into a reality. Or at least that's how she'd explained it to her son.

Studying the photograph on his desk, the one of Maxine astride a camel, a smattering of smallish pyramids behind her, Harry knew there was more to the story. The picture was actually taken in Sudan, as close as Maxine ever came to Egypt. Something about dysentery. Sudan was basically the same, minus the Sphinx and stuff. That's what Maxine always said.

Harry'd never understood his mother's infatuation with Sudan, or Egypt. Both were worlds away from the cypress knees and cotton fields they called home. Whenever Harry asked, his mother would get this faraway look in her eyes as she explained that she'd just wanted to ride a real camel and meet a cute Muslim boy with clean dark hair, light blue eyes, and a long brown penis. Another anecdote from Maxine's African adventure: Muslim boys, Harry's mother once told him, had surprisingly dark members.

The congressman's eyes went to the open window on his study's far wall. Then they went through it to the five-hundred-acre farm his mother had named "Sudan." Harry tried to remember the farm as it was before. Back when there was a gorgeous woman tucked away in each of the house's thirteen rooms. Lord, it had been beautiful. The live oaks out front were still imposing, but the grounds were disheveled now. Weeds grew up through the cracks in the walkway. Rusty light fixtures. Broken limbs and splintered windows.

Despite the disarray, Harry had still managed to keep his antiques collection in prime condition. World War II bayonets, Blue Willow China sets, sterling silver flatware, and a bevy of intricately crafted maps from the early 1800s lined the walls in the congressman's study. The shelves, however, held Harry's most prized possessions.

A ceramic tobacco jar, which opened by removing the "head" of a Black shoeshine boy, sat on the shelf to the congressman's right. To his left, a fabric mammy doll, hair wrapped in a tiny red kerchief, grinned back at him. Harry's shelves were lined with more of the same. He'd started this special collection after he heard that antiques from this era were being bought up and destroyed. Which was ridiculous. They were just as much a part of American history as his World War II bayonets, and Harry took great pride in preserving them.

One of the congressman's cell phones dinged.

Harry hated those damn slabs. Made his life twice as hard as it used to be. Used to, Harry had one phone in his office, another in the kitchen, and that was it. Beige rotary phones with curly cords. Now, he had to keep a box of burners in his desk like some kind of two-bit crook. A whole box of beeping black plastic and charging docks dangling out everywhere.

Email was worse.

Harry had a government email address he hadn't checked in five years. The Freedom of Information Act was a royal pain in his ass. Ever since he'd borrowed the governor's jet to go visit all those college football towns, Harry'd been chipping away at FOIA, coming at it from a different angle with each new legislative session. Kept reminding his fellow congressmen that Mississippi FOIA laws had gone largely unchanged since 1967, that glorious time before email, cell phones, and text messages. The way the law read now, a Chinese state-owned company operating in Mississippi could use their employees to FOIA for internal government documents, which, in Harry's personal and professional opinion, was a ridiculous waste of taxpayer money. The less people—*Chinese* people, especially—knew about what he did or how he did it, the better.

The phone dinged again.

It was a text message from "Bruiser" Brandt Conrad, a link to a YouTube video. Harry put on his reading glasses and held the phone at arm's length, recalling the last time Chief Conrad had sent him such a link. How that video of Speer Taylor dancing around the locker room had, in some ways, led to the mess they were in now. Harry braced himself and tapped the screen. The video started, reflecting backward in the congressman's non-prescription, half-framed readers. Harry watched every second of the five-minute clip, and then the screen went dark.

The congressman lifted his letter opener, the one with the handle shaped like a fleur-de-lis. He brought the pointy end down on the heart of the burner phone, then repeated the motion three more times. The old Luddite relished the sound of the crunching plastic, the sight of shattered glass. When he was finished, Harry shook his head at the mess. He felt silly. It wasn't like him to be so brash. As much as he hated those slabs, they were still expensive.

The congressman swept the mess into the wastebasket beneath his desk, took a fresh phone from his stable, and placed a call to Chief Conrad.

"Hey, boss. Coach Taylor's blowing up," the police chief said between heavy breaths. "He's gone viral. You read the comments?"

"I could barely bring myself to suffer through the video."

"This one guy, 'MississippiMudCat78,' said the houndstooth hat reminded him of his grandaddy."

"Mississippi *mudcat*?"

"That's the guy's handle."

Harry said, "*Lord*," tapping the flat edge of the letter opener's blade against his forehead, picturing Speer again, his yellow hair hanging out the back of that fedora. He'd never expected the coach to make such a mockery of his proposal. Harry didn't know what to do with Speer Taylor now.

More grunting from Bruiser, then: "This changes things, don't it?"

The letter opener lay flat over the bridge of the congressman's nose. Harry stared up cross-eyed at the blade. "We knew the service was being recorded. There were news vans everywhere."

"Prism News," Bruiser huffed. "They're the ones posted that video, and they've got damn near ten million subscribers to their YouTube channel."

"Ten million what?"

"Subscribers. You know, people watching whatever them rainbow warriors are putting out."

"Ten million people have seen that video?" Harry'd spent the bulk of his life manipulating the masses, but that much influence, that fast, was beyond him.

"It's only been up a half hour, but there's already over a hundred thousand views," Bruiser croaked. "Just read the comments, Congressman Christmas. That's the best part."

Harry peered into the wastebasket at the remains of his shattered smart phone, "Fine, Brandt. But I need you to send me that link again."

A few seconds after Harry recited the new number a different burner dinged. This time, the congressman noticed that the clip had been professionally edited. There was a backing track and fancy captions citing every line Speer had plagiarized. It was a hit piece. No doubt about it. Prism News had achieved its goal, but in doing so, they'd also provoked some sort of angry virtual mob.

Harry made it through the first three comments before he stood and said, "My God. They *loved* it. This man here, 'gunsup4jesus,' says, 'These hippies got no rite attackin a God fering man like Coach Tayler.'" Harry brought the phone in closer, fighting to keep his hands steady. "And 'TheGipper' just wrote, 'Speer Taylor for President! #SpeerTheLibtards.'"

Bruiser's grunts grew deeper, morphing into something like a low growl, a series of primal groans. The congressman couldn't be certain, but it almost sounded as if Bruiser was crying.

"Brandt?" Harry said. "What on earth are you doing?"

"Ordered up some a them at-home, low T injections," the former linebacker said. "You know, like for testosterone and stuff? Got the 24-gauge needle, right here, just like what it says on the box, but damn, it still hurts like a sonabitch."

Harry Christmas didn't have a clue what Chief Conrad was talking about. He didn't care. He said, "Those comments, Brandt, they change everything. With supporters like this, a whole new burgeoning conservative base, Speer's got a fighting chance at next year's Senate race."

"What about . . ." Bruiser said, still catching his breath. "What about Eddie Pride?"

Harry was so caught up in the news of the video, he had to say the bagman's name in his head, then roll it over one more time before it registered. "Eddie Pride *Junior*. Yes, that's right. We need to make sure he still has his end of the deal covered."

"You want me to string him up again?"

Harry remembered the sound of the porch beam creaking, the way the fat man's toes had twitched. "No," he said. "No rope this time. This time, let's keep things civil. You've spoken with the owner of the Buffalo Nickel, correct?"

"Yessir. Mr. Estes said he had a camera on the roof, but it wasn't working. Hadn't worked in years."

"A malfunctioning camera would be very hard to explain in court."

"How about I call Mr. Estes back and ask him to kindly take that camera down? That way we don't have to worry with it at all."

"Good boy, Brandt. Now go fetch Mr. Pride and bring him here. I'd love an update on our new quarterback."

"You want me to bring Eddie out to Sudan?"

"Yes," Harry said, running one finger over the letter opener's blade, "but please, keep my home address private."

21

Darren's Monte Carlo eased through the intersection and out from under the shadow cast by the electric guitars, each one built to resemble a Gibson ES-355, the kind of axe B.B. King made famous and named Lucille. Nothing like the one Robert Johnson kept strapped to his back all the way up until the day he died. Only three verified photographs of the clandestine bluesman remained, and Rae's daddy kept a print of one hanging in every office he'd ever had.

Chuck Johnson never could get into hip hop. He was too old school. Early Jimmy Buffett albums were his go-to jam, but Chuck also enjoyed the blues. The blues offered him a common ground with his players. Chuck couldn't get enough of "Hellhound on My Trail." Said it was the perfect coaching song; somebody was always after your job, your players, especially once you made it to the top. To the best of Rae's knowledge, Chuck Johnson had never been to Clarksdale, and that was a shame. He would've loved the Crossroads.

Darren steered the Monte Carlo north up alongside the Sunflower River. Ground Zero, a former cotton-grading warehouse turned world-renowned blues club owned by Morgan Freeman, the man Rae considered to be the voice of God, came and went on the left. Scenes from *The Shawshank Redemption* played in her mind. The Monte Carlo rolled on, following the river upstream until they were out of Clarksdale's crumbling downtown and into the heart of the Delta. Mile after mile of flat farmland. Rae let her mind unwind and felt the tug of her past calling up to her from the cracks in the blue highway. All those years she'd spent on her daddy's field, learning the game as she brought his players water and listened to their tales. Rae understood why Darren had let her tag along. Why he'd brought her to Moses's hometown. Darren thought she was a journalist, and he wanted her to hear the quarterback's story.

It was fitting, Rae thought as they pulled off the highway onto a dirt road named Ivy Lane, that Moses was from the same place as Robert Johnson. The blues ran deep in their blood, so deep it had forced both young men to put all their hopes and dreams into something like a guitar, or worse, a football.

A ramshackle structure—a onetime tenant house, if Rae had to guess—appeared at the end of Ivy Lane. The sheet metal roof caught the morning sun and gleamed. Rae pulled the vanity mirror down, shading her eyes as the Monte Carlo came to a stop. When she lifted the mirror again, Moses was standing on the front porch alongside the largest woman Rae had ever seen.

"Darren?" the woman hollered. "You got a white girl with you?"

"Excuse me?" The special agent slid out of the passenger seat and cupped both hands over her eyes. "My name is—"

"*Rae*," Darren said, stepping in front of her. "I'd like you to meet Momma G."

"Christian name's Geraldine," the woman said. "Geraldine McCloud."

Rae waited for Geraldine to say more. Silence followed. Enough time for the cotton rows to connect Rae back to her father. She pictured Chuck Johnson standing on doorsteps of similar houses, caught in the crosshairs of some bone-hard mother's gaze, maybe tossing out a Robert Johnson line, something that would make her trust him.

"Rae's a journalist," Darren said. "She's working on a story about college football."

Geraldine cocked a hip in the redhead's direction. "Well, Moses say he got a story to tell. Something big enough he brought his ass back home but wouldn't say a word about why to me. Not till Mr. Darren got here."

Rae watched Moses. The boy had his back to her, pulling the flimsy screen door open behind his grandmother. He seemed shy for a quarterback, almost scared.

"I'm here now, Momma G," Darren said. "You wanna let us step inside?"

"Do I *want* to? Nope. But what I want don't matter none." Geraldine's bootheels clacked over the porch planks. She stopped at the door, just long enough to say, "Y'all come in quick now. Don't let the bought air out."

The inside of Geraldine McCloud's house smelled like stale cigarette butts and Palmolive, a lemony, chemical aroma that made it hard to breathe. Geraldine fired up a fresh one as she plopped down in a faded recliner and snapped at Moses, saying, "Fetch me one them blue China bowls."

Darren was smoking too, leaned up against the doorframe in his joggers and white Chucks, the sun already on its way down behind him. Rae wondered if every real smoker left in America had migrated to Mississippi. Or maybe it was just the fact that things moved slower in the Magnolia State, like the whole place was still a couple decades behind the rest of the world.

There were piles of clothes on the sofa. The kitchen table, a Formica laminate–topped square with dingy chrome edges and legs, was positioned out a couple feet from the sink. Rae was considering the red vinyl chairs when Moses tossed a ceramic bowl clean across the kitchen and into the living room. Geraldine caught the flying dish with one hand and tapped her cigarette on the rim with the other. Like she'd run this play before, putting on a show for all the coaches and bagmen who'd stopped by on recruiting visits, an exhibition of the McClouds' athletic prowess.

"You gonna put that in your story?" Geraldine said, grinning around her cigarette.

Rae said, "Sure."

"You either is or you ain't." The recliner creaked as Geraldine shifted her weight. "And I need to know, honey. Before I get to talking—before Moses say one damn word—I need to know exactly what you writing this story about."

Darren pushed off the doorframe, hand raised, mouth open, ready to take it from there. Maybe Rae should've let him, but she needed Geraldine to trust her. Moses too.

"The story's about college football."

Geraldine said, "Uh-huh . . ."

"But not like what you see on ESPN. Not even those *30 for 30* documentaries. This story's got nothing to do with the scoreboard. It's about what goes on off the field."

"We off the field now, ain't we?"

"The story I want to write is about moments just like this. It's about boys like your grandson."

"Moses been at UCM six full months," Geraldine said, one hand on her hair, the other holding the cigarette a few inches out from her lips, the smoke a thin gray screen, a cloud that masked her eyes. "Coach Taylor made him come in early, back during the summer, and that was fine, but then he left him on the bench all season. Kept that lanky-ass white boy ahead of him. What's his name?"

Rae said, "Matt Talley's dead," and watched Geraldine jab her cigarette toward the window-sized flat-screen television mounted on the far wall.

"Been all over Action News 5. That's why you here, ain't it?"

Moses was sitting at the kitchen table now, leaned forward a little as if he were bracing himself.

"Rae's here because I invited her," Darren said and took the seat next to Moses. "She's cool, Momma G."

"She the odd man out, what she is," Geraldine said. "My baby's finally the quarterback. Got everything we been after for forever, but something ain't right. Something got Moses running all the way home to see his Momma G, and I ain't fixing to talk family business in front of no *journalist*."

Darren said, "Why don't we ask him, then?"

Geraldine hooked an elbow over the armrest. "Come on, D. Moses don't know what's best for him." The old woman talked over her grandson as if he wasn't sitting right there. "Raised that boy up from nothing, and I mean no-*thing*. After I just got done raising my baby girl, his momma. Then she run off with that fool Keyshawn, left me here to start all over again . . ."

Geraldine inhaled and the tip of her cigarette sizzled, hot enough for Rae to realize Darren had known just how hard to push Geraldine to get her out of that recliner, stomping around her living room now, ready to tell Rae the story he'd brought her there to hear.

"Had me a man by the name of Codell everybody used to call 'Code.' Looked like Karl Malone. 'The Mailman.' Remember him? Strong Black man rode a Harley and always kept his mustache clean. Me and Code was gonna get the hell outta Clarksdale, see the world without any windows, just ride the sky down and never look back. But then Keke—that's my daughter—and Keyshawn, they beat us to it. Took off for L.A. Maybe it was San Diego. Don't make no difference now. They never made it."

Rae heard something tapping to her left, turned, and saw Moses drumming his fingers across the top of the kitchen table, each beat a little harder than the last.

"They found Keyshawn's little busted-ass Buick up north of Oxford a couple miles, wrapped so thick in kudzu vines you couldn't tell the car was there, even if you was looking straight at it." Geraldine lit another cigarette off the tip of the last. "Least that's what the *po*lice told me. What they didn't tell me—the shit they didn't have to say—was that it took them lazy-ass, donut-eating sonsabitches damn near forty-eight hours to find my baby."

Moses was tapping the table hard enough to rattle the laminate. He still had his head cocked toward his grandmother. Darren was leaned back with his legs crossed, eyes closed, as if listening to an old blues tune he knew by heart.

"Weren't no guardrails," Geraldine said, flicking ash into the blue bowl, "and that kudzu was everywhere. Only reason anybody found them at all was 'cause some wino walked by and heard the baby screaming."

The way Geraldine said it straight out like that caught the rookie agent by surprise. Rae said, "Baby? What baby?"

"What you mean *what* baby? You think I'm telling you some story about my cousin's kid?" Geraldine planted one hand on her hip and brought the other to her mouth, smoking as she stared at the ceiling. "Moses weren't even five years old but he made it two full days down deep in that kudzu. No food. No water. Sheriff said one more day would've been one too many. I looked him straight in his face and said, 'Ain't no such thing as too many for my Moses.'"

Geraldine plodded across the living room and stopped at the window beside the front door, staring out at the dirt road winding its way back toward the Sunflower River, Clarksdale and the Crossroads waiting somewhere beyond the water. Rae felt the weight of the story, but still wondered how much of it was true. A four-year-old kid, alone in a car for forty-eight hours? Nothing to eat or drink at that age? It seemed like a stretch. It reeked of the Delta, a place where stories got tangled up in kudzu vines and grew wild with time. A down-on-his-luck blues singer learns to play a mean guitar and the Devil gets thrown in the mix. Monuments are made, but somewhere along the winding highway between then and now, the truth is lost.

It was a lot to think about in the short time Rae had before Geraldine said, "God saved my Moses for some special thing. You believe in God?"

Rae realized the woman was talking to her and said, "God?" feeling her way back into the conversation, the smoke thick in the cramped room now. "I believe in a higher power, if that's what you're asking."

"That ain't what I said." Geraldine turned from the window. "I'm asking if you see my boy like I see him. Like God saw him that day in the kudzu. If you wanna write a story about my Moses, then that's what I need to know."

Moses wasn't tapping his fingers anymore. Without the sound, all was quiet in the tiny house. A silence so thick Rae could feel the weight of it, the pressure Moses carried with him always, the hometown hero, a legend in his grandmother's graying eyes.

"I see a kid," Rae said, then stopped. She had to get this part right if she wanted to hear Moses's side of the story, and "kid" wasn't the right word at all. That wasn't who Rae saw staring back at her from the other end of the table. She summoned the highlight video Frank had shown her, the clips where it wasn't just Moses's speed or arm strength that had piqued the coach's daughter's interest.

"I see a young man who knows the game, inside and out. Does he have talent? Sure. The electric touchdown runs. The seventy-yard dimes. That's all anybody notices." Rae glanced at Moses. She had his attention now. "But nobody talks about what's going on under his helmet. It's always the same story with quarterbacks like Moses. *Athleticism. Agility. Talent*," Rae said, wondering how many times her father had used those same words on his recruiting visits. "But Moses is smart too. Smart enough he rarely makes the wrong read. That's what sets him apart. The way he lets the game come to him and doesn't force anything."

Geraldine raised one eyebrow, her left one. "Ever since that boy could walk he been throwing a football around. Swear to the Lord in heaven I saw Moses knock a Miller Lite can off Keyshawn's head at a reunion a couple weeks before the kudzu crash. A beer can! You believe that?"

"Yeah," Rae said. "He's got a great arm. But it's the stuff that can't be measured that makes the difference."

"His *heart*," Geraldine said, starting for the kitchen table. "That's what makes Moses so special. My boy's got the heart of a lion. Done my best to keep him straight. He tell you I send him texts sometimes?"

Rae shook her head.

"Just the other day I sent him one about that USC quarterback."

"The DUI charge?"

"That's right. Got to make sure Moses know how fast it can all go away. One bad choice, and he's right back here with me." The old woman stared down at her cigarette, what was left of it. "But if he do right, if Moses stay straight, just how good you think he can be? You think my boy can go all the way?"

Images of Moses out on the field firing fastballs and lobbing high floaters into the back of the end zone flew through Rae's brain. She said, "Toss in a few well-timed interviews, a couple features like the story I'm working on, and there's not a doubt in my mind Moses could make it to—"

Rae was about to say "the League," meaning the NFL, but Moses's gaze stopped her. She felt the weight of her lies adding up, each one coming out easier than the last. Moses was standing now, towering over the kitchen table.

"Make it where?" Geraldine said. "You think he good enough to get drafted? Maybe in the first round? That's what you was about to say?"

Rae looked up at Moses. "If that's what he wants, then yeah, sure."

"If that's what I *want*?" Moses said. "We talking about the same thing, right? A multimillion-dollar contract, a fat-ass signing bonus?"

"*Moses McCloud*," Geraldine snapped. "Watch that mouth in my house."

"Everybody all the time telling me what to say, how to say it. I got a class this semester on Tuesdays and Thursdays called Media Management. A whole class trying to teach me how to talk to people like you."

Rae said, "Me? No, listen, I'm not—"

"I don't even know who you with," Moses said and spun on Darren. "How about you, D? What you know about her?"

Darren said, "Easy. Rae's cool. She's with—"

"Go ahead." Rae shrugged. "Google me."

Phone in hand, the quarterback went to work unearthing the fruit of Madeline Mayo's labor, saying, "*New York Times*. *USA Today*? Looks like you work for everybody."

"I'm a freelancer," Rae said and paused, nervous but taking her time, letting the play develop. "Which means we can work together on this story, nail it down, so it says exactly what you want before I send it out."

Moses massaged his face. "Everything Momma G just told you—all that stuff about the kudzu?—it was true. My whole life been just like that. Like some crazy ass rollercoaster and I ain't got no say in which way to go. How fast, how slow. Nothing. Not unless I'm out on a football field."

Rae wished for her Trapper Keeper, or better yet, a legal pad and a pen. A real writer would've been taking notes. Rae Johnson wasn't a writer, though. She was a federal agent, moments away from learning a part of the story Frank had missed. Moses wasn't just a player on the UCM football team, he was their new quarterback, the centerpiece. If Rae could get him talking, if she knew what he knew, then she'd be one step closer to cracking her first case.

"When I got that ball in my hand," Moses continued, "I'm in control. Can't nobody touch me. Been like that since peewee. Didn't matter what was going on at school, or back here at the house. When I'm on that field, I call the shots. Every hit I ever took, every touchdown I scored, that was me just trying to shake them vines loose and climb my way out of Clarksdale."

"You done it, baby." Geraldine sniffed and wiped her nose. "You done good. I know you scared, but—"

"No, not scared," Moses said. "Not anymore. I'm mad, pissed because . . ." His voice died away, then came back stronger, louder. "Because I done just like what you said. All those texts you send? I done right, Momma G. I been careful, real careful. Which is why this conversation is over."

Moses glared at Rae as he stalked around the table, completing a half circle on his way out of the kitchen. Geraldine whispered her grandson's name, but he didn't stop. Rae could still feel Moses's gaze, studying her, questioning her, long after his bedroom door slammed.

Geraldine ran both hands over the laminate tabletop. "Something don't feel right, D," she said, digging for her cigarettes again. "Something besides this girl you brought up in my house."

22

There was a bar at one end of the Ground Zero blues club, a stage on the other, some tables and chairs in between, every square inch covered in scribbles. Names, dates, locations, and other drunken notes like: *Mrs. Sippy and Spunky wuz here.* Or, Rae's personal favorite: *Hi, Morgan. Your a great actor.*

Hours had passed since the meeting at Geraldine McCloud's place. It was dark now, a little past dusk, but still muggy. Darren was bent over a pool table, sliding the cue back and forth along his left index finger and thumb as he said, "That boy played us, talking all that serious shit about being stuck down in them kudzu vines, about being in control. Then he just got up and left?"

Rae knew it was her—her presence—that had kept Moses from saying whatever it was he'd called Darren there to tell him. Darren knew it too. He hadn't said a single word the whole drive over to Ground Zero, just kept smoking and pitching the butts out the window, leaving a trail of sparks behind his Monte Carlo. Marking a path back, maybe? Rae wasn't sure, but she liked the way the bagman was working his cue now, smooth, fluid thrusts, the way a conductor builds to a crescendo.

The white ball smacked into the pyramid of colored ones, sending them scattering across green felt. Rae didn't know the rules of this game, but her neck was hot, palms clammy. It felt like weakness. She wiped the sweat away.

Darren pushed up from the pool table. "You were right about Moses. What you said back at Geraldine's?"

"He's smart."

"I ever tell you he wants to be a veterinarian?"

Rae said, "Really?" sidling up to the table now, trying to picture Moses McCloud in an animal clinic instead of the huddle, the locker room, anywhere other than a football field.

"Craziest damn thing. Kid's good enough to make it to the NFL, but all he ever talks about is his 'plan.' How he's got to keep his GPA up so he can get into vet school."

"He can do it," Rae said. "If Moses works hard and doesn't quit, good things will happen."

"Not many brothers in vet school, but shit, not many concussions either."

Rae decided on the ball closest to the far-left corner pocket, the burgundy one with Moses's jersey number on both sides. She was spreading her feet, trying to mimic Darren's stance, his well-practiced motion with the cue, when her phone vibrated.

It was a text from Madeline Mayo. The text Rae had been waiting for. The rookie agent stood and scanned the message then read back through it again. Thanks to something called a "rootkit" (Rae didn't ask), Mad had gotten a sneak peek at Matt's autopsy results. The quarterback's blood alcohol content was .21, which was high but not lethal. The rest of the report detailed a series of cervical fractures and blunt force trauma to Matt's head, chest, shoulders, and torso. In other words, Matt Talley had died on impact.

Rae was still staring at her phone when Darren eased up behind her and said, "Here, let me show you." She felt his hands on her hips, moving down her forearms, positioning her fingers around the cue. There it was. That rhythm she'd noticed before, the stick gliding back and forth above the felt like a violin's bow.

When the cue tip tapped the white ball, it felt so natural, so smooth, Rae wasn't sure if she'd struck it at all. Not until she heard the soft *plunk* of the 7-ball dropping into the corner pocket.

"See?" Darren said, still leaned forward, his chest pressed against her back. "Nothing to it."

Teamwork makes the dream work. That wasn't one of Chuck Johnson's lines, there was a limit to his clichés, but there was some truth in it. That's why Rae'd gone against her senior partner's direct orders and told Darren Floyd she was an investigative journalist. That's why she'd let him put his hands on her hips like that. She needed his help.

Now that the autopsy report had come back clean, Darren was Rae's only hope. There had to be some connection between UCM, the dirty cops, and the money that went to the recruits, all those bags nobody talked about. If there was anybody who knew the ins and outs of the whole shady business, it was Darren Floyd.

Rae had her star player, and she didn't want to lose him. What was it Frank had said? That fortune cookie line? *A muddy puddle clears best when left alone . . .* Something like that. He'd said other stuff. Kept telling her to slow down. The case would still be there in the morning. Maybe, Rae thought, if she played the game just right, Darren would be there too.

She leaned back and felt his hand come up, caressing her chin as Rae's phone started vibrating again. Darren didn't move, his lips so close now they brushed hers as he said, "You gonna get that?"

"Yeah," Rae said and ducked out from under his arms. "What if it's my—" She cut herself short because it was her partner, Agent Ranchino, calling with news that thrilled Rae even more than the bluesman had.

23

Frank said, "I've got 'em, kid. 1466 County Road 103," reading the address off a mailbox as he put the Subaru in park. "I just pulled up. You coming or what?"

"Got who, Frank? What are you talking about?"

The veteran special agent took a long drag off his e-cig and said, "I went back to the field house. After I dropped you off? I wanted to get eyes on Speer Taylor. You know, set up surveillance and see if there was any fallout from the eulogy . . ."

Except, Frank hadn't gone to the field house. He'd stopped at the nearest McDonald's, ordered a Quarter Pounder with cheese, a large fry, and a McFlurry. The ice-cream machine was broken, so he'd settled for a Diet Coke and hit the road. Frank was never more comfortable than when driving. That's what almost thirty years as a special agent did to a man. A cramped cab, a couple grease-stained bags and a watered-down soda usually put Frank's mind at ease, but after Matt's service, none of his old tricks were working.

Frank didn't tell Rae any of that. He stuck to the facts, short, descriptive details about what had happened, what he'd stumbled upon, pushing down the thoughts of his new partner that kept slipping through. Frank couldn't put his finger on how, exactly, Rae Johnson made him feel. Rae was the kind of woman who beat you out of the bathroom. Didn't waste any time in the mirror. Didn't have to. *Christ.* She was a good-looking broad. A redhead with a rocking bod. A *pole vaulter.* But that wasn't it. Rae was out of Frank's league. She was out of her own league too. The rookie just didn't know it yet.

Frank couldn't quit thinking about how she'd called it quits after the memorial service. Didn't say shit about Speer Taylor's speech, much less how her morning had gone at Floyd's Fresh Fish. It was weird. Weird enough Frank went cruising after he dropped her off at her apartment.

Frank had still been thinking about Rae as he eased his Subaru to a stop at the intersection of College Street and Main, the Dollar General to his right, the Waffle House to his left, the very parking lot where he'd last seen Matt Talley alive. Eddie Pride's Ford was in the lot, almost the exact same spot. Had it ever left? Frank couldn't remember. He blinked and the truck was still there, parked beside a Compson PD cruiser, the driver-side window down. All Frank could see was the cop's meaty hand, a little bit of his forearm too, the skin tight and well veined.

A car horn honked.

Frank checked his rearview and saw a pimple-faced college student using his middle finger to let the veteran agent know the light was green. Frank hooked a left into the Waffle House parking lot and watched the kid damn near take off his side mirror, the same mirror that was inches away from the cruiser, the Compson Police Chief looking straight at him. To the man's right sat Eddie Pride Junior, riding shotgun with what appeared to be a grocery bag on his head.

Frank had backed out of the parking lot, slowly, and tailed the police chief a couple blocks, taking time to get his story straight before he called his partner.

"So, yeah," Frank said. "That's it. You coming? Where are you?"

Rae answered his question by asking him two more: What's the place look like? Who owns it?

Frank wasn't sure who owned the crusty-ass plantation at the end of county road, but he knew it gave him the willies. Looked haunted, and not by any white-sheet ghosts, neither. The spirits Frank imagined wore shackles, heavy, rusted chains. Had sour-milk eyes and keloid scars from their master's cat o' nine tails. *Slave ghosts*. That's what had Frank spooked, and he wasn't even a Southerner. Frank was from Brooklyn, originally. Went to St. Francis of Assisi, the Catholic school where he smoked Camels in the bathroom and chased girls like Juliet Floriani up and down the halls. How the hell did these rednecks do it? That's what Frank wanted to know. How'd they go on living in a place where so much blood had been shed? How'd they sleep at night, or look at themselves in their bathroom mirrors?

Eddie Pride wasn't looking at anything except the inside of a brown paper bag. Through his binoculars, Frank noticed a cartoon pig wearing a butcher's cap printed on the front, *Piggly Wiggly* stamped above it in red. What kind of name was that for a grocery store?

Frank shook his head and realized he'd forgotten about Rae. His partner, still on the line, saying, "Talk to me, Frank. Who's all there?"

Chief Conrad, the muscle man, blue sleeves stretched tight around his biceps, was there, but it was the other guy Frank wasn't sure about, the one he'd never seen before, or if he had seen him, he hadn't thought enough about him to remember. It was the old man's clothes, his lack of style, that made him so easy to forget. Looked like somebody's Grandpa Bill, but the guy was in charge. Frank could tell that much without the binoculars. Brandt Conrad had brought Eddie Pride to the old guy's house, the filthy friggin' plantation where Frank was crouched behind a wrought-iron fence now, binoculars in one hand, cell phone in the other, e-cig powered down and tucked into the breast pocket of the federal agent's Hawaiian shirt. Now wasn't the time for a smoke, not even a fake one. They had Eddie tied to a chair in what appeared to be an office of some sort, a study. Yeah. That's what the dry fart in the windbreaker had called it.

His "study."

Frank was too far away to hear the men speaking but with the binoculars he could see their mouths moving just fine. Frank really was deaf in his left ear. Never made a big deal of it. Just something he'd lived with after taking a pipe to the head his first year on the job. Frank adapted by paying real close attention to people's mouths. You could learn a lot about people from their mouths. How often they brushed their teeth, the type of salad they'd had for lunch, or, if you happened to be stuck in Butthole, Mississippi, their favorite brand of smokeless tobacco. Twenty-some-odd years of staring straight into everybody's kisser, and Frank eventually learned to read lips. Got so good at it the Bureau gave him a cardstock certificate with a frilly blue border he kept in his office back in DC.

The secret to lipreading was knowing the context of a conversation. Visual cues were key. From his place behind the fence, Frank was too far away for such aids, but he was still able to gather bits of what was going on inside the study. Like the fact that nobody'd called the old-timer by name, which was why Eddie had that grocery bag on his head. This guy was important, maybe even more important than Speer Taylor. *Maybe*, Frank thought, Gramps was the piece of the puzzle he'd been missing, his one-way ticket out of Mississippi.

The old guy was asking Eddie something about a noose. How'd he get down from the noose? The guy's voice sounded like a Kentucky Fried Chicken commercial in Frank's head. Now the geezer was laughing and talking about a thoroughbred horse from—Frank squinted through the binoculars—*Dublin?* Yeah. "That racehorse really got you down from there, Edward? *Good Lord . . .*"

That's what the old guy said.

Frank frowned, unable to make sense of what they were talking about, not sure they were even talking about anything regarding the University of Central Mississippi. Not until the geezer mentioned "Moses McCloud," followed by what looked like either "proposition" or "preposition."

The bag on Eddie's head came to life then, crinkling as he squirmed in the chair and spoke words Frank couldn't hear or see. Frank could see the tiny dagger in the boss's hands, though, the blade glistening in the study's dim light. The bagman's back bowed when the dull blade sunk into his right thigh. Frank winced, then realized it was a letter opener, not a dagger.

The old guy started pacing around his chubby victim, twisting the letter opener with each pass, driving his point home. Frank was so wrapped up in the sudden gush of new information, he'd forgotten about his partner, Rae Johnson, asking more questions he didn't have time to answer.

"Can't read lips and talk to you at the same time, kid."

"Wait. What? You're reading their lips?" Rae said. "You're a lip reader?"

"Certified and everything. But hey, let me call you right back, okay?"

24

Rae said, "Okay . . ." and kept the phone pressed to her ear even after Frank had hung up. Behind her, Ground Zero was buzzing, more patrons filing in, ready for the show. There was a band on stage now: a drummer, a guitarist, a bass player, and three Black women huddled around one microphone in the back. Another mic stood alone, front and center. Darren was still at the pool table, giving Rae space to talk.

Darren was a good guy, levelheaded and cool. So cool, Rae probably could've told him the truth. She could've said she had to step outside and finish her call, but what if he asked questions? What if Darren wanted to know who she was talking to?

Do the right thing and you never have to worry. Another Chuck proverb, a riff on his overarching mantra mixed with that Mark Twain quote about lying. He used it for off-the-field speeches, mostly. Recruiting visits. Rotary clubs. Rae was as far away from her father's game as she'd ever been, but not so far she'd forgotten the lessons he'd taught her.

Phone still pressed to one ear, Rae waited until Darren looked her way then mouthed, *I'm sorry,* before slipping out the club's side door.

The air outside was heavy but cooler than it'd been in the day. Rae trudged her way through it to the far corner of the blues club's gravel lot, past a green dumpster filled to the brim with broken bottles and Styrofoam trays. The scent of warm suds and day-old pork pushed Rae on to the highway, headed north up Highway 49.

Her phone rang.

Rae slid her thumb over the glass and said, "What's happening now?"

Frank said, "Hell if I know," his accent off, a half-assed Southern impersonation. "Bruiser closed the blinds."

"Why are you talking like that?"

"Shit," Frank said, getting every ounce of Yankee back into that one word. "Too much lipreading."

"Who's the guy, Frank. The old guy you mentioned?"

"Christmas. *Congressman* Harry Christmas. The police chief let it slip, and that's not all. Listen to this . . ."

Rae pictured her partner in another time, another place, feet propped up on his desk in the Jacob K. Javits Federal Building, a gang of rookie agents huddled around him, recounting what he'd learned while reading lips outside the gates of Sudan. Frank said that's what the congressman had called his place. *Sudan.* Said the entire deal was like that, like something from the old days.

"There's this court case out west, something to do with a video game," Frank said. "They're worried it'll change everything. Make it so the players get paid real money. Real contracts. Advertising deals out the ass. A power shift. Yeah. The congressman said the case would 'negroize' the sport."

"What?"

"Confused the shit out of me too. The way the guy's mouth moved, I thought he was talking about ophthalmology, but he wasn't. No ma'am. He stuck a letter opener in Eddie Pride's thigh too. I mention that?"

The woman Rae'd been forty-eight hours ago would've never believed the words coming out of Special Agent Frank

Ranchino's mouth. How the congressman had single-handedly arranged the Chiefs' meteoric rise, how he'd sold a bunch of farmers in town on this idea that college football was their next big cash crop.

"And they bought it," Frank said. "All those rich white farmers are pumping gobs of money into Harry Christmas's campaign, money he funnels straight into the Chiefs' football program. The hotels? That bar downtown? All the money the football team's pouring into Compson—that's what's at stake here."

Rae knew, firsthand, the importance of college football in small Southern towns like Compson, or even back in Fayetteville. The Razorbacks were the closest thing to a professional sports team the Natural State had to offer. Arkansas didn't make it into the national media much, not unless some meth head got loose in a Walmart or her daddy's Hogs were playing. The emotional wellbeing of the entire state depended on how well the University of Arkansas's football team performed. It wasn't like that everywhere, but in states like Arkansas or Mississippi, the games were more than games. They were everything, the only thing.

"I mean, I understand what Harry's trying to protect," Frank said. "The part I don't get is how he's trying to do it? Matt Talley. Moses McCloud. What do the quarterbacks have to do with anything?"

Something about the question reminded Rae of her father. The night sky helped too. All those times she'd sat beside him in a darkened room, watching twenty-two miniaturized players flicker across a glowing screen. That's where her daddy had taught her that every team had a weakness, a tell, just like in poker. A linebacker who clapped twice before he blitzed the B Gap. A receiver who adjusted his face mask then took off on a deep route. There was always something. The same was true of this case. Rae had been so busy running around Compson, she hadn't taken time to properly consider the whole scene. She hadn't watched her film, but the reel was unspooling in her mind now.

Rae imagined herself flipping to the INCIDENTS tab in her Trapper Keeper. She scrolled back through the scene at the Buffalo Nickel. She recalled Matt Talley climbing into Eddie Pride's Ford. She pictured him stepping back out again— *empty-handed*?

"Matt never got paid," Rae said, talking more to herself than her partner, still working through it. "Even after he pulled off the biggest play of his career and saved the Chiefs' shot at another championship season, Matt still walked away with nothing. It doesn't make sense."

Frank's voice on the line said, "It never did, kid. That's why I was so torn up about it. There wasn't any money."

Not until a couple seconds before Matt's swan dive onto College Street, Rae thought, remembering the way the bills had fluttered like confetti at the end of a championship game. Where had all that cash come from?

Rae's imaginary world morphed into the one she'd just left behind. The blues bar and the pool tables. That text she'd received from Madeline Mayo. The autopsy proved Matt had died upon impact, but what about the toxicology report? A .21 blood alcohol content was toilet-hugging drunk. Wasted enough it wouldn't have taken much to send the quarterback over the edge, and there was only one other person up there with him.

Ella May Pride.

Rae almost said the girl's name then remembered she was playing a different game than her partner. Frank wasn't interested in the murder investigation. It was "out of their jurisdiction." That's what Frank had said. He wasn't saying anything now. Neither was Rae, but she was starting to think the bagman's daughter might've gone far beyond a Gridiron Girl's call of duty. Regardless, that part could wait. The motive, on the other hand—the reason Matt Talley was dead—was obvious now.

"They were trying to rig the game," Rae said and started speed walking back toward Ground Zero. "They wanted Matt to lose to Southern Miss, and now they're trying to get Moses to do the same thing."

"Holy shit," Frank said. "You're right. And game fixing, especially when a politician's involved. That's a public corruption. That's—"

"—white-collar crime," Rae said. "This is it, Frank."

"I hear you. But nothing we've got now'll hold up in court."

"What if . . ." Rae said, pausing to get the words right in her head. "What if we went undercover?"

"That's not what we do. We sit back, we—"

"I'll do it, Frank. If you're too scared, I'll do it."

Rae pictured her partner sucking from his e-cig, that wrinkled Hawaiian shirt open at the neck. The silence lasted long enough Rae realized she'd hurt him, hit Frank in his soft spot, the weakness that had left him stranded in Mississippi at the end of his career. She felt bad, all the way up until Frank said:

"Two things gotta happen before I agree to something like

that. First, you gotta call Barb. We'll need the SAC's clearance, no doubt about it. Second, we gotta have an inside man. Somebody with connections to Congressman Christmas, or at least an in with the bagmen. Somebody who could set up a meeting, which takes time, Johnson. Months, *years*, even."

Rae said, "I hear you, Frank," staring up at the mural on Ground Zero's western wall, portraits of dead musicians and guitar shapes painted across the bricks. "We need to be patient and all that, but hey, how fast can you make it to my apartment?"

Back inside Ground Zero, Rae spotted Darren Floyd at the opposite end of the bar. He had his back to her, watching the stage as the house lights dimmed and Morgan Freeman's prerecorded voice came out low over the monitors. "*Ladies and gentlemen,*" the voice of God said, "*prepare to take a trip down to the Crossroads.*"

A spotlight clicked on, tracking the top of a black umbrella slicing through the crowd. Rae stepped in behind the sunshade's wake but kept her distance, thinking of what she'd say when she made it to the bar.

"*In the dark of a night not so different from this one, Robert Johnson carried his guitar to the intersection of Highways 49 and 61 where he made his infamous deal with the Devil. And now, nearly one hundred years later,*" Morgan Freeman's voice boomed, "*I'm proud to introduce you to his grandson, Bobby 'Bald Foot' Johnson.*"

The band launched into the opening bit of "Hellhound on My Trail" as the umbrella came down, revealing a huge Black man stuffed into a pure white suit, lumbering barefoot onto the stage.

Rae was at the bar now, pressing into Darren's left shoulder as she said, "Let's get out of here."

The way he shifted his weight, Rae thought he was on to her, but then his hip bumped hers. There it was again, that same playful nudge; Darren slow dancing, singing a few lines from that Robert Johnson tune before he said, "Was gonna ask what took you so long, but now I'm thinking something else."

"Yeah? What's that?"

"Your place or mine?"

Rae raised up on her toes, lips inches from his ear, and whispered, "Mine."

25

Eddie preferred the grocery bag to the feed sack. It was lighter, for one thing, and it didn't stink. The house did, though. *Mothball Mansion*, Eddie thought and laughed until his thigh seized up on him.

"You're telling me Moses McCloud, a poor Black boy from Clarksdale, Mississippi, turned the money down? Fifty thousand dollars, cash?"

The old man's voice fizzled in and out. Eddie wasn't listening; he was bleeding. His neck hurt. What would his thigh feel like tomorrow? His knees already sounded like a popcorn machine when he walked. Now this.

"Edward?"

Eddie blinked and the bag was gone. The study looked just like it smelled, like the man standing before him. *Old*. If Eddie hadn't been tied to the chair, he could've zone stepped that little bastard into the wall and snapped his neck. Sweat dripped into his eyes. The man was still there, smoking a skinny cigar. *But wait . . .* Eddie'd seen this guy before. He knew him, and that made it worse. Like figuring out Santa Claus isn't real; he's your stepdad, or in this case, some wrinkly-assed politician.

"Congressman—" Eddie licked his lips. "Congressman *Christmas*?"

"The wool has been lifted from your eyes, Edward. You know what that means, don't you?"

Eddie watched the Compson chief of police move from window to window, closing the burgundy curtains.

"Before we wrap up here," Harry said, "I thought you'd like to know the latest on the Matt Talley investigation."

"Investigation?" There was blood in Eddie's mouth. He swallowed it down. "Matt was drunk. He fell, right?"

The study was darker now than it had been. Eddie could hear the old man's windbreaker swishing as he slipped in and out of the shadows.

"That's what we thought too, Edward, but then we saw the tape."

"The security footage," Bruiser's voice said from somewhere. "There was a camera on the Buffalo Nickel's roof. One of those old school ones that's got a blinking red light and turns on a swivel."

Eddie said, "So?"

A small orange ember crackled a couple inches from the tip of Eddie's nose. The congressman's face emerged behind the glow.

"We know what happened," Harry hissed. "We know what your daughter did."

Eddie whispered, "*Ella May*," picturing her back in third grade, a white bow in her hair, still missing a couple teeth. "Listen here, you slimy—"

Harry leaned in close enough Eddie could feel the warmth of that skinny cigar on his cheek. "Nobody has to know what Ella May did. Chief Conrad can make all that go away, as long as you hold up your end of the deal."

"But Moses didn't take the money. He wouldn't—"

"Money's not the only way to persuade a young quarterback. You, of all people, should know that."

The red-hot tip of the cigarillo sizzled when it touched Eddie's cheek, triggering the bagman's lizard brain. The burn boiled all his thoughts down to simple stimulus and response. Eddie wanted free of the pain so badly, he shouted, "*Wait.* Jesus! Moses has the hots for Ella May!"

The congressman adjusted his fedora. "The what?"

"The *hots*. Yeah . . ." The cigarillo was gone, but Eddie's cheek still hurt like a sonofabitch. He opened and closed his jaw, hating the words that came out of his mouth. "Maybe we could use it. Maybe I could ask her to—"

"Why, yes, Edward," the congressman said. "Maybe you could."

26

The drive from Clarksdale back to Rae's apartment took longer than she'd expected. Frank's Subaru was already parked outside her door when Darren pulled the Monte Carlo into the lot.

Rae didn't like being late, but the extra time had given her time to think over how she'd handle the meeting. No, "meeting" wasn't the right word. What was about to transpire in her apartment was a setup, a blind date between an aging federal agent and a former wide receiver who played the blues. Rae had to be careful. Guys could be sensitive, especially a guy like Darren who'd been putting the moves on her all night. Rae didn't want him to get the wrong idea.

"Hey, uh . . ." Darren had one arm draped over the back of her seat. He left it there and nodded. "Who's that?"

It was Special Agent Ranchino, stomping toward the Monte Carlo's passenger door.

"Listen, Frank. Give me five minutes." Rae had her head out the window, talking fast. "Five minutes and I can explain everything."

"I'll give you two, but not out here. Whatever you've got to say, you can say it inside."

Darren slid his arm out from around Rae's seat and pushed open the driver-side door. "Hey, man. Who you think you are, talking to her like—"

Frank placed his hands on his belt, holding his blazer open far enough Rae could see his shoulder holster, the Glock 19M hanging there. Darren must've seen it too. He wasn't saying anything now.

"Your new friend stays here," Frank said. "You hear that, buddy? You so much as move a muscle, and I'll take you down, way down. You got me?"

Darren had both hands on the wheel, ten fingers raised, palms pressing into the leather casing, when Rae stepped out of the vehicle and followed Frank into her apartment.

"What the—I mean, seriously—what the *fuck*, kid?"

Frank had a dirty mouth. Most feds did, especially old timers from Brooklyn. This felt different. Frank had never dropped an f-bomb in front of Rae before. She looked past him to the apartment door, thinking of Darren Floyd and how Frank had made him stay outside. Maybe it was better that way. There wasn't anywhere to sit. No table, no chairs, not even a mattress. Just a completely bare studio apartment, and files. Stacks of them.

Rae slid her backside up on the kitchen counter and let the heels of her Jordans clang against the cabinet doors, listening as Frank told her what she already knew. How she'd put the whole investigation in jeopardy.

"My last case, that's what this is. Did you tell Darren what we're doing here?"

"No."

"He don't know you're a fed?"

"I don't think so."

"You don't *think* so?"

Of all the Franks Rae had seen over the last two days, she liked this one the least.

"Don't lie to me. Don't sit there and act like I don't know who you are, why they sent you down here."

"Who am I?" Rae folded her arms then unfolded them. "Huh, Frank? Who do you think I am?"

Frank, like it was the most obvious thing in the world, said, "You're Coach Johnson's kid. Kept waiting for you to mention it. One week later, still nothing. Little Miss Tight Lips . . ."

All this time, Rae'd thought she'd pulled one over on Frank, thought he was clueless when it came to her daddy. It made her think of Ella May Pride, that new angle she'd thought up about Matt's big fall. Was it time to fill Frank in?

"Except," Frank said, "that's not right, is it? Because you told Darren something. You had to. What'd you whisper in his ear?" Frank's face flattened out to where Rae could almost see the man he'd been thirty years ago, back when he was her age. "I thought you were supposed to be good, first in your class, all that shit."

"I'm close, Frank. We're close."

"Squeezed your way in there, got up real *close* and personal with Darren Floyd."

"It's not like that."

"Tell me about it, then," Frank said. "Tell me what I'm missing."

There weren't words for what Rae was feeling, what she'd felt, for Darren. Weren't all relationships the same? A couple dates, a few drinks, then you got in bed with a stranger. It all came down to trust. An investigation worked the same way.

"Was what I did risky?" Rae said. "Sure, but you said it yourself, back when you called from Sudan. You said we needed somebody on the inside, somebody who could set up a meeting with the congressman."

Frank cocked an eyebrow. "And you think Darren Floyd's that somebody?"

"He's a good guy."

"He's a bagman."

"No, Darren just looks out for the players. He's like an agent but he doesn't get a cut."

"That how your daddy did it?"

"What?"

"Your dad, the football coach you never mentioned," Frank said. "Is that what he called guys like Darren? *Agents?*"

"Watch it, Frank."

"I'm serious. That's why Barb sent you down here. Because of all that time you spent with your dad. So, how'd he handle guys like Darren and Eddie?"

Rae said, "It wasn't like that," thinking of the years she'd spent with her father, all the hours she'd volunteered in college. "My dad never dealt with guys like Darren at all. I mean, sure, he had to appease a booster every now and then, but boosters—"

"—aren't bagmen." Frank frowned. "Yeah, that's what I told you. Told you a lot more than that too. All that stuff about how it works in Compson? You seriously didn't have a clue?"

"No," Rae said without hesitation. "My dad's just a coach, a damn good one."

"And what does that make you?"

"Me?"

"Yeah, you, kid. What'd you tell Darren you were doing in Compson?"

"I, uh, well . . ."

Frank didn't wait around for Rae's explanation. He was gone, already out the apartment door before the rookie agent noticed the pressure that had formed in her chest. Where had that come from? As much as Rae had disliked Frank's tone, all those f-bombs he'd dropped, she knew her partner wasn't to blame. No, this sort of worry came straight from the heart. It was reserved for one man only, and it wasn't the guy Frank was marching back into the apartment now either.

Darren Floyd said, "You're a fed?" loud enough to derail Rae's train of thought, the concern she'd felt for her father. "A *federal* agent?"

"Okay, so you weren't lying." Frank shrugged. "But if you didn't tell him who you are, what you're doing in Mississippi, what did you tell him?"

"Said she was journalist," Darren said, "down here to write a story on college football."

"*Jesus* . . ."

"I looked her up. She's got a website, all these articles online."

Frank turned to Rae, grinning, maybe? She couldn't tell. "Glad to hear you at least did something right, but I told you not to go undercover. That sort of operation takes time."

"Took one day, a couple hours, for Darren to let me tag along," Rae said, studying his expression, trying to gauge where he stood on all of this. The way the corners of his mouth were curved down surprised her. Darren didn't look angry or scared. Not even all that surprised. He looked hurt.

"I get the feeling," Frank said, "that that didn't have nothing to do with your digital footprint. You tell him the other bit?"

Rae didn't have to tell Darren the other bit. Frank told him everything. Her whole life story, every little detail about her father, the football coach. Rae felt like her partner was punishing her, making a joke out of her daddy's occupation, her childhood, as he said, "You remember her from SportsCenter? She was like nine, this cute little redhead . . ."

Rae remembered liking the lights. The makeup lady who'd loved her freckles. Most of all, Rae remembered how she'd felt sitting on that soundstage beside her daddy, throwing out lines like "Our tight ends should have a field day against Bama's outside backers," or "Coach lets me call the plays sometimes, if we're up a few scores in the fourth? Yes, sir. I'm serious." The broadcasters got a kick out of it, and Chuck really did let her call a couple plays. He let her help him all through her time at the University of Arkansas, but he wouldn't let her coach.

Maybe Chuck had been right. Maybe his daughter really was too smart for football. One thing Rae knew for sure: She was smarter than Darren Floyd and Frank Ranchino.

The two men were still cutting up when Rae stepped between them and said, "Y'all done?" and waited, giving them both a second to notice the shift in her tone. She spoke her partner's name, soft but serious, and Frank said, "Yes, your highness?"

"You said we needed two things to go undercover."

"I said that?"

"You said we needed an inside man, and look, I got him. Darren's in."

"Hold up." Darren straightened. "I don't even know what y'all are doing here."

Rae told Darren everything she'd already told him but substituted "investigative journalist" for "federal agent," and "tell-all college football piece" for "white-collar fraud case."

Replace a few words here and there, and it was basically the same thing.

"All that stuff you told me on the way to Clarksdale?" Rae said. "That's what we're trying to fix. We have reason to believe UCM isn't playing fair and—"

"*Fair?*" Darren said. "College football? Come on, the whole system's rigged against the players."

Rae said, "Not true," and saw her father, asleep behind his desk at the end of a grueling practice week, working all day, all night, doing whatever it took to get his team ready, to teach his players the value of hard work, perseverance, and determination, lessons that would serve them long after their football careers were over, the same lessons Rae had learned so well. "There are good coaches out there, teams that play by the rules. UCM just isn't one of them."

"I'll take your word for it." Darren surveyed the apartment, his gaze bouncing over the bankers boxes, the accordion files. "But I still don't see how I can help."

Frank hitched his pants and stepped forward. "What the rookie's asking is if you've got any connections with Congressman Harry Christmas."

"Never heard of him."

Rae said, "Seriously?" then remembered that grocery bag over Eddie Pride's head. There was a level of secrecy at play here, or "window dressing" to borrow another of her father's terms. Harry Christmas was running college football's most intricate screen play, and although Darren Floyd was still involved with the game, he wasn't in the congressman's inner circle. "Okay," she said. "What about Chief Conrad?"

"Bruiser?" Darren said. "Me and Brandt played ball together.

He's just as dirty now as he was then, but I still don't understand what y'all need me for. Why can't you just put them away?"

Frank formed an *O* with his lips then bared his teeth, but didn't speak. He paused, then did it again.

Darren said, "The hell you doing, man?"

"He's trying to make a point," Rae said. "Everything we've been talking about, all our new intel, came from Frank lip reading out at Sudan."

Rae watched Darren's eyes for any signs that he recognized the name of the congressman's plantation. There were none.

"And lip reading," Frank continued, "well, it's not an exact science. It's an art. Damn sure won't hold up in court. But we stick a wire on you, let you go have a nice long chat with your former teammate, then we got them dead to rights."

"*Dead,*" Darren said. "That's what I'd be if I showed my Black ass at this dirty politician's place. Ain't no way I'm going out there, man."

Rae slid down off the counter. Her feet were asleep, her toes prickly like her mind. She realized she still hadn't told Frank about her Ella May theory. She wasn't sure why. Did she want the glory? Full credit for cracking the case? That was probably partly true. Rae'd always imagined herself as a quarterback, but there was more to her silence than credit or praise. Frank should've known. He'd been given the same clues as Rae. He knew Ella May was on the roof. He'd seen the money in the street, but Frank hadn't said a word about Ella May Pride. Then again, he hadn't said anything about Chuck Johnson until just a few minutes ago either.

"What if I went with him?"

Darren said, "Nope," and shook his head.

"Yeah, maybe we set up a meeting," Frank said, "let you go in with Mr. Floyd, go undercover, but do it right this time and get the SAC on board."

"Barbara Lawrence?" Rae said. "That could take weeks. The Chiefs play Mississippi State in five days."

"And if they win, they'll still play in the SEC Championship, then the Cotton Bowl after that. The big show. That's when we make our move."

Rae's shoulders slumped. "What am I supposed to do till then?"

"You could start by sprucing this place up. Maybe do some laundry?" Frank said, glancing around the apartment. "Relax, champ. It'll be game day before you know it."

HALFTIME

At Georgia Southern, we don't cheat.
That costs money and we don't have any.
—Erk Russell, Georgia Southern
football coach

27

Nineteen private jets, twelve turboprops, and one yellow crop duster—the same single-engine Air Tractor that had been flying up from Ocean Springs for Chiefs' home games as far back as Harry Christmas could remember—were all parked in the grass surrounding the University–Compson Airport. Parking in such a prime location, only a ten-minute shuttle ride from the campus, cost the aircraft owners upwards of a thousand dollars per day, depending on wingspan. Space wasn't the issue; an expansive hundred-acre cow pasture surrounded the airport's single runway. No. Harry just figured the bigger the plane, the deeper the pockets. Everything came at a price in Compson, especially on home-game—*conference*-game—weekends.

The Mississippi State Bulldogs, the Chiefs' biggest rival, were already in town. They'd had a lackluster season but a win tonight would make the Bulldogs bowl-eligible. A loss for the Chiefs, however, would end their hopes of a second national championship. Harry doubted he'd get that lucky. Oh, no. Harry'd have to wait until he'd heard back from Eddie Pride regarding his daughter.

When it did come time for the Chiefs to lose, though, there would be a part of Congressman Christmas's withered old heart that would revel in watching the home team squander their chance at a second championship. It was the valve that had been stomped on when he was a child at the Apple Blossom Orphaned Boys' Home, constantly tormented by bullies who'd taken joy in hurling pigskins at young Harry and watching him try, in vain, to catch the torpedo-shaped balls. Harry still carried the scars, a boxer's nose and chip on his shoulder, sixty-some-odd years later. That particularly painful memory had come in handy as he'd gone about morphing Compson into a money-making machine. Harry had no mercy when it came to football fanatics, charging them top dollar for everything from hotel rooms to tent space in the Glades.

That's where Harry was now, pulling his rusty Ford Ranger into a private space alongside the prime tailgating spot nestled in the heart of the 173-year-old campus. The airport was always his first game-day stop. The thirty-plus planes were a good sign. The high rollers had come to town and were already deep in the throes of their tailgating rituals.

Harry kept a low profile as he surveyed the Glades, moving slowly from tent to tent beneath the centuries-old oaks. Each tent, every ten-by-ten patch of grass, cost seven hundred dollars for the duration of the tailgate, which usually started at dawn and ran up until kickoff. Parking was also big business. Spaces a half mile from the stadium still went anywhere from fifty to seventy-five bucks. Once everyone was parked, the real party began. Some fans opted to never leave the tailgate at all, watching the game from flat-screen televisions they'd installed inside their camps. Some of the tents had chandeliers and gaudy floral arrangements. Some were done up like teepees with feathers and animal hides. Regardless of the décor, they all had coolers packed to the brim.

Harry had spent many an hour trying to concoct a way to charge them for their pregame drinks. In the end, it wasn't worth it. Alcohol fueled the game-day profits. The longer the fans had to drink, the more money they spent. Night games always yielded the highest proceeds. The extra hours provided fans more time to imbibe and peruse the local establishments. Once they were all finally packed inside the stadium, everything came at a cost. A beer, a single Bud Light, went for twenty bucks at any one of Sutpen Stadium's thirty-four concession stands.

This, of course, had taken some doing.

Despite Mississippi's debutante style, it was still in the heart of the Bible Belt. "Right behind the buckle . . ." That's what Harry had told the board of trustees when he'd made his pitch to allow the sale of alcohol inside the stadium. He claimed the shift would cut down on binge drinking at the tailgate. Harry wasn't sure if the student section drank less now than it had before. He didn't care. He did know that the University of Central Mississippi generated over fifteen million dollars from the sale of alcoholic beverages in the first year of Harry's new deal.

The congressman continued his pregame stroll, running more numbers in his head.

Students, and sometimes volunteers from neighboring high schools, manned the ticket booths, the concessions stands, and the UCM apparel stores. Most worked for free. Last season, the Chiefs had accrued nearly fifty million dollars in ticket sales alone. The whole operation—the fraternity and sorority houses, the private fundraising dinners, even the university's enrollment, which had seen a significant increase after the Chiefs' championship season—was fueled by the game.

So much depended on a ball stitched together from thirty-two panels of waterproofed leather. The fans came to see what the players did with that ball: the blazing touchdown runs, the high-flying, bone-crunching hits. And the players played for peanuts. That was the only way any enterprise could achieve the sort of profit margins enjoyed by universities with nationally ranked teams. The trick, though, was convincing the rest of the country that college football was not a business, but instead a game, a contest played on the field of higher education, which also served the Chiefs well when it came time to file their taxes.

Because the University of Central Mississippi was an educational organization, it enjoyed a 501(c)(3) status, which meant nearly every dollar the institution made was exempt from federal income tax. It was the same exception granted to churches.

Harry lit a fresh cigarillo and took a long, contented drag as he finished his stroll through the Glades, past all the tents stuffed with war-painted fanatics donning their Sunday best. Yes, Mississippi was in the Bible Belt, but the real holy day, the day when every true Southerner bowed at the altar, was game day. And in just a few more hours, the congregation would gather inside their recently renovated, five-hundred-million-dollar cathedral, bought and paid for by the old man walking alone through the shady oak grove.

28

All that money, and the turkey was still dry, the green beans tasteless. Like chewing little plastic tubes. That's what Moses McCloud was thinking three hours before kickoff, sitting in the Sinclair Assembly Hall, this side room connected to the UCM cafeteria. Same meal for each of the eleven games so far in his first season. Tonight, Moses would take the field against Mississippi State, the Chiefs' biggest rival from just down the road in Starkville. Moses had grown up watching the Magnolia Bowl in his grandmother's house, a football in one hand, a cold turkey leg in the other. Dry as it was, the turkey in Moses's mouth had enough juice to transport him back to those early days. Made him think of Momma G and what was best for her but also him and all the dreams they'd dreamt together.

"Eat up, cuz."

Cerge was the only other player at Moses's table. The running back's plate looked like it'd been licked clean. Neither of them had spoken over the course of the pregame meal. The rest of the assembly hall was quiet too, the players focused, staring steely eyed out the windows to the Chiefs fans gorging themselves in the Glades below.

Moses held the turkey leg out for his running back. Cerge took it and said, "You scared?"

"No, not scared."

"Just got your game face on, huh? Extra serious now that you the man."

"Something like that."

The muscles in Cerge's jaw flexed as he chewed. Moses watched him, trying to refocus his mind on the game he'd play in a few more hours. How he'd refused Eddie's dirty money. Forget him. Not Ella May, though. Ella May still gave Moses the gooseys. Made every hair on his forearms stand straight up. He wanted to show her what he could do. Wanted to show everybody: his friends back home, Momma G way up in the nosebleeds, all the frat boys in the good seats. Moses wanted to show them too. Wanted to score and jump up in the student section, let those Z-Bar-popping future investment bankers slap him on the pads and holler, "Moses, *Moses . . .*"

Was that really what he wanted?

Still gnawing on the turkey leg, Cerge said, "Remember how I showed up late to camp? Couple days after y'all was already sweating it out, had half the offense installed?"

Some of the other players were standing now, taking their trays to the washing station, that little metal slot where Black hands reached out and grabbed the plates. Moses followed his running back to drop off his tray, the air thick and damp from the hot water spray. A gloved hand emerged from the slot, the latex like thin white skin stretched tight over brown leather.

Moses blinked and the tray was gone, replaced by a football. He couldn't recall the walk from the caf to the field house, but that's where Moses found himself now, sitting in locker number seven as Cerge performed a downward dog in front of him on the rubberized floor.

"Anyway," Cerge said, back arched, looking at Moses through his legs, "I's way down at South Beach, sitting in one of Eddie Pride's beach chairs when this little homie came up and started making fun of my socks."

Moses knew about Lazy Dayz. He didn't know why Cerge was telling him this story, though. Maybe he was nervous. Maybe Cerge wasn't as sure as he said he was about Moses calling the shots for the Chiefs. The way the offense was set up, everything hinged on the quarterback. Run plays, pass plays, they were all packaged together and the QB decided what was best before each snap. Sometimes the choice was made during the play, if, say, a linebacker shot down to stuff the run? Then the quarterback could whip the ball over his head to a slot receiver slicing up field on a slant. It was a lot to compute in just a couple seconds, like a calculus equation running in real time. The quarterback had to solve for X using a handful of O's before some defensive end broke free and speared him in the kidney. It happened. And might be happening to Moses soon.

"Can't stand the way the sand feel between my toes."

As Cerge started in explaining why he wore socks to the beach, Moses glanced around at the rows of LED lights outlining the lockers, like they were in a club, low bass notes rumbling down from hidden speakers. A pair of defensive backs sat in barber chairs, getting faded up by the brothers who brought their clippers into the field house on game days. A couple linemen were playing ping-pong. A gang of white boy linebackers were walking around with nothing but their eye black on. Nobody was talking much. The flat-screen TVs mounted to the walls relayed highlights from around the country. Moses saw his own face on the screen now, a picture of himself from six months back, chubby-cheeked and cheesing.

"This kid, probably still in high school or just dropped out, he keeps standing in front of me, man, talking about my socks.

Trina's with me. Said she wanted to see Miami, so I took her down and we stayed with my cousin Savion."

"Savion Blanc?"

"Yeah, he's my daddy's brother's kid. Uncle Hercule's a wino, man, but Trina . . . that girl straight up *loved* the water. Kept going out ass-deep in the Atlantic Ocean. Third, maybe fourth time she did it, I asked what she's doing? Trina tells me she going 'pee pee.' Said it just like that, like a little girl. *Pee pee.* Then she tried sliding her hand up my thigh later that night, after I whooped that homie's ass? Like I hadn't seen her pop a squat in the ocean."

Moses said, "Wait. You whooped whose ass? Why?"

"That homie was making fun of my socks. He started in on Trina when she came back from taking a piss, started trying to spit some game. So I asked him did he want to step into my office . . ."

Cerge transitioned from downward dog to child's pose, knees flat on the floor, arms extended straight out on either side of his head. Moses stared at him, still not sure what to make of Cerge's story, but thinking it felt right somehow, the wildness of his tale in tune with the flashy locker room: the nude white boys, the ping-pong table, the barber chairs. This wasn't real life. It was all a dream, a four-year fantasy the players paid for with their lives. Even if they did make it to the League, even if they got paid, they still paid for it. And it wasn't just their knees or shoulders, not even their brains. It went deeper than that. Once their playing days were over, they would be booted out of Eden, resigned to the stands to watch as the next crop of finely tuned athletes took their place. As extravagant as a Saturday spent tailgating in the Glades was, it did not compare to the roar of the crowd. Only gladiators know true glory. Was that what Moses was? A gladiator?

"The OLPD picked me up the next morning, had my ass sweating in a holding cell until Coach Taylor sent Coach Cato down to get me," Cerge said, voice muffled against the floor. "So, yeah. That's why I had to miss the start of camp."

Most of the other players were at their ventilated lockers now, faces aglow in the light of the little screens that displayed their weight charts, sleep routines, and up-to-date statistics. There were no stats on Moses's screen. Thus far into the season, he'd been redshirted. Any late game clean-up duty had gone to a walk-on quarterback named Sam Billingsley. As he reached for his pads, Moses said, "Why'd you just tell me all that?"

When Cerge spoke again, he was so close Moses could smell his breath, the faint scent of Skittles. "Thought I'd left that life behind, then, *zap*, I was right back at it. Showed me how close I was, how close I am, always. That shit scared me. That look on your face back at caf? Thought maybe you was scared too. Wanted you to know whatever you was worrying about weren't nothing like what Big Cerge been through already, and look at me now."

Moses didn't nod, didn't speak.

"What I'm saying is," Cerge said, massaging Moses's throwing shoulder, "you ball out tonight—we win—then you ain't got nothing to worry about. That's just how it is, baby. This America. Winners don't never lose."

29

Eddie Pride Junior didn't make it to the Glades for the tailgate, but he still had his headdress on, watching the game on his sixty-five-inch plasma TV. Ella May was there too, sitting on the sofa beside him. After everything that had happened, she didn't feel like going to the game. She wasn't saying much either. Hadn't said one word about her daddy's busted thigh, but damn, it still hurt something nasty.

The stabbing wasn't necessary. Poor coaching, really. Congressman Christmas didn't know shit when it came to motivating his players. A guy like Eddie, you don't have to make threats, and you damn sure don't have to follow through with them. All you had to do was explain how what you were doing was good for the team.

Eddie'd played on the offensive line, left guard, spent two hours kick stepping and punching at the air, pushing his buddies around, a bunch of meaty white boys with upper bicep hair working to slow down some big fast Black dudes. Rarely saw a white nose tackle anymore. Definitely not any defensive ends. Not in the SEC at least. Line those guys up next to Eddie's unit, compare their height, weight, bench press, squat—it wouldn't look fair. Didn't seem fair in real life either. In real life, it looked like the Dallas Cowboys against some jayvee squad from North Dakota. High school seniors versus kindergartners in dodgeball. But there weren't any balls in the trenches and that's how guys like Eddie were able to hang. All he had to do was slow those freakazoids down. Just get in their way for a couple-three seconds on a drop-back pass. Even less on a run. Zone step, zone step, throw the hands, roll the hips, then—

"Bring your dick!" Eddie shouted at the television, the same phrase his old coach used to holler at him from the sideline. That's where Moses was now. The home sideline. Half the defense still didn't know he had the ball, and the half that did couldn't catch him.

Eddie watched that long-legged Black boy sprint eighty-some-odd yards and thought of Matt Talley, the difference between them, night and day, black and white. Moses was that damn good. Good enough to take the Chiefs all the way. Yessiree, Bob. Except . . .

Shit.

Eddie fingered a fake feather on his warbonnet and propped his good leg up on the couch, thinking of the last thing Congressman Christmas had told him, the only reason he was still alive. His daughter, a stone-cold killer? No way. Harry hadn't stuck around for questions. He'd just given Eddie a new phone, a burner with the congressman's personal number programmed into the contacts. Eddie was supposed to call after he'd had his talk with Ella May, and there she was, legs curled up on the sofa beside him.

"That Moses sure is something," Eddie said, easing his way into it. "Look at him go."

Ella May hugged her knees.

"If he keeps this up, he could be the best quarterback UCM's ever had. Break every record in the book."

"What happened to your leg?"

"This?" Eddie patted his thigh. "This ain't nothing to worry about. What I am worried about is you, hon. How you been?"

"Fine."

"Haven't seen you with any boys around campus."

She turned. "Are you serious?"

"As a heart attack, or hell, how about a broken neck?" Eddie poked his brace with two fingers. "Need to ask you something, okay?"

He tried to picture Ella May pushing her boyfriend off a roof. Matt was so tall, it wouldn't have taken much, a love tap on his throwing shoulder, but why? Had she done it for Eddie, her daddy, the man she hadn't spoken to for weeks, no, months, after the divorce?

"If this is about Matt—" Ella May put a hand to her mouth. "Listen, I'm not ready to talk about it, okay?"

"Well, hon, other people are talking about it."

That got her attention. "What kinda people?" Ella May said. "What're they saying?"

"Some real powerful people are saying you—"

"*No.*"

Eddie could hear her breathing. He watched her shoulders rise and fall. "Yeah, I heard it straight from the Compson chief of police. Said he had a video."

Ella May sprang from the sofa as Moses McCloud stepped up in the pocket and scrambled for another first down. Eddie could still see the TV screen over the top of Ella May's head. That's how short his baby girl was, how little.

"He's lying, Dad. There's no video."

"So, you, uh . . . you didn't do it?"

Ella May hesitated, no longer than a second, the difference between a touchdown pass and an interception. "I didn't do anything. I wasn't even up there when Matt—"

She got his name out this time but choked up before she could say whatever she was going to say next. Eddie hated to see his daughter cry. He opened his arms and was surprised when she fell into him. Eddie held her tight even though her tears stung that little burn mark on his cheek.

"Chief Conrad's lying because Moses didn't take the money," Ella May said, face still buried in her father's chest. "They're trying to get you to—" She jerked back. Mascara rimmed her eyes, narrow slits of white and light blue glaring up at her daddy.

Eddie knew that look. He raised both arms, keeping his hands where Ella May could see them, and said, "Easy. Just take it easy. Ain't no need to—"

"What do they want you to do?"

"It ain't me." Eddie kept his hands up, for protection, and said, "It's you, hon. Something you could do for me, for UCM, but I ain't gonna force you, okay? I wouldn't do that."

"Just say it. Whatever it is, just say it."

So he did, and every word hurt Eddie more than the thigh wound or the rope burn, but at least it was out there, the hard part over and done with. The rest was up to Ella May.

30

Seventy-thousand powwow drums rattled as one then died away, replaced by the Sutpen Stadium sound system. The house speakers were so loud they rendered the Mighty Chiefs' Marching Band obsolete. Same way everybody mostly watched the Jumbotron instead of the action happening on the field. Matt Talley was dead, but look, there he was on the video board, throwing touchdown passes then posing in a green room while "Kernkraft 400" by Zombie Nation blasted in the background. It was the same offensive highlight the UCM production team had used to start every drive of the season, except it didn't make sense now.

The Chiefs were up three scores going into the fourth quarter and Moses McCloud was still in the game, a bunch of Black faces behind bars staring back at him, the same guys he'd been outrunning for the last two-and-a-half hours. He recognized the strong safety, an upperclassman from Clarksdale High who had dreads like Cerge, squatting to Moses's left, not a single scuff mark on the running back's powder-blue jersey.

Maybe it was time to hand one off, Moses thought, then barked, "Leo, three ten. *Leo, three ten!*" The *L* in Leo told the linemen the inside zone was headed left, the three-ten pure bullshit, a way to keep the defense guessing like they'd been for the first three quarters.

"*Down* ..." Moses shouted, feeling invincible with four rushing touchdowns under his belt, each one a message to the man, whoever it was that had told Eddie to tell him to throw the game. Nah. Moses was running the rock. That's how good he was, how good he'd always been but was just now realizing it. Didn't matter how many Bulldogs lined up in the box, Moses could run around them, through them, or jump clean over their heads like he'd done his boy from Clarksdale right before the second half. Made it to the end zone as the scoreboard buzzed with time enough to turn and watch the replay on the Jumbotron; the safety going down on one knee, then the other, arms swiping at the air Moses had just flown through like a fight scene from *Dragon Ball Z*.

"... *Set* ..."

One more word and the snap count would be over, the next play in motion, another chance for Moses to drive his point home. He wasn't just some puppet on a string. He wouldn't dance for nobody, especially not Eddie Pride Junior and his lousy fifty grand.

"... *Hut!*"

The ball shot back between the center's thighs. Moses caught it and held it out for Cerge, but that big-ass D-end was biting down again. *How many times I got to pull it and leave you in the dust?* Moses thought, then did just that, legs like bike spokes blurring together they were moving so fast, already breaking contain. The only thing between him and the end zone was that same strong safety he'd hurdled before half. Maybe he'd use the B button and drop a spin on him this time. Moses could see it working, just like he was playing his favorite video game, *EA Sports NCAA Football*, the same game that had the University of Central Mississippi's backup—a dark-skinned QB from Clarksdale—listed at six foot three, his weight one-ninety-something. Got all that right but only gave him an 84/100 speed attribute?

Not after tonight.

After Moses juked this little bowlegged safety clean out his girdle, EA Sports would know all about Moses McCloud, just like the rest of Mississippi. The whole country. Damn straight. Moses was finally on the field, finally in control, timing up the perfect angle as he spun and the safety went flying past him.

It was beautiful, and kind of funny too. Moses would've laughed but the Bulldog defenders were already catching up to him. The young quarterback kept his head turned as he stepped over the sideline, his eyes back on the gang of linebackers and d-backs nipping at his heels. That's why he never saw the photographer squatting near the sideline, his 600mm outdoors sports lens aimed straight at Moses McCloud's left knee.

The sharp pop that followed came from somewhere deep inside, the place where Moses stored his hopes and dreams, everything riding on his legs. His left one was on fire now, burning as he made it to the bench and stopped. Moses did not limp. He wouldn't give them that. The man was still up there watching, searching for signs of weakness.

Mouth dry, palms sweaty, Moses spotted the photographer flat on his back, the long lens detached from the camera, both pieces lying ten yards apart. The young quarterback had been hurt before—fractured ribs, sprained ankles, a dislocated pinky or two—but blowing your knee out on a camera? That was new.

Moses had one hand on the bench, propping himself up, knee numb now but working, when Coach Taylor called off the dogs and sent in the backups.

Cerge, who'd failed to reach the end zone for the first time all season, pitched a fit and kicked an orange Gatorade cooler so hard, so far, Moses had to dodge it, but *hey*, his knee felt fine. Didn't it? The young quarterback took a seat on the bench and kept asking himself that same question long after the game was over.

31

"**I'm sorry,** sir, but you're not allowed to smoke in here."

Harry Christmas kept his eyes on the front of the conference room, studying the two microphones with corresponding bottles of purple Gatorade spaced out evenly over a long white table, the word "Pepsi" printed in a thin gray script over a blue backdrop. The soft drink company had been a great sponsor, much more involved than the boys from Coca-Cola. The Pepsi team didn't just provide the drinks and the backdrop, they'd funded the entire Jim R. Kirby Conference Room. The "R" stood for "Richard." Last time Harry'd seen ol' Jim Dick was at his private hunting club after the Florida game. Harry was thinking he would've rather been sipping Woodford Reserve at the L'Anguille Bottom Lodge than attending a postgame press conference when the girl said, "*Sir*," and Harry lowered his gaze.

Looking at her now, Harry saw past her skin. Beautiful? Yes, very, and saucy too, standing there with her head tilted disapprovingly at the old man in his windbreaker holding a cigarillo. Harry wondered what she thought of him, or if she thought of him at all. Did this girl whose nametag read TRINA realize how much better her life was compared to back when Maxine was still running Sudan? Now, a light-skinned girl like "Trina" was all the rage, on damn near every commercial and online advertisements because she fit almost every demographic except one. There was one thing "Trina" would never be, and that's why it surprised Harry to hear her talking to him like that, saying, "Sir, you can't be smoking in here. You—"

"Run along." Harry made a motion with his free hand, looking past her, through her, to the table and the blond man pulling out a chair, positioning himself behind one of the mics.

The girl stood her ground, bound and determined to get this old man to stop smoking inside the stadium. The toe of her left sneaker came up then down on the concrete floor, not a stomp but close, before she said, "*Fine.* I'm getting security."

When she was gone, Harry lit a fresh cigarillo, a power move in the already packed conference room. The flick of his lighter drew the attention of the reporters, glancing around just long enough to notice his windbreaker, or maybe his houndstooth hat, same style as the one Speer Taylor had removed from his head and positioned neatly between the Gatorade bottles, the coach leaning into his mic now, saying, "I'd like to open us up with a word of prayer . . ."

The chair next to Speer, the same place Matt Talley had sat after every home game of the season, was empty. Harry shut his eyes and felt a new kind of tiredness spreading up from his bones, the kind that comes after seventy-something years. Twelve hours ago, he'd been walking the airport grounds, then the Glades, rushing past the fraternity houses because the congressman didn't have a use for those boys yet. Not until they'd graduated and gotten jobs from men who'd been boys who looked, talked, and acted exactly like they had once. Like they still did when their wives weren't looking. Those men had never looked even remotely similar to the eighteen-year-old Black boy the congressman saw the second after Speer Taylor said, "Amen."

Harry blinked, giving his eyes time to adjust to Moses McCloud. He was shorter than Matt Talley had been. Dressed in a black hoodie and skintight sweatpants, the Chiefs' new QB didn't look like he belonged. Harry had a Rolodex full of former UCM quarterbacks—CEOs, CFOs, insurance and real estate agents—who could be counted on when the university needed donations. Men who married cheerleaders and reserved tent space in the Glades. Harry was trying to imagine Moses at a tailgate ten years from now, when Coach Taylor pointed to a reporter in the front row and said, "Fire away, Dan."

The man said, "Dan Tuttle, *Clarion-Ledger*," and stood.

Dan Tuttle had covered every one of Congressman Christmas's campaigns as far back as Harry could remember. Dan was an old school newspaperman and a bleeding-heart liberal to boot. A critic, that's what Dan was, a man with a thousand questions but not one answer. Why in the hell Speer had called on Dan Tuttle out of all the reporters in the room, Harry had no idea.

"This question's for Moses," Dan said, cell phone in one hand, notepad in the other, "if you don't mind, Coach?"

Of course it was. Every question from this point forward would be for, or about, Moses McCloud. Which was why Harry Christmas had come down from his private suite and was now surrounded by the enemy in the Jim R. Kirby Conference Room. The congressman had to know what he was up against. How would Coach Taylor handle his new, defiant star, the young quarterback who'd rushed for damn near three hundred yards and four touchdowns, setting a UCM record in his first-ever start?

"Moses," Dan Tuttle said. "Great game. I mean—"

"Dan?" Speer Taylor had one hand up, waving at the reporter. "You didn't let me answer your question."

"Sorry, Coach. My question's for Mo—"

"You asked did I mind?" Speer picked his houndstooth hat up then sat it back down. "You said, 'This one's for Moses, Coach, if you don't mind?' Well, see, I do mind, actually. I want you to answer something for me. Okay, Dan?"

The reporter said, "Yeah, Coach. Sure."

"Where you from?"

Dan Tuttle opened his notepad. "Oxford."

"Home of *the* University of Mississippi. The Rebels, right?"

"Not anymore."

"Oh, yeah. Colonel Reb got the boot a few years back. Got replaced by a bear?"

Harry didn't know where Speer was going with all this. He couldn't see the coach's angle. He could, however, see Moses McCloud frowning and tapping his microphone's black foam windscreen. That Gridiron Girl was back in the picture now too, stomping across the conference room with a pudgy security guard in tow. Harry slipped a hand into his jacket, going for his phone.

"What I'm saying," Speer Taylor said, "things are changing in Mississippi, changing for the better, I think. Y'all hear about that group that's been working to get a new state flag?"

Dan Tuttle from the *Clarion-Ledger* said, "I'm a member of that group, a proud member."

"You don't say?" Speer said. "Tell me about it."

"Well . . ." The reporter cleared his throat and glanced around the room, checking the pulse of the other members of his flag-changing constituency, if Harry had to guess. That many damn journalists crammed into one place, no way Dan Tuttle was the only one who spent his free time trying to rewrite Mississippi history. The other members in attendance must've given Dan the go-ahead. Harry listened to that left-handed journalist say, "You see, the Mississippi state flag closely resembles the Confederate flag. Which, for some people, is a symbol of hate," then begin citing the dangers, the ethics, of such a symbol. It was almost enough to make the congressman leave the conference room. Instead, he pressed his cell phone to one ear and took a significant drag from his cigarillo.

"There he is," the light-skinned girl said and pointed. The security guard followed her aim. When the guard was within arm's reach, Harry said, "Hello, officer," and exhaled a cloud of cigar smoke before extending his phone. "This is for you."

The security guard took the phone and Harry turned his attention back to the press conference; Speer Taylor nodding next to Moses McCloud as the newspaperman rambled on, and on, about all the work he'd done to get the state flag changed to something less vile, something like a magnolia leaf, maybe.

"Or how about a cotton boll?" Speer said. "No. Wait. Cotton? That might get us in trouble too."

Murmurs spread across the crowd, all those liberal-minded members of the media whispering to one another, trying to gauge the political correctness of cotton. Coach Taylor rested his chin on his fists. Harry couldn't tell if he was serious. That's how good the young coach was, speaking into his microphone now, saying, "What about a blues guitar, or a tractor?" his voice taking on the same highfalutin tone as Dan Tuttle from the *Clarion-Ledger*. "No, not 'tractor.' It's 'farm equipment' these days, right?"

The Jim R. Kirby Conference Room was abuzz, the

murmurs so loud Harry Christmas barely heard the Gridiron Girl whose nametag read TRINA hollering at the security guard as the boy handed Harry back his phone.

"Sorry about that, Congressman," the rent-a-cop said. "It won't happen again."

Harry pointed the hot end of his Black & Mild at the light-skinned girl and held it there until the security guard took her by the elbow and began escorting her out of the room. On the phone, "Bruiser" Brandt Conrad asked how the press conference was going. Was there anything to worry about?

"It's hard to beat cotton in Mississippi," Speer Taylor said, his voice amplified through the PA system. "So, yeah, I'd say go with the cotton boll. Which reminds me. We've got a game to get ready for."

Speer stood after that line but didn't exit the stage, not until Moses McCloud stood too, looking somewhat relieved, thankful he'd been excluded from the circus. That's when Coach Taylor placed the houndstooth hat back on his head and said, "Hey, Dan? What's wrong?"

"Well, I mean . . ." Dan Tuttle from the *Clarion-Ledger* said. "Where are you going, Coach?"

Speer made a show of checking his watch. "I'm afraid our fifteen minutes are up. The press conference is over. Really enjoyed the chat, Dan."

Every reporter in the room jumped to their feet as Speer Taylor and Moses McCloud shuffled off the stage, going out the same door the portly security guard had led "Trina" through moments before.

Harry Christmas had forgotten about the call he'd placed to Bruiser and was surprised to hear the police chief breathing heavily on the other line, saying, "Well, uh, how'd it go? Did Moses try anything funny?"

"No, nothing funny," Harry said. "Moses never had the chance."

"What about Speer?"

"Speer did fine." The congressman took a final drag from his cigarillo, going over everything he'd just witnessed in the Jim R. Kirby Conference Room. "Better than fine. Matter of fact, Coach Taylor's turning out to be quite the politician."

THIRD QUARTER

Same motherfuckers talking about racism don't exist be the same motherfuckers shaking our hands, giving us hugs, telling us how you really love us. Fuck you phony-ass, fraud-ass bitches.

—Eric Striker, Oklahoma defensive lineman

32

The guy's name, the one his mother had given him, was *Verlon*. That's what the man behind the bar had told Rae when she walked into the Buffalo Nickel and asked to speak to the owner. He'd said, "You're looking at him. Name's Verlon."

That was five minutes ago, past tense, just like the rest of Rae's investigation. So much had happened over the first two days. Then nothing for so long. Three straight weeks, or was it four? Time enough for Rae to go out and get a couch from the Goodwill up in Grenada. That was it, the only addition she'd made to her apartment. Just something to sleep on, eat on, sit on like Darren had done when he'd visited Christmas morning. Rae'd passed the rest of her days doing body-weight exercises, watching college football, and looking up gardening articles online. She'd completed five hundred squats, ten sets of fifty, while the Chiefs whipped the Mississippi State Bulldogs so bad it was almost boring. The following Saturday, UCM won the SEC Championship game by demolishing the Alabama Crimson Tide. Seven more days and the Chiefs would face the undefeated Ohio State Buckeyes in the Goodyear Cotton Bowl.

The weeklong wait felt like forever. Like time had stopped, the same way it does inside a bar during the day, the morning, especially, a little past eight but Verlon already had his apron on, both palms flat on the scarred bar top like a butcher, staring down at the redhead who'd come in asking about her cardigan.

"Your what?"

"My cardigan. It's like a sweater except with buttons. Anybody turned anything like that in?"

Verlon said, "No," without moving his lips.

"Mind if I look around?"

Verlon picked at something on the bar then wiped it away. "If somebody found your sweater, it'd be back here, under the register."

"But what if nobody found it? I think I left it up in the loft." Rae glanced past him to the stairs. "That's the last place I remember having it. Right before I finished my third Tipsy Tomahawk. The heck's in that thing, by the way? Gasoline?"

That got a smirk from Verlon, a small one. "The bartenders," he said, "they're the only ones that know, and they don't know everything. I pre-make the mix myself."

"Your secret's safe with me, Mr. Verlon, but I'd really like to see if I can find my cardigan. It belonged to my mother."

Verlon peered over one shoulder to a clock mounted on the wall. Rae followed his gaze. A stuffed owl wearing an eyepatch stood guard from its perch above the bar. She thought the bird was just some sort of strange decor until she noticed the blinking red dot behind the owl's good eye. The security camera reminded her of why she'd ventured into the Buffalo Nickel in the first place.

Rae still hadn't heard anything from Barbara Lawrence. One whole month and no word about the requested clearance. Which was why she'd returned to her Trapper Keeper that morning, or more specifically, the notes she'd taken on Ella May Pride: five foot two, curly blond hair, "built like a cannon ball." Rae'd written those exact words her first night out in Compson, sitting in the Dollar General parking lot with Frank. The rookie agent hadn't written anything about a pulsing red light on the Buffalo Nickel's roof. It wasn't even a fully formed memory. More like a hunch, a gut feeling that was strong enough to finally get her out of her apartment.

Rae was still looking up at the owl when Verlon said, "Okay. Fine. Go see if your sweater's in the loft, but be quick about it."

Rae said, "Deal," and spun on her heels, headed for the stairs.

Strings of turquoise beads dangled from the loft's ceiling. Framed pictures of former Chiefs lined the walls. The spaces in between were covered with more sports memorabilia, dyed feathers, and imitation arrowheads. Everything looked cheap and new. Like Verlon had googled "college bar" and "Native decor" then ordered whatever popped up. The Buffalo Nickel was a far cry from the blues bar where Rae and Darren had shot pool. Ground Zero was the real deal, a historic site where Christone "Kingfish" Ingram, James "Super Chikan" Johnson, and Bobby Rush had all performed. The discrepancy between the two establishments made Rae think of the Compson city slogan. *An oasis of culture and thought.* It sounded like a Harry Christmas line, a sales pitch for old white dudes.

Rae peeked over the loft's railing before starting for the stairwell. Verlon had his back to her, scrubbing glasses in the sink. Rae slipped through the exit and eased the door shut behind her.

The air was cooler on the roof, the morning sky clear. The whirlybird vent was still spinning its lazy circle, right where Rae remembered it. But what about the red glow, the faint pulse that had called her there? The roof was like the bar, different in the daylight, too bright for electric lights. So bright Rae noticed the screw holes in the bricks. Four of them. Enough to hold a security camera's mount, or maybe just a light fixture.

Rae ran a finger over each hole, trying to recall what she'd thought she'd seen. Her mind was clouded by thoughts of Verlon. How many glasses would he wash before he came to check the loft? Rae turned to the roof's ledge and looked down. The Waffle House's yellow-and-black sign stood like a Southern totem pole a block up the road. The traffic signal at the intersection, the same one where Frank Ranchino had pulled to a stop on the night Matt died, ticked from red to green and Rae decided it was time to go.

Speed walking across the bar's first floor, Rae lifted a hand and said, "No luck, but thanks anyway, Mr. Verlon." She almost made it to the door before the man said:

"Hold your horses."

Rae's Jordans squeaked, a basketball court sound drowned out by the water still running in the sink. Verlon cut the faucet off and slung a towel over one shoulder.

"You really drink *three* Tomahawks? A girl your size?"

Rae said, "Come to think of it," and started walking again, not rushing but moving with purpose through the door. "It might've been four."

Thirty minutes later, Rae was back in her apartment, still uncertain about what she'd just done, why she'd done it. String lights glistened from the shops lining the Compson Square, about half as many as there'd been all through December. Rae wouldn't mention her little outing to Frank. What was there to tell? The ingredients of the Tipsy Tomahawk remained a mystery. She still needed her partner to believe she was following orders and being a good girl.

Rae checked her phone. Nothing. No missed calls from her SAC.

Special Agent in Charge Barbara Lawrence was in her late forties but looked older, the woman Rae might become at the end of another twenty years filled with sterile apartments in towns like Compson, Mississippi. She brought the phone to her ear and noticed her reflection moving in the window's glass. Rae had on slim-fit khakis and a white dress shirt unbuttoned far enough to see the clasp of her red bra, the kind that gave guys trouble, or at least it *had* given them trouble ten years ago. Maybe guys were better at stuff like that now. If Darren stopped by for another visit, maybe Rae'd find out.

A voice said her name, distorted through the phone's tiny speaker but loud enough to clear all thoughts from her mind. A man's voice, which wasn't right. Barbara Lawrence wasn't a man. She was the boss. The only one who could give Rae what she needed to move forward with her undercover sting.

The voice said, "Rae?" and she could see the man it belonged to sitting behind a desk in an office a couple hundred miles away, that picture of Robert Johnson on the wall behind him next to one of Rae with a ball cap on and a whistle around her neck.

Rae said, "Hey, Coach," and reached out, steadying herself against the woman in the window.

33

The conversation between Rae and her father played out like this:

Chuck: What's up?

Rae: Just checking in.

Chuck: You've "checked in" every day since Christmas.

Rae: You're complaining?

Chuck: I'm busy. If we ever have to play in the "GoDaddy .com Bowl" again, I might call it quits.

Rae: And do what?

Chuck: Some gardening, maybe?

Rae: You got my gift?

Chuck: I got a book, right here. *The Zen of Raised Bed Gardening.* Came in the mail a few days ago. Not sure what to make of it.

Rae: Merry Christmas. Sorry it was so late. You can trash it.

Chuck: Or I could use the pages as a weed barrier. Go get some compost, topsoil, mix it all together but not too deep. Six inches for lettuce and greens. A foot or more for radishes. Any rooted vegetables, really.

Rae: Thought you said you were busy?

Chuck: I am, but you know what I always say: A man has time to be great at—

(—*three things*, Rae thought, completing one of her all-time favorite Chuck Johnson lines in her mind. Rae'd first watched her father give that speech at a post-season banquet, or maybe it was some sort of award presentation. She couldn't remember, but she could still hear her father saying, "Notice, I didn't say 'good,' gentlemen. I said 'great.' If you want to be truly exceptional in life you've got to stay focused. By the time you get to my age, two of your three things will have been decided for you. Most of you are going to be husbands and fathers. So that leaves one other thing. Just one. You can't be a salty fisherman, a scratch golfer, a great husband, *and* a great father. Don't forget your job. Where does it fit in? That's my third one. I spend my time striving to be a great husband, father, and the best damn football coach I can possibly be." Chuck didn't curse much, especially not in front of his team, but when he did, his players loved it. Just like they loved that speech. It was something they brought up whenever they saw him, even if they'd been away from the program for years. Rae always thought it was funny, listening to her daddy talk about his "three things," because she knew the truth. She'd known it ever since Lola Johnson—also a redhead—skipped town right after Rae's first day of public school. Pigtails and a backpack dangling down past the back of her knees. Rae the kindergartner, getting off the bus and coming up the sidewalk that led to the front door of 404 Whippoorwill Way. They were living in Kansas at the time. Chuck was at practice. He was always at practice, or on his way to another game. Maybe that's what had sent Lola running. Maybe that's why nobody answered the door when little Rae knocked, kept knocking, then tried the bell a few times before she went back to knocking again. Chuck Johnson made it home at a quarter till six and found his daughter still pounding on a door no one would ever answer. Chuck drove Rae to school the next day instead of making her take the bus. He dropped her off under the awning outside of Sequoyah

Elementary and didn't say a word, not one word, about Lola. The point of that story, the truth Chuck never included when he gave speeches to his players, was that he had had only two things to focus on: his daughter and football. That's why his third thing had vacillated over the years. Rock climbing for a little while, back when Rae was in high school, then woodworking when she was in college, and now gardening. Chuck had never been the best carpenter or cragsman, and Rae doubted his raised beds would yield much, but he was one hell of a father. He'd had to be.)

Chuck: I would've sent you something, but I still don't know your address.

Rae: I'd tell you if I could.

Chuck: Classified and all that. I get it, but can't you at least tell me how your case is going?

Rae: Slow.

Chuck: That's okay. Take advantage of it. Get your three things in order. Let's see. You've got your job . . .

(And that was it. Chuck was ahead of her in the gardening department. He'd at least built a bed.)

Chuck: . . . and you're already a great daughter.

Rae: What?

Chuck: You heard me.

Rae: I still can't disclose my location.

Chuck: I'd sleep better if you could.

Rae: Fine. I'll give you a hint . . . You never coached here.

Chuck: I never coached lots of places. That's not a hint.

Rae: It's as good as you're going to get.

Chuck: I'll take it. Heck, maybe I'll break out all those old binders you made before every season. The ones with the year, the team names on the front? Scouting reports for my next opponent. Remember?

Rae:

Chuck: Yeah, if I worked my way through them, started marking off cities and states, anywhere I'd coached, I could treat it like my own little investigation.

Rae: Sounds more fun than gardening.

Chuck: Damn straight. Anyway, you see the Chiefs are headed back to the Cotton Bowl? Coach Taylor's got them in the big dance two years running.

(Was he messing with her? Did her father already know where she was, or worse, where she wanted to be? The Goodyear Cotton Bowl would take place inside the Dallas Cowboys' billion-dollar stadium. Rae had been to "Jerry World" before. She'd sat beside her daddy watching the hundred-million-dollar retractable roof fold back on itself, revealing the night sky after eighteen anxious minutes. They'd even gotten to meet the man himself, Jerry Jones, former University of Arkansas Razorback football player turned oil man turned multibillionaire owner of the Dallas Cowboys. It was a connection Rae'd overlooked, a memory she'd almost forgotten.)

Chuck: Didn't think they had it in them. Not after the Southern Miss game.

Rae: Oh, yeah. We watched the end of that one together.

Chuck: The UCM quarterback, Matt Talley. They ever figure out what happened to him?

Rae: Coach, listen. I'm sorry, but—

Chuck: No problem, sis. I better run too. Time to prune my garden.

• • •

Rae'd laughed a little at that garden joke after she ended the call. It wasn't that funny; it was sweet. Chuck was still trying to connect with her. Growing vegetables gave them something to talk about other than football. She could've played it cooler when he brought up UCM. Just because Chuck had once met Jerry Jones—just because he'd mentioned Matt Talley—didn't mean he knew anything, and so what if he did? Yes, Rae was investigating a college football team, but she was there to root out a bad seed. When Rae finally exposed Harry Christmas, Speer Taylor, and the rest of the Chiefs' crooked establishment, Chuck Johnson would be happy. No, he'd be more than that; he'd be proud.

Her phone rang.

Rae read the name on the caller ID. Then read it again before she answered. "Good morning, Director Lawrence."

"Hello, Agent Johnson. I'm calling to follow up on your request."

Rae rolled her eyes. "Appreciate it."

"You can start by telling me more about Congressman Christmas. How you plan to approach him?"

Rae explained her relationship—no, that wasn't the right word—her *in* with Darren Floyd. How he had agreed to set up a meeting with the congressman.

"But what's your cover?" Barbara Lawrence said. "I mean, why would Harry want to meet with you?"

This was the best part. Rae didn't need a cover at all. She was already Rae *Johnson*, daughter of Chuck *Johnson*, the football coach.

"That's why you put me on this case, isn't it?" Rae said. "Because of my dad? Guys like Harry flip shit over football coaches, national-championship-winning coaches, especially."

"But you're not a coach. You're just his—"

"—personal assistant. That's my cover, and it works because positions like that never get talked about. I won't even need an online profile. Harry Christmas has been around the block long enough to read the room. He'll know why I'm there."

"You'd be there to discuss your father's future? A possible employment with UCM?"

"That's right."

"And what's to keep the congressman from calling your father?"

Rae snorted. She couldn't help it.

Barbara said, "Excuse me?"

"I'm sorry. It's just that, well, you don't know my dad. He'd never take a call from some dirtbag like Harry Christmas. He's too busy, for one thing. And for another, he's not that kind of coach. Dad's old school, salt of the earth. Every cliché you've ever heard about championship caliber men— that's my dad to a T."

"You're not worried about his reputation? There will be risks if you involve him in this."

The call with Chuck replayed in Rae's mind. He had asked her, specifically, about the Chiefs. He'd even mentioned Matt Talley. Then again, UCM was in the national championship game for the second consecutive year, and the subject of most all the Johnsons' conversations revolved around college football. But that wasn't what Barb had asked. She'd asked about Chuck's reputation. Rae hadn't considered that. The oversight surprised her. She didn't want to get her dad in trouble. It was the exact opposite. Rae wanted to prove that Chuck had been right; his baby girl was destined for bigger, better things than football.

"I don't see why my dad has to know," Rae said. "If everything works out, then—"

"That's a big if, which is why it's taken me so long to evaluate your request. Besides, UCM has a coach already, correct? Aren't they winning?"

"Yeah, but they're trying to lose. Agent Ranchino, he was—"

"—lip reading? That's your source?"

The string lights in the shop windows seemed dimmer now. Rae's suspicions about Ella May Pride, the extracurricular work she'd put in at the Buffalo Nickel that morning, it felt the same way. Rae squinted at the lights, listening as Barb said, "Harry Christmas has been the representative for Mississippi's Forty-Eighth Congressional District since the Stone Age, forty-three years, but he's clean. Not so much as a traffic violation."

"Of course he's clean. The worst ones always are."

"*The worst ones?* The worst ones are in Juárez, or Kyzyl. Come on, Agent Johnson. This is white-collar crime we're talking about."

Rae took that line on the chin. It hurt to hear her SAC put words to the very same notion she'd had upon first receiving this assignment. "If this case is such a joke, what am *I* doing here? I'm the best rookie agent you've got."

"You don't lack confidence, that's for sure," Barbara said. "And you're right, there's a ton of money on the line. Just last year, the NCAA cleared over ten billion dollars in media rights from its deal with CBS Sports. To put that in perspective, the GDP for the country of Liechtenstein is barely over six bills."

"Cookie-cutter case or a big money operation? Which one is it?"

"It's not counterterrorism. That's for sure. It's football. Which is a priority to most of the country. It's our job to make sure it's clean, or at least *cleaner*. You're in Mississippi to put a little pressure on these people. That's all. Just make sure they know we're watching."

"If you give me the clearance, I could do more than watch."

"That's what I'm afraid of."

"So you're denying my request?"

"I'll let you know by Sunday."

"*Sunday?*"

Rae had nowhere to go, nowhere to be, nothing to do all day except take this call. Through the window, she spotted a middle-aged man wearing a baggy shirt out for a morning jog.

"That's almost a whole week away," Rae said, realizing it was also the day before the Cotton Bowl. "What am I supposed to do until then?"

"How about some actual fieldwork? You know, set up surveillance, gather intel."

The jogger was closer now, close enough Rae could see he wasn't wearing a shirt at all; it was a UCM jersey with a big red number 7 stitched across the front. The same number was on the back of his jersey too, but there wasn't a name. Names were against the rules. Names spelled it out.

"What if I could secure an informant?" Rae said. "A kid on the team who's willing to talk?"

"Who?"

"The new quarterback, Moses McCloud."

"If Moses went on record, he'd be putting his entire career in jeopardy."

Would Moses really be willing to sacrifice his scholarship,

along with any chance he had of making it to the NFL, just to help her with the case? Maybe. Rae recalled her encounter with him back at Geraldine's place. How Darren had said his sights were set on veterinarian school.

"I'd need to promise him he'd be safe afterwards, his future secure," Rae said. "Surely, we can offer him some sort of protection."

"*Protection?* We're White-Collar Crime, Johnson, not the kid's offensive line. Besides, who's he need protection from? The NCAA?"

"You read the report I submitted. Harry Christmas is as crooked as they come. He's got this whole town, including local law enforcement, in his back pocket."

"But you can't prove it."

"Not without your blessing."

"You'll need more than a single player's statement. You'll need to corroborate his testimony with actual evidence."

Rae knew what she needed. She needed Moses McCloud to talk, but he was smart. Even if she offered him protection, what was in it for him? "How about compensation?" she said, knowing exactly how much the FBI could pay an informant.

"*Money?* I just told you—"

"You said college football is a billion-dollar industry. I'm not asking for much here. Just enough to cover Moses's tuition, books, room and board."

"On top of the clearance you need to set up a meeting with Congressman Christmas."

"Yeah," Rae said. "That should do it."

"Agent Johnson, listen . . ." The Special Agent in Charge paused just long enough to raise Rae's hopes. "You remind me a lot of myself when I was a rookie, always rushing ahead, bulldozing anyone or anything that got in my way."

"Appreciate it."

"Not a compliment. A warning. One I wish you'd heed until I've had time to process your request."

"Do you really expect me to wait until Sunday?" In just a few more hours, the Chiefs would be back in Sutpen Stadium for Monday's practice, their first practice of the new year. "That's the day before the—"

Rae heard a soft click and lowered the phone. The rookie agent Barb had said she'd been was framed in the window. Every version of the woman Rae was—the woman she might be one day—was right there in front of her, but all she could see was Compson, the sleepy Southern town still blinking itself awake as the winter sun warmed a new day.

Rae slid her thumb over the phone screen. The glass was cool like Darren Floyd, the bluesman trying to hide the sleep from his voice when he answered, saying, "Rae? Hey, yeah. What's up?"

34

Over the last month, Speer Taylor's eulogy video, which had been edited by a crack team of millennial hipsters, had garnered well over fifty million views. Speer'd made guest appearances on television before: *SportsCenter*, *Around the Horn*, *Pardon the Interruption*, even *Good Morning America* once. All the regular shows any other national-championship-winning coach might visit, but this, everything that had come as a result of that video, was bigger than football.

Across the country, people who didn't know the difference between a touchback and a touchdown were still ranting or raving about the coach in the houndstooth hat. It worked like a Rorschach test. Everybody who watched the clip either saw Speer Taylor as the Second Coming or a two-bit fraud. There was no in-between. Prism News had caught lightning in a bottle. Which was why they'd kept their film crew in Compson, pointing their cameras at the enigmatic young coach as he prepared his team for the Cotton Bowl.

Speer was well aware of the cameras. He'd almost called for closed practices until he realized that without that video, he didn't have a political career. Prism News was everywhere—lurking in the stands, creeping down the breezeways—trying to recapture the fervor that had so enthralled the nation.

Throughout nearly every minute of every practice leading up to the Cotton Bowl, Coach Taylor had done his best to re-create the magic from before. He'd been playing music at his practices for years, but now he'd hired a real-life DJ to stand at the fifty-yard line and blast tunes by Florida Georgia Line, Bubba Sparxxx, and Cowboy Troy. Normally, Coach Taylor alternated between country and hip hop, trying to keep both his Black and white players happy. His newfound conservative voter base wouldn't stand for A$AP Rocky, though. Not even Eminem or Drake. Real hip hop didn't fit the target demographic. So, Speer had settled on country-rap mashups, also known as "hick hop," which did not go over well. Neither did the magician and the sock-puppet show he'd booked to perform in the field house lobby.

After that video went viral, Speer had spent the bulk of his energy trying to morph his football program into Kanakuk, the church camp where his life had changed the summer before his senior season. He wanted—no, he needed—more perfectly framed footage to feed his future voters, and there was nothing more perfect than Kanakuk.

Which was why a hundred-gallon Rubbermaid horse trough filled with hose water sat discreetly behind the goal posts in Sutpen Stadium's south end zone. The horse trough trick had worked in Memphis, back when Speer'd been having trouble with a standout receiver, the same sort of issues he'd been having with Moses McCloud since the Mississippi State game. The quarterback was still pouting. Upset about his coach's antics at the postgame press conference, maybe? Speer wasn't sure, but the water held the answers. It would make great content too. Which was why practices had been moved to the game field, the brand-new stadium rising like a modern-day Colosseum in every direction, a fitting background for what Speer had in mind.

The trough had gone mostly unnoticed over the course of

the practice. The players probably thought it was there for an on-the-field ice bath, despite the fact that there were six Cryo-Spas in the training room, each jetted tub costing a little more than a brand-new compact car. The trough sat Speer back eighty-seven dollars, a purchase he'd made with the team credit card at the Tractor Supply on the outskirts of town.

Speer blew his whistle, signaling an early end to the day's repetitions and waved the team over. The boys started his way as a gang of beefy assistant coaches lugged the trough into the end zone and the DJ switched Kid Rock's "Cowboy" out for Amy Grant's "Better Than a Hallelujah."

When all were finally in position, Coach Taylor winked at the nearest Prism News cameraman and said, "Every eye closed, gentlemen. Every head bowed . . ."

35

Moses still had his helmet on, peeking out through the bars of his face mask. Sam Billingsley, the backup, walk-on quarterback, knelt to Moses's right. Ever the rebel, Cergile Blanc had assumed a squatting position in front of the QBs, heels flat on the turf, elbows spread wide between his knees.

"Big-ass white stallion," Cerge grumbled, "gonna come running through that tunnel—same one we bust out before the games?—any second now. Real talk. Coach might even hit the smoke and shit. Let off a few fireworks. Then, what?"

A wild stallion wouldn't have surprised Moses. Not after all Coach Taylor had put them through over the last month. Moses could barely see the black plastic horse trough through the jumble of shoulder pads, dreadlocks, tapered fades, frohawks, and 360 waves.

"That horse start coming at me?" Cerge said, voice strained from holding the squat. "I'm a go all Luca Brasi on that bitch. *Bet.*"

Moses was about to correct his running back, tell him that there was no way to know who had actually decapitated the horse in *The Godfather*, but Coach Taylor beat him to the punch, saying, "Heads *bowed*, gentlemen."

Moses lowered his head.

Somewhere, someone was lightly strumming an acoustic guitar, or maybe it was just a new track coming out of that DJ's portable PA system. Moses's eyes were still open, hidden behind his tinted visor, but he wasn't about to turn around to check, not after the way things had been going ever since Matt Talley went down. First, Eddie Pride and Ella May. Then, Darren and that redheaded reporter rolling out to Momma G's place. And now this . . .

Moses knew what Coach Taylor was doing. Another power play. Like that shit he'd pulled at the press conference, talking about the Mississippi state flag, a cotton boll. Coach Taylor was slicker than he let on, slippery, like that black plastic trough he was pointing at, saying, "There comes a moment in every young man's life when it's time to get serious."

Serious? Coach Taylor wasn't serious. He wasn't even coaching, that was for damn sure, but all his assistants still were. The Chiefs' offensive coordinator and quarterback's coach, Todd Sessions, had put together one hell of a game plan for Ohio State. They were going to pick the Buckeyes' Cover 3 defense apart.

"And no, I'm not talking about the Cotton Bowl," Coach Taylor said, wearing a white robe now, some sort of gown. "That game is the furthest thing from my mind. I'm talking about this moment. The here and now. Can you feel it?"

Cerge whispered, "Here come that stallion. Watch . . ."

"Keep those heads bowed," Coach Taylor said as the guitar in the background plucked a minor chord. "If you've got guilt in your heart—any guilt at all, about anything—I want you to raise your hand."

Moses eyes tracked left to right, scanning the crowd.

"Ah, *yes.* There's one," Speer said, "in the front row," but there wasn't. Not a single hand was raised that Moses could see. "Maybe you're feeling guilty about cheating yourself out of a power clean rep during this morning's workout?"

Moses had, actually, skipped his entire fourth set on power

clean that very morning, worried about his knee, remembering that sharp pop on the sideline of the Mississippi State game. Coach Taylor didn't know the full extent of Moses's injury, nobody did, but Moses got the feeling his coach was talking to him, trying to trick him into something.

"Doesn't have to be anything crazy. Doesn't make you a bad person. We've all fallen short. Go on, get those hands up where I can see them."

None of Moses's teammates had their hands up. Coach Taylor wasn't fooling anyone, not even when he said, "Yes, *yes!* I see you over there. Keep that hand up high. I know there's more. We're all guilty of something. How about plagiarism, huh? Anybody ever cheated on a test?"

Little Sam Billingsley's tiny left paw, the same hand that barely fit around the back end of a football, started rising from his kneepad. Moses noticed the movement and reached out, reflexively, catching the walk-on quarterback's wrist. The sudden movement drew the desperate coach's eye.

"Yes!" Speer yipped. "Moses McCloud, our new leader, just raised his hand in the back row!"

There wasn't a single head still bowed in the south end zone. The whole team was looking up, staring straight at their quarterback.

"Come on," Coach Taylor said and bent to touch the water. "Don't be scared, Moses. Let's lead this team to the Promised Land."

36

From the comfort of his soundproofed suite—complete with high-backed stadium seats, an expansive floor-to-ceiling window, and a custom mahogany bar—Harry Christmas surveyed the scene in the bowels of Sutpen Stadium. Despite Speer Taylor's rabid gesticulations, Moses McCloud had not budged from his spot at the back of the pack.

"Maybe we'll get lucky," Bruiser Brandt said, mixing himself a Rum Grizzly at the skybox bar, "and Coach'll drown the poor kid. Twenty bucks says Moses can't swim."

Harry doubted the Black quarterback could swim but didn't say as much. Moses didn't need to swim, or even drown for that matter. Harry Christmas just needed the boy to throw one goddamn football game. Was that too much to ask? Maybe so. The young quarterback seemed to have a real disdain for authority. Speer Taylor had told him three times already to stand and come forward. Yet there Moses was, still kneeling as his coach splashed around in the makeshift baptismal font.

"It's fine." Harry slid a fresh cigarillo up from his windbreaker and began peeling back the plastic. "Everything is fine. We're still on track."

The Compson police chief dribbled bitters over his cocktail.

"The mob is fickle," Harry continued, "but as long as Prism News keeps pumping those videos out and kicking the conservative hornet's nest, I don't see how Coach Taylor can lose."

"But we still want him to lose, right?" Bruiser plopped down in the recliner next to Harry, cradling his drink in both hands.

The police chief was out of uniform, wearing a loose-fitting UCM sweatshirt and a pair of overly tight jeans. It appeared as if Bruiser's chest had expanded since Harry'd seen him last. Fresh pink acne dotted the man's usually grizzled cheeks.

Harry ignored the changes and said, "I'm speaking of the forthcoming campaign. Speer Taylor's a household name. All we've got to do now is maintain momentum, keep those cameras rolling, and Coach Taylor will soon be *Senator* Taylor."

The bottom half of Speer's baptismal gown was soaked so thoroughly Harry could see the coach's Nike shorts through the sheer white fabric. The congressman knew where Speer Taylor was headed. The rest of the players knew it too, parting like the Red Sea as the sodden coach made a beeline for Moses McCloud.

"Come next fall," Harry said, the cigarillo's wine-flavored wood tip clacking over his teeth, "no one will care about Speer Taylor's *plat*form. We won't even have to go through the motions, prepping his stances on gun control, abortion, or immigration. No sir. Our boy's gonna stick to what he knows. The one thing every true Mississippian cares about most—college football." Harry paused to light his Black & Mild. "That's the ticket. How Speer's going to save the game. I can think up a half dozen Civil War allusions right now. *Reconstruction.* That's exactly what'll happen across the college football landscape if we let this name, image, likeness crap slip through the federal courts."

Bruiser, still staring sideways at Harry, said, "Because the players would be getting paid, right? Just like how after the war, the slaves—"

"No, Brandt." The tip of the congressman's cigarillo cut

through the air and stopped dangerously close to the police chief's pimpled cheek. "That is not the right word. Don't even think it. Understand?"

Bruiser nodded, slowly.

"Reconstruction, on the other hand . . . That's a fine word, because that's what it'd be. Except this time, there'd be no Compromise of 1877 to save us. Oh, no. There would be no end to the *de*construction of the sacred traditions we've upheld for so long. No Howard's Rock or the 12th Man over in College Station. Chief Osceola would never again plant his flaming spear in the center of Doak Campbell Stadium." Harry's eyes were glassy, and it wasn't from the smoke. "All those longstanding rituals would be replaced by the dollar. Pure greed would reign supreme. If we start paying these boys real money, loyalty'd go straight out the window. The players would simply sign with whichever school offered the best deal. Can you imagine?"

"Well, yeah." Bruiser sipped his rum drink. "I mean, it ain't too far off from the way things are now."

"What the hell is wrong with you? All those pimples on your face, your chest. It looks like you're wearing a Wonderbra, and if you aren't, you should be."

Bruiser cradled the lowball glass between his breasts. "Remember how I told you about them at-home, low T injections? Well . . ."

Harry studied Bruiser staring down at a turf field he'd never played on. Sutpen Stadium had been completed just two years ago, right before the Chiefs' first championship season. The project had been funded through a combination of tax-free municipal bonds, cash payments, long-term tax exemptions, and operating cost subsidies. The result was a new-age arena featuring club-level seating, a three-story Chiefs' Museum, and a high-tech canopy designed to maximize crowd noise. All that engineering, all that money, just to showcase Neanderthals like the still-blathering Bruiser.

"Save it for your wife, Brandt," Harry snapped, cutting the police chief off midsentence. "This is bigger than us. Bigger than Compson. We've got to stop that goddamn NIL case before it makes it to the federal courts, and Speer Taylor is the man to do it. Look at him down there, parading around like some sort of Old Testament prophet. He's clueless yet determined. He's *perfect.*"

There was a player in the trough now, a small white boy. A kicker of some sort, or maybe a backup QB. Coach Taylor only had eyes for Moses. He was standing directly over his quarterback, flapping both arms in the direction of the end zone.

"And I'll tell you what else is perfect," Harry said, turning away from the field as the Prism News crew moved in for the kill. "The way we've got Eddie Pride pinned. That bit about his daughter?"

Bruiser straightened. Ice rattled in his glass. "I called up Mr. Estes, like you said, and asked him to take that security camera down. Verlon was happy to help. He's a big-time supporter, a proud Chiefs fan."

Harry trusted Brandt. The two men had been through so much together, but they were in uncharted waters now. They'd tampered with an actual crime scene, which was a much more serious infraction than simple bribery or fraud. But what choice did they have? They had to find a way to properly motivate Eddie Pride. Leading the bagman to believe his daughter was about to be charged with murder, or at least manslaughter, was more than just a calculated risk. It was their only play. But what if Ella May had really done it? What if she'd actually pushed Matt Talley off the Buffalo Nickel's roof?

"Well, I'm glad to hear Mr. Estes is a team player," Harry said, deciding the girl's innocence didn't matter; she would be whatever they needed her to be. "And apparently Ella May Pride is too. Eddie called this morning, on that phone I gave him? His girl's making her move tonight."

"Tonight? Shit . . ."

"Oh, don't be such a worrywart, Brandt." Harry leaned over, tapping ash from his cigarillo into the police chief's half-full glass. "That girl's a pistol. She'll do fine. I'll tell you what isn't fine, though. That boy down there making a fool out of Speer Taylor."

Bruiser was gazing into his ruined rum drink when his phone rang, the shrill sound shattering the silence inside the soundproof suite.

Harry ignored the noise, watching as Speer Taylor continued to tug fruitlessly at Moses McCloud's shoulder pads. Then the ringing was gone, replaced by the police chief's voice, saying, "Darren, huh? Darren Floyd?"

The congressman turned.

"Yeah, I can hear you," Bruiser said and hefted the soiled glass to his mouth, grimacing as he swallowed the murky mess down. "The hell do you want?"

37

"Wanted to talk to you about the Cotton Bowl," Darren said into his phone, pacing the stadium's north tunnel, the field, the horse trough, less than fifty yards away.

Rae'd met the bluesman in the parking lot an hour before and told him that Barbara Lawrence had postponed her decision until Sunday. Darren didn't like that. Said it'd be tough to set up a meeting with a man like Congressman Christmas, a man he'd never even met, on such short notice. What he liked even less was what he saw when they'd made it to practice. The scene on the field rubbed the former receiver the wrong way, Coach Taylor's white robe, especially.

"Listen, I need to get with the boss." Rae watched Darren keep his cool and deliver the lines they'd just discussed. "Yeah, man. *The boss.* Got somebody I think he'd like to meet. Somebody that could help . . ." Darren waited, letting the police chief get good and curious before he dropped her daddy's name. "You know Chuck Johnson, that coach over in Arkansas? Well, he saw Speer's eulogy on the internet, man. He hit me up. I used to be over there all the time, playing these shows in West Helena and Little Rock. Anyway, listen . . ." Darren asked the dirty cop did he want to meet Coach Johnson's daughter or not? Brandt Conrad said, "His *daughter*?" loud enough Rae could hear it through the phone. Darren said, "You'll love her. She's his personal assistant or some shit. This good-looking redheaded chick," and winked at the federal agent standing next to him in the dark, his hands trembling a little, voice steady. "She'll be in Dallas for the game. Just wants to talk. Think of it as a recruiting visit, except the other way around."

That got the police chief's attention. Rae liked how Darren was playing it, getting his point across without saying too much. Except there was silence now, a couple seconds' worth before Darren said, "Gate 8, huh? Right before the start of the game? See you then, Chief," and hung up, quick.

The music from the field drifted down the tunnel, some weepy, alt-rock Christian tune.

"Well?" Rae said, staring into the shadows around Darren's eyes, the color draining from his cheeks. "What?"

"You forget about that noose? The one they used to string Eddie's fat ass up?"

Rae hadn't forgotten.

"What you think they'll do to me," Darren said and slapped his chest, "if this deal goes wrong?"

Rae said, "I'm sorry," and meant it, but she'd made sacrifices too. Getting her father involved, dangling Chuck's good name in front of the congressman—that was a risk. Just like Barbara Lawrence had said. It hadn't stopped Rae from pushing ahead, though. Nothing would. Football was dangerous, guys got hurt, but that didn't keep them from playing.

"You hear me?" Darren said. "I'm gonna head back up to Detroit till the end of the week. Give all this some time to blow over."

Rae nodded and noticed movement behind him, a new commotion taking place on the field.

"That's it?"

"If you're wanting me to say thanks," Rae said, "you're gonna have to wait. Matter of fact, why don't you stop by my place when you get back from Detroit?"

"You got some leftover eggnog?"

"Oh, buddy," Rae said. "I've got more than—" Her eyes jumped to the south end zone. It looked like a scrum, a fight, maybe? Rae'd seen her fair share of melees break out at her father's practices, but this was something different.

Darren said, "What you got, huh?"

Rae, eyes still locked on the field, scanning the crowd for Moses McCloud, said, "I gotta go."

38

Speer Taylor had been tugging on Moses's practice jersey for 248 seconds. The freshman quarterback kept count in his head, just like his elementary school counselor had taught him to do after Keyshawn crashed his Buick into the kudzu. It wasn't working, though. Each second felt like a vine wrapping tighter around Moses's heart as the rest of the team, all the other players, closed in.

Sammy B's bitch ass wasn't helping, scooting around in that trough like a baby seal, doing his best to get Coach Taylor's attention. Speer didn't care. He just wanted to baptize Moses for all those men and their cameras. Yessir. Cerge saw what was happening too, kept whispering Haitian-sounding stuff under his breath: "Aye, zozo. *Zonbi!* Great gods cannot ride little horses . . ."

Moses wished it was that simple. He'd take a white stallion running wild across the field over this any day. Moses stood and watched Coach Taylor stumble back over Cerge still squatting on the turf. The coach shouted something Moses couldn't make out, not with the way the wind was whipping through his helmet's earholes now, the same holes Rock Cato, the running back's coach, told his studs to stick their dick through anytime they pancaked a linebacker and got him pinned down.

It sounded too crazy to be true, but this was Moses's life, his only hope at something better than the tenant house he'd left behind in Clarksdale, just like he was leaving the football field behind now, hurdling a blocking sled on the sideline then sprinting for the tunnel, the dark corridor from which Cerge had claimed a horse would come running, and he was almost right. Except the white stallion was a Black quarterback, slicing through the darkness into the locker room, a horde of assistant coaches and cameramen huffing behind him, hellhounds on his trail. Moses's cleats clacked across the concrete walkway that led to Gate 5. His Altima was in the far back corner of the lot, the same place he always parked, careful with the vehicle that had once belonged to his mother. The mob of coaches and cameramen was getting closer. Last thing Moses wanted was his great exodus broadcast for the world to see.

He made it one stride into the parking lot before the Chevrolet Impala cut him off. The tires squealed as the back end fishtailed to a stop, throwing the driver's hair down in her face, bright red hair Moses recognized when the woman brushed it from her eyes and said, "Need a ride?"

Yeah, Moses thought and yanked open the passenger-side door, but what did that redhead reporter need from him now?

39

A siren yipped and Rae checked her six. Lights pulsed liquid blue in the rearview as the Impala barreled toward the stadium's south exit. Compson was a small town. Not many back alleys or parking decks. One wrong turn and she'd be caught, her cover blown. Rae was thinking she could hook a right onto College Street and make a run for the highway, take 49 all the way to Clarksdale if she had to, when Moses McCloud said: "Left at the light, then take Durant down to the corner. Don't stop till you cross the tracks."

The Impala nicked the curb, roaring west along Durant Avenue at upwards of seventy miles per hour, the renovated downtown shops and colonial-style houses blurring through the windows. Rae was driving so fast, she didn't feel the Impala bounce over the C & G Railroad. She didn't notice the way the town changed as soon as they crossed those tracks, not until Moses spoke again.

"Another left right here."

The new street was like the last street, rundown vehicles with jumbo-sized wheels lining both curbs, leaving a narrow corridor of cracked concrete in between. The Impala slowed to a crawl. Rae's knuckles flashed white over the wheel. Though she'd been in Compson for more than a month, she had never ventured into this part of town. There were no pictures of this neighborhood in the University of Central Mississippi's recruiting pamphlets.

"Slow down," Moses said and leaned forward. "We're here."

It was full dark now, the night blanketing the downed bas-ketball goals, the bikes with broken chains left to rust in side yards. A double-wide trailer appeared at the end of the cul-de-sac. Two rows of flickering solar lights lined the walkway leading to the door. A white cross fashioned from what looked to be railroad ties rose from the well-manicured lawn. Beyond the cross was an open patch of grass, a field, thirty, maybe forty yards long. Both sidelines were rimmed with cars, their head-lights aimed at the boys in the middle.

Moses said, "Look at that kid go," and Rae watched a pock-et-sized quarterback zip around the edge holding the ball like a loaf of bread, swinging it as he ran. The kid flickered between the headlights. There for a moment, then gone, then back again, an act of teleportation—of magic—that transported him from one end of the field to the other. There was no scoreboard, no fireworks, no stadium full of cameras and drunken fans, but there were horns. A chorus of car horns and flashing high beams. The small boy's shadow grew long in the lights and split in every direction. A coach appeared and raised one hand. The lights leveled out again.

In the stillness, Rae watched the coach squat and position the ball properly along the boy's right arm, wrist above the elbow, five tiny fingers splayed tight over the tip. It was some-thing she'd seen her father do hundreds, maybe thousands of times. Chuck Johnson was a drill sergeant when it came to ball security. This felt different. More real despite the grade-school kids and the dim-lit field. The coach blew his whistle and the boy trotted back to the huddle, still holding the ball high and tight, just like he'd been taught to do.

One more drill, ten wind sprints, and the coach called his

team up. Moses stayed quiet as the boys popped their chinstraps and shed their pads. Rae wondered what he was thinking. Did he see himself out there like she did? Rae'd never gotten a chance to play ball with the boys, but she still felt at home on a practice field.

"Every battle is won before it's fought."

Chuck again, quoting Sun Tzu's *The Art of War*, trying to motivate his players at practice. Rae didn't need motivation. She was prepared, but what about Moses? What had happened back at Sutpen Stadium? Why had he run away? And, most importantly, was he willing to take part in a federal investigation?

Rae told herself to slow down and cocked one ear, listening for the sirens that had prodded them there. The night stood silent like the field. Rae clicked on the Impala's headlights. There were no yard lines in the grass, no goal posts, but there was a football, forgotten in the back corner of the end zone. A small one, some sort of youth-size ball. It wasn't much, but Rae knew exactly what to ask Moses now.

40

"**Do I** wanna play catch?" Moses said, watching the redhead slip out from behind the wheel and walk around the front of the car. The headlights made her face even whiter than it was.

"Catch, yeah," she said and clapped. "Come on."

Moses didn't want to play catch. He wanted to go home. All the way back to Clarksdale, far enough maybe he'd forget about that horse trough and everything else. Let Momma G cook him up some biscuits and gravy in the morning like she used to before every one of his high school games. Moses was sick of caf food, sick of UCM and Speer Taylor. And now this crazy-ass reporter lady was asking him to play catch?

Moses opened the passenger-side door and said, "Nah, I'm good," but the woman was already running, sprinting away from him with what appeared to be decent form. Knees up, hands swinging ear to pocket like she was competing in the hundred-meter dash. Moses didn't see the ball until she bent to pick it up. Then it was airborne, a torpedo spiraling straight for the Impala.

Moses jumped up and extended both hands out as far as they would go, snagging the ball before it smacked into the windshield. The pigskin was lighter than he'd expected, a peewee ball. Which made sense, considering how far that woman had just chunked it.

She was still on the far side of the field, fifty or so yards away. Moses hollered, "I ain't playing. You hear me?" and let loose a pass, so high, so far, it got lost in the moon. He smiled as it started down, knowing the ball would land well past the far edge of the field where the grass hadn't been mowed and the headlights didn't reach.

The woman ran on anyway, maintaining that same tight form.

Moses squinted when she reached the shadows. He cupped one hand over his brow, tracking her pale arms slicing through the darkness, then rising, stretching out longer than seemed possible. The way her body went flat, perfectly parallel to the earth, a straight line over the knee-high grass—Moses thought she'd tripped. He heard her grunt when she hit the dirt and moved the hand over his eyes down to his mouth, ready to shout out an *Any Given Sunday* quote, or maybe keep it PG-13 and stick her with something from *Remember the Titans*. "Zero fun, sir." Yeah. That line Petey tells Coach Boone.

Instead, Moses heard, "Nice pass!" coming from the place where the woman had fallen. Then he saw hands, rising, the reporter's hands, holding that ball up like she'd caught it.

Moses said, "Nuh-uh," when she was close enough he didn't have to shout. "No way you snagged that."

She lobbed the ball back to him underhanded. "I can catch whatever you throw at me, Moses McCloud."

He laughed.

"Don't believe me? Let's make a deal. For every pass I catch, you answer one question."

"So that's what this is? Some kinda interview?"

"Sure, and it's over after my first drop."

"One catch, one question?" Moses said and slid his fingers over the leather until they found the laces. "All right, I'll play."

41

The next pass, the first one of Rae Johnson's new game, was a ten-yard floater. She caught the ball easily and said, "Why'd you leave practice?"

"That's your first question?"

"You lobbed me a softball to start. I'm returning the favor."

Rae rifled the ball back to Moses and he caught it with one hand. "Coach Taylor was being a asshole. Trying to break me. That's what he was doing. Get me to kneel down and roll over. Like a dog."

"Looked to me," Rae said, "like he was trying to baptize you."

"Already been baptized. See that church back there?"

Rae gazed past the crudely fashioned cross to the double-wide trailer she'd noticed when they'd first arrived. There were words written in the center of the white cross, each blue letter painted by a steady hand: MOUNT ZION AFRICAN METHODIST EPISCOPAL CHURCH.

The rookie agent said, "Yeah, I see it," and turned, just quick enough she was able to get her hands up before the pointy end of the peewee football hit her in the nose. "*Hey!*" The word came out hot. "You cheated. You tried to—"

"One catch, one question. Those were the only rules I remember."

"Okay, then," Rae said, deciding to up the difficulty on her end too. "Let's talk about your recruitment. What made you decide to sign with UCM?"

"I had a friend," Moses said, "back in grade school. This white kid—"

"I asked about UCM."

Moses said, "I'm getting there," and adjusted his shoulder pads. He was still wearing all his gear except his helmet. "But first let me tell you about my little buddy. His daddy was the principal at our school. Booker T. Washington Elementary. One day, we're out at recess, and this kid tells me he wishes he was Black. I ask him why? And he says all his favorite athletes are Black, favorite actors, comedians too. We're in fourth grade." Moses hooked his thumbs in the loops of his practice pants. "So, I tell him how every morning when I wake up, first thing I remember is that I'm different. Asked him had he ever thought like that before? Didn't wait for him to say nothing. I knew the answer already."

Rae held tight to the ball but couldn't feel the leather or the laces. It was as if a timeout had been called, the game they'd been playing interrupted by reality.

"That kid moved out of Clarksdale the summer before fifth grade. Said his daddy got a job teaching kindergarten over in Madison." Moses was pacing now, moving farther away. "That man was willing to go from being the principal to a *kindergarten* teacher, just to get his ass out of Clarksdale."

Rae said, "You still didn't answer my question. I asked how you got to UCM?"

"And I'm telling you about how, when I was in ninth grade, this fancy-ass 'academy' came calling," Moses said, backpedaling, jogging in reverse toward the far end of the field, "trying to get me to do like what that boy's daddy did. Get me on up to some lily-white town in Alabama. Get me a *good* education. Get me ready for that *big-time* college ball . . ."

"But you stayed," Rae said. "You graduated from Clarksdale High."

"Yeah, I stayed in Clarksdale, but I left my boys behind." Moses was so far away, he had to shout the next line: "Ain't no way to really 'stay' when you getting calls every day from coaches, getting on planes to go see all these universities. Every time I came home, I'd think about that little buddy I had back in fourth grade, how his daddy went out looking for greener pastures, a snowy field, and found it."

Rae didn't move, Moses didn't either, but the distance between them had widened, a gap that spanned much further than any field. The ball felt heavy now too, like it wasn't hers to hold. She reared back and ripped off another fifty-yard bomb. Moses caught it with ease.

"Yeah, I was ready to get mine," he said, patting the ball, slapping it. "Momma G was ready to get hers too, finally get paid for pulling me out them kudzu vines, working overtime, raising up her daughter's kid because her daughter was gone. My moms was—" Moses's voice cracked. He started bouncing around as if he were in the pocket, sidestepping defenders, all the obstacles life had thrown at him already. "Remember how I told you I liked football because I'm in control when I'm out on the field?"

Rae nodded.

"That's how this is." Moses kept his eyes up as his feet pulsed beneath him. "How it used to be back when I was the same age as them kids practicing earlier."

Rae remembered the coach, the one she'd almost mistaken for her father.

"It's different now. Ain't nothing like what I thought, like how it looked on TV. Spent my whole life dreaming, trying to make it here, right here, and now they trying to—"

The ball took the place of his words, rocketing out of the quarterback's right hand. This wasn't some high arching floater; this was a flash of light and sound. Rae could actually hear the laces whizzing as the ball cut through the night. It was a laser, a missile that never got more than ten feet off the ground. The ball hit Rae in the gut so hard it knocked her off her feet. If she hadn't had her Jordans laced, it might've knocked her clean out of her shoes.

But she caught it.

The ball was still in Rae's hands when she stood and said, "Who are—" The pain in her stomach stole her words away. Rae swallowed it down and shouted, "Who are *they*? The bagmen? Eddie Pride Junior and—"

"Hey, now," Moses said, trotting toward her. "Don't be getting my name mixed up with all that. If that's what you trying to write your story about, then this game's over. Might need to stop anyway. You okay?"

Rae was fine. She'd have a bruise on her stomach soon. Might be one there already. A cross, or an X, above her navel. Rae knew the strange mark well, the shape the tip of a ball left on bare flesh.

"But Darren . . ." Rae said, still catching her breath. "Darren Floyd. He's your bagman, right?"

"Darren's my dude, yeah. He hooks me up with some fresh kicks, some groceries every now and then."

Rae remembered Darren's JCPenney bag at the Waffle House. How he'd said he'd gotten Moses a shirt. Something he could wear to church.

"What I'm saying is . . ." Moses bent forward until his eyes were level with Rae's. "Nobody gives me money. Not Darren. Not Eddie. Nobody."

"*What?* Why not?"

"It ain't easy, I can tell you that much. Between class, practice, position meetings, and study hall, I'm working over sixty hours a week. Sometimes seventy, if, say, we fly to an away game. You believe that?"

Rae believed it. She knew how hard her father's players worked.

"And," Moses said, "I don't get paid for it. Not one real dollar I could use to go buy a Big Mac when I get sick of the caf. You ever eaten in the UCM cafeteria? Taste like hospital food."

Rae pitched the ball back to Moses and clapped her hands. "No way. That last pass just about killed you."

"Come on," she said. "I've got one more question."

"You got a screw loose. Don't know when to quit."

They were closer now, barely ten yards away, and Moses was right. If he fired her another heater, Rae doubted she'd catch it, much less survive it. But what choice did she have? Rules were rules.

"What do you know about the Gridiron Girls?" Rae said, hands raised, protecting her face. "Ella May Pride, in particular?"

Moses gripped the ball tighter and cocked his shoulder.

"She was Matt Talley's girlfriend, right?" Rae watched the quarterback's eyes, trying to read them. "Were they a happy couple? Or was there trouble in paradise? Did Ella May have any reason to—"

The toe of Moses's rear cleat twisted in the grass, a lever that started a chain reaction up the length of his body, the muscles in his thighs, hips, and torso torquing like a catapult, preparing to fire a pass that would put an end to Rae's game for good.

The rookie agent braced herself but did not back down. She was still standing there, both hands extended, when Moses said, "The hell is this?"

It was blood, Rae's blood, all over the youth-league ball. With her hands still up, she could see that her left one was bleeding. Moses's last pass had torn the webbing between her index finger and thumb.

Rae wiped the blood on her shirt and called for the ball.

"Sometimes you've got to lose the battle," Moses said, "to win the war. Know what I'm saying?"

Rae didn't get it. She wasn't there to lose. None of her father's coaching maxims ever mentioned *losing*. "Listen, I just need to know about Ella May and Matt. I need—"

The way Moses dropped the little pigskin, the way he stared back at her, made Rae wonder what he saw. Though she'd never competed in a real game, Rae had played a lot of catch with her dad. It was the same sort of setup, a go-until-you-drop-one game. That's where she'd learned the lessons that could only be taught on the field. Chuck had given his daughter so much wisdom, so much grit, through such a simple contest. Over the last half hour, Rae had put her father's training to the test. Thankfully, the young quarterback knew the score.

"Whatever Ella May and Matt had going, that's their business," Moses said. "My business is football. This game's all I got."

"But you're a smart kid. You've got school. Your grades."

"Don't nobody care about my *grades*. I can't even walk down the street at night wearing a hoodie, but you put a helmet on this head, hide these brown eyes behind a face mask, then I got the whole state of Mississippi hollering my name. White women in the Piggly Wiggly saying, 'Go get 'em, Moses.' Patting me on the back. Hoping like hell I'm gonna take the Chiefs all the way," Moses said. "If I take money from some bagman— if I get caught with a bag in *my* hands—then all that's gone. Everything I been working for since I was a kid. All it'd take is one mistake, one drop goes wrong, and it's my name in the headlines. Them same articles Momma G's always sending me."

If Rae really had been there to write a feature on college football, she would've had enough meat to pen a real bang-up piece. But she was in Compson to investigate Speer Taylor and the Chiefs. She was there to nail Harry Christmas and bring his whole shady establishment down. After playing catch with the quarterback, Rae realized she couldn't involve him. Moses had a dream, and being a federal informant didn't fit into it. She felt the gash in her hand, a cold sting rising through warm blood. Rae'd lost the battle—she knew that much—but what about the war?

42

The eighteen members of the Chiefs' full-time coaching staff, plus ten "quality control" coaches and seven graduate assistants, were all crammed inside the staff meeting room. With nearly one hundred and twenty "student athletes" on the UCM roster, the large staff was necessary, especially since Speer Taylor insisted that every play of every practice be graded before anyone went home.

The grading system was simple. If a player performed his job, he got a "+." If he didn't, he received a "–." After all the marks were tabulated, each athlete was given a grade. For example, nine positive plays out of ten over the course of one practice earned a 90 percent. Coach Taylor was aloof when it came to many aspects of his football program, but he was a stickler when it came to practice grades. They were tangible. Something he could cite when decisions had to be made, hard choices like what to do about Moses McCloud.

"Coach Sessions?" Speer said, addressing the Chiefs' offensive coordinator. "What was Moses's grade from today?"

Todd Sessions was older than Speer Taylor by exactly twenty years, the yin to the younger head coach's yang. The Peter to his Paul. Todd slid a pair of slim rectangular glasses down from his salt-and-pepper hair, positioning them carefully—the way he did everything—on the bridge of his nose. "Seventy-nine out of ninety-nine," he said. "One play away from grading out."

In order to "grade out," a player needed an eighty percent or better for the day. A string of failed practices meant an athlete could be removed from the starting lineup.

"One play," Todd Sessions said. "One practice. That doesn't mean—"

"What about Billingsley?"

Todd Sessions' eyes rose behind his spectacles. "Samuel Billingsley graded at a hundred today, Coach."

"A hundred percent?"

"We're talking apples to oranges. We're talking about practice."

"You know how I feel about practice."

"But Billingsley only got ten reps. Moses got damn near a hundred."

Speer knew it would take more than one bad practice to justify benching Moses McCloud. He moved around behind the coaches and flipped two switches on the near wall. The room went dark. A projector screen rolled down from the ceiling.

"You said Moses completed ninety-nine reps at practice today," Speer said, "but you're forgetting one."

Speer tapped at the laptop plugged into the projector. Todd Sessions and every other coach in the room had witnessed Moses fleeing from that horse trough as if it were a tub full of snakes. The less-than-stellar practice grade was one thing, the product of a few missed reads, a couple late throws. The way that boy had turned his back on his team, his coach, *that* was a different situation altogether. Bad enough to warrant a reprimand, maybe even a suspension. Speer brought up the video Prism News had posted after practice, hoping the on-field, high-def footage would help drive his point home. He clicked play and full color, moving images of Samuel Billingsley splashing around in the horse trough filled the projector screen. The third-string quarterback's whole body fit inside the tub, cleats and all.

Fingers on the laptop's trackpad, Speer was planning to skip the rest of Sammy B's self-administered baptism, but then his cell phone buzzed. As the rest of the coaches watched the diminutive quarterback try, in vain, to free himself from the depths of the trough, Speer read the text he'd just received from an unknown number. The message was simple yet direct, concrete like the practice grades, but better.

Much better.

When Speer's eyes rose from his phone, Sammy B was gone, replaced by Moses McCloud, sprinting off the field so fast the film crew had trouble keeping him in focus. A half second later, Moses was at the sideline, running straight for a blocking sled. As the young man's feet left the ground, Speer paused the video, freezing the high-flying quarterback in a hurdler's pose.

"Let's take a moment," Speer said, eyeing Coach Sessions, "and make sure we're all on the same page here."

"Listen, Coach," Todd Sessions said and turned. "Moses is eighteen. He deserves a mulligan. I know that horse trough trick worked back in Memphis, but you can't just baptize every prima donna on the roster. Besides, if you bench Moses over this, we won't have an ice water's chance in—"

"Grade him, then." Speer pointed his phone at the projector screen. "Grade what you just saw on film."

Todd Sessions removed his glasses. He tapped the left temple against his bottom teeth. "Well, I mean, his running form isn't bad, and that hurdle . . . The kid cleared a five-foot-tall blocking sled."

Without looking at his most trusted assistant, Speer said, "So, you'd give him a plus?" both eyes fixed on Moses McCloud, the quarterback suspended in midair, unaware of the trap that had been set for him when he landed.

"I would, yeah," Todd Sessions said. "I'd give Moses a plus for the hurdle alone."

Speer closed the laptop and flicked on the lights. The projector screen creaked as it receded into the ceiling. The other coaches were still rubbing their eyes, waiting for clarity, when Speer said, "Then that means Moses scored an eighty out of a hundred today, correct?"

Todd Sessions folded his glasses. "You're saying he graded out?"

"He either did or he didn't," Speer said, thinking of the Gridiron Girl that anonymous text had just mentioned, her sacrifice. "I just want to make sure we're on the same page."

Todd Sessions ran a hand over his chin, shook his head, and said, "I hear you, Coach. We all do," pausing to give the rest of the staff time to grunt or nod, signaling their allegiance. "Loud and clear."

43

Sandy-eyed, Moses watched Compson drift by through the Impala's window. The redhead behind the wheel wasn't saying much, and that was cool. She was cool. Rae was taking him home, back to Starlight Apartments where he planned to sleep all the way through till noon. Hadn't done that in forever. Moses could catch a ride from Cerge. Pick his Altima up after practice. No problem. Give everything time to blow over. What was Coach Taylor gonna do, bench him?

Moses blinked and they were there, sitting in the Starlight Apartment parking lot, the miles between the C & G Railway and the UCM campus nothing but a dream, a manmade dividing line that didn't seem so solid anymore. Maybe things would get better. Maybe Moses would do like Cerge had told him on his recruiting visit and make things better. "*A Black quarterback in Compson, Mississippi . . . You know what that would mean?*"

Moses said, "Thanks for the ride," and waited, expecting the white woman to say something because, well, she was a white woman. A redhead that didn't act nothing like any reporter Moses had ever encountered, and he'd dealt with a few, at least one after every game all the way back to junior high.

The way this lady was leaned back in her seat, one hand on the wheel, hooded eyes moving in the dark, always moving, Moses almost realized what she looked like, the role she was playing, different from the one she'd told him. He almost had it. Might've even asked her straight up—*Hey. Are you a*—but she beat him to it, saying, "This little excursion is gonna cost me."

"Sorry about your hand."

"No, it's your pads. Forgot how much those things stink." Rae nodded at the shoulder pads in his lap. "I'll have to get my car detailed in the morning."

Moses wondered why a woman like Rae would know anything at all about shoulder pads. And where had she learned to catch like that?

Rae leaned across the cab and popped the door for him. "When you make it to the League, I'll send you the bill."

Moses grabbed his pads and said, "Deal," as he pulled himself up from the passenger seat. The night was cool, almost cold. His sweat had dried and felt sticky now, a thin scab coating his skin. Before he shut the door, Rae looked straight at him, green eyes focused like they'd been back on the field.

"You be careful out there. You hear me?"

Moses almost said *Yes, ma'am*, but gave her a thumbs up instead and turned for his apartment. He kept thinking about Rae, all those questions she'd asked, the questions he still had about her, while he slid his key into the door. When he made it to his room and spotted a pair of cyan-blue Lululemon leggings on the floor, same color as the sports bra a couple feet closer to the bed, Moses wasn't thinking about Rae anymore. The oversized Chiefs' T-shirt and the pair of tan UGGs, the kind with the real sheep's fur lining, had his full attention now.

Moses said, "Hello?" and took a small step forward, following the trail of women's clothing. A couple more steps and he was standing beside his bed, trying to remember the last time he'd changed his sheets. Been a minute. Couple weeks, at least.

All Moses could see was the girl's hair, a few stray curls slinking up and down over the pillow. His shoulder pads thumped against the wall nearest the door. He could smell the sweat on his chest, the stale scent of his breath.

The girl was flopping around like the old women at Momma G's church did anytime the keyboard player called down the Holy Ghost. Moses reached for the comforter and started to peel it back but felt weird because he was still thinking about church. What was even weirder, though, were the handcuffs the girl was holding up by one finger, just letting them dangle there.

Lying butt naked in bedsheets that hadn't been washed since the Southern Miss game, Ella May Pride rolled onto her back and said, "You gonna put these on me, or do I got to do it myself?"

Moses said, "Here," and slid the handcuffs off Ella May's pinky. He maintained eye contact, a bedroom stare, as he latched one cuff to her left wrist then clicked the other around the nightstand drawer.

Ella May said, "*Hey*," and jerked her hand. The chain between the cuffs pulled tight. The nightstand wobbled. "What the fuck, Moses?"

"Yeah, that's right," he said, still staring at her. "What the fuck?"

44

The motel maid liked to come by late. Frank hoped it was because she knew he'd be there and wanted to see him. The veteran special agent had never thought to get an apartment. What'd he need an apartment for when he had the Super 8, a cute little Mexican girl said her name was Yamilet who came by and changed his sheets for him every night? Took the wet towels hanging over the bathroom door and brought back new ones. Even folded the first square on the toilet paper roll into a triangle, which she was doing now. Frank watching her from the bed, hands behind his head, eyes on the mirror where he could see Yamilet bent over the toilet in her light gray skirt.

Must've been harder than it looked, getting that thin white paper to stay folded like that. Yamilet sure seemed to be having trouble with it. Or maybe, Frank thought, she's putting on a show, gyrating her hips side to side, pointing her plump little can straight at him.

Did it ever go away?

Frank's daddy'd told him it did. Tony Ranchino, a beer bottle in one hand, a smoked-down Camel in the other, grinning as he said to his son: "There's three great pleasures in life, Frankie . . ." His old man would bring the cigarette to his lips and take a long drag here, then wash the smoke down with a sip from his Heineken, making it obvious what the first two were, but waiting for his son to ask about life's third great pleasure, maybe wondering if little Frank already had it in him. (He did. There was a nun at his primary school Frank had had a thing for all the way back in second grade. Sister Clara sure could fill out a tunic.) Time for the punchline: Big Tony talking around the cigarette dangling from the corner of his lips, a line of smoke drifting up between his eyes as he said, "The third one's the best one, Frankie, but it gets taken from you in the end."

What Tony'd never told his son, though, was that even after his dick turned to mush, he'd still be thinking about it all the damn time. Like Frank was doing now, watching Yamilet stand and run her hands down the back of her skirt, smoothing the wrinkles out as she turned and said, "Will that be all, Mr. Ranchino?"

"How many times I got to tell you? Call me Fr—"

Frank's phone vibrated.

He reached for it, had the device in his hands, moving it toward one ear while cutting his eyes back at the bathroom, the place where Yamilet had been but wasn't anymore. The motel room door clicked as it latched behind the maid and Frank said, "The hell you calling so late for, kid? Yeah, I talked to Barb."

Barbara Lawrence was an old friend of Frank's. Okay, "friend" wasn't the right word. She was his boss. He knew how she worked. Frank knew what Sunday meant too: Barb delaying the inevitable. He didn't tell the rookie agent that. "If the director said she'd get back to us by Sunday, then she'll get back to us by Sunday."

Rae said a man's last name, followed by his first, like she was reading it out of that damn binder she lugged around everywhere. No, it wasn't a binder. It had a Velcro strap. What was it?

"The hell's Eddie Pride got to do with anything?"

Frank pictured her finger moving across the pages in her Trapper Keeper. *Shit.* That was it. A *Trapper Keeper.* Came back to Frank just like that, like nothing. The same way Rae was asking him to run Eddie Pride's tags, keeping her tone cool, nonchalant. She remembered Frank saying the big blue Ford belonged to Eddie Pride Junior, but she wanted to be sure. So, yeah, go ahead and run the plates, partner.

Phone wedged between his shoulder and his left ear, Frank grabbed the government-issued laptop off the bed beside him and opened it, grinning at the way Rae'd just called him "partner." Except it sounded more like "*pard*ner" when she said it. All those different degrees, the year she'd spent practicing law in DC, and Rae still couldn't get that Arkansas drawl out of her voice. Like she was auditioning for a part in a Western; Barbara Rush as Audra Favor in *Hombre*, the one where Paul Newman plays an Apache-raised white man and nobody knows his Christian name till he dies at the end. Fifteen years ago, Frank would've made his move already. Shit, he would've made *ten* moves.

It was better this way, Frank thought, typing 7-8-6-B-F-S into the Automated License Plate Reader before clicking the button that would tell him all he needed to know about the owner of the vehicle that had his partner worked up.

Rae said Eddie's name again, same way she'd said it before—last name first, first name last—as Frank read it off the screen, delivering a punchline of her own, setting him up for something. Frank didn't have to wait long to find out what. Rae said they needed an informant to corroborate any evidence they might produce from their meeting with Congressman Christmas.

"*Might*," Frank said and reached for his e-cig. He took a long, slow hit and thought of his father. Tony Ranchino with an electronic cigarette instead of a Camel Turkish Gold. No way. Never. Frank was older now than his old man had ever been.

Not a new revelation, but still, it was weird. "You hear me, kid? If Barb doesn't give us clearance, we won't have any evidence to corroborate. What a word. *Corroborate . . .*"

Rae didn't laugh. She wasn't joking. That wasn't why she'd called at a little past ten on a weekday night, right in the middle of Yamilet's visit. This was about Moses McCloud. Rae explained how she'd spent the last couple hours with him, and, get this, the quarterback's clean. He's never taken a penny from a bagman. Too scared. Worried he'll get caught and it'll be the end of everything.

Frank didn't ask about her visit with Moses. He didn't want to know when or where, why or how. He knew Rae was up to something. Just like she'd been up to something her first week on the case, making that move on Darren Floyd. It scared Frank. That was it. That's exactly how the rookie had made him feel ever since she'd arrived in Compson, *afraid*, and something else too. The way Rae's daddy must've felt watching her sprint down the runway with that pole in her hands, flying thirteen, sometimes fourteen feet in the air. Exhaling when she landed safe on the mat, the crowd clapping, maybe even chanting her weird name. Frank respected the girl's grit, her tenacity. But Jesus, now she wanted him to go have a chat with Eddie Pride Junior in the morning, see if he could get the bagman to squeal.

Frank said, "I'm not going undercover."

Rae said it was hard to ask someone to be an informant without letting them know you're a fed.

"An *informant*? The hell makes you think Eddie'd cop to a deal like that?"

Rae told Frank he could ask Eddie that same question, first thing in the morning, *partner*.

45

After four weeks, Eddie Pride's rope burn had scabbed over, but the neck brace was starting to itch. Stunk too. Boy, did it stink. A sickly-sweet stench like two-week-old General Tso's Chicken. His leg was even worse. The meat of his right thigh still oozed where the letter opener had pierced the skin, then the muscle. Tiny thing had damn near hit bone. Eddie knew that much, and this:

Ella May was one tough cookie.

His daughter had a 3.8 GPA and was studying to be an elementary school teacher. Eddie'd always envisioned Ella May getting hitched to some white quarterback who would take her all the way to Dallas, or maybe Atlanta, a Southern city with an NFL team. What made Eddie the proudest, though, was how Ella May didn't need him or nobody else. The girl could handle herself. If she did end up marrying the Cowboys' starting QB and living in a Highland Park mansion, Eddie knew she'd have some sort of side hustle going. Maybe get on one of those *Real Housewives* shows, let the world take a good look at her, show everybody up in New York how a Southern Belle handled her shit, staring straight into the camera on the season finale as she recalled this whole crazy ordeal, three little tow-headed kids running around the kitchen behind her with UCM shirts on, climbing up on the table and slamming cabinet doors but not bothering their momma one bit.

Eddie was back out on the old trailer porch he'd had his contractor attach to his new house, that damn noose still dangling above him. He'd left it there for motivation. Eddie didn't want to forget what he had to do and why he was doing it. This was for Ella May. After what Congressman Christmas had told him, Eddie didn't have any choice but to let his daughter go over to Moses McCloud's apartment. He'd spent the rest of the night and this far into the morning working on his other problem, his gambling problem. Eddie still owed that bookie in Tunica a buttload of cash. Which was why he was sitting in his grandpa's old rocker with his laptop on his belly, a sweet tea by his side, checking the odds for weird shit because that's where the money was.

Ten to one the Chiefs scored a touchdown on the first drive. *Not bad*, Eddie thought, beady eyes jittering over the computer screen. Fifteen to one Moses McCloud was the one who scored it. Now there was a bet Eddie hadn't thought of before, an angle that might play. If Ella May did her job, Moses McCloud wouldn't score shit. It was something to think about. Eddie still had a couple days. Didn't have to drive over to the Horseshoe and place his bets with that dirtbag bookie. Didn't even have to call him anymore. Eddie could just click a button on a screen and *voilà*. The wonders of the internet.

The noose danced above the bagman's head as he leaned forward, reaching for the sweet tea on the side table. The tea was in a Mason jar filled all the way to the brim. So full, Eddie didn't even have to turn the jar up; he could just press his lips to the rim and slurp some off the top. Eddie had the jar in his hands, craning his chin over the brace, when he noticed a car coming down his gravel road. Looked like something a woman might drive. Eddie kept his eyes on it and called his daughter's name then remembered Ella May was still off doing Lord knows what with you-know-who.

Eddie watched the car coming, thinking about how he'd always wanted a son. Told his wife, Darlene, that the day she gave birth. Told her boys were easy because you only had to worry about one dick; with a girl, you had to worry about every dick in the world. Eddie'd said some other stupid stuff and then Darlene was gone. Left him for a real estate agent named Chad Lancaster who lived up in Memphis. Eddie only got to see his daughter every other weekend for a while after that. Then Ella May came to school at UCM and he got to see her damn near every day. Never thought his little girl would become his right-hand man. His secret weapon. Eddie might've lost his pull, but after last night, Ella May would have that dual-threat QB by the balls. All Eddie had to do now was figure out the right way to play it.

The car came to a stop in the gravel drive. Up that close it looked less like a mom van and more like a station wagon. Made Eddie think of Darlene and the three boys she'd had with Chad Lancaster. The dude behind the wheel didn't look anything like a real estate agent. Didn't look like he belonged in Compson, that was for damn sure, just sitting there, staring up at the front porch with both hands on the wheel.

46

A noose? Frank thought and killed the engine. *Jesus*, these hicks really are stuck in the past.

Frank stepped out of the Subaru and flashed his badge at the porch. "Special Agent Frank Ranchino," he said. "I'm here to ask you a couple questions about your involvement with the UCM football team." Getting straight to the point with the overweight bagman. No more messing around. It felt good, better than he'd expected. "And before you go running your mouth, I want you to know I know what you've been doing."

Eddie said, "What?"

Frank, still standing behind the Subaru's open door, said, "I've been watching you for over a year, Mr. Pride. I know all about the money you've been paying the players."

"Is that a crime, Agent Ran . . ." Eddie shook his head.

"Ranchino."

"What's that, Cuban?"

"Italian."

Eddie took a sip from his Mason jar and set it on the table beside the rocker. "Listen, it's my money. Always thought I could spend it how I saw fit."

"Sure," Frank said. "Long as it's your money, you got nothing to worry about."

"It's my money, all right. I'm a Chiefs fan, through and through. Couldn't think of a better way to spend it. UCM football's a family tradition. You know my daughter's a Gridiron Girl?"

"You're saying your daughter's in on it too?" Frank shut the car door and stepped back, standing out in the open now.

"There ain't nothing to be in on."

"Does she pay the players?"

"Shit, she can't even pay her tuition."

"Nobody's talking about Benjamins, Mr. Pride. I'm talking about blue-chip athletes who don't play ball for nothing."

"Nothing? These boys come from *nothing*, pard, especially the Black ones. I'm just trying to help them out."

Frank saw Matt Talley's pale, lifeless eyes staring into the pitch-black sky after he'd hit the street outside the Buffalo Nickel, Eddie's dirty money settling all around him. Frank almost put his thought into words but that goddamn noose was still hanging right there, like some kind of backwards-ass windchime.

Frank said, "So, it's like a charity?" and looked down from the noose, leveling both eyes on Eddie. "That's what you're saying?"

"It ain't exactly a tax write-off." Eddie grinned. "I can tell you that much. Some people—people who got a lot more dough than me—they try to give away just enough dough to drop a tax bracket. That ain't charity. That's capitalism. The American Dream."

"So you pay the boys in cash. Make sure you don't leave a paper trail."

"There you go again, making it sound like I'm the bad guy."

"Just telling you what I know."

Eddie hitched his pants. "You know what would happen if the NCAA caught one of them boys with some extra spending cabbage in his pockets?"

Frank knew.

"Poor kid would get kicked off the team. Sent back to whatever cotton patch Coach Taylor plucked him from. Three months later, he's brought in for possession, or maybe steals a loaf of bread from the Piggly Wiggly, just trying to survive. That's how it goes around here, Frank. That's why I don't mind helping these boys out."

"A loaf of bread, huh?"

Eddie leaned over, going for the Mason jar on the side table. Sweet tea sloshed onto the porch. "Never met a real Yankee before. Always felt kinda bad thinking what I thought about people like you, especially since I ain't ever talked to one in real life." Eddie brought the Mason jar to his mouth and took a drink. When he finished, he went, "*Ahhh*," real loud and sat the jar back on the table. "Don't feel so bad about it now."

"You and me," Frank said, moving across the gravel drive, "we're not that different. These boys you been 'helping,' giving all that money to, they're the ones caught in the middle. Been stuck right there between us for a long time." Frank stopped when he got to the porch's first step. The noose was so close now, he could see all thirteen coils in the hangman's knot.

"I'm guessing it weren't just any boy you came out here to talk to me about."

Frank said, "Now we're getting somewhere," and started up the steps. "I'm here to talk about Moses McCloud."

"First thing you need to know about Moses, he's got his eyes on my daughter like a buck in rut."

"What's the next thing?"

"The next thing?"

"You said, 'First thing you need to know about Moses . . .' So, what's the next?" The oniony stench of body odor caught Frank by surprise. He held his breath and said, "What's the kid's story?"

The old rocker moved back then forward, groaning over the porch decking. "Well, all these boys got a story," Eddie said, "but Moses's got a *story*. A pure-dee shitkicker, if you know what I mean."

Frank said, "No, I don't," and exhaled. "Tell me about it."

47

Ella May Pride was still handcuffed to the nightstand when Moses awoke on the floor. At some point in the night, she'd put on one of his shirts. The black and yellow Wu-Tang tee was three sizes too big, large enough to cover her.

Moses's back hurt. His neck was sore. There was a phone tangled in the sheets, the same phone Moses had spotted propped up on the nightstand after he'd walked into his room eight hours before. The way it'd been positioned, the camera aimed at the bed, it was like spotting a safety creeping down before the snap. The freshman quarterback recognized the blitz. He knew, right then, Ella May was trying to sack him, catch him on camera with his pants down, in a compromising position or two. It made him recall the last time he'd seen the Gridiron Girl. Back at her apartment when Eddie'd asked him to throw the game then hauled out the money, the bag Moses wouldn't take. That's why Ella May was there. Poor thing. She was all her daddy had left to offer.

Moses reached for her leg, but noticed her thigh, all that exposed flesh rippling out from under the T-shirt's hem, and tapped her shoulder instead.

"Wake up."

Ella May smacked her lips and rolled over.

"Come on," he said, digging in his pocket for the handcuff key. "Get up."

Hair mussed, Ella May peeled herself from the bedsheets and stretched her free arm. "What time is it?"

Sunlight slanted sideways through the room's closed blinds. It was a little past eight already, but Moses still couldn't shake the bad feeling that had settled in his gut. Same way he felt anytime he'd had too much to drink. Which had only happened once over the course of his first college semester. Only happened that time because of "Big Cerge's Hunch Punch." When Moses's eyes opened the next morning, his lips were still red from the Kool-Aid Cerge had mixed with Everclear and NyQuil in his big orange Gatorade cooler. His eyes hurt anytime he moved them. His chest was worse, trapped under a heavy blanket of guilt. Like he'd done something he shouldn't have or said something he shouldn't have, even though he hadn't. Yeah. That's exactly how he felt staring at the half-dressed Gridiron Girl shackled to the nightstand beside his bed.

Only reason Ella May was still cuffed was because she wouldn't talk. Wouldn't tell Moses what she was doing, why she'd come to his apartment, but shit, now she was crying.

Moses took a long, slow breath, reached for her hand, and said, "What's wrong?"

"Everything."

"*Everything?*"

"They're saying I—" Ella May ran the back of one hand under her nose, unaware of herself in a way she hadn't been all night. For a moment, Moses thought he could really see her. "They're saying I pushed Matt. You know, on the roof that night? When I—"

Wails replaced her words, a high-pitched cry that made Moses's head hurt worse than Big Cerge's Hunch Punch. This was worse than hangxiety. Moses thought of that redheaded reporter from the night before. What had she said? Something about Ella May's and Matt's relationship.

"Who?" Moses swallowed. "Who thinks you . . . you know?"

"I don't know who they are, but it doesn't matter." Ella May threw her legs over one side of the bed. "Because I didn't do it."

Moses stood and started crawfishing until his heels touched the far wall, the one with his favorite Kobe Bryant poster tacked to it. "You were up there, though." He said, "I saw you go up on the roof," then thought, *Thank God for Cerge*, remembering how the running back had slammed the stairwell door. How he'd told Moses to let Matt and Ella May handle their own shit, and he did. Moses left the Buffalo Nickel and went to the Burger King on Durant where he'd had it his way and ordered the number nine Double Whopper combo meal.

Ella May said, "We got into it. Me and Matt," both feet on the carpeted floor now. Thanks to the handcuffs, the nightstand, that was as far as she could go. "It was nothing, really, a silly argument. I came back downstairs and ordered a Tipsy Toma-hawk."

"That ain't all you did," Moses said. "You called *me*, Ella May. Told me to come over to your apartment the next morning."

"That was different." She smiled and Moses noticed the dimples in her cheeks, similar to the ones on her lower back he'd spent the whole night trying to ignore. "That didn't have nothing to do with this."

Back to the wall, shoulders framed by the "Mamba Mental-ity" poster, Moses said, "This? What the hell is *this*?" and felt bad when Ella May flinched. Momma G had raised him better. "Listen, I'm sorry. I shouldn't have—"

Before he could finish the sentence, Ella May lurched forward and started dragging the nightstand across the lam-inate tile. The lamp toppled sideways. Cords ripped free of the wall. It was like something from a horror movie. *Attack of the Five-Foot Cheerleader.* Ella May was stronger than she looked, gaining ground with every step, and then she was there, close enough to reach out and wrap both arms around Moses's waist.

He said, "No, wait . . ." but didn't push her away. Moses liked the way she fit into his arms, the warmth of her head on his chest stirring sympathy in his heart. Ella May didn't want to be there; she'd been sent there. She'd sacrificed her body for the team, for UCM. Moses understood that. His back and neck had been sore long before this morning, but what choice did he have? He still had to play the game, and so did Ella May. Moses felt a new bond forming, something deeper than their current embrace. They'd both been duped but for different reasons, tricked into believing the same lie as everyone else in Compson.

"I didn't do it. I swear to God, Moses. I didn't . . ."

Still holding onto her, Moses said, "If you didn't, who did? Who killed Matt Talley?"

Ella May leaned back and frowned. "He fell."

"You sure about that?"

"I mean, he was really drunk."

Moses remembered watching Matt bird walking around the bar, how much trouble he'd had with the steps. Something clicked over in his mind, a new path forming, a crease in the defense. "Okay, yeah. Matt was drunk," Moses said. "*Really* drunk. Which means we don't have nothing to worry about."

"Um, no?"

"Yes, Ella May. That's it. We just gotta keep our mouths shut. These guys, whoever they are, they're just using you to get to me. All because I didn't take that money, because I wouldn't throw the game."

"And you still won't? Even after what I just told you?"

Moses thought of his dream, his plan, and how a cheating scandal was worse than taking a bribe. Cheaters didn't just get punished, they got banned, banished from ever stepping foot on a field again.

"I can't lose. I won't, okay?" Moses extended the handcuff key. "Promise."

Ella May said, "Sure make things easier if you would," before grabbing the key and unlocking the cuffs. She snatched her leggings next, followed by her sports bra, her fuzzy shoes, her phone, then marched out of the bedroom wearing nothing but his T-shirt and a cheeky pair of UCM panties.

Moses stood in the doorway and watched Ella May go, thinking about another woman in his life, the one he'd played that game with the night before. Rae had caught everything he'd thrown at her. Ripped her hand clean open then clapped for more. But what about this? How would Rae handle a story like this? Moses reminded himself she was a reporter, a woman who wrote articles like the ones Momma G sent him every week, and shut his apartment door.

48

"**One whole** year I been in Compson, trying to put all those pieces together," Frank said, still leaned back on Eddie Pride's porch rail, Eddie in the rocker, an empty Mason jar in his hands, "but now that I heard that kid's story—the whole thing from start to finish—I'm starting to think I could've been here ten more years and never gotten it straight."

Eddie rested the jar on his stomach. "It's different down here. Can tell you that much. Just means more."

"I call my buddies back in Brooklyn, these lonely, retired guys, and try to tell them about it. They say, 'Come on, Frankie. You gotta be shitting me.'"

The Mason jar on Eddie's belly bobbed up and down, timing up with his laugh.

Frank watched him, wondering why he was talking to the bagman like he was from Kings County. Like they were old pals went way back to St. Francis of Assisi. Frank didn't know Eddie. Not really. The guy had just told him this real sad story about Moses McCloud. How the kid got stuck down in the weeds or some shit. Frank saying, "*Kudzu?*" when Eddie got to that part, watching the guy nod off the porch to the thicket of trees covered in vines. Frank had seen the stuff everywhere around Compson—some of the buildings downtown swallowed whole—but he'd never wondered if it had a name. Now all he could think about was a little Black kid stuck down deep in there for two whole days.

No wonder Eddie wanted to help Moses, and that was fine.

Honorable even. Made Frank see that neck brace in a new light. He felt himself starting to like the guy he'd been going after for so long. Except Eddie was the wrong guy. The fall guy. Just a middleman. And he stank too. So bad, Frank guessed it was some sort of condition and didn't bring it up.

"Listen, I know I just told you a whole buncha crap, but you're still a fed and I'm still upside down with some bad dudes," Eddie said, squinting as he lifted one finger from the Mason jar, pointing up to the noose and the cracked porch beam. "What I'm saying is, I can't say nothing else."

"Yeah," Frank said. "I know."

Crows cawed from somewhere in the cotton field surrounding Eddie's house. The sun hung low out over the horizon, a darker shade of orange than the sun Frank remembered up north. Or maybe he'd just never seen it get that low before. Too many buildings.

"All right, then," Eddie said, pushing up from the rocker. "Guess it's about that time. I still gotta crunch some numbers."

"Numbers?" Frank slid down off the porch rail. "What numbers?"

"Gotta find me a longshot. A prop bet that's gonna pay out."

"Sport betting's illegal in the state of Mississippi," Frank said.

Eddie sat the Mason jar on the side table and reached for his laptop.

"But I'll let the bets slide," Frank said, "if you answer one more question."

"One, my ass."

"You said things went sideways after Matt Talley muffed the big one."

"Talley didn't muff nothing, and that's the problem."

"So, that's what you're doing on your laptop there, cooking up something that pays better than just throwing a game. Big enough you didn't mind getting your daughter involved in it."

Eddie's upper lip curled at the mention of Ella May.

"Easy, I get it." Frank lifted both hands. "They got you backed into a corner, and the kid ain't some punk loser. He's just Black, which is still a big deal down here."

Eddie's lip relaxed, a little.

"I'm thinking out loud. That's all. Just ol' Frank thinking . . ." The special agent stared up into the porch's ceiling and noticed for the first time it was blue, a baby blue that didn't match the rest of the house.

Eddie said, "Yeah?"

Frank wondered about the weird blue paint, how it was worn away where the rope wrapped around the beam, but he'd asked for one question, and this was it, what he'd come all the way out there to say: "If you're willing to come clean, you know, go on record, then I could get you off the hook. Offer you protection, immunity, the whole nine yards." Frank shrugged then scratched his armpit. "How's that sound?"

Eddie tugged at the fabric of his polo shirt, pulling it off his belly. "Not sure how y'all do it up in Yankee-ville, Frank, but it takes ten yards to get first down around here." The bagman stomped his feet so hard he almost dropped the laptop.

"Come on. That sort of information could bring a pretty penny."

"How much we talking?"

"Six figures, maybe more, depending on the dirt."

"After taxes," Eddie said and reached for his tea, "that wouldn't be shit."

Frank said, "Okay," and started off the porch. He stopped

when he was out from under the noose. "Hey, Eddie? This conversation, it never happened. Okay?"

The bagman brought the Mason jar to his lips and frowned when nothing came out.

"I'm serious. My job's on the line here," Frank said. "Which is why I looked into your beach-chair business."

"Lazy Dayz?"

"Tax evasion's a federal offense, a bigger deal than sports betting. Minimum sentence is right around five years' time. Two thousand days. Fifteen hundred if you're on your best behavior."

"Yeah, well," Eddie said, picking at the brace's Velcro strap, "at least I'd be alive."

"This thing plays out like I want it to, you won't have nothing to worry about. You'd be in the clear with the government's money in your pocket. Just think about it, okay? You get a wild hair, call the Super 8 and ask for Yamilet. She knows where to find me."

Frank made it back to his Subaru, Eddie behind him, muttering, "You can't help me, Frank, and I can't help you. We're just too damn different. Been like that forever, and it's only getting worse."

Frank left Eddie on his front porch talking about the past, the future, how it was brother against brother, the whole country still at war. Frank thought real hard about that on the drive back into Compson, the highway lined with vines he'd missed on his way out, acre after acre, covered in kudzu, the creepers like a curse, a plague that hung heavy over the South.

49

Rae went for a drive Sunday morning and made two laps around Sutpen Stadium. Moses wasn't there, of course. Moses was in Dallas already, along with the rest of the Chiefs. She didn't have anywhere to go, no leads to follow, but the drive kept her from thinking about the big game tomorrow and the call with her SAC that was scheduled for today, the conversation where Barb would tell Rae if she was finally going to let her play.

When she got back, Rae was surprised to find Darren Floyd sitting on the curb outside her apartment, a battered guitar case standing on edge between a pair of gator-skin shoes.

"Miss me?"

Darren in a bowler hat and cream-colored cardigan. Looked like something Mister Rogers would wear, but still looked good on Darren Floyd. Rae answered his question by pecking his left cheek on her way to the door. She had missed him. Darren was fun. Those first two days on the case had been wild, running all around the Delta with a real-life bluesman.

In the time since she'd last seen Darren, Rae'd been back to a couple more practices. She'd watched the Prism News crew follow Coach Taylor around, Moses and Cerge slicing up the scout team defense. The horse trough was gone, packed away with the water cows in the stadium's underground utility shed. *The hay's in the barn, the horses fed.* Something her daddy always said on Fridays after a good practice week.

Rae wondered what her daddy was doing now. Probably kicked back in the eight-bed, eleven-bath mansion Texas Tech had paid for with those monthly buyout checks. The same home where Rae had spent the evening part of her youth. The three covered patios, the pool, custom hot tub, lighted sports court with the infrared, recessed heaters. Chuck stayed out in the guest house, mostly. That's where Rae imagined her father now, watching Speer Taylor on ESPN, poor-mouthing his team at the pregame press conferences, citing their freshman quarterback as a "definite question mark." Which, Rae guessed, was true. Even though Moses McCloud had dismantled the Bulldogs and the Crimson Tide, the Buckeyes were a different story. What would he do when the lights clicked on and a hundred thousand fans started screaming, more than half of them from Ohio? There was no way to know, not until tomorrow.

Today, however, was the day the rookie special agent had been waiting for. The day she'd learn if her hay was in the barn. After Rae's night with Moses, and Frank's worthless chat with Eddie Pride, any hope they'd had of securing an informant was gone. Thanks to Darren, though, the meeting with Harry Christmas was still on. All Rae needed now was her SAC's clearance and she'd be watching the Cotton Bowl from the congressman's luxury box.

Darren said, "Like what you've done with the place," as he walked into Rae's apartment. She watched him lay the guitar's hard case longways on the floor and begin flipping the brass latches up. "Wrote you a song."

Rae was wearing same outfit she'd worn to the Waffle House that night with Frank. *Frank*, Rae thought, imagining him behind the wheel of his Subaru, or maybe watching *The Sopranos* back at the Super 8. She slipped her phone up from her shirt's breast pocket and saw three missed calls from Agent

Ranchino. A couple texts too. No word from Barbara Lawrence, though. Not yet.

"Didn't know you wrote your own songs?"

"I didn't," Darren said, opening the case's lid, revealing a wine-red velveteen lining. "Not until I went back home."

"Home?"

"Told you I was going up to Detroit, remember? Better than getting hauled out to Sudan. But all that time away made me realize what I'd left behind."

Rae bit her bottom lip.

"Two types of blues songs," Darren said. "There's blues about a man—*the man*—and blues about a woman."

Rae said, "Two types, huh?" thinking about Ma Rainey and Sister Rosetta Tharpe. Etta James too. Miss Peaches was as good as it got but apparently not good enough for Darren Floyd. Or maybe he was just trying to make a point. People did that sometimes. Said things they didn't mean.

"Yeah, see, you got songs like 'Real Real Gone' by John Lee Hooker, or 'Country Girl Blues' by Memphis Willie B. Kept listening to that Willie B. tune, trying to put my own spin on it while I was in Detroit."

"Are you calling me a country girl?"

"Listen how you just said that. *Kuntry gurl.*" Darren paused, proud of his impersonation. "Me? I grew up in *De*troit. Almost forgot how big the city is, just block after block of empty towers and parking garages. So big it made all this stuff we got going on down here seem small."

"Cowboys Stadium is over three million square feet."

"Been doing your homework, huh?"

"Most of the skyboxes have their own bars, theater seating."

Darren had the guitar out of the case now, perched high on his right knee. He dropped a brass slide onto his fretting hand's pinky and began pulling low blue notes from the Dobro's strings. Rae touched her neck, the skin there warm already and getting warmer as the bluesman worked his way up the fretboard. Each note higher than the last. She kept waiting for him to sing. Rae wanted to hear the words Darren had written for her in Motor City. Maybe it wasn't that sort of song. Maybe there weren't any words for whatever it was they had going. Without the case, was there anything at all?

Rae moved in behind him, ready to find out.

Darren's laugh timed up with his tune, the one he said he'd written for her that sounded familiar now. Rae was trying to think where she'd heard it, or if she'd ever heard it at all—maybe it was just the blues she recognized—when her chest started to pulse, her phone, vibrating over her heart.

She pushed up from the sofa, half hoping to see Frank's name on the screen. She swallowed and said, "Hello? Yes, *yes*, I can hear you . . ." Rae steadied herself by watching Darren work the frets, but she couldn't hear the guitar anymore, just her SAC's monotone voice giving her the news she'd waited all week, all month, to hear.

"You're serious? No . . . I mean, yes. I understand. But let me tell Frank. Okay? Okay. Yeah, thanks, Barb." A pause. "Tickets?"

Rae pictured Barbara Lawrence's Botoxed forehead, the lines that should've been there but weren't. The rookie agent brought a hand to her mouth, biting the meat of her palm as she said, "Sure, but can I get three?" then nodded and hung up without saying goodbye.

Darren turned, the last note still vibrating deep inside the resonator. That's how quick the call was. So short Darren didn't get it. "I was thinking maybe we should go over the details. You know, talk everything through. How we're gonna play it at the game tomorrow."

Rae gripped her phone, the conversation with Barbara Lawrence rewinding in her mind. A weaker woman might've cried. A muscle in Rae's jaw pulsed. That was it. Her only visible sign of distress, and Darren missed that too.

"I mean, we gotta get Harry talking." He hooked one elbow over the back of the secondhand sofa. "The way we got it set up, it's like you're scoping out the Chiefs for your daddy. You wanna know how they handle their business. Right?"

"Sure."

Darren stood. "Hey, what's wrong?"

He was on his feet, coming around the sofa now, a few more seconds, a couple more steps, and he'd be there, close enough maybe he'd finally see the truth, then what? What would Darren do if she told him her SAC had denied the clearance?

Rae didn't wait to find out.

This time, her lips didn't peck his cheek. This time, they found their mark and pushed past it, so hard Rae's front teeth touched Darren's. The bluesman didn't have any trouble unclasping her bra, and that was nice, different from her college days. Darren paused just long enough to sit the Dobro in its case. The lights were still on when they rolled backward over the sofa and slid in next to the guitar.

50

Eddie Pride Junior stared down at the "mission-style rocker" Harry Christmas had said might bring a pretty penny at the Antiques Roadshow. The bagman's eyes ticked to the left, stopping on the side table where he'd sat his burner phone, the one Harry had given him.

"Fucking Frank," Eddie muttered, thinking back on his talk with the fed. Ella May had come home from Moses's place an hour later. Pissed. That's what Ella May was, telling Eddie he was her daddy, he should've never sent her over there with those cuffs. Like he didn't feel bad enough. What Eddie wanted to know was did she do it? Did she have the video?

A gleam in her eye, Ella May'd said, "Nope."

"Shit, baby girl. This is your ass on the line here. They're saying you—"

"Moses wouldn't touch me."

"Wait. What? Is he—"

"That boy's straight as Highway 61. Won't bend for nobody. Not even me."

Was Eddie disappointed? Sure, in himself, mostly. He'd asked too much, pushed too hard, and things had gotten out of hand. Eddie told Ella May to go take a shower, a nice long bath. He didn't care if she went and jumped in the creek, so long as she came back clean.

Ella May said, "*Clean?*" like she'd never heard the word before, but she had heard it, at least once, back before Darlene left Eddie and moved to Memphis with Chad. Maybe that's where it all went wrong. Eddie wasn't sure, and Ella May didn't wait for him to figure it out. She stormed off the porch, stomped up the stairs, and slammed what Eddie hoped was the bathroom door.

Still standing on his front porch, Eddie Pride Junior found himself caught between the federal government and a crooked congressman. His baby girl's future was at stake, and it was all his fault. Eddie'd gotten her mixed up in this. He'd given her that money bag after he'd kicked Matt Talley out of his truck. Damn kid wouldn't shut up about Favre. Didn't care one lick about what he'd done, what he'd set in motion by scoring that last-second touchdown. That's when this whole new game had kicked off.

Staring up at the noose, the same rope the Compson PD had wrapped around his neck, Eddie reached for the burner Harry Christmas had given him. The congressman had also stabbed him in the thigh. The wound seeped in the mornings. It still hurt, but goddamn, Frank Ranchino was a fed.

The phone rang before Eddie could place the call. Hand to his heaving chest, eyes scanning the shadows beyond the porch, the bagman answered, saying, "Yeah?" hoping to set the tone but the old man on the other line was a step ahead of him, like always.

The conversation was short and to the point, Eddie's final job, a blocking assignment, delivered in less than a minute.

As soon as the call was over, the wind picked up from the north. The noose swayed in the breeze, but the rope didn't scare Eddie so bad anymore. Neither did Frank Ranchino. It was Ella May. He couldn't stop thinking about his daughter. She still had her whole life—the NFL QB, the reality TV show, and the houseful of kids—out ahead of her so long as Eddie executed the congressman's new plan.

51

Six hours later, Rae was finally alone.

Darren had fallen asleep on the sofa, mouth open, making zoo noises until Rae shook him awake and said, "That couch ain't big enough for the both of us, bub." Darren rubbed his face and gave her a one-sided, sleepy grin. She fastened the latches on his guitar case, then walked him to the door, telling him to get some rest, she'd pick him up first thing in the morning.

Ten more hours, and she'd be there, empty-handed, all dressed up with nowhere to go. *"A cover like that can't be back-stopped, Agent Johnson. It doesn't pass the smell test."* The smell test? That's what Barbara Lawrence had said before telling the rookie to sit back and watch the game. Said the tickets were on the house, so go on. Dallas was fun if you didn't mind cowboy hats and concrete.

Rae didn't get it. She'd been there over a month. She had inroads with Darren Floyd. Even if he wasn't a real bagman, he still had enough pull to set up a meeting with Congressman Christmas. If Harry ran her credentials, he wouldn't find a ghost or any gaps in the story. Rae *was* Chuck Johnson's daughter.

Frost rimmed the apartment's lone window. Rae was back there again, the same spot she'd stood when she'd called Barb at the start of the week. She thought of her SAC mostly as "Barb" now, a thorn in Rae's ass. Her reflection moved in the darkened glass. It felt like watching someone else. The woman Rae'd been on that practice field beside the church, catching everything Moses threw at her. Even after her side cramped and her legs went wobbly, even after the ball ripped her hand wide open, Rae kept going. If Moses hadn't stopped her, she might still be out there.

Sometimes you've got to lose the battle to win the war.

That's what Moses had said, but he was just a kid. What did he know about losing?

Staring into the window's glass, Rae noticed her Trapper Keeper lying open on the kitchen counter. She hadn't gone through it in days. She knew the case by heart. Everything came down to Harry Christmas, getting the congressman to talk. Their meeting was still scheduled for tomorrow, but Barb didn't care. Barb didn't see it like Rae saw it. She hadn't spent the last month organizing every detail, making sure the case was airtight.

Shadows hid the dirty dishes, the trash bags piled by the door. Rae stepped around the mess on her way through the kitchen. She pulled back the Trapper Keeper's Velcro flap, still not sure what she expected to find. Every note she'd taken had led her here, to this, a dead end.

Paper rustled. Sheet after sheet. It wasn't until the last page had been turned over that Rae spotted something she'd missed. A note she'd scrawled on the binder's back flap two decades before.

Work hard, never quit, and good things'll happen.

Rae had been sitting in her father's office when she'd first heard that now infamous line. A frantic Sunday afternoon spent at the field house, helping her dad get a head start on his next opponent. His team had lost the day before, the week prior too. Another loss, and Chuck feared his team would quit on him. Rae traced his words with one finger and could hear his voice again, trying to find the perfect message to motivate his boys come Monday:

"Water boils at two-hundred-and-twelve degrees Fahrenheit, gentlemen, and boiling water makes steam. Steam has the power to propel a locomotive, to cut through—" Chuck kept stopping and starting, feeling his way into the speech. "But what if you quit before you reach your boiling point? I'll tell you. Nothing. If you make it all the way to two-hundred-and-eleven and stop, all you got is hot water."

Rae recalled Chuck liking the imagery but fearing the metaphor would be lost on his players. He needed something simpler, a single line even the meatiest of meatheads could discern.

"Work hard, never quit, and good things'll happen." Chuck had grinned as he uttered the sentence. He liked it so much he'd said it again, and again. Rae liked it too, enough she'd written it on her binder's back flap. She'd done more than that, though. Rae had lived by those words.

Which made her wonder: Why stop now?

FOURTH QUARTER

When an athlete, no matter what color jersey he wears, finally realizes that opponents and teammates alike are his adversaries, and he must deal and dispense with them all, he is on his way to understanding the spirit that underlies the business of competitive sport. There is no team, no loyalty, no camaraderie; there is only him, alone.

—Peter Gent, *North Dallas Forty*

52

When Frank answered the door at the Super 8, Rae had her lines ready. She told him she wanted to drive. Dallas was a seven-hour haul west through Arkansas, her old stomping grounds. If they didn't stop for lunch, they'd make it to the Big D by four, still have three hours to grab a bite, get their bearings, and get set up for the game. She didn't mention anything about her call with Barb.

It wasn't until she stopped talking that Rae noticed Frank's outfit. The veteran special agent was wearing a black sport coat over a teal-green sweater, a new pair of oxblood loafers peeking out from under his jeans. No scuffs in the leather. No wrinkles. Like he'd gone out and bought the whole outfit just for today. The badge clipped to his belt sealed the deal; Frank Ranchino finally looked like a fed.

Sounded like one, too, when he said, "You ain't driving, kid. We're taking my car. Let's go." His voice different, serious, as he turned and shuffled down the stairwell without reaching for the rails.

They drove through downtown Compson in silence, the sun slipping between the old brick buildings and into Rae's eyes, making her squint so bad she almost missed Sutpen Stadium, a giant concrete bowl with a tiny green rectangle in the heart of it. Rae studied the scoreboard, the same one Moses McCloud had lit up the Saturday after Thanksgiving. It was early January now, still two weeks left in UCM's Christmas break. The campus was mostly empty, vacant like that look in her partner's eyes.

Another part of Frank's new tough-guy routine? Rae wasn't sure. She felt the same way about what she was doing, going against Barbara Lawrence's direct orders. Going rogue.

It wasn't as crazy as it sounded. Her meeting with Harry Christmas was still on. All she had to do was make it up to the skybox and get the congressman talking. The more she thought about it, the more Rae realized she didn't need Frank to come at all. She tried picturing him in the stands. The green sweater, that black coat, sneaking hits from his e-cig like he was doing now, the red tip flashing on and off like a traffic light.

It made the rookie agent stop. Made her curious. A couple more miles, and they'd be at Floyd's Fresh Fish. Rae said, "Cut the crap, Frank. Whatever you're thinking, just say it."

53

Frank was thinking all sorts of stuff, same shit he'd been thinking since he talked to Barbara Lawrence real late the night before, but he said, "I been thinking about Christmas . . ."

"Harry?"

"No, the holiday. How'd you do it growing up? Have to split time between your parents' parents? That's the way it was for us. A friggin' whirlwind. The kids could barely get their presents open before it was time to go."

"I said cut the crap, Frank. Not tell me a Christmas story."

The way Rae had her head turned, Frank couldn't see her face. He didn't have to see her to know the bridge of Rae's nose was all wrinkled, lines that would go away after a while but come back and stay forever when she got to be his age. That's the Rae that had Frank worried, the woman she'd become after today. After he'd talked to his Special Agent in Charge, after Barb had delivered word that the jig was up, his final case closed, Frank had spent the rest of the night rereading his partner's files. Rae was younger than he'd figured. Just turned thirty in September, a Virgo who thought she knew what she wanted, but Frank knew better. Nobody knows nothing before forty.

"Wait," Rae said. "You have *kids*?"

"That's what I'm talking about. Partners I had in the past, we covered stuff like that over coffee. Felt each other out so when the shit hit the fan, like it's about to do here in"—Frank checked the time on the dash—"here in a few more hours, we'd know what to expect."

The veteran agent paused, giving the rookie time to come clean, to tell him, straight up, about the little stunt she was trying to pull. When she didn't, Frank said, "A married guy's gonna react differently in the line of fire."

"You're married too?"

"I was. Her name was Jamie. We went to high school together but didn't get serious till later. So serious we never really knew each other. Not with the way I was working back then. Shit. Nothing's changed. That's what I'm trying to tell you."

The wrinkles across the bridge of Rae's nose were so deep Frank couldn't help but grin, which made it worse. His partner looked like some sort of *Star Trek* creature, a Klingon, as she said, "If you're saying there's more to life than being a federal agent. *Hey*—quit smiling at me like that. What's wrong with you?"

Frank had all sorts of problems Rae didn't know about. He'd joked with her about his deafness, how he couldn't hear so good in his left ear, but never told her the whole story. Frank shot a guy named Stanley Loperfido—white male, age twenty-four—in the chest his second year on the job; year three of life with Jamie, their last one together; two toddlers in diapers tearing their one-bedroom apartment—their lives—apart. The Bureau took his badge and kept it for six months after that. They sent Frank to see a counselor, a young guy with glasses in a leather chair; Frank beside him on the sofa, a patch of white gauze taped to his hurt ear, telling the shrink, "The punk hit me with a pipe. Damn near took my head off," every time the doc asked him why he'd shot Mr. Loperfido. Jamie got the kids, and eventually Frank got reinstated, stuck behind a desk answering the phone and filing papers for twenty years until somebody in a suit decided to send him to Compson, Mississippi. Being back in the field made it hard to forget that night in the alley outside The Wrong Number, the dive bar where Frank sat watching the Mets in a doubleheader against the Red Sox when he should've been back in that one-bedroom apartment helping Jamie put the kids to bed. Four Heinekens and a shot of Jameson later, Roger "The Rocket" Clemens retired the side, Frank walked out into that alley, and the first game was over, the one where he'd been half-assing his role as a husband, a father; that part of his life finished the moment Stanley Loperfido stepped up to the plate.

"I'm worried, kid. That's what's wrong with me." The Subaru came to a stop at a Chevron, still a couple miles away from Darren's place. He brought the e-cig to his lips and inhaled, then hit it again. "I'm worried how this is gonna play out for you."

"*Me?* Wait, Frank. Why did you stop?"

Frank said, "I'm running low on gas, and I still want to talk to you about Christmas." He watched Rae make her Klingon face as he stepped out of the Subaru and left the door open. "Just listen to me, okay? Twenty years from now, and every year in between, you're gonna be sitting across the dining-room table from your daddy, passing him the cranberry sauce without looking him in the eye. Both of you feeling weird around each other for all that time. Because of what? This game? Your first investigation?" Frank counted the reasons off on his fingers, stopping after two. "Think about it." He paused, watching the rookie trying to figure out what he was saying, how much he knew. "The cranberry sauce. Twenty years is a long-ass time."

Rae said, "They don't have cranberry sauce at Ho Ho's," surprising the veteran agent like she always did. The girl was really something.

Frank said, "Ho Ho's, huh?"

"It's the only place in Fayetteville open Christmas Day. Ho Ho's. It's a Chinese buffet."

"Kinda like in that movie. What's it called?"

"You'll shoot your eye out, kid."

"Yeah, that's what they keep telling him. *A Christmas Story.* That's it. Little Ralphie wants a BB gun, then gets one and goes out and shoots himself in the face. Not the eye." Frank slipped the gas nozzle into the Subaru's tank and pulled the trigger. "Bet it still stung like a son of a bitch. Hurt bad enough maybe the kid learned a lesson without losing anything." Frank gave that line a second to sink in, still holding the trigger down, the e-cig dangling from his lips. "The neighbors' dogs bust through the screen door after that and eat all the turkey."

"You're losing me, Frank."

"Ralphie's family, they wind up at a Chinese joint for Christmas dinner, the waiters singing, 'Deck the halls with boughs of holly, fa *ra ra ra ra* . . .' The cook brings out a roasted duck, the head still attached to the body?"

"Okay, yeah. I remember that part."

"But do you know what I'm saying?"

Rae took a strand of red hair down from behind the ear closest to Frank and started twisting it around a finger.

Frank said, "We both know what's happening here, what's happened already," as the trigger clicked then went slack in his hand, the tank full now, ready to go.

Just like Rae, still twirling her hair as she said, "I don't know what you're talking about," then took hold of the door handle, itching to get off the sideline and into the game so bad there was nothing Frank could say that would stop her. So, he didn't.

He took his receipt and got in the car at the same time as Rae got out. Like she could feel what was coming. The girl had strong instincts, a sixth sense that would serve her well in the world of federal investigation. Rae had her whole career in front of her.

"Whatever you're thinking," the redhead said, talking through the crack in the window, repeating the first words she'd said to him on their last day together, their last moment, maybe, "just say it."

"You, partner. I'm thinking about you."

Rae's red hair danced in the wind, framing the confused expression on her face as Frank jerked the Subaru into gear and pulled away.

54

The car made it out from under the Chevron's blue awning twenty, maybe thirty feet, before the brake lights flashed. Rae could see Frank's bad ear in the side mirror. She pictured his face, grinning like he'd been when he was talking about Christmas. Like this was all just one big joke. Rae watched the white lights replace the red as the Subaru started to reverse.

When the driver-side window came down, Frank's eyes were up, staring straight into the rearview mirror as he said, "Forgot to tell you, the tickets are at the will-call booth. All three of them. Barb put them under my name for some reason."

Rae slapped the Subaru's hood, hard enough Frank had to look at her. "You called the SAC?"

"Oh, so I got your attention now? And no, she called me."

"I told her not—" Rae stopped, but Frank knew what she was about to say. "You were talking about a Christmas movie, Frank. And then you left. You just drove away."

"Yeah, I did, and I'm about to do it again, soon as we get this part over with." He shrugged and there was sadness in his shoulders. "Whatever you got cooking—whatever you think you're doing—I can't be a part of it."

"And what, exactly, do you think I'm doing?"

"Come on, kid."

Rae scanned Frank's eyes. He had pretty eyes, long lashes she'd never noticed before. "Listen, I'm going to—"

"Don't say it. I've worked too long to get here. I know it don't sound like much, but government pension's no joke. This is it, the end of my career. Let me do it my way, okay?"

Rae saw Frank's outfit in a different light now. How, at some point, before she'd knocked on his motel room door, he'd had to make a choice about what to wear and decided to ditch the don't-give-a-shit Hawaiian shirt for something more formal, like what he might wear to his retirement banquet, the one where the Director would give him that plaque he'd been talking about their first day together. Maybe the big boss would say a few nice words, tell a couple Frank Ranchino jokes. Maybe not. It all depended on how things played out today. A man clipping his badge to his belt and pulling the tags off a teal-green sweater over in the Super 8 before the sun came up Monday morning—that's the image Rae had in mind now, wondering what other choices Frank had made. What had she missed?

"The tickets." Frank kept his eyes straight ahead and the e-cig clamped in his teeth. "They're at the will-call booth under—"

"—your name. I heard you the first time."

Frank nodded and the Subaru lurched forward again. Rae's hand shot through the open window and latched onto his wrist. She trotted along beside the moving car, then slowed to a walk, then finally stopped altogether. Rae could feel his pulse rising beneath her fingers.

"Already said everything I got to say," Frank said.

"And you're still letting me go?"

"*Letting* you? If there's one thing I've learned over the last month, it's that you don't listen to nobody, me especially."

"So, you expect me to do what, exactly?" Rae said, still holding onto him.

"Just go. Get outta here, kid." Frank placed his hand over hers and plucked Rae's fingers, one by one, from his wrist. "Before I change my mind."

55

Darren said, "Where's Frank?" when he opened the restaurant's back door. Rae stared up at him, perspiration dotting her lip even though it was cold for Mississippi, lows in the upper forties.

"Frank?"

"Yeah, your partner."

It surprised Rae he didn't mention the sweat or the fact that she was late. A little after ten already and they still had five hundred miles to go.

"Frank's back on the wagon. Doesn't want you and your Marlboros tempting him all the way to Dallas."

"He's taking his own car. That's what you're saying?"

"Yeah."

"And you . . ." Darren said, his voice rising, reaching a worried pitch. "You *walked* here?"

"Dallas is a seven-hour drive. I wanted to stretch my legs."

"Stretch your legs my ass. We ain't taking my Carlo to Texas. Don't y'all get your gas covered, mileage and all that?"

Rae said, "Yeah, we do," still thinking of Frank, her partner clouding her mind like he had for the two-mile walk over from the Chevron. There was a new distance between them now, and that was fine. Better, maybe. Yeah. It would've been hard dragging Frank along. Darren, on the other hand, Darren was easy.

"Come on, D. We need to get moving. We need to get there *fast*."

His eyes lit up, like he'd just remembered Rae was a fed, a

white woman with a badge and special privileges. Grinning, Darren said, "How fast we talking?"

One twenty on I-40 headed west through Arkansas. A little slower getting there through the traffic in Memphis but they were rolling now, so fast Rae didn't have time to think. She could just feel the tires churning, the road moving beneath her, the little white lines blurring together into a big long one, a string pulled tight between Mississippi and Texas, Arkansas lost somewhere in between.

Rae barely recognized the state she thought of as home. Darren's voice helped, the bluesman throwing out lines like: "Played a show in Forrest City once. That's Forrest with two Rs, like Nathan Bedford *Forrest*. The Civil War general who started the KKK?" He'd go quiet for a while, zipping around semi-trucks, passing cars in the right lane, then say, "Brinkley. Cotton Plant. Towns so tiny they got the same exit. *Cotton Plant*. Reminds me of the King Biscuit Blues Festival over in Helena. Snagged me a shirt there once with this brother playing a guitar in a field on the front, the words 'Cotton-Pickin' Blues' printed above his head in fluffy white letters."

Through the window, Rae noticed kudzu, dull brown in the winter months, a blanket of bony vines covering everything until eastern Pulaski County, Little Rock—a dividing line between the Old South and the New, or whatever the rest of Arkansas was called. It damn sure wasn't the Delta. Darren didn't have any stories about Benton or Bryant. Not even Arkadelphia or Texarkana, patchwork names pieced together from other places, faraway cities, surrounding states. The line between east Texas and Arkansas was nothing more than a road sign, a little ink on a map, but at least it wasn't familiar. The Pine Curtain didn't remind Rae of anything except maybe Christmas. *Damn.* Now all those green trees had her thinking of Frank in his teal sweater and oxblood shoes, probably propped up somewhere, riding the last day of his last case out just like he'd wanted from the start.

The pines were gone, replaced by Lake Ray Hubbard, a fleet of sailboats with white masts and big orange buoys floating in the manmade body of water. Nothing in Texas looked natural. At least not this stretch of it, the Dallas skyline just a few small humps at the end of the long flat highway, like children's blocks left out in the sun.

Darren kept calling the metroplex the "Mixmaster" like it was a term Rae should've known, like that's what everyone called it. "Off-ramps. On-ramps," he said, "half a million cars making the same laps every day."

The closer they got to the Mixmaster, the more Rae missed Arkansas, or even Mississippi. The South was a lot like high school, she realized. Students talk a lot of crap about high school—the outdated procedures, the drafty buildings, the cliques—but by the time their ten-year reunions roll around, they can't wait to go back. That's how Rae felt about the South, the real South, the dirty South, the exact opposite of the sprawling concrete maze that lay before her now.

"DWI at night?" Darren said, reading lines off a billboard on the side of East Randol Mill Road. "*Coffay* in the morning. Get it? It's a law firm. The Coffay Law Firm."

Rae got it.

"See that woman on there, the one in the cowboy hat and the shades? She must be Ms. Coffay," Darren said, craning his neck. "Got a big ol' revolver on her hip and everything. In Texas it's legal to carry a six-gun around, long as it's in a holster."

Rae wondered if she should've brought her Glock 19M instead of leaving it back in Compson. Then again, not many personal assistants packed heat, and that's the part Rae was playing. She was Coach Johnson's personal assistant. Chuck was her in, her ticket to the big dance. He was still her dad too. Rae refocused on the gun she hadn't brought, trying to convince herself she'd made the right move.

Darren said, "There it is," and lifted one finger, pointing to the domed roof gleaming in the distance. "Cowboys Stadium."

Of all the differences Rae had noticed along the six-hour drive that should've taken seven, the one rising before her stood out the most. UCM's home stadium did not compare to Jerry World, the difference between the two a matter of millions. No, *billions*. Rae saw the future reflected in the retractable roof, the early afternoon sun beaming down on the thousands of cars already packed into the lot. It was fitting that this was where it would all end, the very pinnacle of the sports business.

56

The Chiefs arrived at the Embassy Suites on Wednesday, went bowling on Thursday, played laser tag on Friday, had practice on Saturday, a walk-thru, and on Sunday, the team went to Gateway Church. Biggest, whitest church Moses had ever seen; Coach Taylor in a three-piece suit, a little microphone clipped to one ear, waving his arms around behind the pulpit. Wasn't even wearing his new hat anymore. Always had fancy clothes on now, tailored suit vests and little clear glasses he kept having to push back up his nose.

Outside of that, the trip hadn't been half bad. There was enough going on Moses hadn't had time to think about what all Ella May had told him. There'd been no new news about Matt Talley. Everything finally seemed cool. The freshman QB even had his own hotel room, which was nice. Just one month prior, when Moses was still the backup, he had to room with this offensive lineman by the name of Mark Rizzo, a Guido-looking dude from Point Pleasant, New Jersey. Rizzo liked to sit on the toilet and leave the door open. He liked to talk to Moses through the crack while he was in there too, grunting and straining, stinking the whole place up like boiled cabbage.

Rizzo was rooming with Sammy B now and Moses was alone. Had him a sweet little setup in room 313C, which was where he was headed, speed walking down the hallway because the rest of the team was already loading the bus to head over to Cowboys Stadium. Moses had kept a low profile most of the morning, dipping in and out of the team breakfast without saying much, making it to position meetings early, going over Ohio State's Cover 3 Shell one last time. Soon as he snagged his Beats, he'd be ready to go.

The noise-canceling headphones were as much a part of Moses's pregame routine as the eye black he only painted on his left cheek or how he always wore his right sock inside out. The headphones made the world go quiet, helped the young quarterback get in the zone.

For starters, he'd thump along to some Miles Davis, keep things low-key, cool, then work his way into some Bone Thugs as he walked the field, Bizzy Bone singing about meeting Eazy-E at "Tha Crossroads." By the time he was wearing his pads, sitting in his locker, right before kickoff, it'd be Hans Zimmer time, string sections and timpani drums all the way up until he came running out that tunnel. His pregame playlist ended on "Now We Are Free," the last song on the *Gladiator* soundtrack, the one that plays at the very end of the film after Maximus whoops Commodus's ass even though that little harelipped Caesar sticks him in the back before the big fight.

Moses could hear Lisa Gerrard singing strange noises he'd read somewhere were this language she'd made up as a kid. *Damn.* He needed his headphones and couldn't believe he'd forgotten them. He'd been working on that playlist all week, moving songs around, imagining where he'd be for each track, envisioning himself doing the thing he was made to do so he could do the thing he wanted to when all this was over. Moses was thinking of the clinic he'd open one day in Clarksdale, his name on a sign out front, his very own business bought and paid for by the couple seasons he planned to spend in the NFL, as he slipped his room key into the slot and the light on the card reader blinked green.

The room was cold, the thermostat set on sixty-four because there wasn't a better feeling in the world than crawling beneath some cool, clean sheets when you'd grown up sweating yourself to sleep. Moses had come a long way from Momma G's spare room, the one with the box fan in the window that never made nothing cooler, just mixed the air up. That's how Moses felt rushing into the darkness, wondering why his fancy new room at the Embassy Suites didn't have light switches beside the door. Had to walk all the way to the bed, past the free swag left out on the kitchenette's counter—an Xbox One, two new pairs of Nikes, and a Dallas Cowboys hoodie with Moses's number on the back but not his name—just to turn on a lamp.

The light came on and Moses saw his headphones on the nightstand closest to the door, the opposite side he'd been using to charge his phone. Was that where he'd left them?

The third red number on the digital clock switched from a seven to an eight as Moses reached for his headphones. That small movement led to a larger one, a feather pillow rising, levitating, then coming down, revealing a little gray hat with a big red O on it. The hat was perched atop a mascot head made to resemble an anthropomorphic nut also known as "Brutus Buckeye."

Moses noticed the snub-nosed revolver in the Ohio State mascot's gloved hand and heard a voice coming from the depths of all that fabric and foam, saying, "Toss your phone on the bed. Nice and easy now, like an option pitch."

57

The sun was starting down behind the stadium when Darren's Monte Carlo pulled into the parking lot. Other vehicles were there already. Camera crews and diehard fans, tailgaters in their RVs with TVs mounted to the sides beneath retractable awnings. Somewhere in Cowboys Stadium the cameras were rolling, broadcasting high-def images to the tailgaters' glowing screens, ESPN analysts in slim-fit suits and high-top sneakers, offering their thoughts on the game:

"It's been a wild couple months for Coach Taylor's Chiefs, Reece. The UCM faithful are still reeling from the loss of senior quarterback Matt Talley. But with freshman phenom Moses McCloud at the helm, the Chiefs haven't skipped a beat. You have to think the boys will be playing inspired football today . . ."

Kirk Herbstreit's voice coming out loud enough Rae could hear him over the tailgate, but she wasn't listening. Even though kickoff was still hours away, Rae was already running over the plan in her head. Taking "mental reps." Something Chuck made his quarterbacks do, imagining themselves out on the field, scampering across the goal line, or in Rae's case, up in Harry Christmas's luxury suite.

All her plan required was a stealth phone app Madeline Mayo had shown her. The app would record audio even when the device was locked, the screen dark and hidden inside Rae's pocket. Once she was in the skybox, she would allude to her father's interest in UCM. She'd let Harry talk ball. She'd look pretty but uninterested, ignorant of the game and all its silly rules.

What Rae didn't know, the part she still didn't have figured, was what to do about Darren. The bluesman was hungry, starving from the sound of it, the smell of the tailgaters' charcoal grills and sizzling patties too much for him.

"I could eat a shit sandwich," he said, speed walking toward the stadium gate, "and I don't even like bread."

Rae caught up to him at the will-call booth. She heard Darren give Frank's name to the lady in the window, an old white lady with curly helmet hair, staring up at the Black man like, *Ranchino?* but still handing him the tickets. Two of them. Darren said, "Thanks. Frank'll pick his up later," and got another look he never saw, already moving toward the security check outside Gate 8.

The number barely registered in Rae's mind. That's how fast they were walking through what felt like an airport with the tallest ceilings in the world, some sort of industrial park. Except there was a field down there, the same shape, same size, as every one Rae had ever encountered. Way back in the early days, Rae had even helped Chuck paint the field. She knew every yard line, every hash mark.

The thought gave her hope.

Despite all that had been erected around it—bronze statues of Cowboys from seasons gone past, high-end art displays, waterfalls, beer gardens, VIP lounges, and concession stands like the one Darren was headed for now—Rae still understood the field.

Across the concrete corridor, Darren stood at the back of a line. Above him, a navy-blue sign read GATE 8. Rae was squinting at the number, feeling something in her chest, a faint recognition, when a man stepped in front of her. A bulging man with broad shoulders stuffed into a uniform the same color as the sign he'd just eclipsed.

Staring at the pockmarks along his neckline, the sheer size of him, the girth, Rae said, "Chief Conrad?" and watched the guy turn. "Hey, it's me. Rae Johnson."

Bruiser glanced at the "Gate 8" sign, the place he'd said to meet before the start of the game, then lowered his gaze on Rae, bloodshot eyes crawling over every inch of her. "Hot *damn*. Okay, yeah. I can take you up."

"Up?"

"To the skybox, away from all these plebs." The Compson police chief laughed and spread both hands wide enough Rae could see the concession stand line under his left one. "Can't stay down here more than a couple minutes or I start to sweat."

"Nobody wants that," Rae said, trying to keep the fear from her voice, her tone neutral, "but I need to wait on Darren."

"Floyd?"

"Yeah, the guy who called and set this whole thing up?"

Bruiser said "Darren Floyd," and unclipped his phone from his duty belt. He cupped one hand around the device and rotated his shoulders so Rae couldn't see his face. She couldn't hear what he was saying either, his voice just *wah-wah*s compared to the rookie agent's thoughts. Rae's inner voice sounded sort of like Frank Ranchino in his Subaru earlier that morning, talking about how the job had cost him his family. There was the other part too, the cranberry sauce Rae'd never passed Chuck at Christmas. If things went the way she wanted them to today—if Rae really brought Harry Christmas and the

University of Central Mississippi down—what would her father think? Would she ever get the chance to pass him the cranberry sauce again?

"Okay, so, I can take you up," Bruiser said, staring down at the rookie special agent he thought was Coach Johnson's personal assistant, "but just you. This sort of meeting, the less people we got involved, the better."

Rae peeked past Bruiser to Darren Floyd, still standing in line, almost to the front, so close to those spicy chicharrones there was no turning back. No way for him to know where Rae had gone either. The rookie agent told herself it was better like this, easier, at least.

"Yeah, the fewer people the better," Rae said and opened the stealth recording app on her phone by holding down both volume buttons at once, just like Mad had told her. "I appreciate y'all taking the time to meet with me."

Bruiser shrugged and said, "No problem," then started across the corridor.

Rae glanced once more at Darren, both hands stuffed with Spanish pork rinds now. He'd gotten her this far, but not any further. Rae told herself again that it was better this way. She didn't believe it but still took a small step, then another, following the dirty cop because there wasn't any better option, no other way but forward.

58

The Brutus Buckeye mascot suit was hot as shit. For another sixty bucks Eddie Pride Junior could've gotten one with the built-in fans, but he was running low on cash. Which was part of the reason he was holding Moses McCloud at gunpoint. Thankfully, the kid hadn't tried anything funny. Did just like he was told, like Eddie had *coached* him to do. Still, Eddie felt sorry for him. Sorry for himself too, and the whole Chiefs' fan base.

"Why you doing this, man?"

Eddie was headed for the thermostat but stopped and turned, staring back at the quarterback through the mesh that covered the nut head's eyeholes. It wasn't just the money, that debt Eddie still owed his bookie over in Tunica. The bagman was there because of his one-minute call with Harry Christmas. Eddie'd told the congressman, straight up, about Frank the fed. How Ella May'd screwed the pooch but not the quarterback. Told him all that, and what did he get in return?

This.

His "final assignment." That's what the old bastard had called it. That was pretty much all he'd said. Didn't say nothing about a mascot suit. Eddie'd come up with that part himself. Harry kept things simple. As long as Moses McCloud never left his hotel room, Ella May was in the clear. Nobody ever had to know the truth about what had happened to Matt Talley.

Moses rotated his eyes, only his eyes, up in Eddie's direction. "You're holding me hostage in my own room. You realize how dumb that is? This the first place they'll check."

Eddie'd been scouting the quarterback all morning. Never saw the boy in the lobby or on his way to the team meals without a pair of headphones on his head. Not just any headphones either. Big red ones. Like something a rapper might wear. The headphones were Eddie's best play, his only hope. Which was why he'd snagged them out from under the bathroom stall ten minutes before the team was scheduled to load the bus, plucked them straight out of Moses's travel bag while the kid was pulling up his pants. Getting into Moses's hotel room took a little more effort, but not much. Since the deadbolt wasn't locked, Eddie'd been able to shim the lock with a laminated room service menu. Easy-peasy. He hadn't thought about that bit Moses had just mentioned, but that was okay. Eddie wasn't the only one Harry had called. Speer Taylor was in on it too. It was up to the coach to come up with a story, something that would keep people from looking for Moses at all.

There were, of course, holes in their game plan, no different from the tactical errors Eddie watched coaches make every Saturday. He was wearing a Buckeye head, for one thing. Which might've drawn some attention. Then again, this was college football; people wore weird shit all the time.

Eddie aimed his Ruger LCR .22 at the quarterback's chest and dropped a pair of handcuffs, the same ones Ella May had used, on the bed. He said, "Put 'em on, pard," talking in a deeper tone of voice than normal, but not deep enough.

"*Pard?*" Moses said, staring at the handcuffs like he recognized them. He looked up, peering through the mascot head's eyeholes in the same way. "Eddie? Eddie *Pride?* Quit messing—"

"Nope," Eddie said, trying a higher pitch this time. "I'm the world's craziest Buckeyes fan. Now put them cuffs on. Ain't telling you again."

"Tell me why you doing this? Why'd you try and get me to throw that game? This ain't just about money, is it?"

A bead of sweat ran down the small of Eddie's back and slipped between his butt cheeks. He was literally sweating his ass off in that suit.

"All right, Moses. I'll shoot you straight." Eddie removed the mascot head. It was pointless now. They weren't going anywhere for at least three hours. More like four since it was the national championship game. Halftime show. All those commercials. "Made me a prop bet. Know what that is?" Eddie said. "A prop bet?"

59

Rae was in an Owners Club Suite, section 1L, a couple hundred feet up from the fifty-yard line. The skybox had six rows of leather stadium seats. The rookie federal agent sat perched in the last seat on the first row, one arm hooked over the chairback to her right, making listening noises as Harry Christmas told war stories from his days on the campaign trail. Ten full minutes, and the congressman hadn't said a single word about football.

Bruiser Brandt was there too, sitting back at the bar, toying with what appeared to be a syringe bag. The beefcake was shooting up, hands moving in the glass behind the bottles, sticking a thick-gauged needle into his thigh. Rae squinted and noticed the mirror had a star etched into it, a big white one.

The setup was different than she'd imagined, but nothing bad had happened yet. Bruiser hadn't even frisked her before he'd let her into the skybox. As soon as the door shut behind her, Rae wanted out again, but she was there now, right where she'd been headed since she first set foot in Mississippi.

"Did you know," Harry Christmas said, an unlit cigarillo in his left hand and what Rae guessed was a bourbon in his right, twenty minutes left until kickoff, "that I once witnessed your father give the pregame speech to end all pregame speeches? That one about Abraham Lincoln? I'm sure you've heard it."

Rae'd heard it, but the fact that the dirty congressman had ever crossed paths with her father came as a shock. Rae kept cool, reminding herself that she was supposedly there on Chuck's behalf.

"In 1832, Abraham Lincoln lost the race for Illinois state legislator," Harry Christmas said, doing his best Chuck Johnson impersonation. "That very same year, he lost his job. Three years after that, his sweetheart died; 1836, Honest Abe suffered a nervous breakdown; 1838, defeated for House Speaker; 1843, couldn't even get nominated for Congress; 1849, rejected as Land Officer; 1854, defeated for the U.S. Senate; 1856, defeated for the vice-presidential nomination; 1858 . . ."

. . . *defeated for U.S. Senate seat, again.* Rae had the whole talk memorized. That was how many times she'd heard her father give that same speech that ended in 1860, the year Lincoln finally won something: the US presidency. That's when the players would start cheering, or the booster club, or even an auditorium full of high school kids. Whoever Chuck was talking to didn't matter—the punchline always landed. But there was more to President Lincoln's story. Despite the detailed timeline, Chuck never mentioned what went down in 1865.

Neither did Harry. Bourbon sloshed from his glass as he shouted, "And then he became the United States' sixteenth president! Never quit, gentlemen. Never surrender. Now let's go win one for the Gipper!" The congressman paused as if imagining a locker room full of college-aged athletes roaring all around him. He turned to Rae, awaiting her approval.

"Yeah, that's pretty much it," she said, motioning back toward the bar. "Is he okay?"

Harry scoffed at the police chief. "Brandt? Tell Ms. Johnson what it is you're doing back there."

"Low T," Bruiser said. "Nothing serious."

"I'm not so sure about that." Harry blew smoke from his nose. "Brandt started this mess about a month ago and now he's carrying around a little pack of needles."

"Better than steroids," Bruiser said and stood. "Back when I's playing, everybody was hitting the roids hard. Never seen a sadder shower scene. All these beefed-up dudes with the world's tiniest—"

Harry cut the police chief short with a flick of his cigarillo. "Why don't you step outside, Chief Conrad?"

"But the game's about to start."

"Run along, Brandt." Harry nodded toward the door. "I'd like to chat with our guest in private."

Bruiser shrugged then lumbered out of the skybox. When the door swung shut behind him, Harry said, "I'm sure you're wondering what sort of man might own a skybox of this caliber."

"Jerry Jones?"

The congressman clacked his teeth together. "Why, yes, actually, this box belongs to the man himself. Lucky for us, Mr. Jones opted to watch the game from his condo in Cabo."

Rae turned toward the thick pane of glass, hoping to catch the pregame warmup, but she'd missed it. Missed her chance to get a good look at Moses McCloud, get a feel for his nerves by watching his hands the way her daddy had taught her to do. Only the kickers were left out there now, booting arching spirals that came dangerously close to the massive video board dangling over midfield.

"Anyway, your father, Ms. Johnson. Tell me about him, why he sent you here."

"That's obvious, isn't it? You're a real power player in the state of Mississippi, the sort of guy who hangs out in Jerry Jones's private suite."

Something flashed behind the old man's eyes, something different than the show he'd been putting on. "I'm a state-level congressman," he said, and the look was gone. "Just a small-town politician, not to be confused with the swamp you see seeping out of DC."

Rae forced a laugh. "Listen to you, talking like you're a nobody."

"I know my place."

"My dad wouldn't have sent me here if you weren't important."

Harry smiled and it almost looked natural. Like a grandpa. That's what Frank had said back when he'd first seen the congressman out at Sudan. Rae tried imagining the old man jabbing a letter opener into Eddie Pride's thigh but couldn't. It didn't mean the congressman hadn't done everything Frank had said he'd done. It just meant Harry Christmas was good. Rae had to be careful. She had to ask the right question without pushing too hard.

As she rotated back toward the window, Rae said, "Right?" over her shoulder, a throwaway word, not really a question at all.

"A man in my position must keep a low profile. That's all."

Rae could see Harry's reflection in the glass, his body ten times the size of the players taking the field now, bursting out of the tunnel through a cloud of CO_2 smoke. Flames puffed up from the pyrotechnics display as "War Pigs" by Black Sabbath blared from the speakers. Speer Taylor was at the head of the pack, donning a new suit vest that made him look like some sort of megachurch pastor instead of a coach, or even a politician.

"And what does a man in your position think about all this?" Rae said, keeping her question ambiguous, curious which way the congressman would take it.

Harry took his time, three good puffs and a sip of bourbon, before saying, "It's all part of the show. That's what football is, what it's become, just one big show."

From the skybox, the players were tiny, ant-sized versions of their six-foot-something, two-hundred-plus-pound frames. On the video board, however, the Chiefs were giants. Rae's eyes danced between the two realities, scanning the blue UCM jerseys for a red number seven.

"My mother," Harry said, "was in a similar business."

"What's that?"

"Show business."

"An actress?"

"Of the highest degree, but only for a time, just long enough to learn the ropes and get her own production running."

"Any films I might know?"

Harry chuckled. His fedora moved in the window. "She would've liked you, Ms. Johnson. Your spunk. That hair. Yes, Lord. Maxine could've used a girl like you."

Gooseflesh rose on Rae's forearms. She didn't know why. "And what did Maxine think about football?"

"Mother didn't think about football at all," Harry said, his mouth a shadow, moving a millisecond behind his words. "I don't either. Not really. It's the show that interests me."

Rae's fingers curled around the phone in her pocket. This was what she'd come for. If Harry Christmas started talking about how he'd funded the "show," Rae would record every word.

"The show serves a purpose," Harry said. "You see, the fans believe what they want to believe. They see what they want to see. The same way a child believes in Santa Claus, despite the obvious logical flaws."

"And that makes you Kris Kringle?"

Harry didn't laugh. "Not me, no, the sport itself. That's where the fans put their faith. They trust that those boys down there," Harry said and nodded, "are playing for the love of the game. For their state. Their alma mater. That point is critical to the future of the sport, the future of America."

"I thought we were talking about college football."

"Oh, I am," Harry said. "I'm talking about this country and the way things are changing. What is America if not a dream? If the average citizen ever became privy to the compromises our government has had to make, the wars it's had to start—and finish—in order to reign supreme, what would he think? Would there be any true patriots left? Any men willing to go fight for the ol' U-S-of-A?"

"Or women."

Harry laughed at that one.

"Sounds to me," Rae said, "like you don't have the highest opinion of the federal government?"

"I try not to think about the federal government either. I know my place, my people, and I'll do whatever it takes to protect them. Without this game, this show, what would the good folks in Mississippi, or even Arkansas, have to call their own?"

Rae said, "Not much," and told herself she could say the next part too. If she did, maybe it would all be over. "Just the other day, my dad was telling me about this court case, some sort of new legislation about paying the players? I didn't have a clue what he was talking about." She waited, counting the beats in her head. After four, she added: "Do you?"

The smoke hung heavy in the room. On the field, captains from each team gathered at the fifty-yard line. A referee flipped a coin. Rae watched it spin on the video board, thinking: *Tails never fails.* The video was so clear, Rae could see rubber kernels scatter when the coin hit the turf. She could see that she'd been wrong too. Could hear it in the congressman's voice, as he said, "No, Ms. Johnson. I'm not aware of any court cases. Maybe we should ask your father about it?"

Something about the way the congressman had said "we" got Rae out of the stadium seat. It was the same way a quarterback senses a blindside blitz. Rae didn't see a threat. Harry Christmas was an old man, and Rae had received over one hundred hours' worth of self-defense courses at Quantico. She'd aced her Krav Maga, Muay Thai, and BJJ classes. Rae could whip the congressman's ass if she had to, but she still couldn't shake the claustrophobic feeling that had settled in her gut, like the pocket was collapsing and it was time to scramble.

"Want me to call him?" Rae said, lifting her phone as she moved along the wall opposite the congressman. "Yeah, I'll just step outside and call Dad. I'm not getting the best reception in here."

Harry Christmas made no attempt to stop her. His stooped shoulders and frail frame were no match for the former pole vaulter's loping strides. Rae made it to the door as a chorus of a hundred thousand voices rose up from the floor, two hundred thousand pairs of eyes watching the opening kickoff spin, higher and higher.

Rae glanced back at the window, the spectacle calling to her, too incredible to miss. On the video board, the ball bounced into the north end zone, followed by a new angle, a close-up shot of the Chiefs' quarterback, a dumpy white boy who looked nothing like Moses McCloud.

Rae's ears started to ring. The high-pitched tone took her back to the start of all this, the night Matt Talley died. She said, "Who the hell is that?" and turned in time to see the suite's door swing open.

"*That*," Harry said, cigarillo aimed at the man walking into the skybox now, "would be your father, Agent Johnson. And he's right on time."

60

A provocatively dressed sideline reporter cornered Speer Taylor as soon as he stepped onto the field. Even if he didn't know where Moses McCloud was or what had happened to him, Speer had known this moment was coming. Harry had warned him. He'd told Speer to be prepared, this was his chance to prove he was ready for politics, but the congressman hadn't gone into any details. All the football coach knew was that his star quarterback would not be available to play in the Goodyear Cotton Bowl.

The sideline reporter said, "Any comments, Coach?"

"You, uh . . ." Speer let his gaze drift upward, looking to the heavens for inspiration. He groaned when he realized the stadium's retractable roof was closed. "You asked about Moses McCloud?"

"He's playing today, right?"

The Chiefs were in trouble without their freshman quarterback. *Big trouble*, Speer thought, still staring up at the roof, wondering if it were somehow blocking his prayer channel.

"No," Speer said and lowered his gaze, staring straight into the camera's convex lens now. "Due to an off-the-field issue, Moses McCloud will not be playing today."

The reporter brought the mic back under her crimson lips. "So, UCM is handling this internally? This is some sort of self-imposed punishment?"

When the mic swung back his way again, Speer was ready. "Actually, it's a *Coach Taylor*–imposed punishment. I imposed it." Speer glanced down at his right hand and was pleased to see his thumb perched neatly atop his closed fist. It was happening. He was finally becoming a politician. "We run a tight ship at UCM," he said, using his *thist* like a gavel, adding emphasis to his words. "Moses isn't just a football player. He's a young man who needs to learn a hard lesson, a lesson that will serve him long after his career is over, when he becomes a husband and a father, a good Christian man."

"Just so we're clear," the sideline reporter said. "Moses McCloud will *not* be playing in the Cotton Bowl. That's what you're saying, Coach?"

"Let my yes be a yes, and my no be a no. Now, if you don't mind," Speer said, watching as little Sam Billingsley led the Chiefs onto the field, "I've got a football game to coach."

61

Chuck Johnson never wore visors. That was Steve Spurrier's deal. Rae's daddy rarely wore hats at all. His forehead was a dark, leathery brown that looked even darker against his silver fox flattop. Rae had urged him to wear a hat, some sort of headgear, especially after the electrodessication, that procedure where the surgeon had scraped cancer cells off his nose. Chuck wouldn't listen, but now there he stood wearing a baby-blue visor and a pair of Oakley shades inside Jerry Jones's multi-million-dollar suite.

Rae was trapped between the memory of her father—all those lessons he'd taught her—and the man in the stupid sunglasses. Despite herself, she still found comfort in his presence, the faint whiff of the same aftershave she'd noticed on Frank. She was glad to see him but at the same time knew Bruiser hadn't stumbled upon Chuck in the breezeway. This wasn't a coincidence. The half-assed disguise told the rookie agent that much, but what about the rest?

"What are you doing here?"

"Could ask you the same thing, sis."

"Why, she's your *personal assistant.*" Harry Christmas pushed his fedora up with two fingers. Beneath the brim, his eyes were smirking. "Remember? Rae came here to talk to me about your future employment with—"

"Cut the shit, Harry." Chuck grabbed his visor by the brim and yanked it off, followed by the ridiculous shades. "And *you,*" Chuck said, turning back to Rae. "Quit looking at me like that."

"Like what?"

"Like you're fifteen and arguing with me about curfew."

"*Curfew?* Jesus Christ. I was the one always waiting up on you." Rae pursed her lips and rolled her eyes, a look she'd never given her dad, not even when she was fifteen. "And how the hell do you know Harry Christmas?"

"Harry's gotten me a few speaking gigs in Mississippi over the years. Touchdown clubs. Quarterback clubs. He's helped out some here and there. That's all. That's why he called, told me about this little 'meeting' you had set up."

They were all still standing by the door, the game marching along behind them, Ohio State already up three scores at the start of the second quarter. The crowd, or more precisely, the Buckeyes fans, were cheering about something. The men turned to look.

Rae still couldn't believe her father was there, just a couple feet away. Close enough she could reach out and touch him, or punch him. A quick jab to the gut. No. That wasn't what she wanted. Rae wanted to disappear. Snap her fingers and go back in time. That's how the whole scene felt. Like she was a kid again. Not fifteen. Younger. That nine-year-old girl who'd sat in her daddy's lap and smiled for the SportsCenter cameras. She felt like the full-grown version of Sheryl fucking Yoast from *Remember the Titans*, except Rae wasn't just playing some part in a movie. This was her life.

"I thought . . ." Rae said and swallowed. "I mean, Harry's a bad guy, the worst."

Harry bent forward and slapped his thighs. His laugh sounded like his windbreaker swishing, a threadbare wheeze.

"Listen, Rae. This is football," Chuck said, "not law

enforcement. There's no such thing as 'good guys' or 'bad guys.' There's just winners and losers."

"But you, you're one of the—"

"I'm your dad."

Even without the disguise, Rae didn't recognize the man standing before her, the same man who'd let her drive his truck as soon as her feet could reach the pedals, the same man who'd tucked her in and given her butterfly kisses every night. Chuck Johnson had taught his daughter how to hold a football, how to play catch and scout a defense. She had all his best lines memorized, but none of them made sense now.

"Work hard, never quit," Rae said, "and good things'll happen."

"Come on, Rae."

"That's how you did it, right? Your binders. The scouting reports. All the extra work. That's how you won. How you got so good?"

"It's not that simple."

"What about 'Do the right thing and you'll never have to worry'? That's another one of your lines. Do you have anything to worry about? That's what I need to know."

"If you're asking if the U of A has bagmen, well . . ." Chuck ran a hand over his flattop the way Rae used to when she was little. "Yeah, of course, we do. Every program, at least the ones that are any good, they've all got bagmen. Entire infrastructures built around paying the players."

Rae felt something inside her chest—a piece of the girl she'd once been, a page in her Trapper Keeper—wither and fall away.

"But that's against the rules," she said. "It's not right, and you—"

"If it were up to me, I'd pay the players out of my own pocket.

Lord knows I've got the money, but that's not the way it is, sis. It's a broken system, and I've done my best to keep you from seeing the cracks."

Rae stared down at the visor in her father's left hand. Everything she'd learned, was still learning, felt just like that. Chuck hadn't just put on a disguise for today, he'd been wearing a mask her whole life.

"That's why you wouldn't let me coach." Rae looked up at him. "After everything I did—all the extra hours I put in, watching film and helping you come up with game plans—you still didn't want me on your staff. You couldn't let me get that close."

"There's nothing I wanted more, but coaching wasn't what was best for you. Trust me on that one. You really loved football, and I used that love to teach you everything I knew."

"No," Rae said. "Not everything."

A new chill started in Rae's chest, right over her heart, and spread fast through her body. Every rookie goes through the same transformation at some point. Frank had been right. All that stuff he was saying about the cranberry sauce.

"But how . . ." Rae said. "How did you—"

"—find out?" Harry Christmas stepped forward and sneered. "Simple. You misjudged my most faithful soldier."

Rae glanced back at Bruiser, still watching the game from his post at the bar.

"No, not him," Harry said. "Eddie Pride Junior. That poor man was a mess after his chat with your partner. Tore up, his allegiances strained. Which is rare, because Edward is exactly what this country, this football program, was built upon. Eddie's a true believer."

Rae thought, *No plan survives first contact with the enemy,* reciting Helmuth von Moltke again, that Prussian field marshal she'd studied while at Quantico. First contact. Was that what this was? If so, did that make her dad the enemy?

"I called Edward," Harry said, "about an hour or so after your partner's blunder. A big Italian man, Agent Rancilio, if memory serves me."

"*Ranchino.*"

"Yes, that," Harry said and shrugged. "Anyway, I was calling Edward to talk over this new blitz I'd drawn up, but Mr. Pride had news for me. He told me all about your little investigation. Which, I must say, wasn't the least bit surprising. The federal government hates nothing more than a winner. Isn't that right, Coach Johnson?"

Chuck said, "Let's go, Rae. You should've never been put on a case like this. It's too personal. Matter of fact, I'm gonna make a call soon as we get this settled."

Rae thought, *Like you did when I was at Quantico?* Maybe she should've said it, but the words were too heavy. The last thing she'd wanted was for her daddy to come bail her out again, yet there he stood.

"Your father's right," Harry added. "I could've handled this differently, very differently, but Coach Johnson convinced me to give you the opportunity to walk away. No harm no foul."

Rae couldn't have walked away if she'd wanted to, and a part of her really wanted to. The girl who'd grown up idolizing Chuck Johnson wanted to run. It would've been so easy to act like this never happened. Rae was a daddy's girl, through and through. She'd believed in Chuck above all others, but now she wasn't sure if her father had been worthy of such faith. Was anyone?

Rae said, "Give me a minute. Okay?" and fell back into a stadium seat. Time dissolved the way it did during games when she was a kid, so lost in the details, the intricacies of every play, she'd look up and ten minutes would be gone from the clock. That's how this felt. In the darkness behind her eyes, years passed, entire decades fell away.

The sound of the men moving around her brought Rae back from the past. Harry was saying something about the score, or maybe the door. That's where Bruiser Brandt was standing now. Like he was on guard, a lowball glass in one hand, his black plastic syringe bag in the other. Harry spelled out, "N-I-L," and for some reason, those three letters registered in the rookie agent's mind. She still didn't move, didn't speak. Instead, Rae did just what she'd come there to do.

She listened.

"That goddamn court case out west, Coach Johnson. The one that started over a video game? If that thing passes, it'll change college football forever. The players will be running the show, calling all the shots."

Chuck told the congressman he wasn't sure about that, but Rae was. When she'd asked Harry about the case earlier, he'd denied even the knowledge of it. She kept her head down, one ear cocked.

"Take our freshman quarterback for example," Harry said. "A boy like that used to know his place. Did what he was told when he was told to do it, but not anymore. Oh, no. Nowadays, boys like Moses . . ."

As the congressman rambled on, Rae recalled the last time she'd seen Moses McCloud, everything he'd told her during their game of catch. It made sense now. This wasn't about Harry, or even Chuck. This was about the players and the game they'd been forced to play. The contest that took place on the field was nothing compared to the battle that went down in Waffle Houses, seedy motel rooms, used car lots, and a laundry list of other skeevy locales. That's where boys like Moses McCloud had been fighting for so long nobody even saw them as boys anymore. These were young men whose talents had been exploited to pay their coaches' multimillion-dollar contracts, secure billion-dollar TV deals, and provide highly visible recruiting for their respective universities. College football wasn't a game at all; it was a business, a completely self-sufficient economy powered by young, mostly Black athletes. There was a better word for what Rae was coming to terms with on this particular Monday night in Dallas, Texas, during a game called "The Cotton Bowl," for Christ's sake, and that word was—

"*What?*"

Rae blinked, surprised by her father's sharp tone. Harry Christmas was grinning up at Chuck, a twinkle in his eye as he whispered, "I said I'm making an example out of that boy, setting a precedent."

Chuck's cheeks flushed red, the color of revelation. "Jesus, Harry. What'd you do to him?"

"I didn't *do* anything," Congressman Christmas hissed, his voice barely audible across the expansive skybox. "Young Moses is simply enjoying an extended stay at the Embassy Suites."

Rae's hand went to her pocket as she stood. Any coach worth his salt makes adjustments, which was what Rae was doing now, shoving her hand deeper into her slacks, digging for her phone, the one with the app that had been recording the entire conversation.

Fingers coiled around her cell, Rae glanced back at Bruiser. The beefcake had another syringe in his paws, staring down at the needle. Even after all she'd heard, all she'd recorded, Rae doubted she had enough evidence to take Harry down or expose Speer Taylor, but if she got out there, right now, maybe she could still save Moses.

Rae took tiny, sideways steps toward the police chief, watching as he flicked his needle. With each inch gained, Rae counted backward down from ten in her head—*Nine Mississippi. Eight Mississippi*—employing the one lesson she'd learned from Frank Ranchino. She couldn't rush this. She had to time it up just right.

When she reached *One Mississippi*, the thick-gauged needle was mere millimeters from Bruiser's skin, then—*wham*—it was in. All the way in. Rae punched the plunger hard enough the needle pierced the meat of Bruiser's palm and nailed his hand to the suite's wooden door.

"Holy shit, kid."

That's all Chuck got out before Rae plucked Bruiser's service pistol from its holster and leveled the barrel on the howling police chief's head.

"You just assaulted an officer of the law," Harry snapped. "What were you thinking?"

A new silence filled the box. On the scoreboard, five minutes remained until the end of the first half. A timeout had been called. The players were jogging back to their respective sidelines. There was no crowd noise, no cheers or powwow drums rattling. Even Brandt had stopped howling, curious, maybe, about Rae's response. The sudden shift felt just like football. Brief but violent surges, yards lost or gained, then nothing.

"I was thinking about what you said, Congressman Christ-mas."

Rae squared the pistol between Bruiser's bulging eyes and reached for the door, imagining herself sprinting down the stairs. When she made it to the Embassy Suites, Rae'd flash her badge at the concierge and request Moses's room number. That was it, as far as she'd gotten, and she still had to get out of the luxury suite.

"All that bullshit about the players, the future of football," Rae added. "For a second, it sounded like you were a coach, giving some sort of halftime speech. I guess it got me fired up."

Harry made a face like he couldn't tell if Rae was serious. "Okay?" he said. "So, you've skewered poor Bruiser. Now what?"

Rae almost said, *When in doubt, attack*, but was glad she didn't. There'd been enough locker-room talk already. It was time for action.

Bruiser yelped as she yanked the door open. A shocked expression took shape in the wrinkles around Harry Christmas's eyes. Chuck, on the other hand, was grinning when Rae slipped into the hallway and started to run.

62

Eddie and Moses were sitting on the hotel room bed, the mascot head between them, watching the game. Or at least they had been. It was halftime now. The ESPN commentators were back on the screen, talking, trying to predict the unpredictable. Eddie had his right hand, the one with the gun in it, propped up on Brutus the Buckeye's little hat. He had the safety engaged but the muzzle was touching the quarterback's shoulder, his *left* shoulder. Not his throwing arm. Eddie wasn't crazy. He didn't want to hurt Moses. He was kinda starting to like the kid.

"Quiz time," Eddie said. "Let's see if you remember what all we talked about."

Moses lifted his cuffed hands. "Take me back to the stadium and I could do more than talk."

Eddie sucked his teeth, surprised Moses still wanted to go to the game. UCM was down five touchdowns with only two quarters left. That sort of deficit had been overcome only once before. Back in 2006, Michigan State scored 38 unanswered points to defeat Northwestern after trailing 38–3 with 9:54 left in the third quarter. The biggest come-from-behind victory in the history of Division I college football. Eddie knew Moses was good, but was he *that* good?

"It took me most the first half to explain all that betting lingo," Eddie said. "Come on. I wanna know what you learned."

"I know you got a whole lot riding on this game."

"There you go."

"Said you made a 'prop bet,' which is like a wager on something other than the outcome, who wins or loses."

"Now you got it. With you here, and little Sam Billingsley back under center, there's only one other player who's got half a chance at reaching paydirt."

"With me here and Sammy B on the field, the Chiefs ain't scoring shit, Mr. Pride."

"But Cerge is—"

"Nope." Moses rolled forward in the bed. "Cerge can't do it by himself. See, the way the offense is set up, the plays are packaged. The quarterback has options." Moses stood, towering over the bagman. "I got a option too. One I didn't see till just now."

Eddie said, "Sit down," and lifted the .22.

"You ain't gonna shoot me, Mr. Pride."

Eddie's index finger slid in around the trigger.

"You need me too much," Moses said. "Yeah, you let me get back in the game and I'll make sure Cerge scores."

Eddie gnawed his bottom lip. "Naw, that's a bad bet. No way for me to know what you're gonna do when you get out of here."

Moses shrugged and turned for the door.

"The hell you think you're going?" Eddie slid off the bed and started after the quarterback. "Huh? You not see this gun in my hand?"

"You pull that trigger, the whole hotel'd hear it. Then what?"

Moses was three feet from the door, looking back at Eddie, when the bagman said, "This here's a .22," then lowered his revolver until it was aimed at the quarterback's left knee. "Barely louder than a pellet gun. Anybody hears it, they'll probably think it's just some kid slamming the bathroom door."

"You'd shoot me in the leg?" Moses said.

"The knee. Same one you been favoring since Mississippi State." Eddie shook his head. "That's right. I noticed how your game changed after you plowed into that cameraman. That's when you stopped running and started passing the ball so much."

Moses said, "Damn. You really been watching, huh?"

"Told you, I was the one that found your highlight. Don't nothing get past ol' Eddie Pride. Now, be a good boy and sit back down on the—"

Three quick knocks rattled the hotel room door, followed by a soft voice on the other side saying, "Housekeeping."

Eddie grabbed Moses by the handcuff chain and jerked him onto the bed. He said, "Don't move," everything on the bagman frozen except the gun in his right hand, swishing like a squirrel's tail, jumping between the door and the quarterback, the quarterback and the door. Eddie was still standing there, thanking the good Lord he'd thought to employ the security chain, when the maid knocked again, a little harder this time.

"*Housekeeping.*"

Eddie whispered, "*Shit,*" and pressed one eye to the peephole, surprised by what he saw. A redheaded white woman holding a stack of towels. Didn't see many ginger maids, but the woman looked tired enough. Like she'd been running her ass off. Still staring through the peephole, Eddie said, "Little privacy, please?"

The woman said, "Come on, man," and lifted the towels. "You called for these."

If Eddie didn't play nice, that maid might run back to the director of housekeeping and file a report on room 313C. Over what? Some towels? Eddie didn't want to cause a scene. He reached for the security chain. Had his hands on the die-cast fastener then decided to leave it latched. Let the maid pass the towels through the crack.

Before he opened the door, Eddie took a moment to compose himself and think about everything he had riding on this deal. Another twenty minutes, shit, less than that now, and Cergile Blanc would be back on the field for the start of the third quarter, sprinting straight for the end zone and the Chiefs' first touchdown of the game. It was a long shot. Hundred-to-one odds because Moses had been running the show lately, but Moses wasn't going anywhere. It was as good as Eddie was going to get. Which was why he'd put all the money he had left—fifty thousand dollars, the very same stack of cash he'd tried to give two different UCM quarterbacks—on this one bet. If everything went to plan, Eddie would collect more than enough to pay off that bookie in Tunica, and then some.

The latch clicked as Eddie pushed down on the handle then pulled back, keeping his body hidden behind the door. His second mistake. Eddie realized his first mistake when the sixty-pound fireproof door hit him in the chest, the sheer force of it unbelievable.

The redhead slipped into the room, kicked the door shut, and dropped the towels, revealing the business end of what appeared to be a service pistol. It wasn't until the woman said, "Get your hands up where I can see them," that Eddie realized she was some sort of cop, which explained the forceful entry.

Eddie said, "Ten-four," and lifted his right hand, but it was empty, the .22 missing, lost in the shuffle. No, there it was, on the carpeted floor, lying right out in the open like a loose ball. A fumble.

63

Moses saw the snub-nosed revolver on the floor at the same time Rae did, about a half second behind Eddie Pride, already down on all fours, bear crawling toward the .22. Rae had speed on her side and made up for lost ground, quick. The way she speared the bagman, how they both went rolling across the floor, it was like a tackling drill. Except it wasn't just some ball they were after.

It was a gun.

Rae wrestled the revolver away from Eddie by breaking the bagman's left pinky finger, quick and clean, almost politely, as if she were snapping a baby carrot at the dinner table. If all the preceding action hadn't tipped Moses off, that last move did. He knew Rae Joyce wasn't a reporter now, but what was she?

Fast.

Moving like Moses moved on the field, digging through Eddie Pride's pockets, his left one first, then his right. She stood with the cuff key in the same hand as Eddie's revolver, still holding her firearm in the other. A second later, Moses was rubbing his wrists and the cuffs were on Eddie Pride. Just one of them. The other was latched around the bedpost.

Moses was following along behind Rae, halfway to the door, when Eddie cried out, "They made me do it!" The bagman kept staring down at his shattered digit, holding it, cradling it in his other palm the way a child might hold a worm. "They've got my baby girl in a—"

"Save it for your lawyer, Mr. Pride."

Damn, Moses thought. Who *was* this woman?

"The only reason I'm not taking you in, right now, is because of him." Rae nodded at Moses then started back across the room. "Come to think of it," she said, "I need to borrow this."

Eddie flinched as Rae reached past him and snatched the mascot head.

"The hell you need that for?" Eddie said.

"Told you already. It's for Moses." Rae held the Buckeye head up. "Put it on, kid. We don't want anybody recognizing you on the way out."

Rae wasn't just fast, she was smart too. Moses didn't need some half-drunk fan snapping a picture of him in the lobby. He didn't need anybody to know about this. He just needed to get back on the field.

Moses could smell the bagman's funky breath trapped in the mascot head's fabric lining. He could barely see Rae through the eyeholes, opening the door. As he walked through it, Eddie Pride hollered something Moses almost didn't hear. The same thing the bagman had been talking about for the last two hours, the first two quarters of the game. "Don't forget my prop bet, pard!"

Yeah. That's exactly what Eddie said. Moses couldn't believe it.

64

Rae looked down and noticed her hands were shaking. Both of them. She hadn't been this juiced since her first field test at Hogan's Alley, the ten-acre tactical training facility owned and operated by the FBI. This wasn't just some mock town, though. This wasn't a set. This was as real as it got. A recently abducted quarterback was breathing heavily in her passenger seat, a mascot head balanced on his knees. Rae jammed the gas pedal down, sending the recently "borrowed" Dodge Ram hurtling backward before she stomped the brake, shifted the stick into drive, and completed her first-ever reverse J-turn, finally putting her Hogan's Alley tactical driving course to good use.

Moses pawed for his seatbelt but didn't say anything about the truck's KEEP HONKING: I'M RELOADING bumper sticker. Neither of them had said anything. They'd gotten a few strange looks running through the lobby to the porte cochère where she'd parked the Dodge, but they made it. In total, the extraction took a little over eleven minutes. Nine minutes remained until the end of halftime. That's how long Rae had to drive the half mile to the stadium and drop the QB off outside Gate 13, the one closest to the UCM locker room. If she did all that, then Moses McCloud would finally be back in action.

Rae blew past a sedan and hooked a left onto East Randol Mill Road. She could see Jerry World now, a spaceship in the distance, the *Mothership* of the modern sports age. Then they were there. The Dodge was in park and Moses was getting out.

It all happened so fast. Too fast, Rae thought, but that was the point, right?

She said, "*Hey*," as Moses popped the passenger-side door. "You're not gonna say thanks? I came back for—"

"—my interview?" he said. "That's what you told me that night on the field. Said you were a journalist, here to break a big story on college football."

They didn't have time for this. Moses had to hustle. He needed to get out on that field, back in the game, *but* . . . the game was rigged. Rae'd realized that much in the skybox. She'd gotten a peek behind the curtain and seen the old men, her father included, who pulled the levers, jerking boys like Moses McCloud around.

"Okay," Rae said. "I'm not a journalist."

"No shit."

Rae tried to read Moses, clean shaven with a cubic zirconia stud in each earlobe, a silver chain showing around the neck of an oversized black hoodie, strong jawline, sharp features, put together in a smart way.

"I'm a federal agent."

Moses, still with one hand on the door, one foot on the pavement, said, "Then you need to go find Ella May."

"Pride?"

"You not hear Eddie hollering back there? People been saying she pushed Matt. Saying she, you know—" Moses scraped a thumbnail over his throat. "But she didn't. Ella May was up on the roof. She told me that. But then she got so mad at Matt she came back down to the bar and ordered a drink."

"Listen, even if I wanted to help Ella May, I couldn't," Rae said, pushing the memory of Matt Talley's death down. Despite the extra effort she'd put into the quarterback's death, Frank had been right. They weren't there to investigate a murder, an accident, or whatever the hell it was that had happened to Matt. "A case like that is out of my jurisdiction. Everything that's happened to you, though, *that's* why I was sent to Compson. I can help, but only if you're willing to talk."

"Talk?"

Rae had to say the next part quick, get it out before she had time to overthink it. "There's a man by the name of Harry Christmas. He looks just like Bear Bryant. Wears a fedora and everything. He's the guy behind the money. He's the reason Eddie locked you in that hotel room."

"So?"

Despite what Rae'd heard and recorded in the skybox, Harry hadn't incriminated himself. He was too slick for that. All he'd said was that Moses was enjoying an "extended stay" in the Embassy Suites. The admission had been enough to tip off Rae, but would it hold up in court?

"You remember what you told me when we were playing catch?" Rae said. "After I ripped my hand open?"

"Told you it was time to quit."

"No, you said, 'Sometimes you've got to lose the battle to win the war.' That's what I'm talking about here." She took a breath, a quick one, then said, "Do you know what an informant is?"

Moses laughed.

"I'm serious. If you're willing to go on record and explain everything that's happened to you, then maybe we could change the game, change it for the better."

Moses cut his eyes at her.

"The money's good," Rae added. "Enough to cover tuition, books, room and board, and you'd be helping take down UCM and Coach Taylor."

"*Coach Taylor?* What's a man like Coach Taylor got to worry about?" Moses peeked back over his shoulder, the stadium, all those rabid fans, calling to him. "What's gonna happen to me, or any them other boys you put down in your report? That's what I need to know."

"Accepting payments is not a criminal offense. It'll—"

"It'll be the end. That's what," Moses said. "And, listen, I know the game's crooked. Known it since those academies started calling back in high school, but it's still my only way out. I got a plan, a dream, and what you talking about now would squash it. How many coaches gonna sign some player got his name in an FBI file?"

Moses made a "0" with his index finger and thumb. He stared down at Rae through the hole then stepped out of the Dodge.

She whispered, "*Wait*," but the people inside the stadium were beginning to stir, a low, insect thrum rising. Moses didn't turn to the sound. Not yet. He waited, still staring at Rae, long enough she would remember this moment. She'd second guess it, overanalyze it. But Rae was no match for the cheers, the crowd, the game and all it promised.

Moses took two more small backward steps, and then he was gone.

The Section 13 breezeway was humming with fans hustling to catch the start of the second half. Rae let the people swarm around her, feeling lost, confused after her conversation with

Moses McCloud. She wished for her Trapper Keeper. Maybe it would've helped organize her thoughts. Maybe just holding it would've given her comfort. Then again, that binder—the layout, the tabs—had been inspired by her dad. Just like everything else.

Fuck Chuck.

That was the thought that got Rae out of the Dodge, got her moving again. The truck was still parked outside the gate, just sitting there, not even pulled up alongside the curb. It might've been towed by now.

Rae didn't care. Whoever owned the Dodge had left the passenger door unlocked and the keys in the glove box. Not to mention that dumbass bumper sticker. *They had it coming*, Rae thought, keeping her feet moving, tracing the quarterback's steps, still trying to see the field like Moses saw it. Like she'd seen it once, before she'd become aware of the cracks her father had kept hidden from her. There were cracks along the concrete corridor, but Rae walked on, following the fault lines until the stadium rose around her, expanding in every direction. It felt like vertigo, all that open space falling away. People everywhere, double fisting Bud Light tall boy cans, ready to refill their recently emptied bladders. Ready for more. That's what Jerry World offered. As much as any one person could handle, and more.

The stadium's retractable roof was open, opening, still in the process of it, revealing a slice of pitch-black sky, but not any stars. The lights were too bright. All the stars were inside the stadium. Giant steel stars. LED stars. Stars like Moses McCloud would be if he pulled this off. A thirty-five-point differential was no joke. Five touchdowns in one half. But that was the point, right?

That's what the people came to see. Winners and losers. When the game was over, people wanted to know the score.

It wasn't that simple for Rae.

The game she'd been playing wasn't black and white; it was opaque. Just like her first investigation and the "bad guys" her father had mentioned. That star etched into the mirror behind the skybox bar had been opaque too, reflecting her showdown with Harry Christmas and Bruiser Brandt. Tackling Eddie Pride had been fun, but was that it? The climax of her first investigation. Was this the end?

A voice said, "Ticket, please," and Rae looked down from the starless sky. A man in a neon green vest, the word USHER stamped into the reflective fabric, stood before her with his hand out. Rae dropped her ticket into his palm and listened as he said, "Oh, I'm sorry, ma'am, but you're in row fifty. You've still got a ways to go."

Rae took the first step, followed by the second, then the third. When she finally made it to Row 50, the retractable roof was all the way open. Rae was closer to the sky than the field, so high she could barely read the players' numbers, but she could hear a man's voice saying, "Leave it to the federal government to skimp on the tickets, the cheap schmucks . . ."

"*Frank?* What the hell?"

"Come on, kid," the veteran special agent said and patted the empty seat to his left. "Take a load off. You've earned it."

65

"**The mustard** seed, gentlemen. Faith like a mustard seed, the tiniest of all seeds . . ." Speer Taylor was saying, stalking between the mass of players, feeling their heat, smelling their sweat, the faint scent of blood mixed with rubber infill because there wasn't any dirt in Jerry World. Speer checked his watch. Halftime was almost over, but he finally knew where he was going now.

"On the road to Jairus's house," Speer said, chest puffed, parading around the locker room like the counselor he'd been once, telling his campers a ghost story. "That's where Jesus was headed, to Jairus's—"

"Jairus right there, Coach," said Markeith Payne, a sophomore cornerback pointing to a free safety named Jairus Jefferson kneeling in the front row, helmet still on, moving it, slowly, side to side.

"Ah, Markeith. No, I'm sorry," Speer said. "This is a different Jairus, the *biblical* Jairus. From the Book of Mark?" Speer winked at a Prism News camera peeking out from behind a bathroom stall. "This is the story of the bleeding woman."

A wave of scraping cleats and rustling pads spread across the locker room. The players groaned as they settled in for what Speer had decided was the perfect narrative to match the moment, a lesson in faith.

"You see, a huge crowd had gathered outside Jairus's house, hoping to witness another miracle. In that same crowd there stood a woman. Her dust-covered toes, her tattered sandals, speckled with blood."

One of the players said, "*Jesus Christ*," and Speer added, "That's right, Cergile. *Jesus.* That's who the crowd had gathered to see. That's who the woman was there for too, the woman who'd been bleeding for twelve straight years, deemed 'unclean' by her friends, her family. This woman was a believer, though. Oh, yes. She knew if she could just touch Jesus's cloak, she would be made clean again. So, she pushed her way through the crowd until the Messiah was right there, close enough she was able to reach out and . . ."

Speer closed his eyes and lifted his right hand, performing the movements of a woman he believed had walked the earth over two thousand years ago. He felt good, alive like he'd been yesterday morning when the lead pastor at Gateway Church had asked Speer to come up and talk about his spiritual gifts. The moment was so clean, so pure, it made Speer feel guilty about what he'd been, what he was becoming. Weren't there already enough coaches and politicians in the world? If Speer wanted to preach, then by God, why wasn't he preaching?

He opened one eye, his right one, and saw exactly what he expected: a bunch of blank faces staring back at him. The people at Gateway hadn't looked at him like that. They understood. Speer squeezed the eye shut again and started to pray. He prayed harder, begging God to grant him the same clarity he'd given that woman in the crowd outside Jairus's house. His request was met with silence. So much silence for so long, Speer decided it was time to cut Jesus a deal.

If You want me to turn my whistle in and give up on politics, Speer prayed, watching the words scroll across his mind. *If You really want me to be a man of the cloth, JC, then at least let me go out a winner. Give me a little help here in the second half, and I'm all Yours.*

The players were murmuring now. Speer was too lost in the spirit world to hear them. He was planning to keep the prayer channel open through the second half—to pray without ceasing like it says to do in Thessalonians, Chapter 5—but then the whispers rose to a roar.

The cheers pried open Speer's eyes.

The boys were congregating around something, someone, their coach couldn't see. Speer began elbowing through the crowd, pushing past Markeith, Jairus, and Cerge. He stopped when he saw Moses McCloud standing in the center of the room.

Speer couldn't believe it. Did this mean Jesus was listening? Had He finally heard his prayers? *Yes*, Speer thought, fighting the urge to pinch the quarterback's legs or squeeze his biceps. A simple touch would do.

Coach Taylor saw that sultry sideline reporter coming and tried to duck behind the injury tent. Despite her four-inch, backless heels, the reporter caught up to the fleeing football coach at the forty-yard line, had her mic in his face at the forty-five, and then, just before they crossed midfield, asked the question Speer knew was coming:

"Coach Taylor, UCM has struggled mightily in the first half. Any chance we'll see Moses McCloud to start the third?"

Speer blinked. The reporter was still there, standing beside the same cameraman who'd shot the interview before the start of the game.

"Well, yes," Speer said. "There's always a chance."

"What about his suspension?"

"Did I say that?"

"Actually . . ." The reporter lifted her phone, reading from a note she'd taken. "You called it a 'Coach Taylor–imposed punishment.' So, no, no mention of a suspension. You did, however, go on to say, 'That boy's not just a football player, he's a . . .'"

Speer could feel the eyes of the nation on him, but after what had happened in the locker room, he didn't think of the viewers as voters anymore. They were his congregation, twenty-five million possible converts listening as this harlot recited words he'd said two quarters ago, an eon in the life of a football coach.

"'. . . a young man who needs to learn a hard lesson.'"

"And that's just what Moses did," Speer said, feeling better already, stronger. "He learned his lesson. You should've seen him at halftime. Just one look, and I could tell Moses had turned away from his sins. He'd repented."

The reporter mouthed the word at the camera, her recently waxed eyebrows raised.

"Moses prayed for forgiveness," Speer said, never once breaking eye contact with the woman in the sleeveless blouse, her sun kissed locks dangling down over toned biceps. "I was right there with him, in the locker room. Prayers were answered."

The reporter lowered her phone but kept the mic up and out. Speer decided this was it, time to carpe diem. He snatched the mic and said, "That's when I realized it wasn't up to me to judge that young man." A great new power surged through him, the manifestation of everything he was ever meant to be. "It was up to God, and God forgave Moses. He gave that boy a second chance, a shot to get back on the field and help the Chiefs win the Cotton Bowl."

Speer felt like he'd run a gasser, ten wind sprints, but his feet had never left the turf. The interview was over. Speer had won it. He'd defeated the silver-tongued, well-tanned temptress, but he still had her mic. He held it out for her, a peace offering, no, a consolation prize.

Instead of taking it, she leaned forward, her painted lips inches from the windscreen, and said, "Uh, stay tuned for the start of the second half?"

66

Ohio State received the kick, an end-over-end wobbler that came down at the nine-yard line and was returned to the twenty-six. A ref blew a whistle as Rae said, "Wait. Where's Darren?"

"You mean your boyfriend?" Frank elbowed her in the ribs. "Just messing with you, kid. Darren's headed back to Mississippi. He texted me, said something about how you left him *hangin'* at the concession stand line. You know how he talks."

Rae wanted to tell Frank she'd left Darren there for his own protection, but that wasn't the truth. The truth was that Frank had been right. In order to do her job properly, Rae didn't have time for a relationship. Federal agents didn't get three things like Chuck always said. They got one. Which was why Rae was sitting in the nosebleeds with her soon-to-be retired partner.

"And what about you?" she said. "What are you doing here?"

"I was sitting on my bed in the Super 8, watching the pregame show this morning when the cameras swept over the UCM fans. Big crowd of white people dressed up like they were going to church. Made me start thinking about the guys I grew up with. Guidos. Guineas. Micks. So many names for basically the same thing."

Rae said, "Huh?"

"What I'm trying to say, I shot a guy my first year on the job, this bum with a bad habit. Stanley Loperfido. Dope-sick eyes. The works. More than anything, though, Stan was scared. I saw that fear on full display the night I put one in the poor guy's heart. Cleanest shot of my life. Only time I ever pulled my pistol. Stanley Loperfido died for twenty-seven bucks. That's how much there was in my wallet. Should've just given it to him. Then again, the guy did take a swing at me with a pipe." Frank opened both hands and turned them over. "So, yeah . . . That's how I was feeling when I left Mississippi. Like I should've done more, but what?"

"You came all that way just to tell me that?"

"No, kid," Frank said and bent forward, reaching beneath his seat. "I came to give you this."

The synthwave sunrise and the purple palms glistened under the slick plastic cover, tattered at the corners from years of use. In Frank's weathered hands, the Trapper Keeper seemed so small, suddenly fragile. Rae took the binder, hugged it tight to her chest, then leaned over and put her head on her partner's shoulder. The tender moment passed before Rae could say thanks, replaced by action on the field: Ohio State in their "Heavy" personnel, grinding out four yards at a time, the numbers on the clock getting smaller after every snap.

"So, uh . . ." Frank said. "Where's Moses?"

Four minutes were gone from the third quarter when the Chiefs held Ohio State on third and short and the Buckeyes punt team got into position. The ball spiraling off the side of the punter's foot lifted Rae's spirits. She sat up straight again, eyeing the video board, a close-up shot of the returner waving his hand, signaling a fair catch.

Rae squinted and said, "*There*," as Moses McCloud came trotting onto the field, helmet unbuckled, mouthpiece wedged into his face mask, walking now, moving toward the left hash as the rest of the Chiefs got into formation around him. An empty set, Cergile Blanc lined up at slot receiver to the quarterback's right.

"Okay, yeah, I see him," Frank said, "but where's he been? The kid missed the whole first half. It'll take a miracle for him to get the Chiefs back in the game now."

Rae leaned forward and placed her elbows on her knees, picturing Moses back in the Dodge's passenger seat. Now that he was on the field, she knew that this was where he belonged. Moses had been right. If he became her informant, no coach would ever sign him again. Not Speer Taylor. Not Chuck. Rae'd been trying to keep from thinking about her dad, everything he'd said in the skybox. None of that mattered now. Without Moses McCloud, Rae didn't have any plays left in her book. The freshman quarterback had been her only hope, and there he was, right where he was supposed to be, barking out the snap count:

"Blue 42. *Blue 42* . . ."

The ball shot between the center's legs and landed in Moses's hands. Only stayed there long enough for his fingers to find the laces then it was gone again. A missile that hit Cerge square in the numbers as he streaked up a vertical seam, the weakest spot in Ohio State's Cover 3 Shell. Cerge was real-deal fast, Miami Beach fast, fast enough he made it to the end zone untouched.

Rae faintly remembered Eddie Pride hollering the running back's name as she'd escorted Moses out of the hotel room. Something about the first UCM touchdown of the game? There was no telling. No time either.

The federal agents were on their feet along with the rest of the nosebleed section, the entire stadium buzzing. Electric. The Chiefs rode the same current through the third quarter and into the fourth, the scoreboard balancing out as the clock ticked down. From up that high, Rae could see the plays take shape, the routes develop. She saw the receivers pop open but never the ball. It was just there, in their hands, right on time, every time.

Moses was unlike anything the coach's daughter had ever seen. A savant, an artist, that's what Moses was, painting the field with his perfectly timed passes, dishing dimes to Cerge in the flats, then zipping darts over the middle to his tight end, his slot back. Fourteen. Twenty-one. Twenty-eight points.

That's when Ohio State finally switched from Cover 3 to Cover 4 and shut down the deep routes. That's when UCM had to settle for a field goal, making the score 35 to 31 with three minutes and thirty-seven seconds left to go and the Buckeyes back in their "Heavy" personnel, ready to run the rock, wind the clock, and go home with another national championship trophy. That's when Frank asked his partner to look up the Buckeyes' running back—he wanted to know how much that white boy weighed—and Rae reached for her phone, the one that was still in her pocket, the one with the stealth app that had recorded every word that had been said in the skybox. That's when she realized the true power of football. When the game was at its best, its most pure, it was beautiful enough to make you forget.

Rae held her phone out with both hands. Frank didn't notice, too wrapped up watching that white running back churn through the Chiefs' D-Line. Frank was blinded by the spectacle like Rae'd been, but she was seeing clearly now. She was focused on her one and only thing. Her job. What was on that phone, the conversation she'd recorded from the skybox, there was more to it than what she realized. All the evidence she needed was right there, but what about—

"Your dad?" Frank said and pointed. "Is that him, down on the sideline?"

Chuck Johnson was standing at the far end of the coaches' box between Harry Christmas and Brandt Conrad. He had the visor on again, and the shades, one arm folded over his belly, the other up so his hand could cover his mouth. Rae'd seen her daddy strike that same pose before. It was a way to keep the opposing team from reading his lips and stealing his plays, but what was he saying to the congressman now? And better yet, where was the Chiefs' head coach?

"This don't look good," Frank said.

Rae said, "What?" and scooted forward in her seat. "What happened?"

"You not see it? Moses just went limping into that red tent."

"The injury tent? He's hurt?"

"Yeah, kid. Where you been?"

Rae was in the same place she'd been a month ago, stuck trying to tell a game from reality, her first investigation like a linebacker blowing up the gap between the two. But what about the coach? Where the hell was Speer Taylor?

67

Speer was hiding inside the injury tent when the Ohio State quarterback shouted, "*Hut!*" and all twenty-two players came to life, fighting for inches on a polyethylene field under a black Texas sky.

"Coach?" Moses McCloud said, holding his knee on the taping table. He still had his helmet on. "Coach Taylor?"

Speer didn't think of himself as "Coach" anymore. He wasn't going to be a politician either. Speer was meant for something else. Something better. He'd felt the Father's hand on his shoulder, guiding him, leading him into the tent. At halftime, he'd prayed for a win, one final victory. Thankfully, the good Lord had been listening. With Jesus by his side, Speer had called the best half of football in his entire career.

"There are three minutes left in the game," Speer said, "and Ohio State has the ball. They've put in a big, white running back. His ball security, his fundamentals, Moses, they're flawless. Do you understand what I'm saying?"

Moses's helmet moved inside the darkened tent.

"I'm saying nobody thinks we'll get the ball back. Nobody *believes*—"

"My knee, Coach. Listen—"

"—but I do," Speer said. "I believe we'll win this game. Is it going to take a miracle? You bet. Another one." Speer stepped forward and placed both hands on Moses's left knee. The skin beneath the thin plastic pad was warm to the touch, almost hot.

"Gracious God," Speer said and closed his eyes. "I call on

you now to mend what is broken. Remove any inflammation, rebuild any damaged cells. Let the power of your healing love pass through this quarterback so that his body may function in the way you intended it to function. Use him like you used me . . ."

The boy began to squirm. A good sign, maybe? Speer wasn't sure. Eyes closed, he pressed on.

". . . back in 1989 when I won that national championship at UT. You were there, God. You were always there. In the valleys and the shadows, before I went to Kanakuk and started this whole journey? You were there. Back when I still had my beaver paddle and got that DWI my redshirt year? You were there. Just like that time I got caught cheating in Comp I, then cheating on my future wife in the ladies' room at that bar in Austin. What's it called?" Speer waited a moment before adding, "The one with red carpet?" then shook his head. "It doesn't matter. You were there, God. You were always there. You're the only one who can handle my junk."

Speer felt the truth in the moment, praying over a boy named Moses. The Moses in the Bible had been a prophet, and the prophets were one motley crew. Isaiah had prophesied buck-naked for three straight years. Hosea married a prostitute. David didn't just hit Goliath in the head with that rock; the shepherd-turned-king killed a whole bunch of other people, including Uriah, husband to Bathsheba, of rooftop-bathtub fame. Speer Taylor had lived a wild life. He'd made his fair share of mistakes, sure, but recalling the prophets' stories made him feel a little better, like he'd finally found his tribe.

"If this is Your will, Lord, give us a sign," the football coach whispered. "Show us the way."

Silence for a moment, then a roar that could've crumbled the walls of Jericho sliced through the tent's plastic flaps as the public address announcer shouted, "Jairus Jefferson recovers the fumble! UCM ball! It's a miracle, ladies and gentlemen. A miracle!"

Speer Taylor opened his eyes and watched Moses McCloud slide down from the taping table. The tent flap opened—the stone rolled away—and the savior walked into the light.

68

Even if Moses's left leg had been broken, an all-out compound fracture, he still would've hauled ass out of that injury tent. The quarterback's leg wasn't broken, though. His knee was just feeling funny. No worse, no better, than it'd been all the way back to when he'd tweaked it against Mississippi State. Eddie had been right. That was the whole reason Moses had started throwing the ball so much. No sense risking a run. Moses had gone into the injury tent because he thought the game was over and couldn't stand to watch it play out. He'd seen Ohio State's big white running back. He'd noticed his fundamentals. No way the Chiefs were getting that ball back, but then they did.

Trotting onto the field, Moses wondered if he could really do it. Could he really make it the eighty-three yards it would take to continue chasing his dream? He didn't have time to think over all the stuff Coach Taylor had just said. Same way he hadn't let what had happened with Eddie or the conversation he'd had with Rae cloud his mind. The Buckeyes had drained the hell out of the clock. With no timeouts and only fifty-six seconds left, any passes Moses completed had to land near the sideline. The clock would stop when a receiver stepped—

69

"—**out of** bounds," Rae was saying, setting up the final drive for Frank. "The clock'll stop on incomplete passes too. Moses needs to be smart. He will be. He is . . ."

Sitting in the nosebleeds, Rae wasn't thinking about the investigation anymore. She was thinking about Moses. What had he said to Speer? What had Speer said to him? She felt helpless, like a coach stuck calling plays from the sideline.

"Quick pass to the flats," Rae said. "An out route."

A second later, Moses whipped the ball to the visitor's sideline for a six-yard gain.

Frank said, "Hey, look. You called it," but Rae didn't hear him. She was too wrapped up watching Moses, hurrying back to the line of scrimmage. "The corners are biting up, getting greedy," she said. "Pump the short pass and go deep. Take a shot."

Seven more seconds ran off the clock before the ball was in the air. It left Moses's fingers while his wide receiver was still faking the out route, just like Rae had said. Perfect timing. Perfect spiral on a rope. This wasn't some high floating bomb. This was a missile fired at the tiniest crack in Ohio State's defense, a small window between the free safety and the boundary corner that hit the streaking Chiefs' receiver square in his numbers then rolled to a stop on the turf.

"He dropped it. The guy dropped the . . ."

Frank was right. The receiver had dropped the pass. The Chiefs still had seventy-seven yards to go and there were only forty-three seconds left on the clock. Time enough for three, maybe four more plays. The Buckeyes were lined up in a prevent defense. They weren't going to let anything past them. Not again. That much was obvious.

Frank said, "Okay, Coach. What's the call?"

70

A smash route: a hitch and a corner on both sides of the formation with Cerge in the backfield to help protect. It was a bad call, but there wasn't enough time to change it. No more audibles.

Moses caught the snap and watched the Ohio State linebackers flip their hips and drift out toward the sidelines, leaving a runway up the middle wide enough to drive the team bus through. Moses stepped up in the pocket, pumped once to the flats, then took off running, so fast the white lines on the green field blurred like they did anytime he took Highway 49 home to Clarksdale, the highway blue in the night like the music in his grandmother's kitchen. Blue like his favorite pair of Jordans, powder blue like the helmets around him he couldn't see. His teammates. The Buckeyes wore gray lids, but Moses couldn't see them either, not even when his knee popped and everything went red. He made it a few more yards, limping from the ten to the six like a semi-truck after a blowout, and then slid to a stop on the two.

71

"**He's hurt,**" Frank said. "Looks bad this time. Real bad."

The trainers were out there already, huddled around Moses McCloud. The clock had stopped at twenty-eight seconds. Rae couldn't watch. Her eyes jumped from the end zone to the sideline where she spotted her father again. The sight of him reminded her of the other game. Her investigation and how she had everything she needed to win already, if she could just figure out the best way to play it.

Phone in hand, Rae said, "I've gotta tell you something, Frank."

"Now? You serious? This is the—" His bushy brows rose when he saw her cell. "The hell's that?"

"It's our case," Rae said. "I used my phone like a wire."

"When you were up in the skybox? You got Harry on that thing, telling all his dirty secrets?"

"I recorded it, but Harry didn't say much. You were right, that first night you took me to the Waffle House? You said the bagmen were untouchable because they don't have any affiliation with the school. It's the same with Harry."

"Not so fast, kid. Let's say we trace the payments, connect them back to the congressman's campaign. We do all that, Harry'd at least get a slap on the wrist, a few fines, probation, even. We might not run him out of office, but we could still show the world what a bastard he is."

There was a better option. Rae knew it but still had to convince herself. She stared up at scoreboard, the frozen clock.

"What if I'd recorded a coach?"

"Speer? Speer Taylor was up—"

"My dad." Rae eyed the man on the sideline in the visor and reflective shades. "He came to the skybox."

"*What?* Why?"

Chuck and Frank had both come to Dallas for the same reason—they'd come for Rae. Unlike her partner, Rae's father had had another motive. He'd come to cover his own ass too. If her case went public, there was no telling how it might impact college football, the coaches, especially.

"Huh, kid? What'd he say?"

"He told me . . ." Rae said. "He told me the truth."

The veteran agent cracked his knuckles against his chin. "*See,* this is what I was talking about. That whole bit about Christmas morning, the cranberry sauce?"

"Frank, listen—"

"No, you listen. I wanna nail these guys too, bet your ass I do, but that's your dad down there. Your father."

"I don't care."

"Yeah, you do. You just haven't realized it yet, and everything I said about Harry goes for Chuck too. We're still talking about fines, a possible probation. So, your dad gets canned. Big whoop. Is that what you really want?"

Moses had said basically the same thing about Speer Taylor. How, even if he got fired, some team would hire him after the dust settled. And Chuck, Chuck had said he'd pay the players out of his own pocket if he could. He'd even grinned when she'd hauled ass out of the luxury suite.

"Look around you, Rae. We're talking about a game. That's all. A friggin' football game."

The video board hung frozen above the field like a giant guillotine, stretching from twenty-yard line to twenty-yard line. Rae saw Moses framed in the middle of the screen, a pair of trainers leading him to the sideline.

"Nobody's getting put away for life," Frank said. "Nobody's committing murder."

Rae said, "But Matt Talley's still dead."

"The kid got drunk, fell off a roof. So what?"

Moses had mentioned Matt before he'd exited the Dodge. He'd said people were saying Ella May had pushed her former boyfriend, but Rae'd already chased that lead. She'd gone back to the Buffalo Nickel and spotted that one-eyed owl behind the bar. She didn't find anything else. No cameras on the roof. Nobody willing to talk. The Matt Talley case was out of her jurisdiction, anyway. She was there to investigate the University of Central Mississippi's football program, but what if she wasn't?

Rae reached for her Trapper Keeper and flipped past all the notes she'd taken, the clues she'd gathered. She turned to the binder's back flap and crossed out the single line she'd scribbled there when she was a kid. It was time to add a new quote to the list.

"There's no bad guys in football," Rae said, repeating her father's latest maxim. "There's just winners and losers."

"What?"

"It's what you've been saying, Frank. There are no bad guys in football. The only rule is winning, but what if we take football out of it? The real world is full of bad guys."

"Guys like Harry Christmas?"

"Since we've been in Mississippi, the congressman's assaulted

Eddie Pride Junior, coerced local law enforcement, and possibly tampered with evidence in the Matt Talley investigation."

"Tampered with what?" Frank said. "When?"

"It's something Moses mentioned, before I came up here."

"But do you think the kid will mention it again, like, say, in a courtroom?" Frank flopped back in his stadium seat. "See, that's the problem. Everybody who might come forward about Harry, they've all got too much skin in the game."

"I hear you. Eddie Pride's a superfan. He'll never turn on the Chiefs. If we take the game out of it, though, then Eddie wouldn't be testifying against UCM. He'd be testifying against Harry Christmas, the same guy who damn near killed him."

"I hear you, kid, but somebody's gotta come forward first." Frank massaged his face, talking through his fingers. "That's how it works with narcs. They're like lemmings. It just takes one little rat who's willing to jump, and then the rest'll follow."

Movement on the video board drew Rae's attention, a zoomed-in shot of Samuel Billingsley lined up under center. Poor kid. The kickers had bigger biceps. Sam turned and handed the ball off to Cerge. Not a bad call with only two yards to go, but the Buckeyes were ready and stuffed the dive for no gain.

The problem with a run, Rae knew, was that the clock didn't stop.

There were only fifteen seconds left when Moses McCloud limped back onto the field. Rae watched him, Frank's lemming line still skittering through her brain, but she'd called that play already. Besides, Moses wasn't a rat, he was a seriously injured quarterback, readying himself for the final play of the game.

72

Moses caught the snap at the six second mark.

Six.

Five.

He knew what he was supposed to do. Moses was supposed to spin around and hand the ball off to Cerge on another halfback dive. Coach Taylor had even taken advantage of the injury timeout to substitute the Chiefs' beefiest personnel group into the game. Speer was coaching like a man possessed. He'd made the right call, but Moses wasn't sure he could get the ball back there in time.

His bum knee crunched with every step. Bone on bone. As soon as he'd gone down, Moses knew, right then, he'd never run again. Not like that, no more flying. But he was still in charge. Moses was in control. And Speer Taylor was stuck on that sideline, flailing his arms over his head, jumping up and down, trying to get his QB's attention.

I hear you, Coach, Moses thought, remembering Speer's prayer in the injury tent, confessing all that stupid shit he'd done when he'd played ball at UT. All the mistakes that man had made and he was still making millions while Moses was the one on the field, in the classroom, the gym, the caf, trying so hard not to mess up. Moses had to be perfect. He'd had to do everything right just to make it this far, and still, his dream turned out to be just that. The same dream men like Speer Taylor had been selling boys like Moses McCloud long before either one of them ever laced up a pair of cleats.

The young quarterback checked the sideline again. Coach

Taylor was still flopping around, but there was another man beside him now, an old dude wearing a houndstooth fedora. The same sort of hat Rae'd said the man wore. *The Man.* The big bad guy who'd been trying like hell to get Moses to throw a game. He was right there.

Four.

Three.

The world behind Moses's face mask blinked in and out. That's how bad the pain was. Bad enough he couldn't hear the crowd or see the stadium. The bright lights faded, replaced by a scraggily patch of grass. That peewee field where Moses had played catch with Rae. Where he'd told her that same line she'd told him outside the security gate: "Sometimes you've got to lose the battle to win the—"

Two.

One.

Moses took the snap but didn't hand the ball off to Cerge. Didn't even try. He couldn't fathom giving up that sort of control. Not now. Not ever again. This was it. The last play of the game. The *war* Moses had been training for his whole life, all the way back to the McCloud Family Reunion when he'd knocked that Miller Lite can off Keyshawn's head.

What if he'd missed?

He might never have done what he was about to do. He wouldn't have had the opportunity, the chance to make a statement, but at least he would've still had two good knees instead of a torn MCL, ACL, meniscus, every ligament busted and burning as Moses McCloud flipped his hips, squared his shoulders, and sent the final pass of his brief but beautiful career, rifling out of bounds.

73

Harry Christmas was so busy belittling his football coach—"Goddamnit, Speer! You fool! You couldn't pour piss from a boot if the instructions were on the heel!"—he never saw the ball coming. It was just there, a spiraling brown torpedo that knocked the words from the aged congressman's mouth, along with a couple teeth too.

The moment of impact was so forceful, it sent Harry's mind spinning back in time, back to the days he'd spent in the Apple Blossom Orphaned Boys' Home. That's where Maxine had found him, saved him from those wretched bullies who liked to hurl pigskins at young Harry and constantly made fun of his ears.

The congressman reached for his fedora. When his fingers slid over his scalp, he realized he was in a football stadium, not an orphanage. Harry could still hear boys cackling, though. Men and women too. The whole crowd was hooting now. All the people Harry Christmas had hoodwinked for so long finally saw him for what he was, what he'd always been.

A joke.

74

A white woman in a red jersey talking about erectile disfunction appeared on Geraldine McCloud's television screen seconds after her grandson smoked some old man in the face with the ball.

Momma G kept thinking about how that geezer's hat went flying, but she didn't laugh. She wouldn't, *couldn't*, not after what all had happened. She wondered who the man was. Almost felt sorry for him, the way the camera had zoomed in on his right cheek, the one the ball hit and knocked him flat on his ass. Made him look silly. Like one of those videos Moses would send her after she sent him links to the articles she found online, the ones where star quarterbacks got arrested, their scholarships revoked.

The commercial was over. Confetti was falling now. Random shots of fans. Buckeyes fans. Chiefs fans. Nobody sure what to make of that final, sideways pass. An ESPN commentator appeared on screen, saying, "Well, now, that was . . . *something*. Moses McCloud appears to have been injured. We're still waiting on an update, but—"

But nothing.

Moses was hurt, all right. Geraldine had seen the trainers cart him off the field, bits of red-and-gray paper stuck to his pants, left knee swolled up bigger than a grapefruit. She wondered what it meant for her grandson. Was this it? The end of everything.

Geraldine swiped at her eyes. She was so sick of worrying,

almost eighteen whole years' worth. She lifted her remote, ready to make it all go away, but the broadcast cut to another commercial, the same damn one they'd just run. Geraldine watched that white woman in the red jersey. She listened to her talking real serious about ED, and then, finally, Momma G started to laugh. She didn't know what else to do.

75

"The kid just threw the game," Frank said, standing on his toes, looking down over the rest of the speechless crowd. "Moses McCloud just threw the national championship game, live on *national* television."

"Yeah," Rae said. "That's what it looked like."

"But why? I mean . . ." Frank tugged at the neck of his teal green sweater. "What's he trying to prove, pegging Harry Christmas in the face like that?"

"Maybe it means he's ready to talk."

Frank turned, one finger still hooked in his sweater. "You think so?"

Rae wasn't sure. Football was a complex game. Madeline Mayo didn't get it. A lot of people didn't get it. The ball's oblong, for one thing, not spherical. Drop it and there's no telling which way it'll bounce. It sounded like something her dad might've said, but he hadn't. Rae had come up with that one all on her own.

OVERTIME

Straight cash, homie.

—Randy Moss, NFL wide receiver

76

Moses McCloud said, "You look different," but Rae Johnson was wearing the same outfit she'd worn to the Cotton Bowl, or, if not the same clothes, something similar. Black slacks and a white dress shirt with both sleeves rolled up. Kinda fancy for breakfast at the Waffle House. She looked like a cop minus the cream-colored Jordans. A *federal agent*. That's exactly what Rae looked like.

"Different?" she said. "How?"

Moses placed his crutches between two empty stools and eased into the bench across from Rae. It wasn't her hair. She had it down today, waves of red outlining a pale, oval-shaped face, two green eyes staring back at him.

"I don't know. Just different."

Rae said, "I could say the same about you," and Moses felt the air brace on his left knee again. After two weeks, he'd gotten used to it. Not the crutches, though. The foam pads rubbed his armpits raw.

"Listen to you, talking about me, just like everybody else in the country. Ain't you heard?" Moses could tell by her face she had. "My favorite was the sports guy on Fox. What's his name?"

Rae shrugged and reached for her coffee. Two fingers around the handle, she brought the mug to her lips and took a small, slow sip, smiling back at Moses through the steam.

"Big bald dude with a beard calling me an *athlete*, a freshman dual-threat QB. He said the stage was too big. That's why I got confused about the time and tried to kill the clock."

"By throwing the ball out of bounds? You should've just spiked it."

What Moses had done still didn't feel real. Like a dream. Like any day he might wake up and find himself in that nice, cold hotel room again. He wouldn't go hunting up his headphones this time. No sense messing with Eddie Pride. But what about the end? Moses's left leg had given out as soon as the ball left his fingers. He'd watched the pass spiral from the turf, every rotation stirring something like regret in his gut. Moses had thrown it all away—his whole career, his masterplan—and look where that had gotten him.

"Don't know how I could've made it any clearer," Moses said, back in the Waffle House, sitting in the same booth as a female federal agent. "I smoked that congressman in the face on the last play of the game."

"You sure did."

"Harry something, right?'

"Christmas. Harry Christmas. He was a real bad guy. What you and Ella May—hell, even Eddie—are doing, it's gonna help take him down. We looked into Ella May's credit card statement, by the way."

"Told you she bought a drink."

"Who knew a Tipsy Tomahawk would seal the deal?" Rae lifted a maroon designer bag up from the bench beside her. "Dumbasses destroyed the camera on the roof but forgot the one behind the bar. A little wireless setup shoved inside a stuffed owl. I almost did too. Not that it would've mattered. The timestamp on the statement proved Ella May wasn't on the roof when Matt went down."

"What's that?"

Rae pushed the designer bag across the table, just far enough Moses could see the banded stacks of hundreds stuffed inside it.

When the former quarterback looked up the federal agent was out of the booth, moving past his crutches on her way to the door. The jukebox was playing some old blues tune, the man's deep voice singing about a woman who'd brought him gasoline. Moses didn't know the song, but the melody felt familiar. It moved him.

"Hey, your bag," Moses said, back on his feet, shuffling after the federal agent. "You forgot your bag."

Rae stopped beside the jukebox. The blue-green bulbs cast her face in a soft light. From the new angle, Moses could finally see what had changed, what she'd become after all this. *Cool.* That's exactly what Rae Johnson was, grinning a little as she said, "It's a purse, kid, and there's more where that came from. A lot more."

77

The cowbell above the Waffle House door rattled, Rae Johnson beneath it, walking with her shoulders back, chin up. If it had been a scene from a movie, the rookie agent might've slipped on some shades. A slick, stylish pair that showed the audience just how cool she was. Nothing like those boxy Oakleys her dad had worn to the game. The director of this nonexistent film might've even spliced in a sunrise shot, a sliver of orange cresting a cotton field, the bolls glowing pink in the first light of a new day.

Instead, a thick wall of clouds hung heavy over Compson. A plastic Walmart sack swirled in the breeze, pirouetting under the Waffle House's yellow-and-black sign. The diner's parking lot was so dark, Frank Ranchino had the Subaru's headlights on as he pulled in to pick up his partner.

"You do it like we talked about?" Frank was back to wearing Hawaiian shirts again. Tiny Tiki men hulaed across his chest as he waited for Rae to shut the passenger door and buckle her seatbelt. "That whole bit with the bag?"

"Yeah, Frank. I did it."

"And?"

"He took it. No problem."

"But did he get it? Did Moses think it was funny?"

Rae shrugged.

"You know how much time I spent talking Barb into that stunt? She was set on mailing the kid a check, but I told her, No, listen, Rae's gonna hand the kid a *bag* . . ."

Frank hooked a right onto Highway 49, headed south. After two weeks spent nailing down the details on their public corruption/obstruction of justice case, the partners had one more stop to make before they caught a flight back to DC.

"Which reminds me," Frank said, reaching behind the passenger seat. "This is for you."

Rae said, "Come on," but took the brown gift bag from her partner. "Is this some sort of going away present?"

"I think so, yeah, but it's not from me."

The bag was heavy. There was red tissue paper stuffed inside it, along with a card. The message was short and sweet: *After all that running around, figured you could use a new pair of these. Hit me up next time you're in Mississippi. D*

The light blue Air Jordan 1's were even sweeter than the card. Something to remember Darren Floyd by, all the fun she'd had with him over the course of her first case.

Frank said, "Shoes? What kinda gift is that?"

Rae smiled to herself. Whatever had happened between her and Darren wasn't any of Frank's business.

"Anyway, listen. The way we had the drop set up," Frank said, "it had everything. Symbolism and all that. A fed pays her informant, a former college football player, by passing him a bag."

"It was a purse, Frank."

"Even better." He slapped the wheel. "It's funny shit. It's perfect. Just like this whole case, how it all worked out in the end."

Things had gone better than expected. That was for sure. The Prides had both issued confidential statements. Eddie's was a little trickier considering what had gone down in the Embassy Suites. Luckily, Moses wasn't pressing charges. So, yeah. All things considered, the case had turned out pretty good, but it wasn't perfect.

"You see Speer retired? Pulled out of the Senate race too. He's trading it all in for a clerical collar."

"Megachurch pastors don't wear collars. You know that."

"Yeah, kid. You're right, I do, and I know something else too. The one thing we still haven't talked about."

There was smoke in the west, a long line of smoldering fire at the far end of a neglected field. Some sort of controlled burn, Rae guessed, watching as the gray plumes puffed up against the clouds.

"You gonna make me say it?" Frank said.

They were getting close, the turnoff less than a mile away. Rae'd almost made it without the phone coming up, the same one she was sliding out of her Trapper Keeper now. She could see her reflection in the darkened glass, her father's hooded eyes gazing back at her.

Frank said, "There it is," as the Subaru's passenger-side window started down.

Rae extended her right arm and dangled the phone out the window. She could taste rain in the air. A storm was coming. She and Frank were about to bring down a flood on Compson. Together, they would cleanse the town of its dirtiest secret, but Rae still didn't know what to do about her dad.

Chuck had tried calling at least once every day over the last week. Rae never answered. She was afraid to talk to him, scared the old ball coach would win her over, recruit her back to his side. Rae still wasn't sure what side he was on. She didn't know where she stood either, and that was the problem. Chuck had been right. He wasn't a good guy or a bad guy. He wasn't even a winner or a loser. Not in her eyes. Not anymore. But he was still her dad.

Rae's fingernails scratched at the phone's plastic case as she brought her hand back into her lap. A moment later, the phone was safe inside her Trapper Keeper, the Velcro flap sealed. Warm tears sliced down her cheeks, contrasting with the cool air on her arm. The window started up again. She kept waiting for Frank to say something like he always did. When he didn't, Rae said, "I'm just gonna hold onto it, okay?"

Frank spun the wheel, turning left onto County Road 103. "Just don't hold on too tight. Don't let it get ahold of you. You got me?"

Rae whispered, "*Thanks*," and wiped her eyes. She pulled her hair back into a bun, the same way she used to wear it at her track meets. The dirt road ahead of them was long and flat like a runway, but there wasn't a pole vault pit at the end of it. There was an antebellum-style mansion, a plantation house that had once been a brothel that belonged to a congressman now.

Frank pulled the Subaru up to the gates of Sudan and parked alongside a fleet of unmarked squad cars and a lone Lenco BearCat. Rae figured there were at least ten officers crammed inside the SWAT vehicle, each one decked out in body armor and ballistic helmets, full-on tactical gear. A separate task force was already set up in the tree line, sniper rifles poking through the kudzu vines.

Frank said, "*Jesus*," and cut the engine but didn't get out.

"All this just to take down a seventy-year-old politician?"

"Don't forget Bruiser," Frank said, pointing. "See his cruiser over there?"

Rae saw it.

"Maybe we'll get lucky and the police chief'll open fire."

"Doubt it," Rae said. "I bet it'll go down like that *National Lampoon's* Christmas movie."

Frank turned to his partner and smiled. "You serious, Clark?"

"That's it. That's what the cousin says. The agents burst through the windows at the end, break down the doors, tear the whole damn house apart."

"Talk about symbolism. All the antiques Harry's got in there, relics from a time gone past, shattering. It's like a metaphor or some shit."

"Yeah, partner," Rae said as the first fat raindrop splattered in the dry red dirt surrounding Sudan. "It's perfect."

Acknowledgments

I started drafting *Mississippi Blue 42* nearly ten years ago. Since then, it's gone through nine complete rewrites, four title changes, and a total overhaul of the lead character. The book you're holding would've never happened without the following team (listed in order of importance):

Josh Getzler: Bagman / "FTE Tour" Coordinator
Jillian Schelzi: "FTE Tour" Co-Coordinator
Jon Cobb: Bagman's Former Assistant
Bronwen Hruska: Athletic Director
Juliet Grames: Offensive Coordinator
Nick Whitney: Quarterback Coach
Paul Oliver: Director of Football Operations
Lily DeTaeye: Operations Assistant
Rudy Martinez: *Not* Rudy Ruettiger
Rachel Kowal: Quality Control Coach
Janine Agro: Team Graphics
Justin Acri: Sports Information Director
John T. Edge: Mississippi Recruiting Co-Coordinator
Neil White: Mississippi Recruiting Co-Coordinator
Peter Lovesey: Booster
Luke Duffield: Shadow Booster
Johnny Wink: Guru
Josh Wilson: Chaplain
Mike Sutton: Team Lawyer
Robin Kirby: Team Doctor

Lilly Cranor: Intelligence Director
Todd Cranor: Head of Security
Shawn Cosby: Linebacker, Mathews High
Gary Phillips: Defensive Tackle, Lutheran Lions
Michael Koryta: Sandlot QB, Arlington Heights Elementary
Alafair Burke: Tetherball Terrorist, College Hill Elementary
Dwyer Murphy: Third Base, Wareham Vikings
Emmy: Water Girl
Fin: Water Boy
Mom: #1 Fan
Dad: #1 Critic
Mal: My hero, my wife, and former U of A pole vaulter